Jacquelyn Frank is a *New York Times* and *USA Today* bestselling author of sizzling paranormal romance novels. She lives in Western North Carolina.

Please visit her website at www.jacquelynfrank.com

Also by Jacquelyn Frank

Three Worlds series:
Seduce Me in Dreams
Seduce Me in Flames

ADAM

Jacquelyn Frank

piatkus

PIATKUS

First published in the US in 2011 by Zebra Books,
Kensington Publishing Corp, New York.
First published in Great Britain as a paperback original in 2011 by Piatkus

A CIP catalogue record for this book
is available from the British Library.

ISBN 978-0-7499-5554-0

Printed and bound by CPI Group (UK) Ltd, Croydon, CR0 4YY

Papers used by Piatkus are from well-managed forests
and other responsible sources.

MIX
Paper from
responsible sources
FSC   FSC® C104740
www.fsc.org

Piatkus
An imprint of
Little, Brown Book Group
100 Victoria Embankment
London EC4Y 0DY

An Hachette UK Company
www.hachette.co.uk

www.piatkus.co.uk

For every last one of my readers.
You begged, harassed, threatened, cajoled, whined, and
pretty pleased your way into this book.
Enjoy!
(And yes, the bitch finally
gets it! . . . Well, maybe. Muhahahaha!)

Printed in the United States of America

"Whosoever wishes to know the fate of Demonkind must consult these prophecies . . ."

". . . as magic once more threatens the time, as the peace of the Demon yaws toward insanity . . ."

". . . it will come to pass that in this great age things will return to the focus of purity that Demonkind must always strive for. Here will come the meaning and purpose of our strictest laws, that no uncorrupted human shall be harmed, that peaceful coexistence between races shall become paramount . . ."

—Excerpts from *The Lost Demon Prophecy*

". . . it is therefore forbidden for any of Demonkind to mate with creatures who are not their equals, not of their nature, not of their strength and power. Those lesser creatures are ours to protect from ourselves, not to be violated in impure sexual abomination. This is the law and the will of nature. The dog does not lie with the cat; the cat does not lie with the mouse. Whosoever breaks this sacred trust must suffer under the hand of the law . . ."

—Excerpt from *The Original Scroll of Destruction*

Prologue

Samhain 2008

"There's too many of them!" Isabella cried out after a moment wasted in catching her breath. The dark ebony cloud of her hair was flung around her head in a wide arc as she whipped it around to look at her companion: her mate and husband, the father of her daughter, not to mention their son, whose impending existence they had only found out about a week ago. He guarded her back just as she guarded his in this fight, and together they were protecting the thing most precious to them both. "*Jacob!*"

The female Druid was forced to turn her back on her attackers as she saw that the odds she faced were nothing compared to his. No matter how strong and skilled she had become as a fighter over her years beside him, no matter how powerful an Earth Demon he was, they would never survive against such forces. Not alone.

But Jacob would not relent.

He *could* not relent.

It was not only because they were the Enforcers and it was their duty to fight these foul aggressors with every last breath in their bodies. It was because their daughter, Leah, was secreted away only a few yards distant from the ground they currently defended. Jacob would sacrifice his last breath before he would see his family harmed. Isabella would do no less.

"Bella!"

Jacob reached for her between one smooth strike at the enemy and the next. He linked his arm through hers, and like the perfectly fitting cogs of a watch, she rotated over his back, her legs windmilling in dual strikes that stunned and stumbled enemies. When her feet hit the ground, she instantly stepped back so the heel of her left foot touched the heel of his right. They braced themselves in that back-to-back position as the forces around them circled like vultures. Fortunately, both fighters knew that baser instincts would prevent these Transformed Demons from organizing themselves with intelligence, cunning, or strategy. The situation was critical enough with their bloodlust berserking; if they were to work in tandem, they would have a horrifying advantage.

Even as Bella struck a mark with a petite arm that packed far more punch than would be expected in one so small, Jacob spread his hands out parallel to the earth, his fingers curling as if they were burying into the soil that, in actuality, was a good four feet below the thick stone under their feet. Shattered quartz and rich loam spewed up toward those commanding hands, starting in one place and rapidly exploding in a circle around him and his wife until they were being swallowed by a perfect cylinder of dirt, rock, and debris.

Isabella wasn't afraid when the ground caved in beneath her and the earth literally sealed its lips above her head and swallowed her up. She instantly dropped down into the chute of the tunnel being burrowed through the soil, her husband sliding swiftly beside her as they fell. Even though she could see and hear the rumble of clean fill collapsing above their heads almost as fast as they fell, she was not intimidated. On the contrary, she was relieved. The monsters above them could never catch them now. It was all Jacob; every grain and every pebble being manipulated around them was under her husband's artful command. He was the most powerful Earth Demon alive. The oldest of his kind. None of the Transformed Earth Demons above them could match the speed and accuracy Jacob used to manipulate the Earth around them, or the way the soil was repacked above them tighter than nature herself had originally done. Now their enemies would have to figure out how to find their way through tremendous amounts of earth in order to find them.

Finally they passed through what was once solid limestone before bursting out of the Demon-made tunnel and into a nature-made cavern. Jacob manipulated gravity so they landed gently on their feet, even giving Isabella an extra moonwalk bounce that made her laugh briefly in spite of their dire circumstances. Then she turned sharply around to face her mate.

"The baby!"

"Easy," her husband reassured her. "She's just through the caverns. I pulled her down, too. What did you think I was going to do?" He reached out and swatted her backside as she hurried in the direction he had indicated. But despite the playful gesture and her smart look over her shoulder, they were both very aware that they weren't safe yet. Granted, most of those above could not follow them, but some . . .

Some could.

"I pulled Jasmine into the caverns as well, but she's hell and gone from here," he warned his wife. "It's going to take some time for her to reach us."

Bella threw up a hand of acknowledgment, even though he already knew she had heard him and understood him. Understood they were on their own.

Isabella's speed as she ran along the twisting corridor still amazed her. It had been six years since she had evolved from a human into a Druid, or rather, a hybrid of human and Druid. The power that had come with that alteration in her genetic makeup, including her ability to run with incredible speed, had been one of many blessings in her life since then. As she rounded a corner, she saw one of her blessings indignantly dusting off the soil the *other* blessing in Bella's life had caused to get on her dress.

"Daddy, I'm dirty," the five-year-old complained, the hands on her tiny hips and the jut of her lips all too reminiscent of her mother's infamous gestures of pique. She completely disregarded the fact that she'd been in any danger.

"Sorry, angel," Jacob apologized halfheartedly as he looked up toward the cavern ceiling, sensing the danger looming above them. "We have to make haste," he said softly as he leaned in toward Bella's ear.

Isabella was already scooping up her daughter as her husband's hand fell into the small of her back to guide and hurry her.

"Mommy, I can walk," Leah reminded her with her trademark stubborn independence, just as she always did when Isabella tried to carry her.

Of course, Leah let her *father* truck her around

everywhere from dusk to dawn if that was his wish, and she never complained *then*, Isabella thought.

"Mommy is faster than you are, sweetheart, and we have to run," Bella explained as she began to do just that.

She didn't lose patience with her daughter's distorted priorities. It wasn't that Leah didn't understand that there was peril around them, because she did. However, Leah had grown up watching her parents run into battle at the slightest threat to their home and homeland, their friends and family, or their monarch's people. She was speaking like a child who wasn't worried in the least about her safety because she knew her parents to be a mighty force, an undefeatable army of two that would never fail to protect her for as long as she lived.

There was a bursting change in the cavern's air pressure, one that all three of them recognized; although in Leah's experience, the force that created that sinus-snapping aftermath was always friendly.

This one was not.

Isabella skidded to a halt, shoving her daughter behind herself so suddenly that Leah's dress hit the dirt once more.

Bella and Jacob squared off to face the traitorous Demon Ruth, who had become a powerful enemy as she'd added potent necromancer magic to her already vast repertoire of ability as an Elder Mind Demon. It was she who had betrayed and Summoned the Transformed Demons Jacob and Isabella had left up above them, layers of earth and rock away.

Worse yet was the presence of the Vampire named Nicodemous, who now shared her power, just as he seemed to share her black magic abilities. Ruth had caused devastating death and destruction when she had defected, first with her daughter, and then, upon her daughter's death, on her own. Now, mated to a Vampire of such age and avaricious might, she was an unfathomable force of evil.

They both were.

The only small thing in the Enforcers' favor was that Ruth's Transformed minions couldn't immediately come to her aid. That wouldn't last long, however. Ruth only needed a moment of concentration before she could begin teleporting them down to her side a bucketful at a time.

Isabella refused to give her the advantage. The Druid released the tight rein she always kept on her ability to dampen the power of any Nightwalker. This was by far her most powerful ability, and it was also the most unpredictable and dangerous to her personally. She even forced herself to acknowledge the unknown damage it could do to the delicate fetus she carried. But she didn't see that she had a choice with the lives of the rest of her family at stake. Even with Jasmine on her way to back them up, the female Vampire was only one person, and it would take an army to defeat these two evil creatures if their powers remained intact. They had learned much about how to use them over these past few years. And it was only going to get worse. Bella and Jacob had to strike now, while they had a chance.

And besides, the traitorous bitch was coming after *her* child. Bella would see to it Ruth paid for even daring to think about touching Leah. Damn the painful consequences she might suffer. If Bella didn't do something, they all would die anyway.

Clearly Jacob felt the same, or he would have volubly protested her impending actions through the telepathic link they shared with one another. He knew what potential harm there was to his wife, but while he'd argued against it in the past on many occasions, there was no time to argue now.

And so she opened herself to the dangerous unknown and drew it into her vulnerable mind and body. Bella had absorbed the power of a female Mind Demon before, but nothing like this blackness of soul. It was sucked harshly into her like acrid ammonia. She *had* taken the power of a corrupted Vampire before. He had stolen the lives of other Nightwalkers, gathering their power into himself through the drinking of their blood. But she knew instantly that *this* Vampire was tainted well beyond that, the stain of necromancer magic on his soul as well. It was like imbibing a double dose of pure, liquid evil. She felt the cloying blackness of dual channels of power from the twin sources; they seeped into her like thick oil and tar. The evil twisted together inside her, suffocating her from the inside out. Her eyes, normally a beautiful violet color, blacked over and she looked down at herself to see pitch liquid oozing out of her skin. She did not realize the vision was only in her own mind.

Jacob felt his mate scream in horror long before she actually found the voice for it. He saw what she saw, just as he knew her every waking thought every moment of the day. He knew she was seeing a hallucination, and he couldn't help the instinct that had him leaping into her mind to convince her of what was real and what was not. He whirled around to catch her in a single strong arm as she lurched in a back-arching seizure.

Leah watched with wide, frightened eyes as her mother was flung backward by an unseen force. Her young heart leapt into her throat as her father spun to catch her mother, the long brown-black tail of his hair whipping like that of an agitated horse. She felt her heart seize fitfully with incomprehension as she watched him quickly ease his beloved wife to the ground as gently as he could, considering the violent contortions of her body.

That was all the time it took for the enemy behind him to strike.

It was the Vampire that moved. Leah watched, paralyzed with shock and fear as he reached with blinding speed into his long, dark coat, grabbing for something that looked sharp and deadly. Even Leah's immature Demon senses could smell the sudden tang of rusted iron, the poisonous metal that was deadly to Demons. A moment later the Vampire leapt onto her father's turned back and drove the iron spike between rear ribs and shoulder blade.

Leah watched as if through someone else's eyes as the spike burst through her father's chest, spearing him straight through the heart. The inconceivable sight of her sire's blood exploding out of his chest was nothing compared to seeing him fall to his knees in total shock, his face full of outrage and a clear frustration that only those who loved him would understand. Jacob looked up into his little girl's violet eyes, so like her mother's, and felt his failure to protect his family so sharply that the last sound to leave him was a keening cry of utter remorse.

Then he fell forward onto her mother, the last exhale of his breath echoing in the suddenly silent cavern.

"Daddy!"

Leah screamed for her father as the Vampire reached to yank him off her mother, baring his fangs. He hissed and then threw Jacob away so violently that Leah heard her father hit the near wall with a sickening smack.

"Dead." A dead Demon with no heartbeat to pump his blood was of no use to a power-hungry Vampire, who could not feed from Jacob to gain one of his many powers. Nicodemous's frustration was keen because of just how powerful a Demon Jacob had been. But he quickly turned his attention to Leah's mother.

Leah had been frozen in terror, but seeing those pale, bony fingers reaching for her mother galvanized her into headlong action. She flung herself between those hands and her twitching, seizing mother, throwing her small body protectively over her, not quite realizing yet that her parents' symbiotic relationship meant her mother's death knell had already begun at the moment of her sire's passing.

The Vampire grabbed her by the neck of her dress, ignoring her scream and easily overcoming the mighty grip she had on her mama's clothing. He plucked her up like a fragile little flower and inspected her with a jaundiced eye.

"It's too small to have any power. I'd much rather feast on the Druid." He cast her aside onto her dead father's chest, the iron spike jutting from his chest stabbing into her, skewering her through a thigh left bare and vulnerable as the skirt of her dress flew up. The iron lodged in her flesh, burning her half-Demon tissue and blood with excruciating pain. Between that and the horror of lying on the rapidly cooling remains of her father, Leah dissolved into screams.

"You idiot! We came here for the little girl! There's nothing like her in the world!" Ruth hissed, reaching for the squalling child, who immediately shut up and found the unprecedented strength to pull herself off the spike that had speared her and scrambled away from the Demon coming after her.

"There's nothing like the Druid in the world either," the Vampire spat at her, "and at least her power is developed! I can only absorb from one at a time! And what is she but a swallow or two?" He scoffed at the idea of feasting on the scrawny little girl.

"Then we'll take it with us," Ruth mused, eyeing the child, who was wriggling her way between two boulders shaded by a natural shelf. "We'll wait for it to grow and show its powers. Then you can eat it and kill it so no one else will have a chance at whatever power it gives you."

Nicodemous grunted noncommittally as he yanked up Bella's torso by her arm, forcing the seizing woman against his chest. He opened his jaws wide, flashing vicious fangs that made Leah cower deeper into her cubby. Too terrified to make any further sound, she whimpered when he stabbed those wicked-looking teeth into her mother and ripped away at her flesh so she gushed blood into his mouth in a sloppy gluttonous mess.

Ruth did the child an unintentional favor when she bent down next to Leah's hiding place and blocked her from seeing any more of the Vampire's cruel feeding on her mother. Ruth reached between the rocks and tried to fish for Leah, but the child wisely kept out of reach, backing up into the dark cubby as far as she could go.

"Come here, girl. Don't make me use magic on you. I'll turn you into a lizard, you little brat."

But Leah knew that as long as her mother was alive and perhaps for some time after that, her attackers would be completely powerless. She knew what her mother could do, *all* the things her mother could do. The Vampire could drink all he liked, but he would only be able to earn one of her mother's powers. For all he knew, he would earn her very benign ability to read any language she saw.

But the child didn't realize just how deadly that could be in a world full of black magic spell books in ancient and sometimes dead languages. Spells and magic that had faded away with the language they were written in. Powerful magics that once upon an age had been seen as biblical events, and perhaps still were.

Suddenly Ruth got hold of the hem of Leah's dress and immediately fisted the material into her fingers, pulling her toward the narrow spot between the boulders she had escaped through. Desperate and panicked, Leah did the first thing that came to her mind. She grabbed hold of Ruth's forearm, opened her mouth, and did some biting of her own. She did it as savagely and viciously as she had seen the Vampire do, taking great satisfaction in Ruth's surprised screech and her immediate withdrawal. Leah scrambled back into her dark corner, this time making sure her skirt was well out of reach.

"You little bitch! Wait until I get my hands on you! I'm going to use you to beat your mother dead!"

"Lovely. That should charm her out of there," Nico said dryly, earning a nasty look from his other half. She was a beautiful woman, tall and tan and cool blond, but her blue eyes oozed utter and exquisite madness, and when she glared at him like that she really came off quite ugly. He took it in stride. He had grown used to her rapidly fluctuating moods. And her volatility kept him from growing bored with her, something that happened easily to Vampires who were as long-lived as he. "Cast a spell to get to her," he suggested. "Our innate abilities may be gone, but surely a spell will work."

"And what spell do you suggest? There is no 'Snag a Rotten Child' spell."

"You could be creative. Surely you can think of—"

Suddenly the Demon/Vampire team went still, both tilting their heads as they sensed the approach of another.

"We had better go," the Vampire said, using a sleeve to wipe at his mouth. It did little good. He was saturated with the blood of Leah's mother, and it was smeared and splashed all over his face, arms, and shirt. "We do not have any power, thanks to her." He flicked fingers dismissively at Bella. "And as you see, it is not a good idea to fight dependent solely on our spell work."

Ruth couldn't argue with that. Instinct told her that whoever was coming was very, very powerful and would be fresh and not battle weary. Ruth and her Vampire were worn out from fighting the Enforcers and manipulating the Transformed minions they'd sent initially to attack Bella and Jacob.

And just like that, they abandoned Leah and the cavern.

Not without sensory abilities of her own, the child was aware of their leaving, and that the farther they went from her, the safer she was. She squeezed out of her hiding spot and raced over to her mother, using her small hands and diminutive strength to turn Bella over so she was faceup. But that was as far as she could pull her. It was as far as she dared to pull her. Every movement she made caused more blood to pump out of the torn flesh in her mother's throat.

Leah's eyes filled with tears. She didn't know what to do. She didn't know how to help. She had been born to the Enforcers, an indestructible team of strength, power, and intelligence that always knew what to do. And now it was shattered all around her, torn and broken. She ought to have been able to do something. Even at five she already had the sense that she was destined for great things, that she was one day going to be a very powerful Demon.

But right then she *was* only five, helpless and vulnerable. Right then there was nothing she could do.

Jasmine found the little girl sprawled over her mother's chest, her tiny hands gripping at Bella's shirtsleeves, her face buried against Bella's breast as she keened softly in an awful sound of despair. The female Vampire was not exactly known for her sentimentality and tenderness, but she would have had to be a stone-cold bitch not to be shocked and moved by the sight that greeted her. Over the past few years as head of the Nightwalker Sensor Network, the law enforcement net that had been put in place all over the world to catch lawless Nightwalkers that slipped through the cracks of their individual race's policing systems, Jasmine had been always two steps short of Nicodemous and Ruth. The chase had gone on long enough for her to recognize their very special brand of aftermath, and she knew that was exactly what she was seeing now.

She moved forward, stepping over the man she knew was beyond help and kneeling by Isabella's shoulder. She gently reached out to touch the back of Leah's head. Her brown and black hair, a mirror of her father's, was caked with dirt and the blood of her parents, but the exceptional tenderness of the female Vampire was everything the frightened child needed. She looked up at Jasmine with wide, violet eyes filled with unshed tears and a traumatization that would no doubt last the remainder of her lifetime.

"Please help my mama," she begged Jasmine painfully.

"Come, puss. It's best we let your mama go," she said as gently as she could, "else she will suffer in the long run." Unlike Leah, Jasmine was well aware of the symbiotic relationship between the Demon and the Druid. Without Jacob's energy to revitalize her, Bella would begin to waste away, and before two weeks were up, she would be dead. It was a long, slow, and agonizing death—especially for those who loved the Druid, those who would be forced to sit and watch it happen, knowing there was nothing they could do to help.

"Please. Please!" Leah reached out for Jasmine, grasping the Vampire's face between her hands and meeting her gaze with a chilling sort of wisdom radiating from her young eyes. "I was mean to her tonight. I don't want Mama to leave me thinking I'm a bad girl."

"Puss, you and I both know your mama would never think that of you. She loves you more than anything," Jasmine reassured her as she pulled her into her lap and hugged her close.

"I know she loves me more than anything, but I don't think she knows that I love her. I was mean to her."

"Oh, sweetheart. She knows. Mamas always know."

"Please. I need to tell her. Please . . ."

The little girl pressed her lips to Jasmine's, right over the spot where her upper left fang was hidden and retracted. Jasmine was well aware that this clever child was manipulating her, pulling out all the stops, doing whatever it took to save her sole surviving parent.

"Damn."

Leah didn't understand what saving Bella for the moment could cost Jasmine for the rest of her life.

Jasmine had never drunk the blood of anyone who wasn't human or Vampire before. The idea offended her every last sensibility. All her life it had been drilled into her that she shouldn't ever drink the blood of a Nightwalker. Until recently it had been deeply forbidden. But then Prince Damien had drunk from a Lycanthrope, who later had become his bride, and it was discovered that the reason the cold and loveless Vampires lived lives of such bland emotion was because they were destined to find their mates in the other Nightwalker breeds . . . in the blood of other Nightwalkers.

But there was no love to be found here. The thing Jasmine was considering was to drink in order to trigger the autonomic systems attached to her second bite, her finishing bite, which would inject coagulants into her victim's body, thus stopping Bella's bleeding. But to drink from Bella would mean to take on an aspect of her power, and Jasmine wasn't interested in altering herself on a molecular level for all time. She liked herself just the way she was.

But it wasn't herself she was forced to consider. It was a pair of pleading violet eyes, a child on the brink of becoming an orphan, and it was that child's mother who would suffer painfully if Jasmine saved her long enough to say good-bye to her daughter.

"I'm sorry," the female Vampire whispered to the babe. "She's gone."

She picked the little girl up and walked out of the cavern that held Leah's dead and dying parents.

One Week Later

Noah, the Demon King, raged with grief, the temper of his volatile element getting the best of him. He hid himself in the very same caverns that had seen Jacob's death and, using the power of his flame and Fire, he burned everything in sight until the rock was charred as black as the wounded places in his heart.

Kestra, his Queen, grieved with love. Leah glued herself to Noah's wife, scrawny legs around her waist and clutching arms around her neck beneath Kestra's sugar-white braid of hair. While her husband burned in anguish, Kes rocked and comforted the orphaned child. They clung to each other, the parentless child and the barren Queen, each fulfilling places of desperate need in the other.

Leah's blood uncle, Kane, brother to her father, couldn't bear to be in the child's presence. Neither, it seemed, could his mate, Corrine, who was Isabella's blood sister. They each saw too much of Bella and Jacob in Leah's features and her coloring, and their avoidance would set a trend far into the future. Leah would feel it most keenly, and she would age knowing very little about them, except to realize just setting eyes on her caused them inconsolable pain.

And they were not the only ones who would behave in such a manner.

She learned not to mention anything about her parents to anyone who didn't talk about them first. Within days she understood that she had no family anymore. That she was alone.

And through the years to follow, a certain female Vampire would watch as the once close-knit Demons began to fall apart over the deaths of two of their finest and most beloved members, anguish and suffocating guilt stealing away what nothing else could have done. She quickly came to realize there was nothing at all she could do about it.

Chapter 1

Ten Years Later

"Adam?"

Leah's dark head jolted up and around in her shock, her violet eyes going wide as she stared at her *Siddah* Elijah. Elijah looked at his foster daughter with amusement. He was well aware the fifteen-year-old had been tuning out most of her lessons up until that point.

"Yes. Adam. Your father's eldest brother was Enforcer before your father inherited the mantle from him."

"But . . . Daddy's only brother is Uncle Kane."

"Trust me, angel, I was very good friends with Adam. You were perhaps just too young to recall your father ever mentioning him."

"But Uncle Kane never speaks of him," she argued.

No doubt, Elijah thought. Kane had not known Adam, having been born after Adam's loss. Then again, the present Enforcer also avoided his niece whenever he could, so the opportunity for discussions about anything was nonexistent. The look flitting over Leah's features told him that she was recalling that very same fact.

Kane and Corrine had never recovered from the tragic loss of their siblings. They had become very insular, taking solace only in one another and avoiding anything that could possibly remind them of Jacob or Bella. At first, Kane had even refused to take on the position of Enforcer, this in spite of the fact that he knew he was the last of his line, the last of a very special legacy of Demon power that allowed him to sense when other Demons were on the brink of insanity.

Eventually, Kane had very little choice. Then again, it wasn't as though any of them had a choice. Life plodded forward, but they were all aware of the pall that had hung over their society this past decade. There were many who believed Jacob and Bella would have destroyed Ruth eventually, or at the very least the plague of rogue Vampires that now threatened to overwhelm the Nightwalker world.

Kane always tried his best and he meant well, but his youth was against him as he struggled to fill his brother's formidable shoes.

Others, like Elijah, simply believed that the blow of the Enforcers' deaths had taken the spirit out of the entire Demon community.

"Adam was gone long before Kane was even born," Elijah pointed out to his charge. "He didn't even know him."

"Gone? You mean he died?" she pressed. As a rule, her *Siddah* was very careful with the words he chose, so the distinction caught the clever girl's attention.

"Actually, I can only assume so. Adam disappeared without explanation some four centuries ago on a Beltane night. We found no clues to his disappearance; however, since we were at war with the Vampires at the time, it was not unusual for even our best warriors to disappear."

"Oh! How terrible!" Leah's violet eyes filled with empathetic tears. She often did this. Leah hungered for stories of her parents and felt a constant need to apply emotions to them. Elijah supposed it helped her to feel closer to them. The tragedy was that Kane and Corrine, the two people on earth who could best fill her hunger for information about Jacob and Bella, were as remote a resource to her as Pluto was to Earth, and it had very little to do with the fact that Leah was being raised in a distant Russian province in the court of the Lycanthrope Queen, Elijah's mate, Siena. Being a Mind Demon, Kane was capable of teleporting at will. He could have brought himself and his mate to Russia whenever he wanted to.

"You know, Noah was Adam's best friend, as I recall. Perhaps you ought to ask him about your other uncle," Elijah suggested.

"Really? I can go to England?"

"Of course." He chuckled. "Kestra and Noah would be thrilled to see you."

"Yeah, I guess," the young girl sighed. "But it stresses Kes out when she sees me. It stresses all of you out."

Leah knew that was exactly the truth of the matter. After her parents had died, there had been something of a terrible war over her custody. Demon tradition stated that upon the death of both parents, a Demon child's *Siddah* would take immediate custody of the child, instead of waiting until the child's power began to show itself in the child's late teens. But Noah and Kestra had fought with Elijah and Legna for the right to raise her themselves until the proper time for her Fostering to begin. They wanted to raise her in the Demon court and in the hub of Demon life. Leah's *Siddah*, Elijah and Magdelegna, both lived with their mates in the Lycanthrope court. A foreign court with foreign traditions.

Of course Kestra's motivations had been strongly oriented to her husband's desires. She was unable to have children of her own and knew how deeply Noah felt for Leah. She had seen it as a perfect opportunity to provide him with the family he deserved. And Leah didn't doubt that the barren Queen had been strongly in favor of the idea for other reasons as well. The fight had, she came to understand, caused some rifts between Elijah and his King . . . and even between Magdelegna and her brother. Legna and Noah had once been very loving and very close, but now the relationship was strained.

All because of Leah.

Eventually it had come down to the Great Council's vote on the matter. The Council had strongly sided with Leah's *Siddah* and Demon tradition, and so she had been raised by Elijah and Legna and Legna's Demon mate Gideon. Siena, the Lycanthrope Queen, and Siena's entourage of Lycanthropes had had their influence on Leah, too.

Leah didn't know if any of them were good or bad influences, or if Noah and Kestra might have been better ones, but frankly she was glad she had been raised outside of the Demon world. There was always so much weight in the eyes of the Demons who saw her mother and father in her looks or her bearing or perhaps even her smallest habits. That weight invariably led to sadness and an overwhelming guilt. Leah's guilt. She felt bad for making them sorrowful, and the older she was, the worse it seemed to get. Apparently her face and eyes made her a dead ringer for her mother, while her build and hair reminded everyone of her father.

"I think I'll just stay here," she said as she almost invariably did whenever she thought of visiting the Demon court. Actually, her thoughts were far more engaged with the fascinating concept of learning about an uncle she had never heard of before. "So what can you tell me about Adam?"

"Adam? Sweet Destiny." Elijah paused to thrust the blade he was forging deep into the hot coals before him. "Why are you so fascinated with him?" he asked his fosterling. He took a moment to look over her willowy frame, smiling as he saw how much she had grown these past few months. She also looked healthy and, considering her history, reasonably happy. But there would always be an element of sadness in this child, Elijah thought. The tragedy of her parents' death was worn deep in her young spirit, and anyone who sat and talked to her for any length of time could see it sitting on her soul.

"Well, you were good friends, yes?"

Elijah didn't see what possible use there was in bringing up stories of other great men who were also long gone, but she was animated and curious and it was infectious to see her that way.

"Honestly?" the big blond Demon said with a crooked grin. "Your father was Adam's best friend even above Noah. When they weren't bickering, that is. Your dad loved to get under Adam's skin and would poke and prod until he got his ass kicked for it."

Leah laughed, and Elijah relished the sound. It

was a rare commodity in her. It was rare in just about everyone these days.

"Then again," he continued, "those sparring matches and their playful rivalry is probably how your father learned all the tricks of the Enforcer's trade. From diplomacy to cunning to battle, Adam was the ultimate instructor, and your father a clever sort of student. Did you know that Adam was the one who devised most of the current punishments we use to deter Demons from straying during the Hallowed moons? There have been others throughout the centuries, but Adam's were by far the most wickedly effective and have stuck the longest."

"Really?" she asked breathlessly, her expression rapt as she leaned in.

"Yeah. Apparently, Adam thought the original forms of castigation and humiliation were a bit too warm and fuzzy for his tastes. What he devised has proved far more diabolical. Adam was . . ." Elijah grinned at her, his green eyes alight with distant memory. "Adam was the definition of a hard-ass. Believe me when I tell you it paid off. Whatever you hear people say about your father being militant, it was nothing compared to Adam. He was the all-time deadliest fighter on the block when he wanted to be. Not to disparage your father, but if Adam were still around, Ruth would have been dealt with long before she could ever have got this far."

Leah frowned as he turned to shift the blade under the coals. "You mean he was better than Daddy?" she asked as she licked the sweat from her upper lip. The forge was hot and close, but she wouldn't have budged for anything.

"Well . . . let's say he was different. Adam wasn't

known for being touchy-feely. Your father was the opposite in many ways." Elijah hesitated. "If I took Adam at the time he died and set him up against your dad at the time *he* died, it'd be a real hard call. But you see, your mother made Jacob more powerful than Adam could ever be alone. However, she also . . . well . . ." Elijah stopped with a wince, realizing he had forgotten whom he was talking to.

Leah wasn't left behind.

"You mean to say Mama was Daddy's worst weakness as well, don't you? It's okay, Elijah. I was there. I know my father wouldn't be dead if he hadn't turned his back on his enemies."

"Actually, no one knows that," he corrected her sharply. "Do you blame your mother for what happened? Or your father?"

"I blame everybody!" Leah bit out sharply. "I blame everyone who ever let Ruth slip through their fingers! I blame the Vampires! I blame you and Noah and even Adam for not being there when my parents needed them the most!" Leah's small hands balled into fists as she railed. She tried to hold back, to rein in her temper, especially when she saw the guilt and pain in Elijah's eyes. "I just . . . I wish it had been different. I bet if my father and my uncle Adam had been there together that day, Ruth would be dead and that Vampire bastard would be burned to ashes instead of my father and mother!"

Elijah looked at her carefully for a minute or two, letting her catch her breath and calm her emotions. Then he said gently, "I think it's a waste of time to think of such things, Leah. If you get caught up in fantasies about 'would have beens,' you forget to appreciate what you actually have in the here and now.

Tragedies happen, Leah, but quite often unexpected good comes from them."

"Tell me what good has come from my parents' murders!" she lashed out, standing up and bearing the fierce heat of the forge in order to go toe-to-toe with her *Siddah*. "You tell me, Elijah! Teach me how to see their deaths in a proper light! Wax poetic on all the happiness among us that was born because Jacob and Isabella are dead!"

Elijah stood in stony silence as Leah reached to dash tears from her eyes. He deserved her anger, he thought sadly. They all did, because they all had failed her. It broke his heart to see her in the firelight of the forge, her mother's violet eyes and her father's brown-black hair leaping out at him from a face made half of Isabella's fey features and half of Jacob's sterner aristocracy. She even grew tall and lean like her sire, yet was developing the curvaceous femininity of her dam. There was no doubt, the instant you laid eyes on her, whose daughter she was.

"I'm sorry, Leah," he said after a moment of weeding his own pain out of his voice. "It was a poor platitude to use. I only meant—"

Leah waved off his explanation with a hasty sniffle. "No," she said softly, "I understand your point. I truly do." She slowly turned her back on him and stepped back toward the stool she had been sitting on. Unable to trust herself, Leah kept turned away and hid her features behind the fall of her hair. "Please. Tell me more about Adam."

Elijah was quiet and still for a beat, but then with a nod to himself he continued to do so.

* * *

When Leah had finished her lessons, Elijah sent her on her way and turned the forge over to the Minotaur that had been assisting him. He then made his way up from the deep caverns to the underground castle that was the seat of his wife's government. There she was, sitting in state, hearing grievances and attending to the minutiae of her political life. Siena looked utterly bored, her chin resting in her palm, her hair absently curling itself into twists. Each strand was alive with its own blood supply and nerves and would reflexively curl around her in protection or if she was cold. When she was changing form, it would spread over her entire body and become the fur of the cougar she could eventually become. But lately the springy, lush golden coils had taken to clinging to her like a constantly protective cloak.

She looked up and directly at him the instant he moved into the room. Imprinted as they were, she was always aware of him, always a part of his thoughts just as he was a part of hers. Their mating was the first one of its kind. In this millennium, in any event. In the past decade, scholars had uncovered certain strange truths and histories about the Nightwalker species that showed history had ways of repeating itself.

Hopefully they would do things better this time around.

Although it wasn't looking very promising. The rogue Vampires and human necromancers were growing in power, and Ruth and Nico continued to wreak havoc.

Elijah had to have hope that the goodness and love of Imprintings like his and Siena's would be enough to counterbalance all of that. But without powerful Demons like Jacob and remarkable Druids like Bella to help defend the Nightwalkers, it was looking very bleak. Once cohesive in thought and action, the central body of government in the Demon courts had fallen apart, agreements a thing of the past, bickering and whining taking up so much of the Great Council's time that Noah had refused to call them to table for nearly three years now. And although he was no longer Noah's Warrior Captain, Elijah was still a Great Council member and still wanted to fulfill his role as such. He wanted to help guide Noah in this volatile time. He wanted to help the man who had formerly called him friend.

But Noah did not feel the same. For some reason, he couldn't seem to move forward without his Enforcers. And Elijah had to admit it was hard. Sometimes too hard. But it must be done. If for no other reason than to show a young girl that it *could* be done.

Siena immediately began to shoo her people away from her, standing up from her throne and displaying her lush, beautiful body in its light, nearly sheer gown. The empire waist brought the material up snugly to her breasts, accentuating their fullness. The silky fabric fell away from the rest of her for the most part. But it liked her hips well, clinging to them and her backside almost lasciviously. It wasn't until she began to move forward that it gave hints of her rounded belly in front.

Siena ought to have been thrilled about her pregnancy, but she wasn't. Not entirely, anyway. What should have been full of joy was marred. And now that she was more obviously beginning to show, it was past time for them to announce the impending birth of the Lycanthrope heir. Most probably those closest to her had managed to figure it out already. Her attendants and aides had very probably deduced as much.

But Siena was trying to protect her child and, more likely, the feelings of her sister. Whatever was left of them. Elijah's belief was that it probably wouldn't matter. If the news *was* going to make any impact, it would be worse if Siena did not confront Syreena herself, instead allowing rumor to reach her sister first. It was quite possible the barren sister would be devastated by the news of the fertile sister's triumph, but Elijah really didn't think it would hurt Syreena quite the way his wife feared.

If Anya had still been alive, perhaps she could have helped advise Siena better than he had been doing. After all, the half-breed General had known both of the sisters best. But Nicodemous had ambushed Anya in the woods last spring, ripping her to shreds for the fun of it, leaving her for Siena to find. Ruth still blamed Elijah for her daughter's death and still took pleasure in tormenting him in whatever way she could, and Ruth knew the deepest way to hurt him was to somehow attack the woman he loved. Anya had been Siena's very best friend, and losing her had been a devastating blow to his wife's confidence and sense of security.

The attack only added to her fear about announcing her coming child. She felt that it would open her up as a target to Ruth's vindictiveness. Siena could remain protected in the bowels of their world; her people and her husband would never let harm come to her there. However, she was part wild animal. To keep her cooped up and under constant observation for all of her pregnancy would no doubt drive her crazy. Elijah had to admit that he was no longer capable of protecting her if Nico and Ruth came at them while they were somewhere in the open alone together. Both had grown so tremendously in power that no one was safe from them. And since Nico had fed from Bella, acquiring the little Druid's remarkable power . . . and Ruth had boldly attacked Syreena . . .

Nicodemous laid waste everywhere he went, and his demented Demon mistress could destroy any mind she touched. It was a recipe for utter devastation and it was eating away at Elijah's world from every direction.

And so his first child, the product of the incredible love he shared with his Lycanthrope bride, was a point of fear and contention in his marriage when it ought to have been just the opposite.

"Hello, Kitten," he said softly as she moved eagerly into his embrace. She reached for his face, the fingertips of both hands smoothing over the blond brows that so perfectly matched *her* hair, rubbing away the creases that had formed between them. It was a common action of late, becoming a habit, really.

"Worrying again?" she asked, although her free access into his thoughts easily told her that he was.

"It's time, love. You know that it is. Your people need to feel secure in the royal line, and ever since Syreena . . ."

"I know," she sighed. "And I am not so able to hide this anymore."

Elijah drew her out of the main receiving room, turning the nearest corner with her. After a quick look around, he reached out for her belly and engulfed it in his big hands. She was just past her first flush of showing, warm with her high body temperature and full enough to fill his hands as he rubbed them over her. She smiled, unable to resist, letting herself enjoy the moment for a change. She had never thought she would be the sort to take to motherhood. To be honest, it still frightened her a bit. But being a substitute mother to Leah all these years had changed her feelings on the matter greatly. It had taken a great deal of clever work to avoid pregnancy during her heat cycles in the interim, her behavior very much the opposite of her sister's. Syreena had barely been wed before she had begun to strive for a child.

The thought of her sister ended all the warmth of her feelings, bringing them crashing down. Elijah felt the change, looked up into her sad eyes, and then reached to bring her close. He hugged her tightly, hushing her softly against her ear when tears pricked at her eyes.

"If only . . ." she said brokenly.

"I know. But we can't focus on our regrets. We can't wish for something that wasn't. And where do we change the past, even if we could? If only Syreena had been protected? If only Nico had never drunk from Bella, giving him and Ruth the power to get to Syreena? If only we had killed Ruth long before she had met Nico? If only Ruth had never been born? I hate to say it, but Ruth was integral to the birth of the Mind Demon ability. She was the first female born with that power. She was the first female to become Elder. All those who came after her learned from her experiences. Even Ruth's madness was necessary. If she had never kidnapped Syreena, Damien would never have fallen in love with her.

"Kitten, we can't play with the past in our heads. We can't do that to ourselves. All we have is the here and now. We must deal with the present and try to shape the future as best we can." He smoothed his hand over her hair, a thumb drifting over her cheek. "We can try our best to be happy."

She sighed.

"I'm afraid that it might not be possible."

A short distance away Leah was eavesdropping on their conversation, her thin arms wrapped tightly around her body.

If only . . . she thought.

Later that night, Leah was sitting in a private alcove located outside one of the busier caverns of the Lycanthrope court. The hub of the court and castle consisted of a well-populated village aboveground that protected the entrance to the more heavily populated underground castle and its outbuildings, which had been carved directly out of the stone of the earth. Most Lycanthropes lived in the large network of underground caverns beneath the wild mountains and forests of Russia. It was probably one of those caverns that had seen the grisly death of her parents. She had been too young to remember the place, but she had heard hints over the years that had led her to make the assumption.

This little alcove was prettily decorated with a hand-carved stone bench and gorgeous pictures on the walls that the talented Lycanthrope stonecutters had created. She liked the privacy of it for reading or for thinking. She sometimes liked to just let her mind wander into the pictures depicted around her, touching the shapes of the carvings, thinking about nothing really at all.

But the problem with picking out favorite places was that after a while they weren't all that secret. People learned of them. And to prove it, she heard the shuffle of a step around the corner.

"Seth, I can hear you," she sighed.

Seth poked his head around the curve in the wall that had so poorly hidden him. He looked sheepish under his too-long *café au lait* curls and the light dusting of freckles over his nose. He was as darkly tanned as his father, so the little dots were hardly visible, but Leah had spent too much time with him not to notice the characteristic.

Leah scooted over and patted the bench next to her. Seth, all long limbs and angular lines, immediately took a seat, leaning back with his hands folded behind his head and his feet crossed at the ankles.

"I don't mean to bug you," he said as an afterthought. "If you want me to go, I will."

"Nah." She gave him a blasé shrug. "It doesn't matter."

The truth was she had been close to Seth since they were kids. Seth was the son of Gideon the Ancient and Legna, the Demon ambassador to the Lycanthrope court. He was also, supposedly, the second half of a prophecy about two miracle children, Leah being the first. The problem was, while Leah had been showing signs of power over the element of Time ever since she had been two, Seth hadn't shown so much as an inkling of the nature of his supposed power over the element of Space. In Seth's mind, this made him somehow . . . less.

"Whatchya been doing?" Seth asked her. "Staring at the walls again?"

"Shut up." She made a fist and punched him in the arm. He was lanky and kind of scrawny in her opinion, so he made a face and rubbed at the spot. But he didn't complain. He felt bad enough about coming up short in other areas; he wasn't about to let a girl know she'd hurt him. Even if it was just Leah.

"Did you know I had an uncle?" she asked him.

"Duh. He's the Enforcer."

"Not Kane! I know you know about Kane. Why would I ask you that? You're so stupid sometimes."

"I am not stupid!"

Seth's face flushed at the insult and he surged to his feet, his hands balling into fists. Leah saw him shaking as a tide of nasty words and insults rushed through his brain and she waited for him to choose the right one, the most cutting insult he could come up with. He was really good at them. Almost as though he had a stockpile of them that he held in careful reserve just for moments like this. He probably did. The Lycanthrope kids their age knew full well what Seth was supposed to be, and they never missed a chance to taunt him for not living up to the Demon prophecy's expectations. He was the son of the oldest and most powerful Demon in the entire world and had nothing to show for it.

"Why are you wasting your time thinking about a family that wants nothing to do with you anyway?" Seth wanted to know.

It was a good one, she had to admit. Even knowing it was coming didn't dull the sting any. She didn't get mad, though. She just absorbed the pain and tried to blink back the urge to tear up. After all, the truth was the truth. Kane and Corrine wanted no part of her. They couldn't stand to look at her, never mind sit and have some kind of conversation. So it really was a waste of time to dwell on her family, past or present.

"You're right," she said softly. "It probably is a waste of time."

As usual, the minute he had spoken the vicious words, Seth regretted them. Leah was his best friend. She was always nice to him. They liked so many of the same things. They thought so many of the same ways. And they were both born out of some stupid prophecy that neither of them felt they could live up to. Leah would give anything to be a normal Demon from a normal element, something simple like Water or Body. And Seth would give anything to have been born to normal, run-of-the-mill parents instead of the most powerful and Ancient one and the King's dynamic sister.

But Seth caught himself in that thought and just as quickly rejected it. He loved his mother. She was the only thing that made living with his father bearable.

"Well . . . what's his name?" Seth asked awkwardly.

"Who?"

"This uncle you had."

"Oh." She shrugged. "Adam. He was supposedly this real kick-ass Demon. He was—"

"Enforcer before your father," Seth finished for her. He nodded and sat back down next to her, but on the edge of the bench only, in case she didn't welcome him after he'd been so mean.

"How did you know that?" she asked.

"History lessons. You know my dad. He's always on me about history. It's easy for him, though. He can remember it all because he was there."

"Oh yeah." Then Leah's whole face brightened

and she slid closer to Seth, grabbing hold of his arm eagerly. "Oh yeah! Your dad lived through all of that! I bet he knew Adam, too."

"Well sure. Until he just disappeared . . . hey, I know that look. You've got something going on in your brain," Seth accused her. "Some kind of plot."

"No plot. Just curiosity. Elijah tends to exaggerate about warrior prowess and all of that when it comes to his friends who are . . . you know, dead. But your dad doesn't ever exaggerate about anything."

"No." Seth gave a beleaguered sigh. He screwed himself up into a proper imitation of his father. "'It makes no logical sense to decorate a story with colorful and emotional flotsam.'"

Leah giggled. "You do that very well."

"Yeah well, I have the benefit of an up-close study."

"Do you think he would talk to me about it?"

"It's hard to say." Seth thought about it a minute, the generous lips he'd inherited from his mother quirking into half a frown. "We'd have to make him think it was his idea or something."

"Or make it seem like a history lesson."

"Why do you want to know about some dead uncle anyway?" Seth nudged his shoulder into hers. "Don't you hear enough about the dead people you missed out on?"

She gave him a grim nod. "True. But . . . I have my reasons. Let's leave it at that."

Chapter 2

"There were yellow flowers in the children's hair last week," Syreena said softly. Her expression turned sad and wistful. "But now they've all died and faded. And I can't find the children." Then she smiled brightly at Jasmine, the multicolored streaks in her charcoal eyes actually growing light. "But we shall find fresh flowers in the gardens. I think bluebells will look lovely. Have you seen the children?"

Jasmine had been on her way out of the citadel when she was waylaid by the Lycanthrope Princess, who was married to Damien, the Vampire Prince, and Jasmine's closest friend. Now she sighed and tried not to roll her eyes. Syreena didn't respond well to negative emotions and hostility, so it was best to talk softly and play along.

"Um . . . I think they're in the courtyard."

Yeah. Right. Just like there were no flowers in the gardens at this time of year, yellow or blue.

"Oh, but I looked there earlier," Syreena said as she absently studied her fingertips.

"You must have just missed them," Jasmine said, trying to hold on to her patience.

"Do you think so?" Syreena asked eagerly. "I will look again." She leaned forward and kissed Jasmine on her cheek. "I am so glad we are friends now."

Syreena drifted off toward the courtyard, the train of her dress trailing behind her, the silken fabric falling crookedly off one of her bony shoulders and showing just how thin she had grown over the past two years. The truth was she often forgot to eat or bathe. Not unless Damien reminded her and held her hand through the entire meal or stepped into the bath with her to keep her focused.

No. Syreena spent most of her time looking for the children.

Children that did not exist.

They had never existed. Would never exist. And therein lay the trouble. When Ruth and Nico had attacked Syreena two years ago, Ruth had plunged into Syreena's psyche and perverted her very worst fears and weaknesses into . . .

. . . into *this*.

Jasmine let her hand fall away from the door handle and looked around the room. She could feel him, knew he was close. He was always close by when Syreena was near.

Damien broke away from the shadows down at the opposite end of the great room. He moved with his usual dark grace as he crossed the room, but all of the strength and power he had once had was now faded. He neglected himself too often, choosing instead to attend to Syreena's needs over his own. He would often go days without hunting, and he didn't dare feed from Jasmine or anyone else to sustain himself, because then Syreena's gentle madness would turn into something else, something vicious and violent.

Jasmine sighed as he spared her only the briefest of looks.

Unsatisfied, she followed him as he tracked his bride's tragic wanderings through his fortress.

"Damien," she called to him as gently as she could. She tried to imbue the address with everything she was feeling, with all the support she could muster. She tried to remind him that she was there for him. She would always be there for him.

Usually he would ignore her or merely nod and continue on his way, but this was one of the rare instances when he stopped and turned back to her.

He looked so sad and tired. His handsome face should have shown nothing of his age, Vampires being utterly ageless, but these past years had altered his looks. He looked older. Weary. Lost. And Jasmine knew she wasn't the only one noticing it. When a Prince grew weak, he could not defend his holdings or his monarchy. There were vipers, young, powerful, strong vipers, waiting in the darkness for the chance to sever Damien's head from his body and thereby lay claim to the Vampire monarchy.

Jasmine was the only one standing in their way. Her strength and her loyalty were protecting Damien's life and his rule.

"Damien . . ." she said again as she reached to put her arms around him. He resisted her hug, casting a worried glance after Syreena, but in the end he was starving for the strength and support of his best friend and adviser. In the end he let her hold him, let her hug him tight and close. He took a deep, cleansing breath, drawing in Jasmine's personal aura, her vigor.

Jasmine bit her tongue so she didn't give in to the urge to spew words he would refuse to hear in any event. "Have you hunted recently?" she asked instead.

"Not very recently," he admitted to her. "But I cannot leave her alone. If she wandered into the wrong place unprotected . . ."

Mad or not, Syreena was still an exotic genetic anomaly. She was a one-of-a-kind Lycanthrope, a changeling who could take on two animal forms instead of just one because a childhood illness had split her abilities in two directions. But what had made her special had also left her barren. At first her barrenness had been attributed to the fact that Vampires and Lycans were not compatible, but as other Vampires began to take Lycanthrope mates and proceeded to have buckets of children together, it became all too clear that the fault was with Syreena's very specifically altered biology. This was Syreena's opinion anyway. An opinion Jasmine had shared. But after Ruth's perversion of her deepest held fears, Syreena began wandering the halls of the citadel like some kind of screwed-up Ophelia, singing to herself and chasing hallucinations in circles. Jas had let go of her enmity toward Damien's wife, feeling too sorry for her in the long run to keep hating her scrawny little guts.

Damien was right. There were lawless Vampires everywhere who coveted Syreena's powerful Lycanthrope blood, and she was now helpless to protect herself. Syreena had once been a magnificent fighter. Jasmine had to confess to that. But now she was an easy meal for any Vampire who bumped into her.

"Damien, you can't do this for the rest of your life," Jasmine said softly, knowing the grim reality of her words would anger him.

"What would you have me do?" he said, but this time there was no anger, and there was no fire in the question. It was as though he was honestly asking for her help. Jasmine's solution had always been to kill the silly bitch and be done with it. But the truth was, for all of Damien's present unhappiness, to lose Syreena would be the end of him. He fancied himself hopelessly heartbound to the Lycanthrope, connected to her in some mystical, spiritual way. Damien had already proven to her that if Syreena died, he would quickly follow.

Jasmine cared too deeply for him to lose him.

And Jasmine needed her anchors, like her friendship with Damien and her appointment as leader of the Nightwalker Sensor Network. It was too easy for her to lose touch with the world around her. Too easy to grow bored and melancholy. It had been that way for as long as she could remember. Perhaps all of her life . . . but more so since . . .

Jasmine shook the thought off. It did no good to wallow in what might have been, what once had been . . . what no longer was. Nor was she going to allow herself to get so depressed that she could no longer bear living aboveground. Damien needed her. Desperately. If she went to ground, some bastard Vampire would take advantage of Damien's present preoccupation, see it for the weakness that it was, and behead the Prince, taking his throne from him in one sweep of violence. Then who knew what would happen to the era of peace the Nightwalkers were trying so hard to enjoy.

She laughed at herself. Her appointment to the Nightwalker Sensor Network was supposed to have been a temporary one. She was supposed to get it on its feet and then turn over the reins to someone else, preferably Stephan, the former leader of the Vanguard, the Vampires' version of an army. But Stephan had been killed, and it turned out there was no one else to take over. Not anyone that all the leaders of the Nightwalker clans were comfortable with, at any rate.

"You need to hunt. You need to keep strong," she counseled her Prince. "You cannot protect her in this weakened state."

"What is this?"

The shrill demand made Jasmine and Damien jump apart, with a guilt there was no reason to feel. They had done nothing wrong.

But the madness in Syreena's eyes blazed and she was pointing an accusatory finger at Jasmine and her husband. "I see! I see it now! You don't love me! You are going to throw me aside because I cannot give you the children you desire!"

"Syreena, that is not true," Damien said soothingly as he tried to gather his rigid, hysterical wife into his embrace, turning his back on Jasmine and the brief moment of opportunity where Jasmine might have made him see sense.

"You've always loved her more than me," Syreena accused him with heavy sadness washing over her and tears filling her eyes. "She's always been better for you than I have. You ought to have married Jasmine. Everyone says it. Everyone thinks it!"

"No one says that," he denied softly, although it was very much a supposition in Vampire circles. "And even if they did, it would not matter to me. It never has. You are everything to me. You are my only love. I need nothing else so long as I have you. I wish you would believe that."

But Jasmine knew Syreena didn't believe him. If she had, then maybe Ruth would not have been able to weaken her mind, tormenting her over children she simply could not create.

Although if Jasmine was going to be fair, Syreena and Damien had once been very happy, strong and content in spite of the Princess's infertility. They had seemed to love each other powerfully enough to overcome this obstacle and learn to be happy with just each other.

Jasmine walked away from the couple. It was just too painful to watch them now. Needing to escape, for just a little while, she flew away from the Romanian fortress and traveled the miles to the Russian provinces of the Lycanthropes. She was drawn to these caverns again and again for one reason. She asked herself for the thousandth time why she was there, why she was so obsessed with checking in on the little Demon orphan she'd rescued that day long ago in similar caverns.

She had no more answers now than she ever had.

Jasmine went in search of Leah.

"Mama, have you seen Father?"

Legna looked up at her son and tried to hide her surprise. It wasn't like her son to seek out his father voluntarily, and it certainly wasn't time for lessons.

"He is in the south wing. Just beyond the baths. Why do you ask?"

"Oh, I had a question for him." Seth shrugged it off, but Legna was a Mind Demon, and that made her a powerful empath. She could sense her son's emotions very easily. She was grateful for that because it

was the only way she would ever know what was going on in his head most of the time. Ever since he had reached puberty, he had become like a stranger to her—and a hostile stranger to his father.

She had to give Gideon credit for his patience with the boy. Gideon was a very direct creature and didn't see much value in indulging in wasteful emotions. Not that he wasn't a devoted and loving father. He was, and he tried to show it as best he could. As Gideon's Imprinted mate she was very well aware of how deeply loving and passionate a man Gideon truly was. And, with her, he was quite demonstrative.

But since Seth had reached ten years of age, they had lost touch with each other. Seth had started to reject his father's attentions and affections . . . now the only way they connected was in their daily lessons. It baffled Gideon no end. He was Ancient and wise, had lived so many ages and experienced so many things, but he had never been a father before and found himself at a loss. He wanted to be direct, address the problem head-on, but luckily Legna had been able to convince him that wouldn't be a very good idea. Seth was very sensitive, even a little brooding. He tended to come around to things in his own way and in his own time. It was best to let him do so without forcing him or challenging him before he was ready.

"I am certain he would love to answer your questions," she said, turning from her baking and dusting off her hands.

"Yeah. I know. He'd never miss a chance at a lecture," Seth said, coming just shy of sounding snide.

"Seth, your father loves to teach you. He wants to prepare you for the world and for the future. He does it to protect you. There are so many dangers out there."

"He should just leave me to my own devices. Seems to me he'd be happier if I got bounced off the earth," Seth said with a shrug.

"Seth! Why would you think such a thing?"

Seth drew back at her powerful response, looking a little trapped for a moment, almost as if he hadn't meant to speak his feelings aloud.

"Never mind," he said hastily, pulling back as his mother reached for him. "I was just talking trash."

"First," she said as she grabbed hold of his arm, "lying to your mother is unacceptable. Second, lying to an empath is futile. Surely you have learned that as my son."

She took the sting out of the rebuke by drawing a line of flour down the side of his cheek.

"Mama!" he protested, swiping at his face. But he stopped trying to escape her. With his head hung, he shrugged one of his narrow shoulders. "It's just . . . I know I am nothing but a big disappointment to both of you. To everyone. I'm a powerless nothing when I ought to have been something special. He hates that I'm not all magnificent and special like he is."

"Sweet Destiny, Seth, nothing could be further from the truth! What is it that you think we are expecting from you? You are only fourteen years old! You have a good four to six years yet before we expect to be on the lookout for your power!"

"That's bull. You all look at Leah and wonder why I'm not as strong and special as she is." The boy's eyes teared up as he withdrew physically from her, wrapping his arms protectively around himself. "She did massive things when she was just two years old. Noah was really young when his power first showed. Jacob was what? Nine? Eight? All of the most powerful

Demons on the planet had so much power in them it couldn't wait to be born. And then there's me. A big, fat . . . nothing."

"The biggest mistake you can ever make is to compare yourself to others."

Seth started at the sound of his father's voice behind him. Shame rushed over him. How could he have forgotten? Speaking to his mother was like speaking to his father at the same time, their connection was so strong, their thoughts so intermingled. But he had seen his mother distance herself from his father psychically before. Stupid of him to think she would have done so now to give him a private moment with her. He turned quickly to face the astral projection of his father, his whole body bristling defensively as he tried to erect some kind of mental protection.

"Whatever," Seth said with a shrug. His eyes were cast downward, studying the rug on the floor.

"Seth," his father said, the tone of his voice far gentler than he was used to hearing from his sire. It was enough to encourage him to lift his eyes. "I have great faith that you will be an extraordinary Demon one day, I do not deny that. But if you were healthy and happy, that would be more than enough for me. Your happiness is everything to me."

Seth had never heard his father speak to him like that before. He looked at him with doubt, wondering if he was using some kind of reverse psychology on him.

"Or," his mother interrupted his thoughts gently, "maybe he loves you just the way you are."

Seth had so convinced himself otherwise that he really found the thought hard to believe. Legna could sense that, and she could sense her husband's dismay as well. It was an idea that would have to be addressed slowly and over a long period of time. But now that they were aware of what was at the root of their son's troubles, they could perhaps go about rectifying the problem.

"Gideon, your son had a question for you," she said, smoothly changing the topic of conversation. Seth was very relieved at the segue. He really hoped Leah appreciated his sticking his neck out for her. Manipulating either of his parents was no easy trick.

He shifted his shoulders and tried to appear casual.

"Actually, it was something Leah was asking about. Let me go get her and we'll come find you. It's kind of a history thing."

"History is crucial to understanding the present and forming a better future. I am glad you are taking an interest," Gideon said. Then he nodded permission to his son, sending the adolescent hurrying to find his playmate.

"Why would you ask about Enforcers aligned before your father?" Gideon asked some time later. It wasn't as though he was especially curious; he was simply gathering information.

"Uh . . . well, odds are I might become Enforcer one day," Leah said quickly. "Shouldn't I be well versed on the lineage and the methods they were known for using?" She shot Seth a look and he gave her a shielded thumbs-up.

"This is true," Gideon said. "But you are young, and time has a way of unfolding in ways we least expect. It could be that Kane and Corrine will have children and one of them will be heir to Kane's present position."

"It isn't very logical to live my life on groundless supposition. I have to assume the truth of the moment is the truth of the future."

Gideon turned to look at her, one of his silvery brows lifting in surprise. Gideon's silver hair and eyes were often unnerving to Leah, but in that moment she thought he was looking at her with a sense of pride. Suddenly it felt like something very special to her. She glanced at Seth again and knew by the look on his face that he felt it, too. The jealousy in his eyes said it all. He wanted more than anything for his father to look at him in that way.

"You are your father's daughter," Gideon said gently to her. "He was a man of practical logic. It was one of his greatest strengths."

Leah very often heard about how she looked, talked, or sounded like one of her parents, but this was something very different. She had never heard Gideon say anything like it before, and there was a peculiar intimacy to the speech that made it exceptional.

"Your father's approach to being Enforcer was very different from his predecessor's. And it changed even more when your mother came on the scene. It was softened, you might say. When your mother became an Enforcer, she made many efforts and changes to see that it became less of a shameful process to be enforced. Your mother was not a part of your father's life when he enforced me. His approach then was very like a—"

"Jacob enforced you?" Seth blurted out in utter shock, tacking on a laugh.

Gideon raised a brow at his son's outburst, and somehow it was a completely different expression from the one he had given Leah. Seth immediately closed his mouth and lowered his eyes.

"Very like a parent drawing his wayward child in line," Gideon finished. "Adam, Jacob's immediate predecessor as Enforcer, was more like a brutal taskmaster. He was powerful, sometimes tempestuous. Like Kane and Jacob, he was not even an Elder yet when he inherited the mantle of Enforcer. But make no mistake, he was good at what he did. He was a warrior like no other I have seen. Perhaps if Elijah had less of an ego, your *Siddah* might admit that Adam was a better warrior than he."

"Better than Elijah?" Leah breathed. "Wow." Then she remembered herself. "So what exactly happened to him? And when did it happen?"

"I think it was about . . . well, 1601. Samhain. No, wait . . . it was Beltane. He just failed to report in one night and that was the end of it."

"Are you sure it was Beltane?" Leah pressed.

"Yes. Your father refused to step into his brother's shoes at first, searching high and low for him. Grieving terribly. He did not accept the mantle of Enforcer until Samhain so I mistook the dates, using your father's ascension to Enforcer as the time of Adam's disappearance. But I am quite positive it was Beltane."

"And no one knows what happened to him?"

"It was assumed he was Summoned. When a Demon is Summoned by a necromancer, pulled out of his life and held prisoner in a pentagram until he is Transformed into a monster, it is often an unwitnessed event. The unexplained disappearance of a Demon is not uncommon. Though perhaps it is felt more sharply when it is a high-standing member of our society."

"I bet an Enforcer like Adam would have caught

and destroyed Ruth long ago," Leah said bitterly, her fists clenching in anger.

"Actually, that is not an unfair statement," Gideon mused. "Your father was much distracted by other things while Ruth was growing in power and wickedness. Adam was far more dogged in his ways. He would have taken all manner of risks to attain victory."

"Do you think he was better than Daddy was?" she asked quietly.

Gideon immediately shook his head. "Jacob had wisdom and age and the power that comes with both on his side. There has never been a more powerful Enforcer than your father, Leah." He took a breath. "But I would hesitate to pick sides in a head-to-head battle of the brothers."

Leah hurried away from Gideon and Legna's quarters, Seth scurrying along in her wake.

"I know what you're planning to do!"

Leah came to a screeching halt and about-faced, glaring at Seth and shushing him fiercely. She grabbed him by his shirtfront and yanked him into the privacy of a nearby alcove, hoping to cut their conversation away from the natural echo of the caverns.

"You don't know anything! Just keep your mouth shut!"

"You're insane, Leah. You don't even have the power to do it. So what, so you accidentally were able to jump through time once. You were two years old! It was a raging accident. Since then what have you been able to do? Send a stopwatch five minutes into the future?" Seth scoffed at the feat. "The great and magnificent child of Time, ladies and gentlemen!"

"You don't know anything!" she hissed at him again. "I'm so sick of you thinking you know so much and being such a jerk to me because I have powers and you don't. The great and magnificent child of Space, ladies and gentlemen, who can—gee, what *can* you do besides whine like a little brat?"

"Shut up! Why don't you just give it up, Leah? Your parents got their asses kicked and now they're dead. Dead, dead, dead! And there's nothing you can do about it!"

Leah swung out her hand and smacked him right across the mouth. The action shocked them both. Leah nursed her smarting hand and Seth nursed his bruised lip. Leah felt the need to cry stinging across her sinuses and burning in her eyes. She felt unable to contain the painful emotions flooding over her. She refused to let Seth have the satisfaction of seeing her hurt, so she ran. She kept running until she couldn't see her way anymore and couldn't breathe. Finally she fell to a stop beside an underground pool, one of many in the castle and the caverns. She knelt down and grabbed up a handful of the always cold water, splashing it over her face. Slowly she got herself under control, drew her sobs in until they were hard snif-fles. She swiped at her eyes, blinked and looked up to see a beautiful brunette standing next to her. Her hair was loose, a black cape all around her shoulders that reminded Leah of her mother. Her legs were encased in shiny tights of an opaque white and a short black miniskirt that barely covered her butt. Her pierced navel was exposed by the short navy blue tank she was wearing. It was her boots that dominated her outfit, though. They were soft black leather with brass but-tons climbing the backs of her legs in a nice steady row all the way up to her thighs. It was as though they alone were announcing her presence, and they were saying she was way too fine to mess with.

Leah had only glimpsed her from a distance over the past ten years, but she would never forget who the Vampire was. It immediately disturbed Leah that Jasmine should see her like this. Weak and out of sorts. She didn't know why it should matter, but it did.

She stood up and faced the Vampire, smoothing her own simple T-shirt down over her favorite pair of jeans. Still, she suddenly felt like it wasn't enough. Like she ought to be wearing something better. Like she ought to be something more. It was a moment Seth must experience every single day he woke up to his father's magnificence and stood in his shadow without anything to show for her parents' expectations of him.

Leah supposed it was because this woman had been her rescuer. Her hero, really. Jasmine was strong and powerful, had a real reputation for being a badass, and dressed with such confidence and panache. You couldn't miss her if you tried.

But there was something in her eyes right then, something Leah would never have thought to attribute to Jasmine.

Vulnerabiity.

"Can you do it?" Jasmine asked.

"C-can I do what?"

"You know what!" she said impatiently. She reached out and took hold of Leah's face by her chin. "If I could go back in time and change one thing, I would see to it that Prince Damien never met the Princess Syreena." She took a deep breath and closed her eyes as she slowly exhaled. "But that would be a selfish thing. A thing designed only to help him and myself.

Perhaps even her as well, when you think about it. But you . . ." Jasmine stared hard into Leah's eyes, and Leah felt the soft coaxing power of the Vampire's influence. It felt like being wrapped in a strange sort of warmth, something safe and caring. "Can you do this thing? Do you have the power?"

Leah simply nodded in reply.

"No," Jasmine breathed, an expression of unbelievable pain lancing across her features. "The past must stay in the past where it belongs. Do you understand me, little half-breed? You cannot play with time in such ways! You will destroy people and you will torment others. You could make things a thousand times worse than they are now! Do not meddle with the past!"

Leah was afraid as the powerful Vampire raged fiercely at her. This was no moralistic scolding like her other mentors had given. They had frequently hammered at her about the massive responsibilities that would come with her element. There was no other Demon of Time in the world and had never been one in history. She was the groundbreaker. But Elijah was very fond of telling her that just because she could do something didn't mean that she should. He told her he could become a category four hurricane that would destroy everything around him, but that didn't mean he should do it. In fact, the damage path would be a very obvious reason why he shouldn't.

Messing with Time could potentially create horrible damage paths. Some would be immediately visible, and others would not show themselves for years.

"I just thought . . ." Leah argued weakly. "Maybe if I could borrow . . . for just a minute . . ."

The young girl teared up and immediately tried to hide her weakness from Jasmine. The Vampire softened a little, understanding very clearly why the teenaged Demon would want to change her history. As Jasmine herself had said, there were things she wished she could change as well, people she would save—people she would protect. But it wasn't her place to try to go back to fashion the world in a way she thought it ought to be.

"There is danger in the idea that we can create a designer life for ourselves by manipulating this thing or that thing in our past," Jasmine said gently. "You might save your parents with one act, but that same act could end up killing Elijah, destroying the political stability of the Nightwalkers, or—I don't know— any number of variables. I understand you have been given these powers for a reason, and perhaps that reason is to alter moments in time to create a better future, but you are too young to be making these decisions now. And you certainly shouldn't be making them on your own. Your power is new yet. You don't know all of what you will be able to do one day. At the very least I must beg you to wait. See how time unfolds. Have patience."

It wasn't an unreasonable request.

Just an unbearable one.

Leah nodded in agreement, her face full of color and tracked with tears. Jasmine could feel the young girl's frustration. It eddied into her psychically like a powerful, stormy ocean tide. It churned wildly with her emotions as all of the plans Leah had been forming were now suddenly dashed upon the rocks of responsibility and morality.

Strange that it had been Jasmine to lecture about restraint and responsibility. Vampires were not known for coloring inside the lines and fully behaving themselves.

But Jasmine had seen too much damage done with out-of-control Nightwalker power. The rogue members of her own society who thought they could go around picking up powers by drinking the blood of innocent Nightwalkers disgusted her. It was one thing to dance along the edges of morality and quite something else to dive over the line again and again, leaving a path of damage. This young girl was a prime example of the harm that could be done when power wasn't properly tempered or respectfully held in check.

"I promise I . . . I won't do anything . . . unless I know for certain . . ." Leah stammered around her words, and Jasmine could appreciate how hard it was for her to rein herself in.

"Look, kiddo, only you can know in your heart what is right and what is wrong, what is selfishly motivated and what is truly for the greater good." Jasmine rolled her eyes. "Great, now I sound like Noah and Damien. But if you really want the best guidance around, go see Noah. He has walked both edges of the line you are teetering on. And he used you to do it. Ask him how he feels about it. Ask him why he hasn't thought about doing what you want to do." Jasmine lifted a shoulder. "Or better yet, ask him why he has thought about it but never approached you with the idea, because I promise you, the first person this would have occurred to is Noah."

With that instruction and a gentle tug on a curl at Leah's temple, Jasmine turned to leave the young girl to her own conscience and devices. But at the last moment, the girl grabbed her by the hand and made her turn back. She waited until their eyes met, her gaze earnest and fierce.

"Is that true? What you said? Is the moment Damien

met Syreena truly the one moment you would change if you could? Is that where you think all of this went wrong?" She opened a hand to indicate the screwed-up world they were living in.

"If Damien had never met her . . . or if he had never followed her the night she'd been kidnapped . . . Vampires would not be drinking the blood of Night-walkers. Before the moment Damien drank Syreena's blood, the act had been taboo—" Jasmine stopped, took a breath. "But I lie. Because the Exchange, the act of taking other Nightwalker blood and then those Nightwalkers taking our blood, was in books in the library we discovered after Elijah mated with Siena. We would have discovered it eventually. So perhaps I would go further back and keep the library from ever being found. That would perhaps mean keeping Ruth from looking for it, which drew our attention to it. So perhaps it's all about Ruth." Jasmine shook her head. "You see? You see how I could play this game? How do you choose? What gives you the right to choose? You believe in Destiny, don't you?"

"Yes," Leah said quietly.

"Then you have to believe that things happen for a reason, and even if you change something, Destiny will find a way to fulfill her needs."

"You mean that even if I kept my parents from dying in that cavern, Destiny would find a way to claim their lives regardless?"

"Possibly. Like I said, talk to Noah. He defied Destiny to take his mate. See what he says about the whole thing."

Leah nodded and this time it was she who turned away, hurrying off, perhaps to find a way to do exactly that.

* * *

Leah could easily have gone to her female *Siddah* and asked her to teleport her right into Noah's living room, but the young Time Demon needed to think . . . or perhaps was dragging her feet. So she was wandering less-traveled caverns, giving herself the time she needed to be alone with everything swirling through her mind.

It was a war between desires and responsibilities.

From the moment the idea had entered her head that perhaps she could redeem herself in the eyes of all those around her who must count her responsible for the deaths of her parents, she had been moving headlong into the possibility. Or so it seemed. She had actually toyed with the concept over and over again through the years, but it seemed every time it entered her mind, her *Siddah* would come up with some kind of lecture about the responsibility of power. It was almost as though they had read her mind, sensed her intentions, and were warning her off the path she wanted to travel. That might be a bit of paranoia, because although Legna was a strong empath, she wasn't a telepath, and neither was Elijah. So she had to assume it was Destiny herself dropping very strong hints in her lap, warning her to leave well enough alone; that she would only make bad situations worse if she meddled in the way things had unfolded.

But Leah watched the world around her quietly and carefully and continually came to the same conclusion. Things would be very different if only Jacob and Bella had not died that day while trying to protect her from Ruth and Nicodemous. What if, she continually asked, someone had come to their aid? What if that someone had been strong enough to defeat Ruth and Nico once and for all?

The question had then always been *who*? Who would be strong enough to do something like that? Noah? Leah couldn't take that risk. What if he wasn't? What if Noah was killed along with her parents? Then what would become of them all under the heavy loss of their King?

But now, suddenly, she had her candidate. Someone who, if taken at the moment of his death, would never be missed throughout time. Someone as powerful as her father. Someone who had it in his blood to fight and defeat a lawbreaking Demon. Someone whose death, should he die alongside her parents, simply would not matter in the grand scheme of things.

But just when she was ready to act, all these warning signs were being flung up in her face again. Jasmine, of all people, being one of them. What were the odds that the Vampire would be there, in that moment, overhearing her and Seth arguing? In Lycanthrope territory? They were infinitesimal.

Leah's eyes began to water with frustrated emotion. She knew exactly what Noah would say to her if she went to him. He would caution her just as Jasmine had. He might even act more strongly to prevent her from doing anything. This was why she had never voiced the idea before. She was wise enough, even at her young age, to understand the far-reaching ramifications that might come with her gifts if she used them without caution and forethought.

"Such a thoughtful child."

The compliment was said so snidely that Leah immediately jerked her attention to the speaker. She had been so absorbed in her moral dilemma, she hadn't realized just how far out of the reach of safety she had traveled.

And she had not realized she had walked right into Ruth's waiting arms.

"Now let us see," Ruth mused, her china blue eyes fixing on Leah in a way that paralyzed her. When Jasmine had entered Leah's mind, it had been almost like a seduction, like falling into the warm embrace of a lover. But having Ruth seize hold of her mind was something cold and terrible. Leah felt her body go dead, as if it weren't any longer a part of herself. And in a sense it wasn't. Ruth had cut off her ability to send and receive nerve impulses within her body.

Leah felt herself falling, dropping to the stone floor like a sack of potatoes. The deadly beautiful Demon moved over her, putting her hands on her knees as she peered down at Leah. Ruth's blond hair was swept to the side and twisted into a fat braid that draped off her shoulder, a strangely incongruous blue ribbon woven into it and tying it off in a big bow. She wore an expensive, luscious evening dress that accented her shoulders and dipped low in front. The midnight blue silk was peppered with sequins that flattered the curves of her figure. But the wide neckline of the dress also accented the vicious bruising and bite marks along both sides of the Demon traitor's neck.

As if the evidence of her Vampire lover's existence called him forth, Nicodemous drifted out of the shadows and appeared at Ruth's side. The smell of them together made Leah gag, making her realize that not all of her senses had been taken from her. What she smelled was the rottenness that filled the flesh of any creature who dabbled in black magics. Selfish, offensive magics. The past decade had shown the Nightwalker world that it was not always so. Natural-born Witches who used well-meant magic in selfless and defensive ways remained clean-smelling and pure. But once they began to dabble in darker arts, they became addicted to them like a poisonous drug, and that drug made them stink of their evilness to any other Nightwalker that came near.

Ruth and Nico reeked of their addiction, their eyes shining in a peculiar way that warned you they were probably a little bit insane from all their power mongering, from all the ways they had altered themselves over the years as they grew stronger and stronger.

"Well, listen to that," Nico mused as he, too, leaned forward to peer at her. "She's barely old enough for Fostering and yet her mind reeks of that self-important righteously moral propaganda you Demons are so fond of spewing."

"Oh, but more than that," Ruth whispered in a breathless way. "She's thinking about *us*, Nico, and how she can go about getting rid of *us*."

Panic infused every cell in Leah's body. Suddenly all the implications of being helpless at the hands of the Demon and, more importantly, the Vampire, who could potentially absorb her power, struck Leah. Since a Vampire could only gain one power from drinking the blood of a Nightwalker, and Leah only had one power to speak of, then that meant . . . It made her sick to her stomach to think that Ruth and Nico might obtain her ability to move through time. Suddenly the small ramifications of her one somewhat selfish act meant nothing in the face of the damage these two could do if they gained control over Time and began to leap back and forth within it, changing whatever they wanted to, sneaking up on unwitting historical figures who could never be prepared for their coming.

"I do so love it when they panic," Ruth mused to her partner, reaching out to fluff a curl near his ear. "They forget we can read their minds and start spewing information in their thoughts."

"Yes, it is rather handy, is it not?" Nicodemous agreed.

Nico reached down and plucked Leah up by her shirtfront, the T-shirt material stretching under her dead weight as he yanked her up closer to his face and the vicious mouthful of fangs he flashed at her.

"So, morsel, you think you have the key to something your betters have never been able to accomplish? You think you have what it takes to destroy us?"

"She may be right," Ruth supposed. "If she found a way to attack us before we were strong enough . . ." The demented Demon straightened her posture and gently stroked her long, graceful fingers down the length of her braid. "Rip out her throat. Drink what you can and kill the little bitch. Then we'll have the power of Time and there will be no one to stop us."

"Finally . . . finally I will be Prince of the Vampires," Nico snarled. "Let Damien find a way to fight me from his crib!"

And in a single savage act he flashed an angry mouthful of fangs at the young girl and sank them viciously into her delicate neck.

Leah screamed. She knew that all it would take was one wrenching pull and she'd be flayed open to bleed to death like her mother had. And all it would take was one swallow and all of the Nightwalker worlds could fall into chaos.

Her panic triggered her power, which whipped through her like the blade of a razor, painful and uncontrolled, nothing but pure instinct. Every molecule of her body began to individually flee from her attacker, leaping through the only thing she had the smallest bit of control of.

Leaping through time.

Chapter 3

About Four Hundred Years Earlier

"Adam!"

Adam's dark head picked up, sweat flinging off his brow as he swung unruly black curls dripping with the salty liquid out of his eyes. They were his mother's eyes, much to his father's consternation. Mother and son both had eyes of the palest green, so clear and so light that it was almost as if they were incandescent. It enhanced the powerful ability both had to seemingly peer straight into someone's soul. Those on the receiving end of that pale jade stare often confessed the total truth, behaving themselves, or rectifying wrongs, whether they wanted to or not.

It was that very same set of eyes that had forced Adam's father, Asher, to confess his undying admiration to a saucy, stubborn, raven-haired female in spite of the fact that he had sworn himself to bachelorhood forever. Now he was two grown sons' deep into the union and had never been happier.

That same female, now three centuries older but

no less saucy or beautiful for it, was calling Adam from the turrets of the family castle. He could see the long braid of her hair hanging six feet down over her shoulder, the fanned tail of it fluttering in the breeze like the family crest she stood near as she leaned over the wall to call him.

"Madam," he addressed her, his deep voice booming up to the ramparts and farther still. "I have asked you not to disturb me when I am at practice." He swept a hand behind himself to indicate the four other Demons lying in various positions of semiconsciousness on the dusty ground, as well as the tall, lanky figure of his brother Jacob, who was leaning casually against the back of a stone statue of their grandfather that stood at the edge of the practice grounds. Jacob almost looked as though he were commiserating with the old man, who grinned deviously down on the practice field where, like his eldest grandson, he'd had a rather nasty habit of tearing through practice partners with god-awful speed.

"It would seem you are due to give your men a reprieve," their mother rejoined boldly, taking note of his exhausted opponents with far too much motherly humor in her voice.

Adam hated it when she did that. Treated him like a son. Of course, he also adored her for it. Being his mother, she could always be counted on to be the one person on the planet who, though she supported and praised him constantly, somehow still managed to be entirely unimpressed and unaffected by the man he had become. Even their father would have shown Adam far more respect for his rank and position in the grand scheme of things. Adam supposed, however, that it was a mother's prerogative to always treat

her son the same as she had when he was just a boy,
and it was a son's prerogative to indulge her in her
desire to do so.

"I suppose you have a point," he conceded, turning
to flash an enormous grin at his baby brother, if a
man 221 years of age could be considered a baby still.
Jacob grinned back, running a hand through the
brown-black hair that he kept far too loose and wild
for Adam's tastes. "Will you require your youngest son
as well?" he asked her.

"As a matter of fact, I should appreciate that."

"What is the matter, Adam, are you afraid that if I
get a few minutes' extra practice in, I will become
better than you?"

"A fear like that would not only be ridiculous, it
would be a complete waste of time," Adam shot back
to his cocky sibling. He would have to make Jacob eat
a bit of arena dirt later on, just to keep him humble.
The upstart was beginning to get as good as he thought
he was, and that had the potential to make him unbearable to live with.

The ribbing and boasts continued as the sons
moved into their home to seek out their mother and
discover what her bidding would be.

Eleanor had come in from the upper walkway, a bit
windblown and breathless, but rosy with merriment
and her clear delight in her offspring as they entered
her salon on the top floor of the north tower. She
took a moment to look over her sons, so different in
many ways, and yet so clearly cut from the same cloth.
Adam had inherited her hair color along with her
eyes, but his towering height and almost beastly build
was a throwback to his grandfather on his father's
side. His best friend, and also his cousin, was a Demon

named Noah, the only Demon in existence who even came close to matching up to Adam's behemoth proportions. Adam sported shoulders that seemed a mile wide, a chest just as broad, and a waist that narrowed fit and tight with straps of well-worked muscles, but was still thick like the trunk of a sturdy oak tree.

In contrast, his younger brother Jacob was lean and athletic, sleek where Adam was more bullish, flexible where his brother was brutally forceful. Eleanor's younger son had his father's hair and build, as well as his dark brown eyes that turned ebony with a rise in temper or other emotive passions.

But even as they differed in looks and build, they rang in perfect tune when it came to morals. Both were obsessed with the nature of the law, crime and its appropriate punishment. Both had a sense of right and wrong that was implacable and unwavering. They were highly moral creatures, something that she demurely credited herself with lending to their makeup. Unfortunately, his conscience gave Jacob the tendency to be very hard on himself should he make some sort of error; and Adam . . .

Adam always wanted to save the world at all costs. Or at least the Demon part of the world. He was protective of humans, respectful of those other Nightwalkers that deserved respect. But he clearly did not know his own limitations. Eleanor herself had yet to see what they were, but she was worried that one day he would find out the point at which he fell short—only after he had raced headlong over the edge of the cliff. She dreaded the day he would subsequently plummet to the ground, brought rudely to earth and awakened to the fact that he would never be able to save everyone and do the right thing on time, all of the time.

As a mother, it was Eleanor's job to worry about her sons' sensitivities and vulnerabilities. It was also her job never to insult their egos by letting them know she still fretted over them in such ways. Asher was always warning her that their boys were far more intuitive than she gave them credit for, and though they allowed her these motherly eccentricities, she'd best not test them too far.

But Eleanor already knew that. She had no intention of ever making her children regret her behavior toward them. They had worked too hard to earn their manhood to be undermined by her.

Of course, that did not mean she would not meddle at all. She was looking forward to grandchildren one day, and if she knew Demon males, they were not likely to go willingly or seek mates eagerly. Well, Demon females could be just as wily as their counterparts, and more than made up for the males' recalcitrance with their own ambitions. She had faith that one day each of her sons would meet his match in a woman, and she made no secret about it.

"Mother," Jacob greeted her, grabbing her extended hands and pulling her close to kiss her peaches-and-cream cheek. Because they'd stopped aging somewhere in their twenties, Eleanor and Jacob could be mistaken for brother and sister, but all one had to do was witness their exchange of fond gazes to see the bond of parental kinship that was there.

"Madam," Adam greeted her more gruffly, as if he were too old and too important to call her "Mother" any longer. However, he drew her into an incredible bear hug that broadcast his undying affection for her.

"Now suppose you tell us," he continued after he finally set her back down onto her slender feet with great care, "why you felt it necessary to drag us from training in the middle of the night."

"I wish to discuss the festival."

Her sons glanced at each other, exchanging pained but patient expressions.

"Mother, we have had the arrangements in place for months. Beltane is tomorrow, and the festival will be flawless as usual. Why are you fretting?"

"Because I am hostess to your cousin's royal event this year, and I would see it done perfectly or not at all. Now, did you invite the Gypsies onto our lands?"

"Of course, Mother," Adam sighed, "It is tradition, after all. And we know you feel it is a good omen."

"Very well," Eleanor conceded. "Have you selected your escorts, then?"

This received the expected sounds of protest from both of them.

"Boys," she said, her tone stern but not too scolding, "you are my sons, and therefore will be expected to bring a proper woman to the table, not just run off and tumble some girl behind a bush later on and consider yourselves as having been social." She ignored their chuckles and mirth-filled glances at one another. "Some other families may not care about decorum, but I do. Please see that you choose decent Demon girls."

"No decent Demon girls will have us," Jacob joked, reaching to tug on her braid in a rascally manner. "I hear that I am far too brooding."

"And I am Enforcer," Adam said, that in and of itself an explanation. "I think my time is better spent enforcing the unruly on Beltane rather than finding some chit brave enough to face her fear of the Enforcer so she may share my plate."

"I swear, you boys would drive Destiny Herself to tears," Eleanor huffed in exasperation. "Adam, I am well aware you will very likely be called away to work, but the rest of the time I expect you to remain here and be sociable. Jacob, I will take no such excuses from you. Choose or I will choose for you, and I do not think you will like my choice half as well as you would enjoy your own."

"Just so long as she comes clothed and does not belch at table?"

"Jacob! Honestly!"

"You try too hard, Mother. You should know by now that neither of us will ever be likely to marry. Adam is far too ugly, and I am far too smart."

Adam reached out and cuffed his brother for his insult, nearly knocking him onto the floor in the process. Eleanor rolled her eyes up toward the ceiling, seeking not only strength, but also possibly reassessing her thoughts on their maturity.

"If we promise to come properly accompanied, will you relax about the festival and allow us to return to work?" Adam asked her.

"Of course," she said with a show of satisfaction and contentment. She knew her sons would keep their word.

"Then we give you our promise to do so."

Adam used only a thought to change from flesh and bone into the form of a mist that allowed him to ride the clouds and wind currents. He rose above the home he had grown up in and let the current of the natural wind carry him over the vast Hungarian forest below. As a Water Demon he could travel as mist or fog or even waves upon the waters, but the superfine mist of a cloud upon the breeze was by far his preferred choice and by far the quickest.

His path of travel ran quite close to the Romanian border, also known as Vampire territory, but the Enforcer was unconcerned in spite of the fact that the two Nightwalker factions—Vampire and Demon—were embroiled in a war. Certainly each side fought with gusto, the Demons believing the Vampires to be unruly and in need of controlling, and the Vampires not liking that idea at all. Adam resented anyone who wasted their time and energy on nothing better than pursuits of pleasure. The Nightwalkers' long lives were precious gifts. They should be used with far better care than the minions of Prince Damien practiced. That, compounded with their delight in meddling in human affairs, made them dangerous. Their behavior put all Nightwalkers at risk. Perhaps King Noah thought that one day Damien would see reason and suddenly start to give a damn about what his subjects did, but Adam did not subscribe to the belief that there was any such thing as a decent Vampire.

It was an attitude shared by his younger brother. Jacob had become quite an efficient Vampire hunter. Quite a notorious one at that, and Jacob ate up his glory just as he would sweet cakes and wine. He thrilled in the war with Prince Damien's bloodthirsty little sycophants. The Vampires had proven that they hungered for bloodshed to relieve their boredom. After all, it was taboo and deadly for Vampires to drink the blood of other Nightwalkers, so they certainly weren't doing it for nutritional purposes. No. The little bastards were simply out to entertain themselves with a few Demon deaths. Unfortunately for them, when they took on his baby brother, all they got was a world of hurt.

Unfortunately for Adam, success was giving Jacob an ego that was becoming unbearable of late.

Another good fighter and a friend of his was the warrior Elijah. He had to say that were it not for the infamy and skills of Adam's brother, Elijah might have made a future Warrior Captain, the leader of all of the Demon King's armed forces. But should the present Captain ever retire, it was most likely Jacob who would fill his position.

At the moment Elijah was a highly ranked warrior who lived on the borders of the Vampire and Demon territories. He said it was to discourage Vampire raids on innocent Demons, but it was more likely so he could wake up every night and be immediately in the thick of battle. There was something of a friendly pissing contest going on between the warrior and Jacob. But it was a little like an apple competing with a pine cone. Elijah was a part of sanctioned battles orchestrated by the Captain and the King. Jacob was a bounty hunter, tracking down specific war criminals.

The thought came to Adam's mind because he was very close to the warrior's holdings just then. In fact, he was almost upon them when a movement below him caught his attention. The sleek-moving shape was too fast and too nimble to be just any kind of forest creature. Curious, he quickly descended into the forest below. As always, the first thing to fill his awareness was all sources of water. Where they were located, which directions they were traveling, the volume of each body of water both big and small. Nothing was too insignificant, no information deemed useless. His senses ran high with the presence of a heavy-running stream nearby, its source coming from up in the high, snow-laden mountains. It ran swift and cold only a short distance away. As he neared it with the March moonlight at his back, he changed back into flesh until he could see his breath clouding on the still and chill air. Then he heard and saw what had drawn him there in the first place.

Crouching down low to the forest floor, moving as silently as a breath, Adam peered through the nearby brush to see what manner of creature was running these woods in the darkest hours of the night. And because the moon was near full, its pearlescent light blanketing every inch of the water nearby, Adam could see with perfect clarity.

It was a woman. She was completely nude as she waded through the freezing temperature of the night and the water. She was pale as alabaster, the moonlight no doubt playing tricks on his eyes, because he had never seen such white perfection before. She was almost aglow as she stood there splashing water up and over her long, luminescent legs, and he could see almost every inch of her was covered in gooseflesh. Most obvious was the hard thrust of dark mauve nipples, as they stood out at the tips of rather generous breasts. Her hair was black as pitch, at least when wet, and a natural curl seemed to ease its way through it. She had the overall figure of a painstakingly crafted statue, although she was a bit too thin at the waist and hips for his taste. But that didn't keep Adam's lips from curling in a smile of appreciation.

She had to be out of her mind, bathing in such frigid conditions, alone in what amounted to a wilderness. The nearest human road was miles away from this place, not to mention any sign of a town or village. He wondered how she had even managed to get there, watching with amazement as she moved to a small fall of water nearby and let it crash into her hair and over her body until her smooth skin sparkled as though she'd been rubbed with diamonds. For that brief moment, Adam had a powerful compulsion to fling himself into his element; to become Water so he, too, could rush down those stones and onto the perfect, porcelain skin and all its charms.

The desire was so powerful, the draw all but irresistible, that he was shocked and stunned by it. He knew, in an instant, that the Hallowed moon of Beltane was what did this to him, and he growled low in ferocious defiance. He was Enforcer. He knew all too well the madness the full moons of Samhain and Beltane wrought on Demonkind. It was his calling, his special Destiny, to punish and control those who desired a member of any breed other than their own. It was not ever going to be acceptable for him to admire a non-Demon female in any fashion. He couldn't afford the luxury of such risks. If he were ever to cross that maddening line, only his blood kin had the senses necessary to detect his betrayal of himself and his people. That would pit him against his young brother or, worse yet, his father. The idea of facing such humiliation was nothing to the proud Demon male when he considered the possibility that in a fit of madness, he might injure, or worse yet, *kill* a member of his own blood family. He knew all too well his own power and strength. After almost three centuries of life, he was more than familiar with his capabilities. People feared him because he was Enforcer, it was true, but they feared him more because they knew he was a savage and artful fighter who had almost no equal.

Adam swore hotly at the thought, jerking back unthinkingly in the underbrush. The girl in the water jolted at the sound and surged out from under the fall, coming toward him with several running steps through the water. Her motion caused tremors along the delectable flesh of the curves of her fair body. She saw him there, narrowing her gaze on him, and for a brief instant he saw the deep mink brown of sultry, bedroom-wise eyes. Then he very clearly saw the flick of a nictitating membrane drop down to cover her pupils as she attempted to define what manner of creature he was by use of her heat-sensing vision.

"Vampire!" he hissed at her in accusation, instantly on his guard as he snatched up the dagger at his belt. It mattered not if the Vampire was a female; she would be as strong and deadly as any male counterpart of her breed.

To Adam's surprise, however, she merely set her hands on her hips, her stance wide and her expression almost bored as she took his measure. Her dark eyes drifted slowly over him, from head to toe, clearly evaluating him as if he were as naked and vulnerable as she was. About halfway down his body, she lifted a single slim brow as though in appreciation, and her lips curved into a wicked little smile.

Adam was shocked when her obvious interest found a mark within his tense body, a queer and robust thrill of heat and chill rushing under his skin and down his spine. *Sweet Destiny,* he thought in stunned disbelief, *I know she is a Vampire, and still she arouses me!* Adam wanted to be disgusted through and through at himself, but he hardly had the time to work up the proper response before she continued to walk toward him, a low little chuckle rolling out of her.

"My, my, they are making your breed quite large nowadays, are they not?" she asked as she rose from the water, climbing the bank of the stream. She looked down at the dagger in his hand, the metal gleaming in the moonlight as she walked up close enough so the tip of it touched just above her left breast. The fearless action completely disarmed the Enforcer as he tried to figure out what her game was. He sensed out for miles for other Vampires, other life forms, but they were alone. Even if she was clouding his perceptions with her Vampire ability to play with his mind, he knew how to remain clear despite that. He was fairly confident this was no trick or trap.

Fairly.

"I am assuming by your less-than-polite greeting that we are, perhaps, enemies?" she asked before affecting a wide yawn. Her whole body stretched, lean muscles flexing under perfectly pale skin. "I have been asleep for some time, you see. Is the war not over yet?"

"Demons and Vampires are still at war. And you can thank your bastard Prince for that," he bit out. But her reaction was quite believable. If she had been asleep as she said, it was natural to expect she wasn't up on recent news. It was not unusual for Vampires to "go to ground" when they grew bored with the outside world, seeking to sleep away a few years, hoping to wake during more exciting times.

"Damien?" She laughed as if it were the funniest joke she'd ever heard, her body dancing attractively under the vibration of her merriment. Hard as he tried, Adam could not keep his eyes on hers, where they needed to be. Even his breathing betrayed him and slid out of his control as he took in the curves of her breasts, the plane of her flat belly, and the wet droplets clinging to her nether curls and her thighs. He had always known Vampires had a natural sensuality that called to all bipedal creatures. It was part hunting instinct, part mating instinct. In a hunt, she could use that body and its sexual magnetism to lure her prey in as close as she needed it. She might even choose to fornicate with her human meal before drinking and leaving her prey to recover in a defenseless heap.

"Well, nothing would surprise me," she noted after she got control of her amusement. "But as for you and me, does this mean I am to get a dagger through the heart? War is so tedious. I was not prepared for it, as you see." She spread out her arms and displayed her body in a rather slinky turn of her hip and proud upthrust of outstanding breasts. The movement caused her to prick herself on his blade tip, and a single line of blood appeared on her pale skin as a bead of red followed a slow path to the tip of her nipple before dripping off. When Adam let a pained little noise escape him, the female Vampire narrowed her gaze on his once again, and he realized with dread that she was seeing into his mind with her telepathic ability.

Adam jerked back and away from her, nearly falling on his ass in the process. She laughed again; completely confident of the disturbing effect she had on him.

"Well, well," she teased, stepping in pursuit of him as he backed away from her, "it seems someone does not have thoughts of war in the front of his mind."

"The mind is a fickle thing, Vampire. Do not let

mine fool you. It is a full moon and a cursed holiday that puts me out of my own control; nothing more. Despite this disgusting display of lust my instincts force upon me, I will not hesitate to kill you. In fact, it only makes the temptation to do so all the stronger."

"Such a waste," she said to him softly, a mysterious contemplation in those dark eyes as they took his measure again. She stopped her gaze at the height of his hips, that little brow rising again as she took easy note of the erection he had developed. "Mmm, now, there is a sight to wake up to. 'Tis a shame you are not a Vampire. I must say, though, you are enough to make a girl reconsider playing outside of her race." She gave a delicate shudder. "*You* at least seem to have learned how to bathe, unlike most others. But the fact is, your race is just as elitist as mine. It would be rather like a cat fornicating with a dog, would it not?"

"Do you Vampires think of nothing but sex and feeding?" he demanded, his voice a hoarse rasp as his mind swirled with the heat of the possibilities her provocative words sent bursting through his mind. Her reminder of the very laws he was supposed to be enforcing did little to quell him.

"Oh, my sweet Demon," she purred, "do not stand there and pretend you are not considering dozens of ways of penetrating me," she taunted him like a cruel siren. "Putting aside the state of your body, Adam," she said, purposely using his name to remind him how easy it was for her to see into his mind, "you are already imagining the feel of coming deep inside me. Perhaps just after I have had a fresh feed, when my body is at its highest heat . . ."

It was a temptation she should not have laid at the door of a Demon who struggled against the full

Beltane moon. For in that moment Adam felt control slip out of his grasp and something wild was suddenly unleashed inside him. He lurched forward, dropping his dagger to the ground, and grabbed hold of her arms. He gritted his teeth as one wild urge after another surged through his mind, and finally he threw himself at her.

He changed form in the blink of an eye, morphing from man to a deluge of water that dashed against her face and body. But unlike normal water, he did not cascade off her and fall to the ground. Instead, he flowed over her supple body, slowly washing over and around her, covering her inch by inch. He felt the smoothness of her skin beneath his touch, the weight of her breasts . . . tasted the hard points of her nipples.

She gasped in shock when he first hit her, but that shock quickly changed to something deeper and far sultrier. The sound that erupted from her as he flowed over her was nothing short of purest sin. He took satisfaction in it.

And even as he covered the most intimate inches of her skin with his exploration, he knew he was going too far. It had gone too far the moment he had sat in the brush to stare at her as she bathed. But this, what he was doing now, it was a whole other level of perversion, and as glorious as she felt, he knew he was stepping way over the line.

With a swirl of fluid grace he pulled away from her and resumed his natural form. They stood like that, in the cold, dark forest, breathing hard and dazed with the mutual arousal he had wrought. But even as their bodies ran hot with physical need, their minds realized they were enemies.

This was forbidden. By law and by nature, a Demon

could never mate with a Vampire. And any Demon who tried would have to face the Enforcer.

The understanding brought the Enforcer sharply back to his senses. He fixed gazes with the admittedly beautiful Vampire and set his jaw. With a nod, he confessed to them both that he had instigated this walk in forbidden territory. But his demeanor made it just as clear he wouldn't be repeating the act any time soon.

Adam burst into a superfine mist that caught on the chill breeze brushing through the forest and let it lift him fast and far from forbidden fruit.

Jasmine laughed breathlessly to herself as the Demon hightailed it out of her range. Her shock at the way he had splashed over her, the incredible way it had felt as he'd literally touched her everywhere at once, was indescribable. She had always thought Demons to be so puritanical, so boringly proper. She knew for a fact they were as racist as Vampires were. The idea of stepping outside of their species for enjoyment was something they simply would not consider.

Well, for the very first time, Jasmine could see some merit in considering it. Oh, not that she would ever really do something like that, but if ever she had been tempted, it had been five seconds ago, when she'd been touched in a way no one had touched her before or would ever be likely to touch her again.

She attempted to shake herself free of the peculiar spell he seemed to have cast on her hungry body. Honestly, she thought with amusement as she recalled his retreat, Demons were by far the most uptight, straight-laced bunch of Nightwalkers she had ever met. Even the annoying Shadowdwellers knew how to have fun as they caused impish mischief everywhere they could. But the Demons . . . for all their varied powers of the elements, the Demons bogged themselves down in so many laws, morals, and self-recriminations, it was a wonder they even knew how to propagate their species at all!

Although, she considered slyly, this Adam seemed as though he'd give a girl a fair enough ride for her money. Jasmine sighed and stretched out her tingling body, the cold of the night warring with the heat of her thoughts. He was a brute, that one, she mused. Perhaps she was intrigued because most of her own race was made up of boyishly slim males, all long legs and lean elegance. When she lived with Damien's entourage, as she was planning on doing again once she caught up to them, she often traded clothing with the males and hardly noticed any disparities of fit.

But that Demon . . .

He'd had a good three inches and at least four stones of weight over Prince Damien, who himself was quite large for his breed. Adam's shoulders had been broad enough to block her view of the moon completely. He had towered over her long height, and his dagger had obviously been special-made for the width and the size of his monstrous hands. She had never seen such enormous hands before, and although at ninety-three she was still considered quite young for a Vampire—for a Nightwalker, truth be told—she figured she had still seen enough.

Jasmine slowly knelt down in the brush at her feet, her hand reaching out to close around the dagger that lay forgotten on the forest floor. It was a thing of deadly beauty, heavy in the heft and bejeweled along the hilt in a delicate pattern of swirling aquamarines.

Usually stones were bulky or coarsely cut, but these were each matched in size and had been faceted to catch any and every light.

How impractical, she thought. It would catch attention far too easily, making a stealth attack completely impossible. And yet she had never seen such a beautiful weapon. She held the length of it against her breastbone and thought about its owner. Again, Jasmine found herself contemplating raw sexual possibilities with a male not of her kind. She surprised herself. She didn't consider herself quite as lascivious as others of her breed. And she wasn't usually turned on by the idea of sex with anyone not a Vampire. Other Vampires might dally with humans, but the idea of having sex outside her species was not for her.

Usually.

Anyway, she much preferred a good book, delving into modern sciences or merely watching the folly of others. Adam had been an opportunity of amusement, and now the moment was passed. He would be easily forgotten . . .

Now she was better off focusing herself on the need for a good long feed. Then she'd find Damien and have him amuse her with stories about this continuing war.

Chapter 4

Damien felt the vibration of a Vampire entering his territory as if it were an earthquake inside him. Of course, he was literally surrounded by Vampires, dozens of them at a time coming and going from his territory as they hunted at a respectful distance from where he lived. But he could always sense the ones who did not belong, the ones who had trouble on their minds, and the ones . . . the ones who were special to him.

She was young yet, too young to have grown past the natural functions of the body like breathing and a heartbeat and circulation. She was close to shedding them, though. Her body would mature greatly in the next few years, completely changing in chemistry and makeup, and all those physical things would cease to be autonomic.

But even as young as she was, he had never seen her as infantile, as he often did with newborn Vampires. She had been wise beyond her years, thoughtful and intelligent, stimulating to his mind.

It had crushed him when, at only fifty-four years

old, she had grown so devastatingly bored with the world that she had decided to go to ground. But he had understood. It had surprised him it had happened while she was so young yet, and that kind of sensitivity did not bode well for her future, but he had understood. He had once become that disenchanted.

Once.

Then he had found purpose in becoming the leader of his people. Managing an entire species of easily bored creatures made for constant challenges. Then there was the additional challenge of keeping his head on his neck. There were always Vampires somewhere that fancied themselves stronger than he was or didn't like the rules he set into place. They would want to fight with him, hoping to defeat him and become ruler in his stead. Admittedly those challenges had grown fewer and farther between as it had become clear he was there to stay. Plus he had quite a loyal following, and his supporters were often able to take care of the smaller troubles before they even came to his attention.

"Stephan!" Damien sat up quickly, dumping a pair of twin Vampires off himself, not really caring where the women landed as he gained his feet and left the salon he'd been lazing around in.

Stephan, a young, eager Vampire with a taste for fighting, came into the hallway just as Damien was entering it himself. Stephan was a high-ranking soldier in the Vanguard and was well on his way to finding a position of charge. He was doggedly loyal, always there when Damien needed him, and a hell of a killer. Vampires and Demons were a bit of a mismatch when it came to fighting, the elemental Demons able to constantly change form and use the elements of the world around them as ammunition. But Vampires like Stephan had savagery and dedication on their side. Any Demon trick could be defeated with a little ingenuity and the powers the Vampires had been naturally imbued with.

"Yes, Prince Damien?" Stephan asked, quickly giving him a bow.

"Jasmine has returned. Bring her to me at once."

"My lord."

Stephan nodded in acceptance and turned to hurry for the nearest exit. He almost ran into Jasmine in the process. She stood with one hand on her hip, a smile quirking her lips and the ugliest, roughest cloth dress covering her body. Stephan smiled, took her by her arm, led her the four steps to Damien and bowed to his lord.

"Jasmine, as you requested, my lord," he said with a cheeky grin.

Damien called him an unflattering word and playfully cuffed him, ruffling his blond hair. Then he quickly pushed him aside and reached to pull Jasmine into a warm embrace. She sighed as she accepted his affection. He petted her tangled black hair, pushing the windblown mess back so he could see her face.

"So only a decade, eh? Little liar. More like four."

"I was sleepy," she argued, smiling up at him.

"So, pleased with yourself to find I missed you?"

"More pleased to find you clean-shaven. Last I saw you, it was pointy beards and mustaches. A ridiculous fashion, if you ask me."

"Hmm. And here I was considering growing it in again," he said as he rubbed at his chin thoughtfully.

"Do what you want. You will anyway."

"And speaking of fashion, what is this horrid thing you have on?"

"It was something clean left to dry on a line. I had no desire to freeze the whole way here. 'Tis still winter, you know. Perhaps I ought to have risen in summer," Jasmine mused.

"No. I could never have borne missing you another three months," Damien declared.

Jasmine scoffed at that. Certainly he had missed her, but she was just as certain he hadn't been mooning about for loss of her every single moment of every single day for the past four decades while she slept. But Damien had a gift for the dramatic and for flattery, and he enjoyed making those he cared about feel special to him in whatever way he could.

"Let us find you a proper dress, love," he said.

"A dress? Must I?" she whined.

"Well, I am certain we can find you some doublet and hose. Regardless of what you choose, our tailor is excellent, keeps well up on fashions, and uses the most exquisite materials he can find. Come with me and you can choose."

Jasmine quickly began to follow him, eager for some nice silks to wear.

"So we are still at war with the Demons, I hear."

Damien sighed. "Yes," he admitted. "It is so tedious, I know. But now that we have been about it so long, I am rather at a loss as to how we should stop it."

"Well, I am certain you will find a way. I would rather not have Demons trying to molest me everywhere I go."

Although, she thought, *some molestations are better than others.*

Jasmine caught herself not only in the thought

but also in a full-blown heated body memory of her encounter with the Water Demon.

Adam.

Noah was completely bemused.

He had known Adam all his life. Not only were they the best of friends, but Gideon, who was the Demon King's *Siddah*, was also Adam's, and Noah being only forty years younger than Adam, they had been raised almost like brothers when Noah had come to be fostered. Therefore, Adam had always been less like a cousin and more like an elder brother to Noah. And although he was well beyond the age of needing guidance, Noah was used to that dynamic. Adam was always the one to impart his version of wisdom, in control of all situations and certain of his morality, while Noah tended to be hotheaded and temperamental. When the King floundered, he often turned to the Enforcer for rescue and guidance.

But tonight . . .

Noah watched with honest fascination as Adam paced a hard circuit across the open floor of his castle's main room. The Water Demon kept both hands at the level of his weapons belt, alternately gripping at the empty dagger sheath on the right or the pommel of the blade on his left. His boots snapped furiously against the stone floor as he paced again and again, his breath coming in a loud fury that echoed through the otherwise silent room.

"*Fine-bred little . . .*" Adam exploded in a growl of frustrated outrage, whirling to face his perplexed companion. "Never believe it when someone tries to tell you women are the weaker sex!"

Ah. Clarity at last, Noah thought with an inner chuckle. He would never have expected it to be a woman that would ruffle Adam's flat calm. There were some who thought the Enforcer to be devoid of all emotion, but those few who were close to him knew Adam buried his feelings deep beneath morals, honor, and duty. Noah understood that Adam's seemingly cold-hearted approach to the business of his life was sometimes all that allowed him to commit acts of punishment against those he saw and socialized with every day. Those he secretly respected. To get emotionally close to someone meant he risked putting a sword through his own heart should he be forced into a battle with them in the name of his duties as Enforcer.

Noah had become one of only two exceptions outside of Adam's immediate family. Elijah, the warrior, was the other. The King took this privilege very seriously, so despite his amusement, he realized Adam was genuinely troubled.

"I imagine you have a specific woman in mind?" he asked.

"Yes! *No!*" Adam countered himself quickly out of an instinct for self-preservation. "It does not matter. They strive to perplex us and drive us to base and ridiculous behaviors, be they mothers, sisters, or lovers. Even a total stranger! A woman can have the power to beguile and confuse a man until he knows not right from wrong! Beware, Noah," he cautioned his friend, pointing an ominous finger at him, "for this is what leads many of our males astray."

"I see." Noah couldn't resist. "So what is it that leads our females astray? Do you mean to say it is they themselves?"

"Yes! *No!*" Adam grunted explosively. "Damn me thrice and let Destiny laugh, *I do not know!*"

"Adam," Noah said quietly, truly concerned now as he stood up to halt his disturbed friend's furious motions. "Be easy, my friend," he soothed carefully. "Remember, 'tis not the temptation that makes us wrong, but the giving in to it. Whatever has happened, you clearly resisted what was thrown in your path. You would not be here confessing to me otherwise."

"Aye, that I did," Adam agreed, finally taking a deep, centering breath. "But I've never come so close to crossing that line before, Noah. I have never fully understood how all-consuming . . . how hard it is for us to pull back from our basest urges no matter how wrongly directed they may be."

"I cannot say I understand entirely, although I have felt more than my share of those cravings for flesh and gratification. But I've never craved outside of my race and, Destiny willing, I never will. I should rather die a horrible death than find myself slaking my lust on a non-Demon woman."

"Never fear," Adam assured him. "So long as I am alive, I will never allow you to get that far gone."

"In that I have complete faith," Noah acknowledged. "However, I realize also that you are forced to be your own last line of defense. Who do you have to pull you back from the abyss of madness as you do for so many of us?"

"My father. Or perhaps Jacob. Maybe even you could sense my disturbance, if you were aware you must be on watch for it." Adam took a deep breath as he further composed himself. "And now you are made aware, cousin. But be assured the threat has passed, and, luckily, is unlikely to return. My duties for the Hallowed holiday begin to press on me and I can already sense I will be quite busy the next few nights." The Enforcer turned to his friend and they clasped arms strongly. "I must thank you. I had meant for this to be a very different sort of visit. But your support has been invaluable to me."

"It is good to be able to lend you guidance for a change, my friend. Perhaps it means there is hope for my maturity yet."

"I highly doubt it." Adam chuckled. "I will see you at the festival. Mother will not hear of your absence."

"I will be there."

Jasmine walked Damien's property with a slow and thoughtful gait. The Romanian stronghold where Vampire government was centered was made of painstakingly crafted stone and mortar, towering far above the barren shale of the mountainside surrounding it, and it loomed over anyone who might lay eyes on it. Though few but Vampires saw it, and they were not easily intimidated. It was deep in Damien's territory, far away from any of the smelly human settlements in the area. Luckily, humans were a superstitious lot and were very easily frightened. They had no desire to explore in an area that gave them chills of dread.

As she walked through the open bailey, under the massive portcullis that protected it, she began to find Vampire servants hurrying about their work maintaining Damien's household. She wondered who it was these days that tagged along after Damien. There was always an entourage of pleasure-seekers, looking for fun and excitement, scurrying after him.

She had barely made it back inside the actual

building before she was plucked up off her feet and spun hard about by none other than Damien himself. Eyes of midnight blue dancing and strong shoulders bulging with the muscles that now held her high into the air, the Vampire Prince laughed up at her in pure delight.

"I cannot express to you how happy I am you have returned!" It was said with relief and scolding all at once, and she sympathetically stroked warm fingers through his hair.

"I am sorry. I suppose my melancholy got the better of me at the time. I simply wanted nothing more than to go to ground and sleep."

Damien nodded, letting her slide down his big body and dropping her back onto her feet. He looked her over with a stern, appraising eye. "You look much better now. Properly attired. After a fashion." Damien eyed the beautiful court dress she was wearing, though without rolls, ruff, or farthingale. The tailor had no doubt stitched and tacked it here and there to accommodate her unconventional manner of wearing the dress. "I highly expected you to be wearing male attire."

"'Tis as bulky and bejeweled as a lady's garb. Fashion has not changed much. I promise I will have a few proper ladies' outfits so you can take me out into public. But should I dress in the English fashion or the Italian? What of the French?"

"Perhaps you can go the way of the Dutch. No heavy jewelry there."

She snorted. "I would make a lousy Puritan. I suppose I will find my way. I just need some time to get my feet above the ground rather than below it."

"I will have a girl assigned to you. Or do you need two?"

"One should be a good start. She can find help if she needs it."

"I have sent for your things from storage, and I will put you in the rooms next to mine," Damien informed her.

"Hmm. Very well. Is there anything else I should know about the world in general? Like the fact that the Demons want to kill us?"

"You exaggerate the thing, really. It is more of a . . . game. We play tit for tat. It is not as though either of us is arranging huge attacks with our armies."

"Hmm. That would explain why the Demon did not kill me," she mused.

"What Demon?"

"I ran into one in the woods. He was no bother," she said, waving the matter off. Well, not unless she counted the way the memory of his intimate wash over her bare body had bothered her. In fact, it had made her crave things. Things that were forbidden on both sides of their cultures. And it was clear from his distaste for her breed that he had done everything against his will or better judgment. "What night is this?" she asked.

"It is Beltane eve. You are just in time for the celebrations on the morrow. With you here, it will make for a tremendous festival!" He hugged her until she thought her ribs would snap. She was beginning to get the feeling he really had missed her.

"How long have I been gone, exactly?" she asked him.

"Oh, I would say a good forty years now. You left me shortly after we visited Queen Elizabeth."

"After Dawn was killed on a French battlefield," she

acknowledged. "How did that freckled little queen make out, anyway?"

"Quite well, actually. She is still alive, last I heard. She never married, never produced an heir, and really never cared what anyone else thought of her. I see a bit of you in her, though you claimed never to like her."

"Hmm. Perhaps I might have been hasty in my judgments," she mused with a grin. "I would not have thought she had it in her to make it through without a man, the way they were always dancing attendance on her. So many think your sex is the be-all and end-all of progress and performance."

"In truth," he said with merriment in his midnight blue eyes, "I think it is women who are the be-all and end-all of most species. You are the ones who must work your minds, bodies, and souls the hardest in order to keep us going."

"Such a progressive thinker," she lauded him. "And yet you war with the Demons. Quite dangerous."

Damien shrugged. "I like dangerous," he said predictably.

"And what of you?" she asked. "Have you a woman? Perchance children?"

She wasn't surprised when he shook his head. Damien had no interest in romantic entanglements. Nor did the idea of hearth, home, and family appeal to him in the slightest. Like Queen Elizabeth, he would probably die alone and unfettered by all those sorts of complications. And it was Damien's predictability in matters like these that made it so delightful to be in his company. Jasmine smiled at the thought and hugged her body against his.

"So it will be just you and me, two lone and contented bachelors, walking the centuries together," she said happily.

"Always," he assured her. "Provided you manage to stay aboveground with the rest of us."

"I shall do my very best," she promised him.

Adam walked through the tightly grouped wagons and tents the Gypsies had pitched on his father's lands the night before. In honor of the Beltane festival, gaily colored banners had been set to fly. These wanderers were often labeled as thieves and whores, pickpockets and criminals, but Adam had never agreed with that harshly judgmental assessment.

Since Demons had begun to find themselves forced to emulate the human culture more and more over the centuries in order to keep from standing out and attracting unwanted attention, they could appreciate how restrictive such narrow-minded thinking could be. However, it had been wise for Demonkind to keep a low profile as humans began to heavily populate the earth. All they had to do was watch how the more blatant Lycanthropes and, worse yet, the Vampires had made targets of themselves and were now hunted by superstitious human zealots. As powerful as the Nightwalker breeds were, they had their weaknesses that the peoples of the sunlight hours could exploit, causing them great harm and even death.

The Gypsies were perhaps the closest things to humans who were aware of what Adam's family's true nature really was. While to most outsiders his kin looked like just another wealthy noble family, the Gypsies had their ways of seeing beyond that facade. They, too, lived mostly in the night, and with their own mysteries and mystical perceptions of the future, they were perhaps destined to one day be the first humans who would earn the label of Nightwalkers for themselves.

Adam was interested in the Gypsies' nomadic lifestyle. It always amazed him how widely things changed from clan to clan and year to year. Sometimes he saw the same face every holiday for years, at other times he never recognized a single one from Samhain to Beltane.

He had been busy since leaving Noah, chasing down a few Demon strays in need of enforcement, so he was ready to enjoy a little time to wander on his own for a while. The Gypsies were just the distraction he needed to get his mind off . . .

Disturbing females. The encounter still clung to him, like a mist hugging low and damp to the ground. The form of the sensual little female Vampire seemed burned into his mind like the sun burned itself into a man's eyes after he had stared at it too long. He needed a healthy distraction, although he couldn't imagine why hunting had not been enough to do the trick. Usually the focus he devoted to his craft was all-consuming and burned away all of life's minutiae. He had been frustrated to discover that was not the case in this instance. Those dark, damnable eyes had dogged his thoughts with unending stubbornness.

Adam turned his attention to his immediate surroundings once again. The tents were open, fires were warm and inviting, and almost everywhere there were gaily dressed young women singing and dancing. Soothsayers were setting up areas where they could read runes, tarot, or other fortune-telling devices for whoever paid a bit of coin in exchange. The men were gambling or peddling, the children running madly about as if there were not a care or danger to be found in all of the world. It was a jolly and exotic atmosphere, one that truly delighted him.

As he moved away from the encampment and into the forest, Adam felt his senses clearing of the clutter of stimuli the Gypsies provided. He began to settle into a peaceful place within himself.

The soft snap of a twig came from above him and he looked up sharply. All of a sudden he could sense the presence of another being. Just the water content in the blood was enough to attract his attention, but it was the sudden appearance of a pale and beautiful face amidst a cloud of ebony hair that really grabbed hold of him.

She was wearing clothes this time. After a fashion. They clung to her womanly figure in most places, or flowed in careless drapes away from her in others. The rich satins and velvets were all tawny and gold in color, emphasizing the brown beauty of her eyes, and it was clear she had no interest in wearing her clothing in a fully conventional manner. But she was laced up into a corset, the snugness of it accentuating the thrust of her breasts over a low, curved neckline.

"Vampire," he growled out, the roughness of his tone making sure she knew it wasn't a greeting and she was not welcome. He was still ashamed of himself for the way he had lost control with her, and he could still remember the divinity of her skin and how it had felt as he had moved over it in a flowing rush.

Just the memory stimulated his mind and body, rousing his interest and piquing his libido. He did not want to be attracted to her like this, but it didn't change the fact that he was. No matter how offensive the idea of taking a woman outside his species, she had a power over this part of him that was hard to control and fight off. It was as if he could feel the Beltane moon burning against his back like a full and glorious sun. It was poisoning him, making him think and feel in ways he should find offensive and off-putting.

The Vampire leapt from the thick branch she'd roosted on and dropped to her feet right in front of him. She rose up to her full height, her posture accentuated by the shining fabric she wore, her heavy skirts swirling into place against her hips and legs. She looked like a richly wrapped gift.

Adam's knee-jerk reaction was to grab for the dagger at his waist, but it wasn't until his hand came up empty that he recalled he had lost it the last time he'd met with her.

"Looking for this?" She held up the intricately made weapon, twirling it expertly against her palm before catching it and waving it under his nose. "I am almost tempted to keep it as a gift," she said, her smile wily, "a sort of fair trade. You took liberties with me, and I can take liberties with this."

Adam was stone silent as she taunted him with his dagger. He tensed from head to toe when she stepped up even closer to him. Close enough that he could feel heat radiating from her. She must have fed very recently to feel so warm. He tried to use that knowledge to harden his will against her, but it was difficult when he could smell the richness of the earth and forest on every clean inch of her. She smelled like a woman should, with all the complexity of her sex hovering right there for the senses to pick up.

"You take chances," he said gruffly, "coming among

my people. You will be perceived as a threat, and they
will kill you for this trespass." He knew even as he said
it that the words were meant more as a warning than
a threat. He reached out to snag hold of her hand
where it was wrapped around his dagger.

"You would kill me because I am coming to return
your property to you?" she asked archly, refusing to
open her hand or relinquish the weapon.

"I did not mean me," he admitted roughly.

"Good." Her smile was sly and her eyes everything
sultry as she reached out with her free hand to grab
hold of the empty sheath on his belt. He let go of her
hand when she turned the dagger toward his body. It
should have been the last thing he did. Why would he
ever let an armed Vampire get so deadly close to his
vulnerable belly?

But he saw no vicious intent in those dark and troublesome eyes of hers. All he saw was her desire to
taunt and tease him. He felt her tug hard at his
weapons belt, and she finally turned the dagger and
slid it slowly into the sheath. She pushed down hard
and firm, the action bringing them together, chest
to breast. She was right under his nose now. He could
feel the sensuality rolling off her in interesting waves.
She even tilted her head back and raised her mouth
to within a breath of his.

Just like that he felt himself flooding full of hard-
ening heat, blood rushing to stiffen his body in reaction to her allure. Adam wanted to curse her for it,
to curse himself, but he was too busy being capti-
vated by the suggestive way she stared at his mouth.
Everything about her was begging for a kiss, and
everything about him wanted to give it to her. He
wanted to forget who he was and who she was and

simply indulge in the chemistry that was flaring so hotly between them.

But the fact remained that she was a Vampire, and Vampires were not to be trusted. Moreover, to kiss her would be to break the law. He also had to consider that she was likely making sport of him, simply amusing herself at his expense.

"You've returned my weapon," he said roughly. "Now you should go before you are discovered or before I change my mind and kill you myself."

The idea made her smile, a slow curling of her lips on one side.

"You want to thrust your dagger deep inside me, Demon?" she asked.

There was no mistaking her suggestiveness. There was no mistaking it because his heart began to race with the very idea of it, the heat in his belly sinking low and hard within him.

"Would that it were a different world," he heard himself murmur to her, dipping his head helplessly to brush his lips over hers. Such magnetism! He'd never felt anything like it! It was electric as it burst across his senses. He simply could not comprehend how he could feel so much need for a creature so very unlike himself. "But it is not," he noted as he drew away from her.

He stepped back, breaking apart from her clingy little body. This made her laugh, her eyes dancing with her merriment.

"Leave it to a staid and elitist Demon to thumb his nose at such an outrageous attraction," she taunted him.

"And if I said yes to you, little tease? If I let my instincts loose upon your person and took the physical as far as I could?" He huffed out a breath of air like a bull becoming more and more irritable. "You would not have me. To play the consummate tease is one thing, but to sully yourself with the enemy would be quite another for you."

"Damn." She pouted, her warm eyes full of mischief. "You have found me out." She withdrew, and with a simple stretch of her arms, she levitated off the ground and slowly began to climb a distance into the air. "Until next time, then?"

"Who are you?" he demanded suddenly, not knowing why he should care.

"I will let you figure that out. Perhaps you and I will meet again in a world much different than this one is now, eh? Would that not be intriguing?"

With that speculation, she flew off, up above the treetops, speeding away toward her home territory. Feeling a bit disoriented, Adam closed a fist around the bejeweled dagger she had seen fit to return. He wondered why she would bother to go so far out of her way.

But then again, he'd been a huge amusement to her as well.

Damn.

She'd played him like a clumsy instrument in the hands of a skilled musician. She'd come expressly for the purpose of disturbing his equilibrium. And she'd succeeded. The brat.

Well, she'd best not think she could return to toy with him again, because next time he would set her straight.

Just the same, he found he was smiling as he made his way back to his parents' holdings.

* * *

"You are something of an ass," Jacob decreed as he dropped hard into the dirt, his body exploding apart and becoming a part of the dust he was falling into. The dust cloud quickly reformed, twisted up into a six-foot column, and in a blink snapped into Jacob's usual shape and features. He made a show of going to dust himself off, but affected surprise when there was no dust to be found. He made a diligent search of himself for a speck, but there would never be any. The Earth Demon grinned at his brother.

"And I am honored you feel such a need to emulate your elder brother," Adam shot back.

He launched himself at Jacob, his body thrusting into a pressured stream of water that dashed hard against his brother, thoroughly drenching him as he took Jacob straight off his feet, yet again, and sent him sprawling in the dirt.

"Son of a—" Jacob spluttered as he scrambled to regain his feet.

"Do not dare disparage our mother, Jake," Adam warned him as he stepped to stand close to his brother. "I will not hesitate to tell her and Father what you have said."

Jacob's reply was to send a fist made of limestone into his brother's face. The coarse rock hit hard and caught Adam off guard. His head ringing and his face burning from the sting of the blow, he staggered back.

"Damn me, that was a fair shot," he praised his brother. Jacob was getting more and more creative when they sparred. If there were any two elements on the planet that made for a difficult fight, Adam imagined Earth and Water would be the ones. Fire and Water might seem the most directly opposite, but the nature of their ability to cancel one another out made for a strangely simplistic fight. He ought to know, he had sparred with Noah many times. The Fire Demon King was very close to him in age and so they were reasonably similar in their strength and the maturity of their powers. It made sense, growing up as they had together, that they would have trained on how best to defeat each other, how best to defeat the polar opposite element should they have to face it down.

But it was still quite straightforward in its way.

Fighting Jacob was something entirely different, and far more creative. Their mother liked to joke that the two of them together made for a mess of mud, and she had seen them make enough of it to know the truth. But his younger brother had developed his power at a uniquely young age. He had been fostered out very young because of it. Luckily it was Noah's father and mother who had been his *Siddah*. The three boys had never been too far apart, because Noah's parents' lands were adjacent to Adam and Jacob's, and they had formed something of a powerful triad, three of the most powerful elements in their masculine form, each constantly challenging the other to greater heights.

Jacob had learned very well. That's why, in spite of the crushing pain in his jaw, Adam spat out blood and smiled at his baby brother.

"Now, that was a good hit," he praised him.

"I used that on a Vampire last week. Only I did not pull the strike like I just did," he had to add smugly.

Adam let it slide and gave Jacob a nod. "I believe you, Jake. You could have taken my head off just then. One day you could make an excellent Enforcer."

That made Jacob pull back, his body language quickly becoming defensive.

"I will never be Enforcer," he swore sharply. "You will pass the role to your heirs. I will be content to hunt Vampires for bounty."

"The war is losing power," Adam pointed out. "I think it is obvious Damien will draw it to a close soon, and you know Noah opts for peace when possible. There will be no Vampires to hunt. Then what will you do with yourself? Come now, you must face facts. We have seen too many of our ancestors die in this job not to understand that I may never live to see those heirs you are anticipating."

"I refuse to speak of it, Adam. You want me to discuss your death blithely? I utterly refuse." It was rare for Jacob to show true anger, but he was showing it now, his dark eyes on fire with growing rage.

"David was Enforcer barely a quarter of a century before he was killed," Adam reminded Jacob gently. Their uncle and Adam's predecessor had been killed in the line of duty. He had been forced to kill the Fire Demon he was enforcing, and had died in the process of the battle. Normally the role of Enforcer would have been passed brother to brother or father to heir, but David had had no children, and their uncle Ariel had already resigned from the role of Enforcer according to Demon law and tradition when he had found himself Imprinted on his mate, Sarah. Asher, Jacob and Adam's father, was not suited to the role of a fighter. He was too much a scholar, having spent all of his life chasing knowledge and knowing only enough of fighting tactics to defend himself if necessary.

But Adam was a born warrior, and the enforcing trait was strong in his makeup.

It was strong in Jacob, too. Whether he wished to address the topic or not, Jacob was the most logical

choice to fill Adam's shoes should something happen
to the present Enforcer.

Adam wasn't trying to upset his brother, and
normally he wouldn't have pushed the topic on him
like this, but after the way he had been behaving
around that Vampire tease last evening, he felt it was
important to make Jacob aware of certain responsibilities that might fall on him.

"You know I have great respect and love for you, do
you not?" Adam asked him quietly. "There is no one
in the world I am closer to."

"Noah," Jacob said with a snort that was trying too
hard to be contrary.

"Even above Noah, Jake. We are brothers. We have
spent so much of our lives together."

"You and Noah have spent more," he felt compelled
to point out. It was true. Noah and Adam had already
been fast friends by the time Jacob came along.

"Do you really think that matters? Do you really
think I hold someone else above my brother in my
heart?"

Apparently Jacob had wondered. Adam could see
the instant of questioning vulnerability in his brother's
eyes. There was appreciation and pleasure over the
honor lighting Jacob's face for the brief moment he
allowed it to show. It was immediately followed by a sly
look of suspicion. The elder brother understood.
Jacob knew he didn't express affection often or easily.
It only went to prove his point, though, that they were
much closer than Jacob realized.

"What troubles you?" Jacob asked him.

And just as suddenly Adam no longer wanted to
travel this route. It was best he admit no weaknesses
to his brother or anyone else. Noah was indeed the

exception, but that was because he was King and it was Adam's duty to report any flaws in himself that might affect his performance. Or that was what he quickly told himself.

"Nothing," Adam brushed Jacob off with a half smile. "I suppose that knock you gave me shook free some sentimentality. Do not get used to it."

Jacob laughed at him, the sound still a bit unsure, but Adam brushed the rest of it away by giving him a good slap against his unguarded cheek. That immediately awoke Jacob's competitive nature again, and before they knew it, both men were back to wrestling in the dirt.

To keep his promise to his mother, appease her and avoid her temper all in one maneuver, Adam had invited Hannah, Noah's elder sister, as his escort to the Beltane festivities. She was at present gladly keeping his mother occupied at a distant tent in the Gypsy encampment where a young girl of indeterminate age was selling beautiful handcrafted jewelry.

To be honest, Adam truly enjoyed Hannah. Perhaps because she was more like a friend than she was an escort, but also because she wasn't as intimidated by his daunting role of Enforcer as everyone else was. Of course, she still had her respectful fears where he was concerned and likely always would. It was to be expected, considering how his position and reputation were received in their society. He had long ago resigned himself to the understanding that he would never meet a woman who wouldn't always be a little bit afraid of him.

Demon woman, he clarified in his head as the

image of sultry brown eyes and fearless laughter filled
his mind. Perhaps that was part of her allure, Adam
mused. She had been so unafraid. She had been . . .
on equal standing.

Adam shrugged away thoughts of Vampires and focused again on his escort of the evening. Mainly, the
young female Fire Demon knew what he did and did
not want her to expect from him. They had good
times together; he enjoyed the temper that came with
her infamous element, as well as her equally volatile
passions. However, they both knew she would settle
down and have a firm commitment to family one day.
Perhaps one day very soon. For all her brassy ways,
Hannah was a domestic at heart. Home and hearth
and a child at her breast was what she wanted the very
most.

Adam was nowhere close to wanting anything like
that, and Hannah was well aware of that. But until the
time came for them to part ways and seek their separate futures, they spent the present keeping each
other company. Especially in situations like this one,
where Hannah occupied and satisfied his mother so
he was able to manage other things. Hannah glanced
his way in the middle of her conversation, sending
him a sly, womanly smile that told him she expected
repayment for being such an obliging companion.
Adam chuckled under his breath, drawing a few ap-
preciative glances from two young Gypsy girls who
were sitting in the dark grass with their bare feet and
calves crossed casually before them. They leaned their
heads together and made a show of whispering while
they blatantly appraised him.

Strange how their dark looks and sensual knowing
touched him not at all, and yet . . .

Angry with himself for yet again obsessing about the Vampire, Adam stepped away from the bustle of the festival and the Gypsies for a moment, moving into the depths of the forest nearby. He needed a moment of peace so he could reach out and test his senses for any trouble among the Demons. While not as taxing as Samhain, Beltane was still hard on the Demon psyche, the full Hallowed moon pressing down on their minds with coaxing force, begging them to let their passions run wild. The Enforcer could sense those who were weakening, who were giving in to those forces. He had been born with the ability as part of his makeup, and it allowed him to hunt down those who were slipping free of control. Those who might endanger innocent lives.

But as he stood there in the silent darkness, he heard no warnings, felt no tension from any other Demon out there. The Enforcer could rest easy knowing there was nothing for him to do but enjoy the Beltane festival with his family.

When Adam emerged from the woods and stepped back into the Gypsy encampment, Jacob caught up with him.

"Very clever, bringing Hannah to appease Mother," his younger brother mocked him straight off, nodding his head to the Demon female in question.

"At least I will not be on Mother's bad side come the morning," Adam said absently, trying to focus on the world around him again, trying to pull away from the senses of his Enforcer self and become more the son and brother.

"Mother does not have a bad side, only a meddling one," Jacob pointed out with a put-upon sigh.

"You blatantly disregarded her request that you bring an escort." Adam put energy into the conversation. "You have earned yourself a steady string of lectures this week. I am glad you have the time for them. I, however, have more important things to do."

"So you say," Jacob goaded, his dark eyes flashing like those of the Gypsy girls. "I prefer to think you are simply Mother's well-trained little boy."

"Thinking like that is how someone finds his face kissing the dirt come training tomorrow."

Jacob was unimpressed by the threat, and it showed in his casual, single-shouldered shrug.

"You gave her your word," Adam pressed.

"No, *you* gave her my word, there is a difference."

"That is splitting hairs."

"Hannah is just the sort of girl Mother would love to see reel you in," Jacob said, changing the topic back to taunting Adam. "She is from the royal household, she is smart, sassy, and sensible, and Mother likes her. I think you would do best to worry about ending up at the altar and stop worrying about threatening me."

"Hannah knows better than to look at me for home and hearth," Adam responded, clearly unconcerned. "We make excellent friends, occasionally quite excellent bedfellows, and nothing more."

"She seeks a husband," Jacob pressed, trying to get a better rise out of Adam. "Not many of us are oriented in that manner, but Hannah is."

"Seeks, yes. Seeks in me, never. She is too smart for that." He flipped an impatient hand at his brother. "Do stop pestering me. Buzz about me like a fly for much longer and I will swat you."

"You can try," was the cocky retort.

Adam ruined his threat by smiling. One day, that threat would actually have truth behind it, if Adam did not keep up with his young sibling. Jacob might gain the upper hand one day because he'd had the luck of being born under the element of the Earth. It was a powerful element, controlling nearly everything that affected the planet. Maybe someday the heavens and the universe beyond would become part of their domain, but it would very likely be a long time before a child was born to an element of that magnitude. And while Demons were far more advanced in science, culture, and logic than humans were, they were admittedly still savages themselves in other ways.

If they had been above savagery, there would be no need for Adam's profession. He knew the majority of Demons wished quite hard that there was no such thing as an Enforcer. Having been tempted himself with forbidden desires, he felt kinship with his brethren keenly. When considering it, Adam would gladly give up his profession if it meant no more moonlit madness or straining Hallowed nights.

Shrugging off thoughts of the impossible, he focused on castigating his troublesome brother. "You are over two centuries old and supposedly a highly respected and successful adult," he remarked to Jacob. "Why is it you only act like one outside of our home?"

"Because if not for me, you would take things far too seriously."

Jacob ducked swiftly to avoid a swat from Adam.

That was when Adam caught sight of the Gypsy girl who lingered not too far from Jacob's back. She was not socializing with any of the others. Instead she hung back and stood cloaked in moonlight, trees, and shadows as well as a burgundy-colored hooded cape, the material unusually rich for a girl of her station. She stood a few yards behind Jacob, her breath clouding on the air. The early spring night was bitingly cold, in spite of the bonfires lit for the festival, but Adam was suddenly struck with the feeling that it was not the cold that made her draw the fabric of her cloak so tightly around herself.

She seemed afraid.

Strange. The Gypsies were usually quite at ease with them. They even shared almost the same religious beliefs and had proven to be quite open and accepting of the Demons. However, he could hardly blame her for her fear when her kind received censure from so many other quarters.

"Jacob, if you will excuse me?"

He had the strangest urge to investigate this odd young woman. As the eldest son, it was his duty to keep a keen eye on all those invited onto the family lands tonight. Her anxiety seemed to strike a particular chord in him, and Adam was very used to obeying his instincts when it came to things like this. Adam felt Jacob turn to watch as he moved around him and began to cross the chill, wet grasses in order to approach the girl who had piqued his interest. He saw dark eyes of undetermined color staring out from beneath the hood.

Adam slowed his steps when he realized those eyes were not focused on him as he had first thought.

They were fixed solely on his brother.

He paused, turning to follow the line of her sight back to Jacob, unable to help wondering why she should look at him in such a ravenous manner. It was quite possible she was merely attracted to him; Jacob was, after all, a seriously handsome heir to very powerfully attractive genes. But she would be disappointed if she thought to lure Jacob to her bed. Demons mating with humans was their priority taboo, after all. However, with the full moon of Beltane lurking above them all, and after having so recently faced his own wayward desire for an inappropriate woman, Adam would have a care for his brother's well-being.

He was momentarily glad to see that Jacob had not noticed the girl even for a second. Of course, Jacob would be the very last Demon to break that particular code. His brother would rather die than act with such harmful dishonor. Humans were too fragile, too frail. It would be like picking up a cat by its tail with the intention of swinging it and releasing it at speed. You knew it was wrong, knew it would be painful and harmful to the smaller, more vulnerable creature, possibly even resulting in death. To do so anyway would be tantamount to coldhearted brutality toward an innocent and defenseless creature.

Jacob was incapable of such brutality. Adam believed that with all of his soul.

At least if Adam had crossed the line and taken his cravings for that fine little Vampire to conclusion, he would have only broken laws of purity. The saucy little Nightwalker was more than his equal in strength, for all her feminine build, and he wouldn't have hurt her in the process.

Much.

The thought was a wholly wicked one and damnably distracting in its potential. Adam shook it off and tried to focus on the concern at hand. A Gypsy girl looking at Demons the way this girl was could be a potential problem. Adam would cut the trouble off at the knees by giving her an ungentle discouragement. Flirting was one thing, but there was something far too covetous in her eyes. Strong as Jacob was, Adam wished him to have no temptations on such a volatile night.

"Are you enjoying our festival?" he asked her by way of greeting.

The Gypsy turned her bottomless eyes onto him slowly, clearly uncaring if he observed her interest in his brother. She then swept an implacable gaze over him slowly and thoroughly, as if she were appraising him for all he might be worth. For some reason, it unnerved Adam. He was not easy to perturb, so her scrutiny put his guard up immediately. Gypsies were known to dabble in magic and, though she did not smell of that vile taint, there was always a chance she was dealing in some unknown variable of it.

She was not like the others. To start, she was far younger than she had first appeared from a distance. It was the eyes that had fooled him. They were aged beyond the years of her body, drawing time to her facial features that did not belong there. This girl, he realized, had seen terrible pain in her lifetime. She wore the weight of the world on her slender shoulders. She was tall for a human girl, even at what was clearly a very young age. She was not pale or darkly tanned, but had coloring that was a cross between the two, a slightly warm toffee that seemed somehow out of place with the swarthy Gypsies and Demons all around her. Still, the pitch-colored hair and shadowed eyes were Gypsy through and through.

"You are the eldest son of the lord of these lands?"

She spoke in his language, but it was awkward on her tongue, her accent heavy and strange. She posed it as a question, but he felt she already knew the answer.

"I am. Adam, by name."

"Adam." She breathed his name as if it was a sacrament, and the tone gave him a chill. How odd that she did not dissemble and call him "my lord" as anyone else would have done. Was she really so bold? She was certainly old enough to know better. Her behavior led him to believe she was plotting something. Perhaps she thought to become the mistress of one of the lords of the household. Despite rumors, Gypsy women were not indiscriminate when it came to choosing a man. They were far more calculating than that. It was something Adam could respect, actually. There was nothing wrong with trying to better one's position in the world. There were many ways of doing so, and the use of one's body was one path. Considering the way he and Hannah used one another for ulterior motives, he would be a hypocrite to think otherwise.

But the chit couldn't be a day over sixteen. That was a great deal of ambition for one so young. Though humans tended to push their females into their sexuality quite young.

"Would you like to have your fortune read, Adam?" she asked before he could formulate some kind of warning to deter the strange child from pursuing his brother.

"I am not interested in your games, girl," he told her firmly. "Nor will my brother be."

She looked back at Jacob, who had long since begun to cross the field and was moving steadily away from them.

"I am not engaging in a game, Adam. I merely see things in your future of great importance and thought you would like to know what they are. If you prefer to remain in ignorance, I will graciously accept your choice."

Adam sensed that it was not as easy for her as she was trying to make it seem. The creases in her young brow were far too serious, and there was something about the stiffness of her body as she made herself turn away that belied her words.

Adam was confused.

And intrigued.

"I suppose you will tell me there is a woman in my future, and she may even look a lot like you," he taunted her dryly.

To his chagrin, she laughed at him, as if it were honestly the most ridiculous thing she had ever heard.

"I wouldn't know about that." She turned back slightly, giving him a shadowy view of her profile. "But I do see danger. Danger you must be prepared for, because it's like nothing you've ever seen or experienced before."

"That is a fair guess. We all see danger in these times."

She actually smiled at his sarcasm. It was a cold smile, however, and it chilled straight through to his spine. There should never be an expression such as that on one so young, no matter how hard life might be.

"The danger does not come for you, Adam, but for your brother."

Adam felt almost as frozen as the breath he exhaled sharply into the air.

"You dare to threaten my brother?" he hissed, reaching for her arm until he was gripping the slim limb painfully.

"I'm only trying to warn you about the future," she

snapped, her anger adding a sudden life to her that her shy and demure act had diminished. "Your brother will die at the hands of a traitor. Someone will murder him while his back is turned, his attention focused on something else. You, however, are nowhere to be seen when he needs you most. Why is that, Adam, the eldest son? Perhaps it's because you didn't listen to a simple girl who wished only to help!"

She jerked her arm away with surprising strength and turned as if to go. Adam did not want to be pulled in if this was some sort of ploy, but the Gypsy people had proven to have a history of strong precognition. Then again, there were those who believed them Witches, the sort who would become necromancers if given half a chance and the spells to do it with.

But despite his fears and doubts about the origins of her fortune-telling, she had struck him on the chord of his deepest vulnerability.

Jacob.

Jacob meant the world to him. What was more, he meant the world to their mother and father. If something were to happen to him, it would be a devastating blow to their family.

"Let us assume I believe you," he said suddenly, halting her withdrawal. "What is it you expect to enable me to do? Jacob is far more capable of protecting himself than a little female like you would ever understand. He would not die easily."

"I understand more than you think I do. You are correct, however. Jacob is more than capable of protecting himself."

"Then—"

"But," she interrupted, "say he was not protecting

himself. What if he endangers himself for the family he loves?"

Now that, Adam realized with painful dread, was very much like Jacob and even a real possibility. Adam's brother would use his own life in trade for those of his family in a heartbeat if it were the only choice left to him.

"I have had enough of your cryptic stories," Adam barked at her, the force of his statement ruined by his apprehensive glance for the brother who had disappeared from his sight. "When will this danger occur that you speak of? Surely one so full of insights can tell me that."

"It will occur today. Tomorrow. Any time you choose it to occur."

Adam instantly came to the end of his temper. His hand shot out and closed around her delicate throat, which he used to drag her back into total darkness. Her back hit the trunk of an enormous oak, but her heart barely picked up a beat and she did not make a single sound under the physical manhandling. He leaned in close to her ear, using the bulk of his body to trap her.

"I am finished with your games, girl. You will tell me how to protect my brother and when, and you will do it this instant."

The Gypsy girl flicked up an unsympathetic gaze in the darkness and her eyes suddenly caught the moonlight. For the first time he realized they were a beautiful violet color.

"Will you give your life for him? Will you trade away everything you know and love to save your brother?" she demanded of him.

"Tell me!"

"Answer my question or kill me, Adam. Those are your choices."

She still had the upper hand, he realized. Even though he held her very life between his fingers, her apparent inability to feel fear in this situation gave her power over him and would keep him forever on the defensive. Adam realized he had no choice but to concede to her demands.

"I would," he hissed. "I would sacrifice everything I have in this world to keep my brother safe."

"This very moment, with no preparation? No good-byes? No promises that you will not die along with him?"

"I said yes! Now tell me what you know!"

"I prefer to show you," she whispered quickly.

Her hands suddenly shot out and hit his chest. The moment she made contact with him, Adam felt his entire body burst with heat. Every autonomic system contained within his skin seemed to flip into overdrive, picking up into a double-time beat before tripling again, quadrupling quickly after. He felt the stress on his systems with the sensation of impending doom. He had no time to react or act or even think beyond that.

The world around him disappeared.

Chapter 5

Samhain 2008

Isabella skidded to a halt, shoving her daughter behind herself so suddenly that Leah's dress hit the dirt once more.

Bella and Jacob squared off to face the traitorous Demon Ruth.

Jacob knew instantly that this was the worst scenario he could ever be trapped in. His family was his one true vulnerability, even though at the same time it was his most powerful strength. Perhaps if it had only been Ruth, he would not have been so worried, but he immediately recognized the Vampire named Nicodemous, who had joined her in her destructive causes a couple of years back, tripling her access to power and advantage over those she considered her enemies.

Jacob felt Bella's knee-jerk reactions as they flew through her mind, just as she felt his; she knew how dire he understood the situation to be. Even though their enemies' minions were out of reach, that would not last very long if Ruth was given a moment to concentrate. She would begin to teleport them down into the caverns any second now.

We're in trouble, Bella thought frantically, her glance back at their vulnerable child a luxury he did not have with two such powerful enemies in front of them.

I know, little flower. But we will not fail. We cannot fail.

Jacob, I have to do it . . .

The Enforcer knew what his wife meant. She intended to dampen the abilities of the Nightwalkers before them, stealing their power and making it her own on a temporary basis. The problems behind that plan rushed through him. Ruth and Nico's powers were tainted with blackness and evil. To take something like that inside herself could destroy everything about her that he loved and knew, everything that she was. She had dampened the powers of necromancers before, but nothing like this. Nothing had ever been like this. As Isabella's power had grown, they had realized she always took something away from her victims when she did this. A part of them would live inside her forever, plaguing her with premonitions or who knew what else. Ruth was one of a kind. So was the Vampire who had been altered because he had drunk her tainted Nightwalker blood and now shared in the blackness of her magical spell casting. In an ideal situation, Jacob would have rather done anything else than allow Bella to risk herself in such a way.

His wife, however, was just as stubborn and protective of her family as he was. Nothing he said or did would stop her once she made up her mind.

So all he could do was quietly resign himself to supporting her.

The Druid released the tight rein she always kept on her ability to dampen the power of any Night-walker who walked the earth. Damn the painful consequences she might suffer in the future; there was no holding back when it came to her family.

Jacob felt his mate scream in horror long before she actually found the voice for it.

Purely by instinct, he whirled to catch her in a single strong arm as she lurched in a back-arching seizure. She did find voice at last, her shrill screech of pain and poisoned terror echoing off every wall of his heart, as well as the cavern. He eased his beloved wife to the ground as gently as he could, considering the violent contortions of her body.

That was all the time it took for the enemy behind him to strike.

Jacob felt overwhelmed as he realized his exposure in the next heartbeat. Before the thought could even complete itself, however, the Vampire moved with the pre-ternatural speed that his breed had been imbued with.

Jacob heard the strike, and then felt the repercussion of it in the air around him.

He jerked around, his wife still clutched to his chest, and looked up at a long, strong male figure that no amount of time could erase from his memory. He met the eyes of a man he had not seen in over four hundred years.

Adam.

His brother was holding the wrist of the Vampire in one powerful fist, crushing it with a stunning grip until the iron spike that had been headed for Jacob's back finally fell with a clatter to the floor.

* * *

Adam had no time to ask questions.

He had felt himself resolving back into solid form one second, and had seen the threat to his brother the next. It only took him milliseconds to focus on the image of his brother doing the inconceivable: turning his back on an enemy to catch the falling figure of a diminutive, raven-haired woman. Jacob lowered the female to the floor with no regard for the threat at his back, concern and tenderness radiating from every last inch of his being.

That left Adam to deal with the fang-flashing Vampire reaching into his jacket for what he knew without a doubt was a weapon. Jacob's elder brother moved with the speed of evaporated water through the air, transforming into a dense mist that arrowed the remaining few yards before he could solidify and come between weapon and target. The Water Demon coalesced so suddenly that the female Demon who stood beside the Vampire gasped in shocked surprise. Adam caught the Vampire's wrist, understanding instantly that the Gypsy had been right, there was a strength and malevolence within these two the likes of which he had never seen before.

How Jacob had ended up in this place, in this situation, with these strangers, Adam had no idea. Neither did he care. The Gypsy had spoken the truth of the matter. His brother was in danger of losing his life to this threat, and Adam was there to see it stop.

As the spike clanked to the floor, Adam met the disbelieving eyes of his younger sibling. Jacob stared up at him as if he were seeing a ghost, still clutching that little woman as if she were his one true security in life. Adam only had time to narrow his eyes on the possessive grip for a minute, understanding that the woman was human and that Jacob's behavior was nowhere near that of an innocent savior.

That was a problem that would wait for later, Adam thought, dismissing the Enforcer within himself for the moment. He had other justice to dispense.

The Vampire reacted to Adam's interference violently. He snarled, fangs sprouting viciously and with gnashing threat that could not be mistaken. Adam understood this threat. What he could not understand was the Demon woman who stood beside the Vampire, reaching for his arm in a clinging manner as she screamed at him to finish Adam off so they could continue with Jacob's destruction.

The Gypsy had warned about a Demon traitor, and by the foul smell of her, the corrupted blonde was all that and more. The whys and hows would wait for later as well. Adam was instantly drawn off his feet and into battle against the Vampire's incredible prowess.

Nicodemous tried to throw the Demon into the stone floor with the hopes of crushing a few of the meddler's bones in the process. To his shock, however, he found himself plunging, arms first, through water where flesh should have been. The deluge dashed to the floor, backsplash sluicing over the hostile couple even as it gathered with blinding speed into the shape of the intruding Demon. Water flew off the curling ends of the Demon's black hair as he back-spun a kick into the dead center of the Vampire's chest.

Adam's metamorphosis had disoriented Nicodemous's balance, so when the Water Demon struck, it took the Vampire clean off his feet. He crashed to the ground on his back, kicking up a cloud of dirt and dust as a satisfactory cracking of bone echoed through the cavern.

At last, Jacob left his preoccupation over the human female to join in the effort to save his own life. He flew at the female Demon with no hesitation for her sex or seeming fragility. Adam was surprised. It had always been one of Jacob's worst weaknesses, his inability to attack a woman. When had he overcome it? The older brother had no idea. But then again, he had not known about Jacob's apparent obsession with a human female either.

Adam took out his confusion and frustration on the Vampire, leaping onto him and beginning to beat the bastard with his bare fists with a pummeling force that could have cracked rock. Jacob's hands were around the throat of the Demon female, but he was too late to stop the string of foreign words she spat out.

A spell.

The inconceivable idea of a Demon uttering a spell took Adam by surprise just long enough to give the Vampire an advantage. With the speed of a striking snake, fangs struck for his exposed throat.

Again, Adam was thrown off his mark. Vampires were relentless sons of bitches, but they never went for the blood of a Nightwalker. It was utterly taboo, and they were terrified of what would happen to them if they did. It was all he could do to shove his palm into the Vampire's path, protecting his neck just in the nick of time. The fangs struck, puncturing clear through his hand.

Ruth's spell flew into effect at the same time. The air pressure in the room was suddenly sucked away, depriving the entire area of all oxygen. The Vampire did not require breath, but the Demons and the human did. Adam jerked around to look for his brother. He knew they were underground, and there would be no hope of replacing the lost air without Jacob's ability to drill through earth and bedrock and all other things in order to provide a vent.

Jacob was forced to release Ruth as he reared back to do exactly that. He could not waste a single second. Bella and Leah could never survive such a complete vacuum.

Jacob leapt for the cavern ceiling, his body moving like a steel drill through the cavern limestone as if it were butter. Adam had no idea how deep they were beneath the topsoil, so he had only one choice. Grabbing the dagger at his waist with his off hand, he unsheathed it and put all of his vital power into the aim he took between the gaping jaws buried in his palm and wrist. The blade nicked through the webbing of his thumb in the process, but it also sank through the Vampire's mouth and into the back of his throat. It crushed through the soft palate, the brain stem, and the skull in one vicious movement.

Then, without a moment's hesitation, Adam plunged off the ground as a powerful wave of water, flushing over the human female, the child behind her he had only just noticed, and the Gypsy girl, who had been watching the entire situation with wide, frantic eyes. The moment he touched them, they turned into water at his command and they all spouted upward through the tunnel Jacob was drumming through the earth.

Jacob broke surface first, gasping for breath and moving out of the way just in time to avoid the pressured geyser at his heels. The water spouted as if released from the blowhole of a gigantic whale, spraying everywhere and landing in four separate streamers.

As they hit the ground, they became Isabella, Leah, Adam, and the strange figure of a young girl Jacob had never seen before.

Jacob immediately sank his hands into earth, making the ground rock and shake until the tunnel he had created collapsed in on itself. Now full of soft soil, it was a dangerous sinkhole that could trap and kill an unsuspecting traveler, so he used a moment longer to concentrate on packing and pressurizing the soil until it was almost hard enough to replace the rock he had destroyed.

"We must move!" he shouted as soon as he was through. He plunged through thickets to grab his daughter up in his arms, and watched as if seeing a dream in action as Adam scooped up Isabella. He turned to look for the strange girl. He need not have bothered. She had already leapt for him, her arms winding around his neck and throat. For a moment, he perceived it as an attack. But before he could react, he realized he was being hugged and that she was sobbing near to hysterics. He awkwardly caught her weight and juggled his daughter at the same time, completely confounded.

The mystery deepened in the next instant.

"I love you," she wept passionately, her arms nearly stealing his breath with their desperate strength. "I love you, Daddy."

Speechless, Jacob looked helplessly toward an equally confusing mystery. His *brother*, who should be dead, yet was now standing before him. Then the constriction around his neck and ribs released, his breath rushing back in as he tried to find answers in the girl's eyes.

All he could see, however, was the dark violet color

of her irises, and the familiarity of them warmed his senses, forcing him to recognize her on a visceral level. From one heart to another. From his father's soul to his daughter's.

"Leah?"

She could only nod, her fingers all over his face suddenly, mapping his features as if she were starved for them.

"Don't be angry with me," she begged him. "I had no choice. They had to be stopped. And I was right. I chose right." She looked back at Adam as her whole body began to tremble. She tried to speak again, but clearly couldn't as her trembles became quakes and then violent jerks of her body. The hands against his face suddenly lost all weight and structure, fading and passing right through him, a condition that rapidly spread through her entire body. Then he was no longer holding her, and Jacob watched as his would-be daughter dissolved away into nothingness in his hands.

"What the hell is going on?" Jacob demanded to know, his heart hurting in his chest though he barely understood the reasons why. He couldn't escape the notion, however, that he had somehow just lost his daughter. And even looking at the more familiar, five-year-old living version of her couldn't shake off the pain of it.

"Later, little brother. I sense company coming."

Adam watched as Jacob turned and closed his eyes for a moment, clearly reaching to feel what it was Adam had sensed. Again, this was different. He had always known Jacob had inherited that special sense that those few of their family acquired, but he had never seen him use it so readily and with such clear ease of familiarity.

The Enforcers, both of the past and of the present, were sensing the coming of the small army of the Transformed that Bella and Jacob had initially gone underground to escape from. Adam lived in a time of readily used black magic, so he was quite grimly familiar with his duty to destroy these unfortunate souls. They had once been Demons, as good and moral as he himself was, but not now. Not after a necromancer had discovered their true power names and had used them in a Summoning spell. Trapped in that controlling magician's pentagram, it only took a short time before those Demon victims would begin to physically and mentally mutate into nearly mindless monsters, fanged and winged and viciously amoral. It was these poisoned creatures that had inspired the popular image of what Demons were within the human population.

Adam was short a weapon, his dagger still imbedded in the Vampire necromancer's skull somewhere below them, but that didn't bother him anywhere near as much as realizing his brother didn't even carry so much as a knife on his person. He had never known Jacob to go unarmed anywhere. For that matter, the mode of Jacob's dress completely baffled his elder brother. Minutes ago they had both been similarly dressed in a doublet and hose. Now Jacob was . . . Adam had no idea what it was he was wearing. And the woman he was protecting was dressed as a boy! If not for her hair . . .

There was no time to consider confusing fashions. Adam could feel the approach of the Transformed. It shocked him to realize how many there were. Everything, it seemed, was shocking and confusing. There was the wicked presence of black magic everywhere. Whoever that Gypsy girl was, she was gone. Had her magic gone with her, or was this all some kind of horrid illusion?

Still, Jacob seemed real enough, for all the change Adam saw within him at a glance.

Adam sought a source of water, another way of arming himself for the coming battle. The landscape was completely alien, he realized, nothing where it ought to be. Rivers, streams, and lakes were skewed and disproportionate to his mental mapping of where things should be. Finding himself too distant from a real water source, he reached for the water above him, seeding the clouds until it began to rain in a violent torrent.

"Get the innocents to safety!" he yelled to his brother. "I will handle these pitiful creatures myself!"

"You cannot possibly! Not on your own!" Jacob shouted back to him.

"Do you think the woman and child will help me, then?" Adam spat back. "*You* certainly cannot while you are distracted by them. Go! Make them safe. I will do this!"

It had been so long since Jacob had heard that obnoxious arrogance, but if he had had any doubts as to whether this man was truly his elder brother, they instantly disappeared upon hearing the unmitigated confidence in his declaration. Jacob took Bella's drenched body from his brother, even while holding his daughter. Together they flew upward into the storming clouds, leaving Adam to his duty.

Surrounded by his element as it streamed down, Adam was aware of its blinding power. But for him it was merely a matter of senses. He felt every molecule of water on its path from sky to earth. He felt the topography of the land around him blossom into three dimensions as each drop of water hit a solid object. He could close his eyes and sense everything, stationary or moving, as the falling water shaped it in his mind's eye. He could see it all without even looking.

The rainfall confused the Transformed. Those that were Water Demons took pleasure in it, not realizing that a powerful member of their former brethren was a part of its appearance. Each former Demon had his powers all intact, but the focus and understanding to use them to optimum advantage was gone. It was enough to leave them floundering and distracted in the rain. They saw no threat, so they did not act in defense. The master who could have guided their actions was not close enough or focused enough to maintain control under such conditions.

Adam was careful to remind himself that there were sure to be necromancers close by, and he would have to watch his back for them. In the meantime, he faded into the drowning fall of his element, drawing his sword for use. Each beast became isolated from the rest by the weather, and Adam darted in and out with little more than the flash of a blade and the subsequent rolling of a decapitated head to mark his presence. He dashed away, leaving the corpse to self-destruct in an explosive burst of flame.

Now *that* could be seen despite the deluge, and after the first four or five flares to warn them, the remaining Transformed realized their lives were threatened. This triggered a base instinct for survival, and Adam began to encounter significant resistance. He managed most of it with deadly precision, until he came up on one who turned to meet his approach through the rain as if fully expecting him. They began to fight, a sword against savage claws and fangs, not to mention powerful wings. The creature seemed able to anticipate his every move, and Adam caught a chest full of talons, the claws ripping him through clothing and flesh alike.

But the true shock came when he was finally set to make a death blow, and the cunning monster suddenly disappeared in a roiling cloud of smoke that reeked of sulfur. Adam had only seen this trick twice before. Mind Demons, he lectured himself quickly. It was a new element, the skills and abilities barely eighty years old. However, he knew enough for his special Enforcer's senses to ring warning of a Transformed presence appearing suddenly at his back. Smoke and sulfur clouded everywhere as the tainted Demon leapt for the Enforcer and found his blade instead.

Fire.

Not only from the falling corpse of Adam's latest kill, but exploding in bursts all around him. It sent jets of steam off in the air as it mixed with his rain. Dread filled his soul as he was forced to contemplate the worst. That one of the Transformed was a Demon of Fire.

He looked up and saw an un-Transformed Demon. The face was instantly recognizable, and Adam couldn't help the rush of relief that ran through him.

"Noah," he rasped.

"Yes. And this would be much easier if you turned off the waterworks, friend," a very familiar voice full of smoke and authority declared loudly.

Adam responded instantly, all of his instincts drawing the storm to a close just as swiftly as it had started. The last sheets of water fell away to reveal what remained of the Transformed and the Demon standing several yards away.

Noah raised his hands, fire immolating them before he resumed throwing molten balls of flame at the enemy, killing them off twice as quickly as Adam had done. Not to be outdone, even if it was by the Demon King, Adam went back to his work as well. Between the two of them, it took less than ten minutes to finish clearing the field. After the last one fell, Adam couldn't help a victorious laugh as he jogged up to Noah with his free hand extended.

"Damn me, Noah, you make that look too easy! You will have others believing my job to be nothing at all!"

Noah had seen some pretty amazing things in his lifetime, but nothing ever so stunningly unexpected and inconceivable as watching Jacob's long-lost brother walking up to him. The King automatically took the hand offered to him, wholly expecting the entire experience to be proved as nothing more than an apparition or illusion. Perhaps some magical trickery.

But the flesh of the hand engulfing his was firm and familiar, despite all the centuries that lay between handshakes, right down to the cracked, rough thickness of his calluses. Back in Adam's time, animal fat and strange home liniments were as close to lotions as anyone got, not that he'd cared much about the smoothness of his hands. The Adam Noah had known had been proud of every hard-worked callus he'd owned.

Despite his shock, Noah had the presence of mind to inspect the inside wrist of the hand he held. Fang punctures and current wounds aside, sure enough, a deep and ugly scar was angrily furrowed up Adam's arm from the seat of his palm to the inside of his elbow. It was more distinctive than fingerprints to Noah. The King had been by his side the day Adam had suffered the injury by iron that had caused it. Despite the skills of a Body Demon medic and his own rapid ability to heal, Adam had taken a long time by Demon standards to recover the full use of his hand after that singular attack.

"Sweet Destiny. Adam?"

Noah's amazement certainly came through. Enough so to make Adam frown darkly.

"Yes, my friend. It has not been that long since we last saw each other. Or is this your way of harassing me to come visit your family more often?"

Noah laughed incredulously.

"Adam, I have not seen you in four hundred years at least! No one has! What the devil happened to you?"

Four hundred years?

Adam chuckled; the slightly numb laugh was the only reaction he could formulate as he stared at his friend. He opened his mouth to deny the claim and even felt the urge to cuff the other Demon playfully for being so wicked.

However . . .

He let his eyes drift down the sturdy form of his King, absorbing the amazing fit of machine-made clothing. Even though Noah wore breeches and Hessians, as he often did, the fashion was dated well after Adam's time. As was the modern tailoring, and the sophisticated royal blue dye used in the silk shirt he wore with casual ease.

Though Demons aged at an infinitesimal crawl, there were signs of time on the Demon King Adam had never seen before; signs of worry and weight that had not been creased into Noah's visage when last he had seen him. Then the Water Demon recalled his brother's equally incredulous greeting and his strange clothing as well.

It all rolled back to not knowing what the Gypsy girl had done to him. Where had she taken him? He wasn't home, he knew that much. Was Noah's claim genuine? Could it possibly be four centuries in the future . . . ?

"No," he denied quickly, a black and indefinable emotion rocking him back a step. He felt dizzy and as though he could not draw a breath. "'Tis a cruel jest you play," he accused numbly.

Noah saw the genuine distress and confusion on the other Demon's face and he realized that even Adam had no idea how he had come to be there.

"I do not jest with you, old friend," Noah said carefully. "I can only tell you that these past few years, I have seen things that could make almost anything possible. You are with trusted friends, Adam, who will help you sort this confusion through."

"Where is my brother?" Adam demanded.

"Close by. He attends to his wife and daughter."

"*His wife and daughter?*" Adam backpedaled another step, holding out a hand in a staying motion when Noah moved forward. "Do you mean . . . do you mean that *human* woman? He is mated to a *human* and she has borne him a daughter?"

"Aye, Adam, and soon a son as well, from what I understand. Provided she comes through her injuries. I can sense her energy is very weak, her life in the balance. I want to help you, Adam, I do, but Jacob is desperately in need of our assistance as well. Can you do that? Can you help me to help Jacob and trust me to find an explanation for all of this later? Can you bear your confusion for a little while?"

Adam didn't even take the time to think about it. Noah had said the words that had always, and would always, work like magic on his mind. He had said his little brother needed his help.

He could never refuse.

Little Leah was crying in near hysterics when Noah and Adam finally found the family in a secluded glen some distance away. She was clutching her unconscious mother's hair, shaking her by it in an attempt to wake her. Jacob was not convinced that they were safe, regardless of his seeming distance from the immediate danger. Ruth was a wily and inexhaustible opponent. She would not give up easily, especially if she was thrown into a fury of insane temper. The female Mind Demon had once been a warrior, and had a track record of not taking defeat well.

"Well now, angel." Noah tsked soothingly as he moved quickly to crouch behind Leah, warming her with his touch and presence. The King glanced at Jacob, who sat beside Bella as though he were only half aware of the world around him. Since Noah knew Jacob would normally never let his daughter suffer such emotional trauma under even the worst of circumstances, the King was concerned by Jacob's distant and seemingly detached behavior. Considering the Imprinted bond the current Enforcer shared with the little Druid he loved, it would not surprise him if Jacob had been caught up in the riptide of whatever it was that had struck down Isabella. "Hush, Leah.

There now. That is a good girl," he praised her as she turned to climb into his arms and smeared her wet face and nose against his shirt, hiccupping out half-caught sobs. "It is going to be all right," he whispered to her softly. "We are all safe now. Okay, lamb? No more crying. We cannot have Mommy hear you crying and worrying about you."

"Why do you say this to her?" Adam demanded. "You will make her feel guilty for an understandable reaction. She is but a babe!"

"Because in this case it is the truth of the matter," Noah informed him carefully. "Bella is a Druid, Adam. She is a hybrid of Druid and human genetics and has remarkable gifts of power and sensitivity. The distress of her child and her husband will resonate with her and will keep her from focusing her energies where they are needed."

"Well, what is wrong with her? I see no obvious wounds."

"She has absorbed all the power of those we encountered in the cavern below," Jacob said at last. He glanced at Noah. "Nicodemous and Ruth. She did it to save us, and it worked. Adam would never have been able to get close enough to kill Nico if she had not done so."

"Ruth *and* Nicodemous?" Noah repeated with horror. "Sweet Destiny. The amount of corruption and evil that must have come into her . . ." Noah shook his head in clear distress as he looked down at the pale, unconscious woman. "Ruth is a Demon turned necromancer," he supplied absently for Adam, "and Destiny only knows what else can be said to fully describe the power she has accumulated and the ways she has done so. And Nicodemous is a Vampire who feasts on the blood of Nightwalkers, which allows him to acquire an aspect of their power. Vampires like him are as black with evil as we can possibly imagine." He looked at Jacob. "Hold on to her, Jacob," he urged. "Only your connection with her will keep her grounded."

"I know. I am doing all I can," he promised as he squeezed his wife's hand between his and stared down at her face in hard focus.

"Damn me thrice and let Destiny laugh," Adam swore on a choke of disbelief. "They are *Imprinted*!"

"Yes," Noah agreed. "They and this child are the fulfillment of a long-lost ancient prophecy. Much has changed, my old friend." Noah paused to stare at him. "Except for you. You look exactly as I recall."

Four hundred years. The King didn't repeat himself, but his astonishment bled through his voice and expression. The words loomed in Adam's thoughts as he tried to absorb everything he was experiencing around him.

"A human and a Demon. This goes against the most sacred of laws," he said numbly. "Laws I am supposed to maintain as your Enforcer!"

"*I* am his Enforcer!" Jacob spat with sudden venom. "You abandoned your post and the right to call yourself that when you abandoned your people and your family! When you abandoned me! You left without a word or a hint of where you had gone! I thought . . . *we all* thought you were dead! After all," he mocked, "what else could possibly keep you from your appointed rounds? But here you are, alive and quite well, it seems. Think you rushing to my rescue will make me forget the past four centuries of your neglect, brother? Do you think it will make me ever forget what it felt like to take on your mantle as Enforcer and all those years of being outcast among my own people? I went from Vampire-hunting hero to Demon hierophant in the blink of an eye. I did not want it, Adam! But who else was there?

"No, Adam, you are no longer Enforcer and never will be again. It is a title I hold proudly now, with my wife fighting by my side. She and I are Noah's Enforcers, and you are nothing! You have no place here! I do not know why you even bothered to come back! You certainly did not feel the need when Mother or Father were killed!"

"*What?*" Adam gasped in horror.

"Jacob!" Noah tried to warn him.

"Take him away from me!" Jacob spat. "Unlike him, I know my responsibilities, and right now I have a family to protect and care for. Give me my child and go. Just go!"

"I have never once shied from my responsibilities!" Adam roared at his brother, infuriated he would suggest otherwise and swimming in a sea of thoughts and questions and information he had no idea what to do with. "And if you were truly concerned with yours, you would not be sending away your only protection!"

"Jacob . . . take a moment," Noah encouraged him softly. "Put the pieces together in your mind. Look at him. You can see he has not spent four centuries living life in exile somewhere, having abandoned all he knows. Look at his clothes. Look at his weapons. The very things he was adorned with the day he disappeared." Noah knew Jacob's outlash of anger, the wild words and accusations, came from shock and grief. A part of Jacob's mind would much rather believe what he was saying than cope with the more obvious truth. A potentially more painful truth.

"One moment I was talking to a violet-eyed Gypsy girl on Beltane night, and the next I was watching you turn your back on a Vampire threat," Adam said.

Jacob looked up as he cradled Bella even closer, his grasp on her reflective of how vulnerable he must be feeling. His dark eyes were awash with emotion. His mind was a confusion of the distant poison his wife was processing in her own brain and body. The Imprinting between them made their heartbeats synchronize, made him weaker at this moment, even as it usually made him stronger. Any damage to her was like walking around with a critical wound in his chest. Or in this case, his mind.

Adam moved toward his brother, knelt in front of him, and reached to grip him by the back of the neck.

"I would never abandon you, Jake," he said fiercely.

"But you did," Jacob said softly, meeting his brother's eyes, although this time with less malice and perhaps less conviction. "Yet you did not," he realized. "It was my child. My girl." He reached out a hand toward the child in Noah's arms. "She was not a Gypsy, but a Demon girl. My daughter. The first Demon and Druid/human hybrid offspring and the first child of . . . of Time."

"You mean this child was that same girl of near sixteen I met?" Adam asked with disbelief and comprehension warring in his overloaded mind. "Time? There is a new element? Is that what you mean? That this girl brought me through time?"

"Actually," Noah said gingerly, "there are two new elements since the time of your disappearance. Leah is the first of Time. And my baby sister and her mate Gideon have the first child of Space. We barely know what Leah is capable of, as you see, and know nothing of Space. Seth is only three and not yet in power."

"I am sorry, but did you say Gideon?" Adam was clearly gaping at Noah. "You cannot mean our *Siddah*!"

"The very same," Noah assured him.

"Damn me. I do not think I can take much more of this," Adam swore, his head reeling. But then he took a breath, smiled half a smile, and shot Noah a look. "So what you are saying is . . . we are all being manipulated by . . . children. Your babe of Time has moved me like a chess piece for her own purposes. Your babe of a sister—and did I hear you say *younger?*—captured the stoic Gideon to mate. And somewhere there is another babe who has powers we have no concept of as yet?"

Noah chuckled. "So it would seem."

"I need a bloody drink."

"Now there's a phrase I haven't heard in that tone in a very long time."

Adam looked up at the familiar voice and found himself captured by the warm familiarity of green eyes set in Elijah's face. But here again there was change. The white-blond hair was gone, replaced by a golden hue as close to the beaten metal as Adam had ever seen.

"Elijah!" And though he'd only seen him, from his perspective, hours earlier, he reached to hug the warrior as if it had been four centuries—because apparently it had been exactly that. And the long absence was evident in Elijah's return embrace.

"Adam. Sweet Destiny, I never thought . . ." Elijah stopped speaking as emotion overwhelmed him. He had lost so many good friends through the ages of his lifetime. But losing Adam had been one of those losses that had hit him particularly hard. "How is this possible?"

Adam laughed a little wildly.

"Ask her," he said, pointing to the little girl Noah still held.

A perplexed look ghosted over Elijah's face, but it was quickly chased away by an expression of cautious understanding.

"Let us wait until later to sort out details," Noah suggested as Siena and Gideon moved onto the field. "Will you protect and care for Jacob and his family? I think it best if I take Adam away with me for a little while. Though I suspect no sure answers will ever come, perhaps I can help him sort through some information, help him acclimate a little. One thing I know, regardless. We'd best not tarry here with Ruth around. Adam has killed Nicodemous, and we all know very well how Ruth reacts to losing someone close to her."

"Nicodemous is dead? Hot damn!" Elijah hugged Adam again, even harder and more enthusiastically. "You have no idea what you've done!"

"You would be right about that," Adam said.

"We've been hunting them for years," Elijah told him. "It was getting so that no one was safe to walk this world by themselves. I promise you I don't exaggerate when I tell you you have saved a great many lives in that single act, Adam."

"And let us not risk any others," Noah encouraged the group. "Take Jacob and Bella to safety," he instructed Elijah and Siena. "Gideon, I think it best if you take Leah for now. Perhaps some playtime with Seth will help calm her after all she has experienced today."

"We will all be at my court. Close together," Siena

said softly when Leah made a sound of whimpering protest. "We will all be able to rest and get well," she continued to soothe the girl as she picked her up into her arms. "And you can see your mama and daddy as soon as we have all had a bit of a nap."

Gideon lifted a brow in Elijah's direction at the sudden maternal streak in the notoriously child-phobic Queen of the Lycanthropes. Elijah shrugged a big shoulder, just as perplexed as the medic was. Then he turned to Jacob and knelt beside him, reaching to rest a hand on his friend's shoulder. Jacob had such a death grip on Bella, his fingers were like rigid talons in her flesh. He jolted a little when Elijah touched him, but settled down when he looked into the warrior's eyes and recognized a friend. The comfort of Elijah's strength seemed to relax Jacob.

"Come with us. We'll keep you all safe now," he assured his friend.

"I will come with you," Jacob said. Then he added vehemently, "But no one is safe until that evil bitch is rotting in her grave."

"I think we're all well agreed on that," Elijah said.

Chapter 6

Transportation. Electrical lines. Modern housing. Technology. These were just some of the things dotting the landscape the Demons covered on their way back to Noah's holdings in England. If Adam had not believed he had been thrust into the future before, he certainly was convinced by the time Noah had brought him home. The fact that the Demon seat of power was now in Britain was alone an earth-shattering concept. But Noah explained that Adam's homelands, the lands once populated by Demons, were now lands of war and contention among humans. It had become unwise for even a Nightwalker race to spend any further time there.

"Humans have made amazing advances in a relatively short period of time," Noah remarked. "Although it remains to be seen if this is a betterment in the long run. I am not convinced of it myself. The very fact that our elemental chemistry interferes with technology, making us unable to use it, leads me to wonder if it is good for the natural world."

"The oceans and the seas," Adam said, heavy grief

in his normally calm voice, "water everywhere is weighted with . . . with disease and polluted with things I do not even recognize. I can feel the poisoning and the tolerances the sea creatures have had to develop. Noah, I can sense entire species are missing . . . or near to it."

"We have always known how thoughtless and uneducated mankind can be in the ways of the natural world's delicate balances. Only now are humans learning the error of their ways."

Noah guided the rather shell-shocked Demon into the Great Hall of the castle he had made the center of Demon culture and society, as well as his private home. The anachronistic décor had some power to soothe the displaced Enforcer as he moved toward the ever-present fire in Noah's hearth, although it was still a far cry from the way things had been done in the Renaissance. Adam drew up short, however, when a woman with hair as white as cotton rose from one of the chairs and hurried into Noah's embrace. Even as he stared at the King, who kissed the obviously human woman with a depth of passion and familiarity, Adam was becoming disgusted with his own state of seemingly never-ending, gape-mouthed shock at the things he saw around him.

He cleared his throat.

"Noah, please excuse me. I . . . I think I need to take a walk. I need some time . . ."

"You should not leave the bounds of my property," Noah said, fully appreciating how Adam must be feeling. "Although the town and surrounding areas are seeded mostly with Demons, you are not familiar enough to navigate safely around, and I would not wish to attract attention."

"No," Adam agreed. "I would not know where to go anyway." He turned away toward the arboretum, which led to the outside gardens, but hesitated a moment to ask, "Is it true?"

Noah raised a brow in query as he cuddled the pretty blonde to his side.

"What Jacob said about my parents," he clarified.

Adam knew it was, just by the expression that fell over the King's features. He didn't need the nod of assent that followed.

"Thank you," he said, resuming his exit.

Once the Water Demon was alone in the gardens, he methodically began to sort through all that had happened, the repercussions and the logic, and tried to reconcile how to fix all of the problems his appearance in this time had caused. There was only one solution, as he saw it. He had to make the Gypsy girl who had started all of this return him to where she had gotten him. He had to force her to return him to his own time, his own country, and his living, thriving family where his little brother did not speak to him with such cold contempt.

But that girl was gone. And yet not gone. Not even of age as yet, if he was understanding things correctly. Why had she done this? He ran it over in his head, all the things she had said to him, all the things he now knew. She had brought him to a moment that, had he not appeared just then, would likely have meant his brother's death. Leah's father's death.

His niece. He had a niece. Named Leah. And his niece had just turned his life around. But hadn't she asked him that very question? Hadn't she asked him if he was willing to give up everything for Jacob? To sacrifice everything he knew?

His answer had been yes without even knowing
what it would really mean. But, Adam realized, when
all was said and done, even if he found out Damien
the Vampire Prince was Noah's best damn friend in
the world, it wouldn't matter. He would accept it. He
would accept it all so long as it meant being able to be
there when Jacob needed him most.

Jacob. As Enforcer? There had never been more
than one Enforcer before. In this time there were two.
The second was a human woman who was also his
brother's wife? Jacob was right. There would be no
place for him here. This was clearly his brother's time.
A fulfillment of *his* Destiny.

So . . . what did that leave for Adam?

He shoved the pitiful thought away. There was no
considering it, he thought firmly. He was not defined
by his role as Enforcer. He had been a man of power
and vital use to his people long before he'd been
passed the mantle of Enforcer, and he would be again.
No matter which way the sand scattered once this child
of Time was through playing with it, he would be of use
and of power so long as there was breath in his body.

The sound of boots on stones drew his full attention. Adam suddenly found himself staring into sultry
dark eyes the color of mink. The beautiful Vampire
was fully clothed, but Adam's breath rushed out of his
body at the sight of her just as it had when she had
stood naked before him. She wore breeches and
boots, both hugging her legs like a second skin, the
fabric smoothed lovingly to the curves of her hips and
her backside. She wore some sort of shirt that barely
reached below her fine breasts as it clung to them
tightly enough to reveal the precise location of nipples
whose mauve color he too easily recalled. She was bare

along her flat midriff, except for the exotic addition of a silver and amethyst chain that circled her waist and linked through a hoop that pierced her navel.

As she stood there, proud and boldly beautiful as ever before, he realized her hair was worn a bit shorter now. She'd cropped the wavy black mass to just a few inches below her collarbone. A shame, he found himself thinking. It had been gorgeous as it had tumbled wet down the length of her bare back. Although he had to concede that there was something attractive about it this way as well.

"My, my," Jasmine murmured in a voice low with lush amusement. "If it isn't the so shy spying Demon. Adam, isn't it?" She laughed, delighted she had recalled his name after so much time. Then again, her brief encounters with him were some of those memories that had just seemed to stick with her over the years. Actually, they had more than stuck, she admitted to herself quickly, as if the admission, like the removal of a Band-Aid, would hurt less that way. Time and again she had been wrapped up in those memories, overcome by a strange longing she couldn't make herself understand. After all, it had just been an amusement. A tease. He had not been the first and he had not been the last she had taunted in such ways.

But he had been the most powerful. The memory had clung to her for four centuries, and she had wondered on more than one occasion where he had disappeared to. She also remembered his flustered reactions to her quite often when she elicited similar ones from others, but while she found her more recent sufferers to be pitiful, she had never recalled memories of him with such disrespect.

The funny thing was he looked almost exactly the

same, from the disorderly curls of his longish black hair to the scuffed and worn leather of the boots riding high on his thick thighs. It was like looking through a portal into the past. He still wore a sword as well. The dagger was missing, yet again, and the scabbard was set empty on his hip.

"Have you spent all these years avoiding me, only to fail now?" she suggested in a blatant taunt.

Adam snapped.

It was all too much, really. He had been through enough in the past hours to shatter a man's sanity. But he swore by Destiny he was not going to let this Vampire harlot stand there laughing at him, getting the best of him. She was on the land of his King, and her intentions couldn't possibly be good if she so boldly strode onto Demon territory. If it was war she sought, well, Adam was ripe in mood to give it to her.

"Right then, my fine-bred little bitch," he hissed as he drew his sword, "let us see how well you laugh through the slit in your throat."

Jasmine barely leapt back in time to avoid the vicious swipe of the already bloodstained sword. Her boots sent the white pathway stones flying as she skidded back to a distance. This time her laugh was wholly incredulous.

"Have you lost your bloody mind?" she demanded, dodging back again when that wicked blade nearly nicked her shoulder.

"Aye. I am feeling rather insane at the moment. So anything is possible." Adam grinned, flashing broad white teeth at her as an excited light entered his eyes for the first time in what felt like ages of confusion. *This* he knew. He knew how to fight and to kill in the name of his King and kind. This at least would never change, no matter how much time might pass.

Jasmine saw the eagerness for blood that shimmered into those amazing pale green eyes and she all but shivered with delight, in spite of her obvious peril. If there was one thing Jasmine could always appreciate, it was a thirst for blood. Of course, he wasn't supposed to be thirsting for *her* blood. Their people were no longer at war, but he was acting as though she were still his enemy. Honestly, she hadn't even been his enemy the first time they had met. She'd been more tempted to tumble the gorgeous brute than fight with him.

But either way, foreplay was foreplay.

"Well then, I am at a bit of a disadvantage, seeing as how you are armed and I am not."

And why was that, Adam wondered sharply. If she had come to cause trouble, why come armed with only her fangs and her powers of the mind?

"Ahh, got you thinking, haven't I?" she taunted him as they danced a couple more steps around each other. "If you wish to stick your sword in something, surely we could find you a better target."

"I doubt that. You are as fine a sheath for my sword as I have ever seen," he parried back with vehemence.

"Do you think so?" Jasmine launched into flight to avoid losing a leg. She flew over and behind him, landing with a flourish and a laugh before sweeping under his next reach and, to Adam's unending shock, disarming him of his sword with just the hard thrust of her palms. She almost cracked his forearm in two with the blow and he roared with pain even as his blade flew several yards out of reach. To his surprise, though, the Vampire danced away from his reach instead of following up on his vulnerability. "Now you

shall have to find a different sword to stick me with!"
She chuckled.

"Why, you little . . ."

The blatant taunt took him beyond logic and all his
years of training. Then again, he'd never been in a
fight quite like this before. Adam couldn't believe it,
but the cunning little minx was amusing him, frustrat-
ing him, and bloody well turning him on all at the
same time!

"And why not?" he muttered to himself. "In a world
turned mad and on its head, where Demons make
babies with humans, why not a Demon wanting to
make a smart Vampire wench scream his name once
or twice?"

Adam lunged for his adversary and caught her in a
fabulous full tackle. They went sailing off the rocky
path and onto the lawn with a hard roll and tumble.
To his amusement, she ended up on top. Her dark
cloud of silky, shining hair formed a black nimbus
around her head, her aristocrat's features lean and
lovely in the moonlight glowing from behind her. She
planted her hands on his chest and purposely slid her
bottom down the length of his torso until she was
astride his hips, riding him like she might a prize stal-
lion with her straight posture and outthrust breasts.
She laughed again, her rich brown eyes dancing with
life and merriment. Then she leaned close to him
until her lips all but brushed against his.

"As I recall," she whispered in rushes of hot breath
against his mouth, "you are quite the well-armed warrior." She rode her heated sex against his to be certain
he took her meaning. "Let us bring your other weapons
out to play."

Adam reached up and grabbed her by her shoulders, dumping her hard over onto the ground until he was in the dominant position. He found himself snug between her strong thighs, her breasts crushed beneath his chest as he pinned her wrists to the ground close to her shoulders.

"I think you might get what you are looking for if you can stay alive long enough!"

"Do not make promises you do not intend to keep," she breathed against his mouth just before she flicked her tongue out from between half-prominent fangs and licked his lips.

Adam jerked back at the contact. What he expected was to feel his skin crawl with utter disgust at the Vampire's stolen intimacy. But what he felt instead was just the opposite. Heat exploded over his face, like a flash of embarrassment without the shameful feeling itself. Adam felt his entire body follow suit, surging with it in rough, overwhelming waves. His heart was already racing from their struggles, but now it was about so much more. Now all he could seem to focus on was the way she was breathing hard beneath him.

Breathing.

Vampires didn't breathe after the first hundred years or so. And she had to be at least four hundred. *Why is she . . . ? Sweet Destiny.*

Adam felt that same shift again inside his psyche. It came on the tide of her rushing breaths, the ones that gave away her level of arousal. It wafted into his senses on the myrrh and clove scent of her skin. Were they fighting or playing? Adam could hardly remember. Or he couldn't tell the difference. All he understood with perfect clarity was the unbelievable draw of her. It had been thus since the instant he had first laid eyes on her.

"Hmm," she purred low in her throat, her long legs sliding to wrap around the backs of his thick thighs. "Haven't you ever heard the phrase 'Make love, not war'?"

"No," he exhaled roughly. "But it is a damn fine idea. Too bad I have no choice but to kill you for trespassing too close to my King."

"Your King has left me an open invitation to come"—she put deliberate emphasis on the word— "and go as it pleases me."

Adam tightened his grip on her wrists so sharply that Jasmine winced.

"Are you implying that Noah would sully himself with the likes of you? That you are my King's mistress?"

Jasmine chuckled at that. "No, darling, I think not. You know as well as I do his wife would have had me gutted ages ago if I so much as looked at him wrong."

"His wife," Adam echoed.

The blonde.

"Kestra has a bit of a temper, I am told. Besides, I was rather considering sullying you instead." She licked her lips slowly, somehow forcing Adam's entire body to tighten in reaction. "But then," she whispered slyly, "so were you."

Damn her and her alluring ways! How did she do it? How did she make him burn as though his life depended on satisfying his outrageous lust for her? It was a trick! He knew damn well it was a Vampire's trick of the mind, but for his life he could not seem to break free of it. Awareness of the tactic should have dissolved her power. Why did he crave her so strongly?

"Ahh," she breathed with obvious pleasure curving up her spine. "Now there is the Demon I remember." Jasmine shifted her hips up beneath the pelvis pinning her to the ground. Adam was highly aroused; he had been since the start of their encounter, just the sight of her obviously having affected him. She could smell it on him, a musky male heat that grew and grew. But now he grew hard against her as well, an enormous erection lying against the length of her own warm sex. Only man-made fabric held them apart, and the knowledge caused her body to flash hot and damp all over.

It was one thing to enjoy a taunting flirtation, but for Jasmine it was quite another to actually feel something in response. Especially a reaction as stunning and powerful as this.

Not of your blood. Not of your breed.

She heard her mind lecturing her sternly on her prejudices. As a rule, Jasmine was completely appalled by the rash of crossbreeding unions among Nightwalkers of late. The worst of them being her own Prince's marriage to a *Lycanthrope*, of all things! Marriage for a Vampire was a ridiculous concept to begin with, because Vampires were so detached from truly deep emotions of affection, but to wed oneself to an outsider? All the trouble it had caused was hardly worth it and more than proved her point!

But she was over five centuries old now, and so little amused her. Almost nothing excited her. Yet as she lay beneath the brute's body, she felt her heart come alive with a wild beat for the first time since she had grown out of the need for regular circulation. She didn't need to breathe, but now couldn't catch her breath. Nothing, *nothing* had ever thrilled her so thoroughly before. Why? Why this time, and of all things, why with this *Demon*?

"You take pleasure in this, do you?" he accused hotly

in response to her taunting. "You tease and manipulate, finding it all so delightful. But let me warn you, Vamp, that I am not having the best of evenings. I find I am rapidly losing all concern for what might be right or wrong. Tomorrow I may even be gone, and all I do until then will never come to matter."

"I find I do take pleasure in this," she admitted, her low voice so sexy it made his body ache with inexplicable longing. "It surprises me to confess it."

"I should kill you," he warned her.

"Why? The war is long over, Adam. We are no longer enemies. Your attack and threats against me are tantamount to treason."

"*Treason!*"

"I am Damien's most valued and trusted aide. Noah has promised me safe passage, and our peoples are rather tediously at peace. An attack against me might be construed as an act of war."

"An act of . . ."

Peace. Of course. What did he expect? A war to last four centuries? She could be lying but . . . he had already known better, hadn't he? The castle was very lightly guarded, she came unarmed and made no effort to seriously harm him, and he had already learned a hard series of lessons that night that said anything was possible.

"Anything is possible," he murmured thoughtfully as he stared down into heated eyes of mink. "Even peace with Vampires. But you, my dark beauty, are quite a different issue, now, are you not?"

Jasmine felt her revived heart stutter under the intense reaction his contemplative words caused to rush through her. It was as though thousands of pins pricked her all along her sensitive skin.

"Tell me your name, little Vamp," he commanded her.

"Earn it, my fine Demon brute," she shot back before she could check the impulse. But the dare made him smile in such a slow and predatory manner that Jasmine wanted to goad him again and again. Anything to invite that awesome savagery in his pale jade irises.

"I think I will at that, Vamp."

Adam vibrated with the stimulation of her invitation, the possibilities churning through his mind as, for the first time, he gave himself complete permission to do so. She was a bold and obviously experienced wench, so he need not be delicate with her. She certainly wasn't the first pretty thing with delicious tits and a fine ass to fall into his lap.

The crude thought came and went in a flash, some part of his mind rejecting it sharply for a reason he couldn't fathom. Then, of all the choices she'd flaunted flagrantly before him, Adam settled on what he wanted most. He lowered his dark head until his lips drew warm and soft against her cheek, and then he set his head lower and lower until his nose was running the length of her fragrant neck and his mouth slowly opened against her raw little pulse.

Jasmine gasped sharply, and then rolled her eyes closed with a slow groan of pure pleasure as his damp tongue flicked against her throat. When he sucked at her strongly, she all but shot off the ground. That particular spot was highly erogenous in her people, and clearly he knew how to exploit it.

"Mmm," she moaned against his near ear in spite of herself. Of all the things for him to choose, why had he chosen this? There was no direct satisfaction for him this way, was there?

The thought disturbed her deeply. Disliking the sensation of confusion, she jerked beneath him and unwrapped her legs from around him to brace her feet on the ground. He lifted his head when he felt her acts of resistance, and now it was his eyes that were alight with amusement.

"So, my little Vamp has borders after all. She prefers to tease but not be teased."

"Get up," she bit out in reply.

"I do not believe I will." Adam went nose to nose with her. "Water is my element. All that is liquid is mine to manipulate and harmonize with. Shall I tell you where you are wet, little Vamp?"

"If you have the balls to say it, Demon, you will find them missing come morning. *Get up!*"

Adam laughed at her threat, unable to explain his delight. As the power play rotated between them, his excitement rose to greet it. He felt more grounded as he regained control of the dynamic of the moment. Yet he still realized that the arousal itself was out of his scope of management. Just the same, he craved indulgence in it. Even if only to get the better of the brassy vixen beneath him.

"Come, come," he coaxed, his inflection making it a double entendre, "you were so eager to play a moment ago. And I have a name to earn from you."

"Bastard! How's that for a name?" she growled.

"Not pretty enough for the likes of you." He chuckled.

Jasmine flashed fangs at him with a hiss. "If I tell you my name, will you get off me?"

"Hardly a fair trade after all you have given to me." He shifted his hips forward against her to remind her of the reactions her teasing ways had wrought. Adam reveled in her nearly airless gasp, watching her sensual nature take her over with her darkening eyes and a delicate flare of her nostrils. She couldn't contain the involuntary sound of pleasure that followed, and he could see her fury at her self-betrayal burning over her features.

Jasmine's head was spinning with sensory and emotional overload. On one hand, she was enraged by this queer turnabout of power, feeling she was meant to dole out, not be victim to such tricks. However, she couldn't believe how easily and thoroughly he affected her. She craved more, the excitement of it making her feel so . . .

Alive.

Adam sensed a measure of surrender, and he risked releasing one of her trapped wrists. Rising up a little, he studied the pretty palate of possibilities she presented. He reached to touch her exposed belly, running a finger under the extraordinary jeweled chain.

"Do all females wear these now?" he asked softly as his callused fingertips scraped over her smooth skin near her navel.

"Some do," she breathed. "I like it."

"As do I," he informed her with an intensity that made Jasmine's blood hum noisily in her ears. "Are you bejeweled elsewhere, little Vamp?"

"Yes," she said on a rushed whisper.

"Tell me."

"Find out for yourself," she countered in a wicked return of her wildly powerful flirtation. The invitation slammed desire into Adam's already heated systems.

"Oh, Vamp. What you do to me . . ."

Adam looked into her eyes, pale jade clashing with

warm mink in a tangle of intensity they both felt far deeper than either thought they wanted to. He suddenly felt as though breathing was beyond his capability, and he found his full attention drawn to her mouth. Her lips were lush and dark, but the pricking of her fangs kept them from appearing sweet or innocent. Instead the image was darkly erotic and strangely tempting.

Jasmine turned her head sharply aside when he feinted for her mouth. His free hand shot up to her chin and turned her back hard to face him, holding her firmly in place.

"Too afraid to kiss me, little Vamp?"

"A kiss is nothing," she ground out. "And my tongue is not pierced, so you need not go looking."

"Your tongue . . ." Adam laughed hard. "I would not expect it to be. Surely not even Vampires would do something so ridiculous."

Jasmine grinned. "No. Of course not."

Adam had a feeling she was having a private joke at his expense, but he didn't much care.

"Kiss me, dark angel. You have nothing to fear from a man who barely exists in this moment."

"Fear?" She laughed at that. "I fear very little and give my kiss to even less. I would not touch my lips to my food if I could possibly avoid it, but, as you see, I have little choice."

"What? Above slitting a throat for your dinner?"

"Not above it, but merely prevented by law and a small shred of decency."

"Oh my," he returned, "what a little liar you are. You are not as lacking in morals as you would have me believe. Tell me, do these quills prove effective in keeping others at a distance?"

"Only certain pricks deserve pricking back."

"Well, let us see how we two might dodge your sharpness, little Vamp," he coaxed softly as he brushed her lips with his. She tried to pull away again but he held her tight.

"Please, I don't kiss . . ." she whispered in final desperation, her free hand reaching to push against one large shoulder.

"Yes, you do. You just have not realized it yet."

Adam's mouth covered hers with heated domination. She was a powerful personality in her own right, but in that moment she was on the defensive, and he could feel the tightening of resistance as it bolted through her. But he could also feel the gasp of surprise she made and the thoughtful turn of her hurried breathing. Tension that had her resisting him suddenly began to reach for him as he slipped a hot, insistent tongue between her lips. He encountered the erotic scrape of her fangs, the points sharp enough to cut him if he moved wrong, but he ignored that small danger so he could focus solely on the sweet darkness that was their kiss.

She hadn't lied when she'd said she didn't kiss. The intimacy was clearly one she avoided. He could tell by the awkwardness of her resistance to his initial invasion. More so, he could tell by the unpracticed way she began to relax and relent into his stolen kisses. It wasn't that she didn't know how to do what she was doing, just that it had been a long time since she had allowed it.

When her tongue finally fully engaged with his and her whole body seemed to lift into him in eager participation, Adam didn't resist smiling down on her triumphantly. She made an obstinate noise and her hands came up to curve fast and strong over his shoulders, covering their expanse in an instant. Her kisses grew fiery and rich, drawing him deeply into her and setting his every inch of flesh on fire. Adam drew back after he felt her fingertips stroking down the entire length of his back, a delicate caress that seemed somehow the antithesis of the wrenching passion skipping between their mouths, yet was deeply stirring just the same. He had to look down into her darkly beautiful eyes, an attempt to center himself or possibly comprehend the depth of what was resonating through him. Could he even begin to understand what he was experiencing? He readily admitted to himself that in spite of his age, he had nothing in his experience to compare this to. Looking into her bewildered expression, he had to doubt it was any different for her. He wanted to fill his hands with her, and it was clear she would have very few complaints if he did.

The Enforcer slid a hungry hand up the lean curves of her side until soft flesh overflowed his palm and the cage of his fingers. Disregarding the barrier of her thin, clinging shirt, he angled her breast and its crest toward his mouth. At first all he did was tease her with the ghostly rubbing of his lips, but it only took a moment for him to realize he had uncovered one of the treasures she had challenged him with. He could feel, on a rushing thrill of excitement, a hard circlet of metal and the two tiny balls accompanying it.

Through with fascinated exploration, Adam shot his hand beneath her shirt and peeled back the skin-hugging fabric. He felt her free hand gripping tightly into the curls of his hair, as though she was undecided about whether to draw him closer or push him away.

But all it took was a single glimpse of the silver piercing through the very tip of a turgid nipple the shade of a flushed rose, and he couldn't have forced himself to stop his next impulse for all his worth in the world. He reached out with the tip of his tongue to hook the inviting ring. With an experimental tug and a quickly followed draw into his mouth, Adam was delighted when she arched her back and all but clutched his head to her in sudden encouragement. She gasped softly, her fingernails dragging down out of his hair and along the cheek that went concave beneath her touch as he took the liberty of toying with her fascinatingly bejeweled body.

The scent of her emanated from her skin in sweet waves of sexual invitation. She made a low, trilling sound of enticement to him, her legs sliding restlessly in renewed temptation. Adam tested her tolerance at the sensitive point, catching the ring and tugging strongly on it until she exhaled a sound of response.

Adam's entire body was raging with need, and he knew he had never wanted a woman with such a sense of sheer insanity. The only exception would have been that moment when she herself had elicited the same strong response from him in what was now the very distant past.

The thought was a highly sobering one. His situation in life was reeling out of his control, nothing making sense and no resolution in sight, and yet here he was with this female, and somehow he felt more grounded than he ever had before. Even though it was wrong to be with her. Or was it? He had no idea what was right and what was wrong in this confusing world he found himself in, and it was making him feel like he had no center. He needed to know the rules. The law. It was how he had always lived his life, and he wasn't going to stop now.

Adam pushed away from the temptation lying in the grass, backing off from her even though very visceral parts of himself protested the act quite violently. He gained his feet and his composure and watched as she slowly sat up and smoothed her hands down over her stimulated body. She touched her mouth with elegant fingers, wiping away the moisture he'd left behind with a pair of sensual little strokes that made his chest ache with longing once again.

"Until next time." She snickered as she rose up from the ground in an easy levitation.

"There will be no next time," he grumbled darkly.

"Sure there won't." Her disbelief was more than obvious.

She headed for Noah's, flying barely four inches above the path as she skimmed along her way. Adam cursed, still unwilling to take her word that the war was over and hurrying quickly after her in case he needed to protect Noah's household.

She entered the Great Hall without knocking, just as she always did, completely aware that the big Demon male was hot on her tail. Jasmine might be acting cool and incidentally flirtatious about their encounter, but she was feeling anything but calm. In fact, her whole body was hot with response and eager curiosity. She couldn't remember when she had last come up against a male who had been so confident and outrageously bold, a male she was also attracted to. And the fact that he wasn't a Vampire simply floored her.

Then again, she hadn't found anyone in her breed to play with in a very long time. They all bored her or were obnoxiously cocky. This Demon male was strong and self-assured, but she could feel the moments of doubt and confusion in him. He was most certainly a puzzle. Why was it she had not laid eyes on him in four centuries? And why was it every time she did see him, they seemed to stick together like irrepressible magnets?

"Noah!" Adam barked out as he reached to grab the Vampire hard around her arm. "She says she knows you. Is this Vampire welcome in your home?"

Jasmine smiled at the way he said "Vampire." As if she were something truly dirty. Well, when she was around him she felt dirty. Very dirty.

"Jasmine!" Noah stood, pushing his wife off his lap and coming up to meet them. He was frowning, just as Adam was frowning as he tried to understand how humans could have become mates to Demons. "Yes, Adam, she is very welcome here. Jasmine, forgive Adam, he has been out of touch with current issues. Adam, she is an important attaché to the Vampire Prince. There is peace between Vampires and Demons . . . for the most part."

"For the most part?" Adam echoed.

"There are some Vampires who have turned to lawless behavior. They endanger us all. Like the one you killed."

"Killed a Vampire, did we?" Jasmine asked, arching a brow at him. He could almost hear her mocking the feat.

"Nicodemous," Noah informed her.

Adam watched with a bit of amazement as she went very still, absorbing the information nonchalantly when all of his senses told him she was quite shocked.

"You killed Nico," she said a bit breathlessly. And

there was something primeval in her understanding of that. The way she met his eyes, Adam could almost taste the arousal and excitement the information sent spinning through her. It was as though he could read her mind, rather than the reverse. But surely his own addled brain was making it up. Why would she take pleasure in the death of her own? Then again, who could ever understand what drove a Vampire?

"I ran him through the brain stem. Last I checked, next to beheading, that is the quickest method of killing a Vampire."

And why did he think the fact that he knew more ways to kill her kind than most turned her on a little? It couldn't possibly be because of that little smile she was giving him, could it?

"Well, he's quite dead, then," she agreed. "I confess I am impressed, Adam. Even your King shied from going head-to-head with Nico or Ruth. I don't know whether to consider you brave or incredibly fool-hardy."

"I would do anything to save my brother's life. And as Enforcer I would not hesitate to hunt the perverted Demon female either. It is a wonder Jacob has not already managed her." Adam pressed his lips together to keep from speaking his theories on that. It was clear Jacob was too distracted by his wife and child to be doing his job effectively. There was a reason Enforcers resigned if they became Imprinted. In his opinion, this situation illustrated that reason.

"As Enforcer? You?"

Jasmine realized a moment after she laughed that it was a bad idea to scoff about this particular notion. The Demon's lip curled and his big body bristled in offense.

Jasmine held up her palms and shrugged a shoulder, trying to ward off whatever faux pas she'd made. Normally she couldn't care less who she ticked off, but she wasn't really all that eager to ruffle this Demon's feathers. When he got ruffled, he started doing things to her that ended up ruffling her. And she hadn't decided yet if she liked that or not.

She didn't think she ought to.

But then again . . . her body was still humming with his last attack on her senses, her mouth still feeling full of his flavor and his heat. She felt as though she had been branded in a way. It took her back four hundred years to the first time they had met, when he had become water and attacked her body in its entirety. She had never forgotten that moment, that incredible sensation. She had never forgotten it because no one since had ever lived up to its potential. It had been an unfulfilled promise, had lasted less than a minute, to be sure, and yet no sexual escapade she could dream up or dabble in had struck her quite as powerfully.

Not that she would ever admit that to him.

"There are two Enforcers, and you are not one of them."

Chapter 7

"Ouch," Jasmine whispered a bit loudly as she turned to look at the Enforcer she was more familiar with. Jacob walked deeper into the Great Hall, looking like he'd been dragged through the bowels of hell and was none too steady for it. Noah moved toward Jacob with concern etched in his features, but Jacob held up a hand to keep him at bay.

"I need to attend to my wife and child, but they are safe for now and this is more pressing," Jacob said as he advanced on his brother, standing toe-to-toe with him for the first time in centuries. "You are not an illusion. You are not some figment of magic sent to trick us. I can see that. I can sense that in my soul. You *are* my brother. And yet . . ." He looked at Noah. "I would never raise my daughter to act in a manner that could have so much potential for harm and negative consequences. I held her and touched her, I looked into her eyes, and it *was* Leah . . . but how could I have so failed her as a parent that she would think this was an acceptable thing to do? To steal someone out of his life like this? To rob him of his own Destiny and to alter the Destiny of so many others in the process?"

"Maybe you did not," Noah said softly. "Jacob, have you considered what would have happened to you and Bella and Leah if Adam had not shown up in that cavern when he did?"

Jacob did consider it now. He blanched as Noah's point sank in.

"But if that is the truth, if Nico would have killed me, how would Leah ever survive when Isabella was incapacitated?"

"Maybe Ruth would have let them live, Jacob. Contemplate, for a minute, what that would mean. You die, but she lets Bella survive. Lets Leah survive."

"Bella could not survive without me. You know that."

"So does Ruth. And forcing Leah to bear witness would make it all the worse. You and I both know that sick bitch is more than capable of it."

"So you are saying . . . you are saying that Leah survived watching her father get murdered . . . and her mother . . ." He cleared the hoarseness in his throat that his thoughts caused.

"Can you imagine what that would do to a child?" Noah said. "A child who grew up with all of us living in the aftermath of something like that? The thought of it alone devastates me, Jacob. It makes so much sense that she would use her power to find a way to come back to change the past, find a way to save you both."

"By going into the distant past to steal my brother to help her? You are telling me this is why he disappeared all those centuries ago? Because my daughter stole him away so he could come and protect me in the future? And if that is so, why did she leave? Why did she not stay and explain all of this to me?"

"You must imagine that the paradoxes are endless, Jacob. That the moment Adam saved you, *that* Leah must have ceased to exist. The future and time line that she had existed in had to come to a crashing halt, had to disintegrate, because it was all based on that one moment in time she had just changed."

"The moment of his death," Adam said suddenly.

"Exactly. Her actions have left you and Bella safe and alive, and Adam stranded here with no way of getting back until perhaps years from now, when Leah is old enough to control her power. But clearly she does not take him back, or you would never have noticed his absence. You would never have become Enforcer. You would never have met Bella or fathered her life. It has to end this way, and begin anew from here. Adam can never go back because if he does, Leah can never exist to take him in the first place."

"My head hurts just listening to that explanation." Jacob said. "But I think I am following you just the same."

"You mean I have no choice? I must stay here in the future? Or rather, this present?"

"It is a house of cards, Adam," Noah warned him. "If you go back, you change everything. You might destroy all chance of happiness for your brothers. For all of the Demon people. Jacob was the first to find and fall in love with a Druid. If that never happens, then I would never find my wife. Your brother Kane would never find his. Elijah—"

"My *brother* Kane?" Adam echoed incredulously.

"Kane was born after you disappeared," Jacob informed him.

Jacob now realized he had no right to be angry with his brother for all of the things he had railed at him

in immodestly skintight clothing and with that perpetually contemplative grin on her lips, he knew she was concerned for him. He knew she understood what he must be feeling. When he had first met her, she had said something about having been asleep for a long while. She must have felt the same as he did now. Out of touch. Confused and disoriented. Behind the times.

"How do you do it?" he asked her bluntly. "How do you simply awake hundreds of years later and assimilate the changes that have gone on around you?"

"Me?" She arched a brow and smiled slyly. "I just embrace the new world around me. The clothes, the food, the smells, and the feel of it all. I want to experience everything about it." She hugged herself as she spoke, but then cocked her head at him. "You, however, don't seem the type. You would probably be better off with a guide."

"What do you mean, not the type?" he demanded, the fine hairs on the back of his neck ruffling with pique.

"Mine are the ways of a sensualist," she told him as she sidled up to him, her tight body skimming against his, "and you don't strike me as the sort to give in to your feelings."

The remark was smug and teasing and he wished he could reach out and throttle her. Instead he found himself flushing at her boldness in front of his King and, apparently, his Queen. Or maybe it was because if she'd rubbed him just a little more firmly, he would have grabbed her and ended up giving her a lesson in sex even a centuries-old Vampire could use. That was how out of control he felt every time she came too close.

Hell, just setting eyes on her . . .

"A guide is an excellent idea, Jasmine. I will take you as a volunteer?"

Jasmine's body went stiff along the length of his, all her teasing washed away under what she saw as a threat to herself. That struck Adam curiously. Why would someone so bold and confident as she perceive a displaced Demon like him as a threat?

"I have more important things to do," she said, her voice snapping cold like the sudden rush of winter. "His brother would be—"

"Jacob has to care for Bella and his daughter. Not to mention his duties as Enforcer. What is it you have to do?" Noah asked archly.

"What I always do. Maintain my connections with our circuit of guardians who are out there protecting Nightwalkers and humans alike from rogue Vampires, Demons, and others. I had actually planned on tracking Ruth. She needs to be dealt with now, before she grows any stronger. It may already be too late."

"Ruth is not a creature you ought to be hunting on your own, Jasmine. No one faces Ruth one-on-one. It would be a death sentence. Between the magic she now uses so adroitly and the natural power of her Demon abilities, no one creature could confront her and expect to survive. Not even me or Damien. She has already killed Gideon." Noah saw Adam react with a choke of sound, and he amended it. "We were lucky enough to get him back, thanks be to Destiny."

"Clearly," Adam said in a strangled voice.

"But she is on her own now. Nicodemous has been destroyed. It is just the opportunity we have needed, just the weakness we have wanted to exploit. And we must do it quickly, before she initiates someone else into Nico's place."

"This is also true," Noah conceded. "So as I see it, you can best kill all your birds if you take Adam with you. As Enforcer, he can sense the Transformed, track them down. Ruth is always surrounded by them. It makes sense that he will lead you to her eventually. Also, he is an exceptional hunter and killer. He has proven that time and again. Being displaced out of time will not change his ability to fight. If you wish to hunt Ruth down, these are my conditions. Take Adam with you. While you search, use the time to introduce Adam to the world as it is now."

"Oh brother," she huffed with a sharp rolling of her eyes. She moved away from Adam, marching up to face off with the King, her body warmth instantly missed by a perturbed Water Demon. "I am not taking him! I do not work with a partner. You're out of your mind if you think I'm going to babysit this anachronism for you!"

"I do not need a governess!" Adam boomed, his voice like a thunderstorm in the echoing Great Hall. "And I certainly do not need this saucy chit of a Vampire to show me around!"

"Quiet! Both of you!" Noah roared back, making both of them startle. Neither was used to Noah using that tone of voice. Noah had always been able to control his temper, always speaking moderately. Clearly the Demon King was losing patience with the tumult of his life in that moment. "Jasmine, either you work with Adam or I will assign a Mind Demon to your ass and have you teleported to Damien's stronghold, where you will stay, like it or not! And Adam," he said, turning to the bigger man, "you realize you need a guide, do you not? And I remember enough about you to know you will not be happy sitting still here in this castle learning about automobiles and computers. Ruth can and will kill you, given half a chance. She is much stronger than you know. I thought a challenge like that would be right up your alley."

"Noah, it is too dangerous," Jacob protested. "Even the two of them together would not have a chance."

"I fear that, too," Noah agreed. "That is why I only want them to find her. Then they can come and retrieve us and a sufficient fighting force. As we all know, just the act of finding her is dangerous enough. But she must be found. This cannot continue any longer. I will send other teams as well, spreading them out as fast and wide as I can."

"Then let us go first," Jasmine said quickly. "We'll start at the caverns where she attacked Bella and Jacob and track her down from there. And give us a head start so others aren't tromping over our path and confusing her trail. I want her, Noah. And I am done playing games."

"You are just to find her, Jasmine," Noah warned her as she turned to stride off with the long-legged grace of a gazelle. The perfection of her posture and the pent-up fury inside her was stunning to behold. Adam would have loved to continue watching her, but he realized he had to move or risk being left behind. "Adam, try to keep a rein on her," Noah said wearily. "And remember she will trick you the first chance she gets if it suits her purpose."

"I will remember that," Adam said grimly. It just went to show that not much about Vampires had changed after all.

* * *

"Find me?" Ruth laughed, the amusement only for herself as it filled her room. "Oh, please *do* find me. I would love that. Love it!" Ruth dashed her hand into the bowl of scrying water she had been using, dissolving the images of Noah, Jacob, and the new male named Adam who had murdered her lover.

For the time being, anyway.

Ruth turned to her bed, a delicate float of silk following behind her as she moved in a flowing soft dress with a pretty rose coloring. She sat down beside her lover's corpse, reaching to smooth back his hair as she slowly wrapped her free hand around the handle of the bejeweled dagger thrust through the back of his mouth. His body was rigid in death, so she had to struggle as she yanked hard to remove it. Luckily for her, unluckily for Nicodemous, the blade was kept very, very sharp. It only took a few tries before it ripped free of the skull and jaws of its victim.

Ruth waited for several beats. In the past when Nico had been wounded in a critical way, it had taken only the removal of the offending object before he had started to heal. Then he would return to life as usual.

But this time was different and she knew it. This time he'd been run through the back of his brain, the crucial connection that he couldn't repair on his own.

But still she waited. She ignored the gruesomeness of his death mask, the coldness of his skin. He'd felt like cold death before when he'd been in need of a hunt. They'd even made love while all his extremities had felt like pure ice. It had been a chilling and erotic experience.

This was not. She had to find some way, some kind

of miracle to bring him back, or he would stay dead forever. Now that she knew what Noah and his cohorts were up to, she could focus on finding that miracle for him.

Ruth hurried to the table filled with compendium after compendium of spells, some hundreds of years old, others she had handwritten herself. That was the beauty of magic, she had learned. If you couldn't find the spell you wanted, you could make it up using components of other spells. It might not always work the way you wanted it to, but it was always fun to discover what a new spell would do. And sometimes it worked perfectly.

She opened to a death animation spell, but shook her head. Not just yet. It would do only if nothing else worked, but the spell had a time period of only forty-eight hours; then the corpse would burn up into dust never to be used again . . . except perhaps as a component for other more complex spells.

"Either way you will help me, darling," she sang out as she rifled through page after ancient page. "But I much prefer you alive and at full strength. And since they think you are dead, that will give us all the advantage."

She slowed as a seeping anger threatened to creep through her. She was really quite blinded by the rages that touched her, so she tried to fight it off. Yes, she thought, they had taken everything from her. The high-and-mighty Noah and his fretting little Demons. And all the while they had each taken on an extra burden, some creature to catch at their hearts and make them a thousand times more vulnerable. She knew that this was where she had to strike if she was going to rid herself of her enemies once and for all.

She and Nico had been trying to get to Isabella and her brat this evening, knowing that to rip them away from Jacob would utterly destroy him. Well, that and the added benefit of having Nico feast on their precious precocious child of Time. True, she was far too young yet, but there was a danger in waiting. What if she developed the ability to jump into the past? Noah could pick his time to attack Ruth, a time she least expected it, and destroy her.

That simply would not do. Ruth wouldn't allow it.

And she had come so close. Adam had spoiled her plans. Adam. A perfect example of the power Leah would wield in the future. She remembered the great disappearance of the former Enforcer, how they had turned the world upside down in search of him. Only to have him turn up here, hundreds of years in the future, and murder Ruth's greatest power resource . . . and her mate. She and Nico had completed the Exchange together, bonding to each other. He had fed on her and gained her ability to teleport. She had drunk of his blood and gained the ability to fly. It had taken her some time to realize that, then to master the ability. It was a delight to be able to travel long distances without being limited to jumps of teleportation that required great concentration and heavily drained her energy.

But power wasn't all they had shared. True, that had been her motive in the beginning, but more than just power had come with the Exchange. It was something she'd never known before. Something quite connective. Nothing like the Imprinting, to be sure. A Vampire could never feel something as powerful as an Imprinting.

And a good thing, too. The Imprinting made a

Demon weak. All of them, Noah, Elijah, and Jacob, all of them were weak. Ruth knew the best place to strike the Demons was through their weaker mates. Or even better, their would-be mates. All of those Demons who had yet to meet their simpering little Druids. All those vulnerable humans with no power yet . . . until that fateful touch. One little touch and power would be born.

So many things to do, she thought with a sigh.

"And it would be better if you were here to do them, dearest," she murmured in her dead lover's ear. "It is already begun. Isabella lies blackly poisoned and in a coma, struggling to survive. They cannot watch over her every moment. And while I am waiting to take care of her, your little friends can begin elsewhere."

She moved off the bed, her fingers drifting across one of her older spell compendiums.

"Let us see . . . perhaps something complex for Noah's new Queen. We will strike at the serpent's head. If we destroy Kestra, Noah will die of a broken heart within a year. You see how Imprinting weakens them? He is the center of what holds the Demons together. I would never battle him head-on; after all, he is the most powerful Fire Demon ever to live. Or so they say. Ideally I would have liked for you to feed from him, obtaining an aspect of him. Can you imagine what you could do with the power of Fire? Or manipulating energy? Even a single aspect of a Demon like Noah could make you unbelievably powerful, dearest."

She sighed as she thumbed slowly through her spells. She had wanted to attack the Demons through their Druid mates for some time, but Nico had forced her to focus on the children of Time and Space. They had determined it was impossible to get to the child of Space, what with the entire Lycanthrope populace, his Mind Demon mother, and the Ancient Gideon, his father, near him at all times. Besides, the brat was powerless at present, having shown no signs of ability as yet. But Leah . . .

"Damn the little bitch. I must remember to destroy her as soon as possible. She has already used her power to defeat us. I will not let her reach an age where she can do it again."

Ruth turned the page, and the colorful imagery of the spell caught her attention even before the hieroglyphs were interpreted in her mind. She was no scholar, the grasp of various languages not her best suit, but she knew enough to muddle through and had attachés who were flawless interpreters. But the beauty of hieroglyphs was that they told a vivid story that even a child could get the gist of.

"Mmm, now, is this not precious?" she whispered eagerly. "If this does what I think it does, it might be very appropriate for our needs. And this reminds me, I ought to look in the Egyptian tomes for a resurrection spell, dearest. They did so have a way with the dead."

She smiled, unable to help herself, and hurried to her door, rushing out of her loft workroom and leaning over the rail. Below her, lazing over the furniture, was her own little nest of corrupted Vampires. There were ten of them visually present. Beneath the loft in another room would be the Demons she had lured her way, who were fast becoming the most powerful collection of necromancers she had ever gathered. She had made errors in the past, using human spellcasters and hunters, but they had proved weak and useless. It wasn't until she had connected with Damien's enemy, Nicodemous, that she had come to understand the most powerful necromancer would be a Nightwalker necromancer. Now she was the most powerful living Nightwalker necromancer on earth. She had had high hopes that Nicodemous would be her second, but he didn't have a head for spellcasting as she did. He preferred to steal his power through blood and learn how to use that instead. Just the same, when they finally defeated Noah and his center circle of Demons, they would be unstoppable.

"Oh, children," she cooed down to the Vampires below. "Mother has a game for you to play!"

Beneath her they began to stir. They were easily bored and could be contentious, but really all they required was constant entertainment and sources of continuing power. Some of them had taken to spellcasting; others, like Nico, preferred to hunt for blood and power. Nico's endgame had always been to dethrone Damien. He really was quite obsessed. And that was fine with Ruth. He could rule the Vampires and she the Demons. Together they would be quite a force to contend with, and they could easily bring the other Nightwalkers to heel.

"What is it?" Isis asked eagerly, her fangs protruding in long, curving readiness. "I want to play!"

"Yes. What game have you for us tonight?"

"And where is Nico?" Benjamin queried. The Vampires were always best handled by Nicodemous, respecting his power more often than they would hers. But then again, they had yet to push her into proving just how deadly she could be.

"He is resting. He will be about later. But for now, there is to be a hunt."

She turned to grab hold of a sheet of silk that had

been thrown over the loft railing for color, and then she shook it out over the rail and the expanse of the room below. As it billowed and curved, an image formed in its center. The image of a woman.

"This, my darlings, is a Druid. They come in all flavors, all kinds of powers. She will make a tasty treat for you, and will give you new and delightful abilities. The only thing you need to do is get past this Demon." The image changed to reveal the dark-haired male Demon in question.

"And what is his power?"

"Do not worry," she assured them. "I am starting you off easy. Kane is a Mind Demon, but he is young and weak. The most he can do is teleport away from you. But keep him separated at all times from his mate and he will not be able to take her with him. At his age, he must be in physical contact to do so."

"And what is her power that we should waste our time on her?" Darren yawned from his position on one of the couches. He was lanky and muscular, half naked as well. He was beautiful and he knew it. If he had his way, he would replace Nico in Ruth's affections and position of power.

"She has the ability to seek out other Druids. Can you not see? We could find them all before their Demon mates do." She laughed loudly into the room below. "I do not know why I did not think of it sooner! If we destroy her and take her ability for ourselves, well, the Demons will have to bow to our will or there will be no more Druids."

"Clever," Darren said.

A perfect new thread in her tapestry of vengeance and power, Ruth thought. Every Demon deserved to suffer for the things she had lost. And it would only begin with Corrine.

"I will also require some complex components for a spell I plan to work." She shook the sheet again and the image changed to show a pretty little mourning dove changing shape to become a beautiful young woman with soft, feathery brown hair and deeply wise eyes.

"Bring me this Siren. Not any Siren will do. I must have this one. She is the eldest of her kind and considered one of the leaders of her people. She should be easy enough to trap. The Mistrals are xenophobic and live cut off from other people, even their own. Choose the strongest and eldest telepaths among you. You will be best able to overcome the enchantment of her song. Be careful and do not underestimate her."

"We won't," Darren assured her. "So long as we get a taste of her when you are done."

"Of course." Ruth chuckled. "I would never deprive you of such a tasty and powerful tidbit."

Adam had never felt so exhausted in his life. The toll of all that had happened that day was weighing on him hard. Yet sleep was the furthest thing from his mind. How could he possibly sleep, knowing all that he knew and facing such an uncertain future? So he was glad when Jasmine wanted to waste no time tracking Ruth down.

"But first," she said with an amused smile twitching at her lips, "first we need to bring you into this century." She gave him one of those thorough perusals that so unnerved him, the feel of her eyes on his body like a physical stroke he couldn't avoid. He resisted the urge to growl at her in threat . . . or for any other reason. What was it about this woman, he wondered heatedly, that threw him into a tailspin?

"What is that supposed to mean?" he demanded.

"It means we are going to find you some clothes. Unfortunately you're bigger than everyone else around here, so we're going to have to go shopping."

"Shopping?" He frowned. "Have you no tailor here?"

"Not here. But at a decent men's store there is. Follow me."

He didn't seem to have a choice in the matter. He followed her outside of Noah's residence and then watched as she levitated into the air. Bursting into a superfine mist, he trailed after her. She seemed to know that his speed was limited, because she took her time. He knew she was as capable as any Vampire and that they could fly very fast when they were in open air. The only way he would be able to keep up with her at her top speed would be if he created a hurricane and rode those winds to tail her. But that, of course, would have an adverse effect on the innocent humans below them.

They reached London in a short amount of time. Adam would never have recognized it. Things had changed so much, he wondered how he was ever expected to get his bearings. He didn't want to be in this future, this strange era when his brother was so different and his family was altogether unrecognizable. He grieved for the loss of his mother. She had always been the strong, equalizing center of their family, a touchstone he and Jacob had always come back to. Now she was gone . . .

His thoughts had him feeling low and melancholy as they touched down just outside the city.

"How much farther?" he asked irritably.

"Just a cab ride away."

"A what?"

She lifted a hand and pointed to the great moving metal beast pulling over to the side of the road.

"I am not getting inside that thing," he declared when she opened the door and entered.

"Yes, you are. Think of it as a very efficient carriage. Trust me. There's a lot to love about this century."

Feeling like an ass standing there, he gave in and wedged his big body into the rather small vehicle. It was a poor substitute for a fine horse, in his opinion, but he had to admit these contraptions moved very swiftly and with very little jostling. Before long they had pulled up to the curb again, only now they were in the heart of the city. Buildings with great glass fronts lined the walkway, names painted on the glass declaring the place as having "fine men's clothing." He thought that was actually very convenient. No guesswork involved. Everything from the clothiers to the cafés was very clearly marked.

Jasmine took him by the hand and led him forward into the store. The first thing he noticed was the fake men with no heads that displayed the clothing to all who entered. The thing that truly fascinated him was the incredibly fine stitching in the clothing. The fabrics were fascinating in their variety, but it was good to see that some things had not changed. Silks were still considered the finest thing to wear, and combined with the extraordinary fit of the shirt he tried on, he rather liked the clothing of this century. The undergarments were strange but comfortable, the "boxers" also made of silk. Jasmine took obvious pleasure in dressing him, and about halfway through the process he got a sense of intimacy from the experience. She had very exacting tastes, but she kept remarking on the temperature of the clothing, and rather inaccurately at that.

"That's hot," she said, admiring the sophisticated combination of shirt and slacks.

"Why do you keep saying that? The clothes are cool and comfortable. Certainly not hot."

She chuckled at him. "When I say something is hot, I mean it looks sexy on you. It's a term we use a lot these days." Jasmine glanced up when the lighting in the store flickered for what seemed like the tenth time since they'd gotten there. "Come on, let's wrap this up. We have a bitch to hunt down, and these lights will start to burn out if you stay near them much longer."

"Why did you purchase so many clothes?" he asked as they walked out of the store with bags full of clothing, including what he had originally worn into the store, since he had refused to give up what he was most used to. It was almost as if it were the last vestige of the things he had known and loved and he was loath to let them go.

"Because these days people change clothes every day. You will need the clothing since you have absolutely nothing. Now, let's ditch this stuff at Noah's and head out after Ruth. I want her so bad I can taste it."

"We are only supposed to find her. We are not to engage."

"Yeah. Sure."

Adam didn't have to be from the future to know she didn't mean that. But he actually didn't have a problem with her attitude. He could handle a corrupted Demon. It's what he did every day of his life. He didn't understand what Noah was so afraid of when it came to this female Demon. Between him and Jasmine they should be able to take her easily. He was just as eager for a fight as the Vampire was, so he saw no reason to rein Jasmine in.

They made it back to Noah's castle in no time at all, and neither of them let on to the Demon King their secret thoughts on how they were going to deal with Ruth on their own. Adam didn't have to be a genius to know Noah would disapprove of them going off on a private quest for vengeance.

At Noah's direction, they took Adam's new things to one of the guest rooms on the third floor. When Jasmine made herself busy hanging clothing, all he could do was sit on the bed and sigh wearily. She looked at him over a shoulder and tilted her head, the cloud of her hair looking beautiful across her shoulders and against her fair cheek.

"Feeling overwhelmed?" she asked him.

He simply nodded.

"It will pass," she assured him. "Try to have fun with it. Take pleasure in all the new and wonderful things you see around you. Don't dwell on what you can't change."

"Maybe that is easy for a coldhearted Vampire to do, but for those of us with deep-seated feelings, it is not so easy to dismiss certain things," he said irritably.

She turned sharply to face him, her warm eyes suddenly alive with temper. "I have feelings, too, you know. Don't make assumptions about me. Your mindset is based on a war that happened four centuries ago. If you even want to call it war. If the Vampires had wanted you all dead, you would have been dead. I think what's happened recently proves that."

"You mean Vampires like Nicodemous? If you have not noticed, *he* is dead. I killed him."

"Maybe. Until we burn the body, I wouldn't be so sure about that."

"Then we should go from here. We have wasted enough time already." Adam grabbed the leather jacket she had chosen for him, shrugging into the garment easily. He had to admit, he liked the clothing of this modern world. It was comfortable and well fitting. Granted, the fabrics and designs were a bit plainer than the cloth of gold, velvet, and bejeweled touches of his time, but he could live with that. Right then he had larger worries. Clearly this tainted Demon female was gunning for his baby brother and his family. That was unacceptable. What he didn't understand was why Jacob hadn't already dealt with her. He was supposed to be the Enforcer. She was the reason his job existed, a Demon gone awry.

To be fair, though, Adam had not sensed this rogue once since he had arrived. Perhaps she was too corrupted, too far from being a real Demon any longer to be sensed in the traditional manner. But that didn't mean she couldn't be tracked at all.

"Let us catch this wretch that plagues my brother," he said to the Vampire as he reached to strap on his weapons belt as well. "The sooner I see it done, the more content I will be. Then perhaps I can focus on other things."

"Such as?" She all but smirked at him. "You have to know you aren't going to be able to go back in time. The young girl who brought you here no longer exists. In this world, she is barely five years old and hardly has a clue as to her power."

"I am well aware of this," Adam groused, irritated

that she so easily saw into his thoughts and desires. He couldn't help thinking . . . maybe if he could get back to his own time, he could prevent the deaths awaiting his parents.

"Clearly you aren't. If you were aware of it as you should be, you wouldn't be thinking of ways you could change what we know history to be. I have no desire to disappear from the life I know and suddenly find myself dead or otherwise. All it takes is one thing changed and the future is destroyed. The good as well as the bad."

"Then someone should have said as much to my niece before she kidnapped me from my life and brought me here!" he snapped at her. "I had a good life! I had loving parents and a brother who was not so bitter!"

She laughed at that, a hard barking sound. "Jacob bitter? Please. He's so sugar sweet in love it's sickening. He adores his family and has a very happy life. A life he won't have if you go back and change things on him. Let's suppose," Jasmine said as she rounded the bed to face off with him, "that you do make it back. That alone would be a significant enough event to change everything. Your brother would no longer be Enforcer in your stead. That means he would not have been doing his job the night he met his mate. Therefore Kane and Jacob and Noah and every other person you supposedly care about would never know that they could find mates outside their species or the happiness they now experience." She shrugged. "Granted, I wouldn't mind it if a certain Lycanthrope biatch never crossed the path of my Prince, but you have to take the bad with the good, I suppose."

"Damien has joined himself to a Lycanthrope?"

Adam leaned in toward her. "You really do not seem pleased by this at all."

"Yeah, well . . ." She frowned darkly. "Their union is the reason why Vampires learned they could survive taking the blood of other Nightwalkers. That it brings them new power to do so. Previously they thought breaking the taboo would mean a horrible consequence—most likely death."

"And you feel he should not have taken her to mate, that he should have made the sacrifice so that Vampires would never learn of the power they could achieve."

"Exactly." She shrugged. "But I'm not going to play shoulda woulda coulda with you. Things are what they are, there's nothing to be done about it."

"Who can say?" Adam gave her a sly little smile as he leaned in close to her. "Perhaps you would like the past to change more than you are willing to admit."

Jasmine frowned. The last thing she needed was temptation from a Demon who barely had a clue about the modern world and all the many things a ripple in time could affect. She would readily admit to doing everything in her power to voice her displeasure in Damien's choice of a bride—everything short of killing her, that is—but she wasn't so selfish that she couldn't see the bigger picture. She liked her life just the way it was, and she wasn't going to risk changing it when she knew things could just as easily be so much worse.

But she had to give him credit for trying . . . and for knowing just the right way to tempt a girl. It made for a very worthy opponent, and she found it beyond hot. Then again, he had been made to turn heads. Wearing the delicious and decadent designs of the modern world, he was enough to make even an elitist like her consider playing outside her species. But she wasn't about to let him know any of that. It was safer to simply team up with him just long enough to kick Ruth's ass and then they could each go along their merry way.

Of course, that didn't mean she wasn't going to have a little fun at his expense in the meantime.

"I think I like things just the way they are," she said with a dip of one shoulder and a flirtatious swing of her body. "You and I going out to play together. We'll track the big bad bitch and hand her her ass for dinner. Then I can go back to hunting rogue Vampires, and you . . . you can do whatever you put your little mind to."

"Rogue Vampires," he echoed, his eyes dropping down over her body in increments . . . breasts, waist, hips, thighs, and eventually her calves.

It was well into winter, and as a result she was clothed almost conservatively, if you could call tight low-rise jeans and a navel-baring sweater conservative. But she wished for her favorite shorts just then. Anything to torment the poor bastard. Still, she wouldn't be worth much if she were only as good as the clothes she wore.

"Funny how that sounds. In my world you were all rogues."

"Well, it's a good thing we're in my world now, isn't it? Otherwise you'd want to cause me bodily harm, and I like my body just the way it is. Don't you?" She ran a hand up her hip to her waist, watching his eyes follow the movement as if he were a compass and she were the North Pole.

She watched his generous mouth turn down into a

full frown and his eyes shoot up to narrow on hers. "I see women have not changed much at all," he noted coldly. "You still try to play with men for your own amusement and ends."

Jasmine snorted out a laugh. "That's rich, coming from a stereotypical Alpha male. If you can't beat something up or screw around with it, it barely gets your interest."

"Why are we having this conversation?" he demanded crossly, turning away from her and marching for the door.

"Because it's fun?" she posited archly.

"For whom?" he muttered as he took to the hallway in huge, ground-eating strides, forcing Jasmine to double-time her pace if she wanted to continue to snap at his heels like an annoying, yappy little dog.

"You don't agree that men are essentially base creatures driven by violence and sex?" she asked him.

"Not to the exclusion of all else, no. I most certainly do not agree with that."

"All right then. Let's test this theory out a little. Right now we are on our way to do violence, and from what I can see you look like you're raring to go."

"So are you," he pointed out as they hit the stairs. "I have never met such a bloodthirsty woman. You are just as eager to have a piece of this Ruth."

"True, but that's because she tried to kill my Prince and held me captive while she prattled on endlessly about what a demented psychopath she is. Not a fun night, I assure you."

"Held you captive?" Adam enjoyed the idea. "Poor you. How did she manage that? You do not strike me as an easy victim."

"Screw you!" Jasmine bit out. "Ruth's a powerful

Mind Demon, more powerful mentally than I was at the time. She seized control of my mind, held me paralyzed in my own bedroom, spent the time until dawn raping my brain of information that . . ." Jasmine gritted her teeth. "Once the sun rose and she knew I couldn't give chase, she left me in order to wreak havoc, using that information."

"How unfortunate for you." He didn't sound at all sympathetic. Clearly, he didn't appreciate the magnitude of what had happened next. "I, however, have been doing some thinking. Seeing that girl, my niece, the way she looked at Jacob like she had never seen him before . . . something tells me Nicodemous and Ruth killed him in that cavern. How the girl survived I cannot say, but Ruth was out to murder my family and would have succeeded if not for the child."

"Leah. Your niece has a name. It's Leah."

That brought him up short in the middle of the stairs and he turned to look at her.

"Leah," he echoed. "He named her after our grandmother on our father's side."

"Someone you admired?" she asked.

"Greatly so. She was a fine lady. A warrior. An artisan. Jacob has high aspirations for his daughter if he named her thus."

"Well, she is a child of prophecy, after all. And she has accomplished much even for one so young. The girl who brought you here—she waited all those years until she was a teen before acting. It means she gave it a lot of thought. It also means she was willing to throw away life as she knew it in order to change what had to have been a life-altering event. Not just for her, but for everyone here. Jacob means a lot to a great many people. As does Bella. I don't see any of them coping easily with their deaths if it went down that way."

Adam thought for a long moment, the expression on his face troubled.

"You are right," he said at last. "I must reconcile myself to things as they are. I have told myself this already, but I continue to resist."

"That is really quite normal," she assured him. "Even though going to ground is a Vampire's way of moving through time, and our whole purpose in doing so is to wake in a different era, it is perhaps instinct to resist and rebel against all the changes we find upon awaking at first. Even though there is nothing to be done about it. And especially when we realize those we hold attachments to did not survive."

He made a scoffing sound. "Vampires have attachments?"

Jasmine could have gotten angry at the thoughtless prejudice in his remark, but she couldn't fault him for it. The truth was, Vampires had few attachments of any significant or emotional depth.

"There are those we grow close to over time. Familiar with. Companions who mean more to us than others. So yes, I would call that attachments. Maybe it is not the grand friendship and love you other races sputter on about, but it is our way and it is how we form affections. Just because it is different doesn't make it any less valid."

She was not speaking with offense or even with any great passion, but instead with intelligent logic—and yet her words had the power to touch Adam. For the first time as he looked at her he saw her to be an incredibly thoughtful and intellectual person, rather than just a flat stereotype of a race he had learned to hate or a creature of remarkable beauty and sensuality. The understanding made her even more irresistible to him; it somehow made her tightly clothed curves and pretty pale skin all the more magnetic.

"And who means more to you than others?" he found himself asking. There was a little bite of insecurity in the back of his brain and he bristled against it. What did it matter to him who was special in her life? She had even just told him that the Vampire definition of special was nothing compared to what a Demon might consider it to be. How much depth could she really feel?

How much depth could there ever be?

Somehow Adam was not comforted by his thoughts.

"Damien," she said without hesitation. "We have walked this world together for quite some time. He is my closest friend." She frowned a little. "Or he was. Until he bonded with a little Lycanthrope twit. He's in *love*." The word "love" couldn't have been any more snide.

"I thought Vampires did not feel love. Or any great passion."

"Apparently there is some great cosmic exception. We can fall in love . . . with other Nightwalkers. Non-Vampires. Then there's this whole ceremony . . ." She waved it all off with the flip of an agitated hand. "Never mind. It is all a waste of time and energy, if you ask me."

"Is it?" he asked her. "I had somehow thought a creature as passionate at heart as you seem to be would crave the deeper passions of love. Or even of infatuation."

"I know Vampires who have been infatuated before.

Some of us are at least capable of that. I watch how ridiculously they chase the object of their infatuation. But it always burns out, and always so quickly."

"Are you telling me," Adam asked her softly as he stepped up and closed the distance between them, "that you have never even been infatuated? Never been roused enough by another to find yourself smitten?"

She had come close once.

Only once.

"Never," she lied to him, lifting her chin and meeting his eyes directly. "Thankfully. Nothing turns a person into an idiot faster than some mindless fascination with another. No one should ever put so much energy into someone else. Others cannot be trusted to do anything but disappoint you."

"As Damien has disappointed you?"

She took a breath to answer him quickly, but then held it as she thought about her answer more carefully. He noticed she did that when she was emotionally engaged. She breathed. Even though she didn't need to. He suspected she felt far more than she owned up to. Despite all her callous exterior, Jasmine the Vampire was sensitive at heart. All of these barbs, he saw, were in defense of that heart.

"I am not half as disappointed by him as I was by you," she said quietly. Then she seemed just as surprised she had said it as he was, and looked around quickly to see if anyone had heard her.

She pushed past Adam and hurried into the Great Hall, grateful it was empty, only the ever-present fire bearing witness to her ridiculous confession.

Stupid, stupid thing to say! she thought heatedly.

"What does that mean?" he asked a little numbly,

more to himself than her because she wasn't likely to have heard him. But he quickly hurried after her, grabbed her by the arm, and forced her to turn and face him. He got a savage little hiss in his face and a flash of fangs for his trouble. He let go of her, holding up his hand in a conciliatory gesture. He had no right to manhandle her, and she didn't like it.

At least not when it came to conversation.

"What does that mean?" he asked her more strongly. "What have I done to disappoint you?"

"Never mind. It wasn't what I meant to say. And regardless, we have other things to do at the moment."

But Adam had never been known for his ability to let things go.

"I will not accept this. You should tell me how I have let you down. I do not see how. I hardly know you!"

"You see, this is why I said to forget about it! I should have known you would say something like that! Hardly know me? You think because I'm a Vampire I let just anyone grope at me and—and stick their tongue in my mouth? Hardly know me? I'd say we're pretty damn intimate acquaintances, Adam! But clearly you don't see me as anything more than some Vampire piece of trash you can poke your stick at a few times, then crumple up and throw away. You sit there with your holier-than-thou bullshit attitude about what lowlifes my kind are, but I'm not the one using a random naked girl for my jollies and then turning my back with no thought to the consequences!"

"Consequences? Like what? Are you trying to say I hurt your shallow little Vampire feelings?" he railed back at her, not liking the discomfort her words made him feel.

"I'm saying, you selfish little prick, that you did something to me! I don't know what it was, but you did something! Then you left me struggling for four hundred years trying to figure out why two brief encounters with an enemy sucked the color out of my world! I may have succumbed to melancholy all on my own the first time, but the second time, when only six months had gone by and all I could do was search the empty earth for the things you made me feel . . ."

Jasmine turned her back on him, her eyes burning with shocking tears. She needed to shut up! Why was she telling him all of this? It wasn't even true! And even if it was true . . .

It was true. It had been so very true. She had gone to ground again after a mere six months, hoping that sleep buried under the earth would make her cravings for ridiculous nothings go away.

"But we could never—"

"I know that! And so did you, but it didn't stop you from touching me, *Enforcer*!"

She growled and swung away from him, confused by her own behavior and the tumult of strange feelings inside herself. This didn't make any sense! Things were coming out of her mouth that she didn't understand. She was feeling things she didn't understand.

Adam did back off after that. She was right. It had never occurred to him how his actions might affect her. He had behaved rather selfishly in all of their encounters, writing off any impact on her because she was a Vampire, an unfeeling, coldhearted thing that didn't deserve his respectful consideration. He'd only considered the ramifications of his actions as far as it concerned himself and his laws and the way others of his kind would look on him because of them.

It was beneath him. She had never once acted the enemy toward him, never once given him cause to be so dismissive. He had neglected to give her even the smallest common courtesy, not to mention being considerate of her feelings, however shallow or deep they might run. And he couldn't even excuse himself by saying that after all he had been through, he couldn't be expected to be on his best behavior. That excuse would do nothing to explain the fact he had been behaving rather selfishly since the moment he had laid eyes on her, taking any manner of liberties with her as it struck his fancy. Even an enemy deserved a certain level of respect. Human men of his time had often behaved like savages, taking from noncombatant women dignities that should never be a part of the battlefield. It had disgusted him.

He should be equally disgusted with himself.

"Wait."

He didn't touch her, didn't force her to his will. He wanted to do so, and on some level he understood that she liked his dominance and naturally aggressive nature, but physicality was one thing and personality something else . . . and respect something else entirely. He had shown her none of the latter and wished to correct that.

"Please, wait," he edited himself.

Perhaps the "please" took her by surprise. She certainly looked surprised when she turned around to look at him. Her reaction only served to make him feel even lower.

"I feel I must . . . apologize." It came hard to say it. He wasn't used to second-guessing his actions. Even less used to admitting his faults to others. "It was never my intention to cause you pain. Whether you feel strongly or very little, that does not excuse thoughtless behavior."

Jasmine hardly understood her own feelings, never mind how they pertained to him. She barely comprehended her own anger with him. But that didn't mean she couldn't appreciate what it took for him to take a hard look at himself and then admit any flaws he found to her. She might be something of a cold-hearted, jaded bitch, but she could still appreciate a generous gesture when she saw one. Especially when she wasn't expecting it. Especially when she usually behaved in ways that made her less than deserving of it.

She sighed.

"I don't deserve much of an apology," she admitted in return. "I have taunted you quite a bit." She shrugged, brushing the entire matter off with the turn of her body. "Let's focus on Ruth. I think we both will feel very much better when we get her in our sights."

And so the matter was dropped . . . for the moment. They were both quite happy and eager to turn their focus toward an enemy that well deserved their enmity. Both of their lives had been bent and twisted in some way because of the Demon traitor. It was well past time she paid for her crimes.

Chapter 8

Windsong was content to spend her long lifetime going no farther than her own little village. She was even happier confining herself to the edges of her property, the borders of her herb garden, the walls of her simple but comfortable cabin home. She had, unlike the majority of her people, done her share of traveling in her life. She had spent time, however short, in almost every other Nightwalker court, lending them wisdom and guidance where she could, or her significant healing abilities. She counted the current leaders of the other Nightwalkers as some of her closest friends. Damien. Siena. In these past years, Noah. She even looked forward to making friends with the Shadowdweller Chancellors. She had met Tristan and Malaya more than once as the Nightwalkers strived to maintain their current peace with regular meetings and communications.

The Mistrals, Windsong's people, did not have a central body of government. There had never really been a need for it. There were one or two village Elders who spoke for an individual village, and sometimes those Elders collaborated on matters of import to all the Mistrals. But that was a rare occurrence. A rare necessity. So when offers to exchange ambassadors between Nightwalker courts had begun, it only made sense that the most experienced and most centrally important village Elders take the foreign ambassadors into their homes.

This was how Windsong had ended up with not only her usual student, Lyric, under her care and roof, but a peculiar little Vampire named Izri. Of all the Nightwalkers, the Vampires were most resistant to the spell of Mistral voices and singing, provided they were old enough and mentally strong enough. Izri was about three centuries old, not very old by Vampire standards and certainly not very old compared to Windsong and the power of her voice. But Windsong had weeded the spell out of her voice, an act that required constant concentration and had slowed her speech down considerably over the past eighteen months, and Izri had focused her impressive mental strength, so they had managed to find a way of living together in an almost musical fashion.

Windsong and Lyric had been used to days full of constant song, and that was the reason Lyric was there. To learn songs. Healing verses and natural power blended together to heal any and all creatures. Some songs were stronger than others. Some were certainly out of Lyric's young reach. She was only twenty years old. Quite the child. She needed time and study to become a true Siren one day. A Mistral who was truly proficient in song and her area of study and expertise would, with time, attain virtuosity. If that Mistral was female, she earned the title of Siren. If male, he earned the title of Bard. There was no fixed age for these things. It happened when the village Elders tested the Mistrals and considered them proficient enough to earn those titles.

Lyric was a long way off from that. And at first Windsong had worried that her teaching would suffer with the presence of another. She had found herself and Lyric constantly curbing their song whenever Izri was present. But the quirky Vampire had noticed this and had begun singing Lyric's study songs herself.

Rather badly.

Lyric seemed to enjoy the fact that there was someone less skilled than she in the house. Though she had been shy and afraid of Izri at first, she now felt compelled to give the Vampire points on how to sing better, passing on what little she knew quite eagerly, and, in time, with a growing confidence that Windsong had never seen in her student before.

Izri's presence in the house had also forced Windsong to expand her dwelling. The two-room cabin had been adequate for a master and one pupil, but for all three of them? It was overdue for a bit of an overhaul and some modernization. However, their village did not have any carpenters so they had been forced to call on outsiders. And so two carpenters, a Bard named Baritone and his apprentice Dove, had come to live in their village. Other homes had opened their doors to them, inviting the carpenters in, something her xenophobic breed was not usually in a hurry to do. She was actually quite proud of her people for the ways they had pushed their own boundaries the past couple of years.

In some ways they had been forced to do so.

One of the more practical reasons Izri had come was to help the Mistrals learn how to defend themselves against Vampires, because it was a well-known fact that not all of her kind were as thoughtful as Izri was. Of all the Nightwalkers, the Mistrals were potentially the most vulnerable to the Vampire rogues. Mistrals relied solely on the spell of their voices and their shapechanging for self-defense, both of which the Vampires could easily circumvent if they were strong enough.

Windsong found it compelling that Izri had volunteered to be a guinea pig. She would allow the Mistrals to learn how to hurt her and her kind, trusting they would not kill her in the process.

As she watched the petite blonde goof off with Lyric in the nighttime meadow, it was like watching two young high school girls, rather than two women centuries apart in age and experience. Their heads were bent together, one fair and one dark, and they were trading whispers as they watched the carpenter Bard and his apprentice work on the cabin. Others in the village usually came to help, more than likely to hurry the process along so everyone could go back to where they belonged, but also out of gratitude. The village of *Brise Lumineuse* owed Windsong a great deal. She was the oldest and most powerful of her kind. She had always protected them. She had always led them wisely.

But tonight no others had come yet, so it was just the Bard and his apprentice.

Windsong suspected Izri had something of a crush on Baritone. She found the thought amusing. In the past, she wouldn't have taken such a thing seriously or given it any worry, but much had changed in just a few years. The Vampires had learned that the only way they could ever hope to know feelings like love was through the blood of other Nightwalkers. It was an attractive cookie to dangle before such sensualist children. Who wouldn't want to feel love for the first time? Why wouldn't Izri be curious about such things?

But Windsong suspected Baritone might not be similarly inclined.

"You had best speak to her."

Windsong looked up from her position in the grass. It was an unseasonably warm night so close to Samhain. She and the girls had decided to picnic in the meadow beside the cabin, to get fresh air while they still could before the winter set its claw into them and forced them inside. Luckily for Baritone and Dove, they were almost done with the exterior work on the cabin, and all that was left was the interior. When all was said and done there would be three bedrooms, a spacious great room, and two baths. It seemed like so much house, but since she had rarely been without a student these past centuries, it made sense. It would just be a little bit of an adjustment. And to be honest, it would be nice to have some privacy back, a place to go where she could close the door and be alone.

She hadn't realized she missed her privacy until it was on the verge of being restored to her.

"Good evening, Harrier," she finally greeted her childhood friend who had appeared at her back. There was only one other Mistral as long-lived as she was. Harrier. At one time their mothers had had high hopes that they would cultivate a great romance between them. Perhaps that was exactly the reason why it had never happened. The idea of making love with Harrier was as ridiculous to her as making love to her brother might be. They were the best of friends, but seriously lacked the chemistry needed for anything like a romance. "I disagree. Izri is a mature Vampire female, and she is very aware of the potential consequences of her infatuation. She has lived among us long enough to know it is very likely any advance she made would be heartily rebuffed."

"You are speaking as a woman of logic. You forget what it is like to be smitten. One does not always think so logically when one's heart is involved."

His observation made Windsong smile a little. "This coming from the most confirmed bachelor in all of history," she said.

"I was not always a bachelor," Harrier reminded her gently.

She didn't need the reminder. No more than he did. It had been centuries since he had been wed, since he had fathered his children—and since he had suffered the unimaginable horror and pain of their deaths. But she knew for him it might as well have been yesterday. He would not let himself forget, even after all this time. And how could he? He had blended it into every component of every song he knew. It was part of what gave his songs such incredible power. It was what made him an incomparable Bard.

Windsong studied him a moment, his tall, well-made physique, his closely cropped hair the color of a new penny, and the aristocratic lines of his features. He was incredibly handsome, what any woman would find alluring, perhaps even in spite of the torch he carried for a family long made into dust. His most startling physical characteristic was the vivid purple heather color of his eyes. But even that was outgunned the moment Harrier uttered a single word. His voice was deep, rich, and hypnotic when he spoke. When he sang, it was positively spellbinding.

"That is true. I suppose that makes *me* the most confirmed bachelor of our kind."

"A mystery to me," he assured her. "You never lacked for suitors in the first half of your millennium. And they are sparse now only because you intimidate them. That and you remain cubbied away here where no one can find you."

"Or they suspect you and I are lovers and do not wish to tread between us."

He chuckled. "I never understood that," he said as he lowered himself beside her. "We both have apprentices and we both lived, until your recent renovations, in close quarters with them. Just when did they suspect we were finding the opportunity for lovemaking?"

Windsong shrugged. "I doubt they are thinking it through that far."

"Perhaps. Which returns me to my earlier warnings. I do not think your Vampire guest is thinking things through very far at all."

"So what if she is or is not?" Windsong looked directly into his eyes. "Life is nothing if not a learning experience. And who are you and I to assume only the negative could come of this? Have you spoken to Baritone? Did he ask you to have me warn her off?"

"No. Nothing of the kind. I only meant . . ." He shrugged a shoulder. "We keep very much to ourselves. We do not like to entertain the idea of outsiders even walking through our village. What makes you think he would welcome one in his bed?"

"Two years ago, would you ever have imagined this village welcoming a Vampire as a member of our family? Granted, it has taken some time, but people have grown quite used to her. I would even dare to say they are fond of her."

"I think they were perhaps blinded by that hair of hers. Or maybe it was the clothes."

Windsong smiled. She looked over and gave serious thought to Izri's lemon yellow and chartreuse streaks of hair, half of which reached her chin on the left side and the other half of which reached the middle of her back.

"I hardly think they would be fazed by exterior appearances. That is not what our people fear, after all. We fear our vulnerability. We do not have the physical strength of other breeds, nor their uncanny speed and senses. We have our voices and our ability to shift into birds."

"And then there is the sun."

"Yes. The sun." They were not as sensitive to the sun as the other Nightwalkers were. They did not burn or become poisoned. They did not feel lethargy or die.

But they lost their only defensive ability.

They lost their voices.

They became completely mute in sunlight. No matter how young or old, how much they struggled, the touch of the sun robbed them of their voices. It made them, for want of a better term, completely human. They had no defenses, no strengths, and no preternatural senses. All of it disappeared. And if they lived regularly in sunlight, they would begin to age as a normal mortal might.

Windsong shuddered. Who would ever want to live in sunlight? Who would ever choose to be mortal? She had lived through so many incredible ages, seen so many extraordinary things. She had great respect for humans and their inventiveness, the ways they strove to better themselves and the things around them, but she also found them sad and tragic. They were destroying the very world that sustained them. The same world that sustained the Nightwalkers. Windsong was very well aware that one day the Nightwalkers might have to choose sides against the humans or risk their own ability to live. It was a frightening thought because Nightwalkers like the Vampires could not survive without their human food sources, and now the Demons were finding their mates in humans who had Druid blood. It could be a tricky little house of cards. But the human trend was moving toward more awareness of the world they lived in. Hopefully it would continue.

"When is the last time you saw the sun?" Harrier asked her.

She gave him a little smile. She didn't even have to think about it.

"It was only a short while ago. A few years back. I saw a sunrise. I confess it is a beautiful thing, for all it hurts my eyes to see it."

"There are many things that are both beautiful and deadly. It has been much longer for me. I have no desire to feel the touch of the sun or to see its questionable beauty. I find it difficult to see loveliness in something that renders me helpless." He looked up at the nearly full moon. "I am very content with this silvery bright splendor."

"Have you come to help the carpenters today?" Windsong asked.

"I find their songs fascinating," he confessed. "The construction songs make such incredibly secure joints. It brings out such beauty in the woods they use."

"I find them very similar to healing songs. In a

sense they are repairing injury they have caused by cutting through the wood."

"I had not looked at it like that. But it is no wonder that we Mistrals make homes last so very long and need so little repair to their frames, roofs, and foundations. Human structures are so shoddy in comparison."

"They do what they can." Windsong drew herself up from the grasses, standing over her friend as she shook out the folds of her skirt. "I am glad you are here. I wish to gather some wild herbs today and I do not like to leave Lyric and Izri alone these days."

"You are not taking them with you?" He frowned. "You should not go alone."

"I have worked them very hard this week with lessons. They should have some time to relax. Lyric tends to get overwhelmed if she does not get a break every few days. She remembers lyrics and pitches far better when she does not feel weighted down with work."

Windsong reached down to pick up her deep willow basket. She would be able to gather hours' worth of roots and herbs and not have to continually come back to the house to empty her basket and make room for more. This would very likely be her last chance to harvest before the snow fell and kept the ground covered for months. She hated trying to dig for roots in the snow.

"You did not address my concerns about *you*," Harrier pressed her as she began to walk away from him. She gave him a smile and raised her brow.

"Did I not? Well, we shall talk about it when I return."

"Wind—!"

Harrier huffed out a breath in frustration. Talking to her back would be no more effective than talking to her stubborn face.

Windsong was actually not very far from the cabin, as the crow flies. A half mile at most. But it was enough to isolate her from anyone else. She was kneeling, uncovering a rare and generously shaped truffle when she felt she was no longer alone. She felt the malevolence creeping up on her well before the stranger came within striking distance. One of the main characteristics that had always made her stand out from all other Mistrals, however, was that she was not easily frightened. She left her basket on the ground, tucking it behind some scrub to be retrieved later and, dusting the dirt from her hands, she moved carefully toward her cabin. She did not change into her alter ego of the mourning dove, recognizing that it was perhaps a far more vulnerable form than the one she was in at present.

The first Vampire appeared right in her path in a sudden, roiling cloud of smoke, the smell of sulfur indicative of a Mind Demon's ability to teleport. It told Windsong that this Vampire had drunk the blood of that type of Nightwalker and gained this aspect from it. Very likely the Mind Demon had died in the process. Rogue Vampires were not known for being merciful when it came to their victims.

"Hello, little dove. Leaving so quickly?" the Vampire asked, his dark eyes almost indiscernible from the night around him. Almost as if he were part shadow, lengths of his body could not be separated from the darkness they stood in. The heavy shadows of the trees interfered with the bright moon, blocking its light.

The second Vampire appeared at her back, almost close enough to touch her. Windsong moved quickly out of reach. She would not allow them the opportunity to drink from her, if that was what they wished to do. But she also needed to bide her time a little. She needed something all the Nightwalkers needed.

Information.

Most rogues acted individually, or perhaps in small groups of two or three, but lately there had been larger bands, and they had seemed very well organized. Her last meeting with the other Nightwalker leaders had addressed this issue. They had told everyone to warn their people to be careful. Jasmine had requested they forward any intelligence on to her so she could rout out the source and destroy the nest once and for all.

"How clever you are to catch me alone," she said to them.

And her speaking voice, the most powerful of her kind, instantly lulled the pair of them. They both relaxed, the shadowy Vampire becoming suddenly solid, his lean and handsome features going suddenly soft with a smile.

"We planned it that way," he said proudly. "But we're not going to hurt you right off."

"No? How kind you are," she said, meaning it. Sarcasm would spoil the spell she was weaving. She had to be sincere. And she did feel sincere. She found their misguided actions to be so unfortunate. So sad. So many people had died so unnecessarily. She wondered if perhaps it was like black magic, or like drugs, an addiction that, once started, became nearly impossible to break. Yes, selfishness and hunger for power might have compelled them in the beginning, but what if they became addicted to the high they got from victimizing others and could not keep themselves from chasing that feeling again and again, whether they wanted the power any longer or not?

She had put forth the idea at the last meeting and met with a lot of disapproving resistance, and this even though a natural-born Witch was sitting amongst them. A Witch who had first come to them many months back and told them that humans who used black magic were redeemable. That she was one who had been led astray because no other option had been put in front of her once she realized she had been born to create magic. She had not realized there were magics that could and could not harm her. That there was even a difference. And by the time she had realized it, she was well into an addiction that had been almost impossible for her to break. It had taken everything she had to rip free of it. It had taken frightening experimentations to learn what was good magic, and what was not.

What if it was the same for these Vampires?

Windsong was willing to risk her life to test her theory.

"We're going to take you away with us," the second Vampire explained.

"How lovely. I am so pleased you are inviting me on this trip," Windsong said. "Where will we be going?"

"Not far. The Demon has need of you. We don't know why."

The Demon?

Suddenly Windsong lost a bit of her calm. She took a breath, trying to regain it.

"You mean Ruth?" she asked.

"Yes, Ruth," a third voice growled from behind her. He grabbed hold of the Siren, yanking her back into his body. Windsong's knee-jerk response was to cry out a single, stunning note, her voice rising wildly into the clear, cool forest.

The Vampire's grip on her went lax almost instantly, allowing her to stumble free of his grasp. She lost all interest in prying information from them. Vampires were one thing, Ruth entirely another. Windsong was not so arrogant as to think she would fare better with the demented Demon than others who had come away brutalized and viciously damaged, if they came away at all. She knew she was strong and powerful, but she wasn't willing to test that strength against someone so corrupted. A wildcard that no one truly understood. And when one didn't completely grasp one's enemy, it was all but impossible to find their weaknesses and mount a proper defense.

Suddenly she was struggling to keep her fear under control. It was imperative that she do so. She could only control her attackers if she controlled herself. The Vampires were getting bolder. She could sense it on them, sense their mental strength. Had she been any other Mistral, they might have already had her captive.

She began to sing, no words, only clear, sharp notes, laying the groundwork to hold their minds and the minds of any others within hearing range. Her voice was powerful and resonant, cutting through the forest for unexpected distances. She doubted they would suspect she was capable of reaching so far. In moments her voice would burst into the cabin clearing where Harrier and the others were.

That was when a sudden, sharp sensation punched into the side of her neck. Startled, Windsong fell silent, her hand jerking up to the dart protruding from her throat. She looked numbly into the eyes of a Demon whose deeply tanned skin set her apart from the Vampires she accompanied. As the powerful sedative flooded quickly into Windsong's blood, she swayed a little. The pretty black-and-gray-haired Demon tugged at a string near her ear, popping free the earplug in it, one of a pair in bright, obscene orange.

"They thought they were strong enough to resist you," she said as she came closer. "I thought it was better to be safe than sorry." She methodically reloaded the dart gun and took aim at Windsong.

"Wait . . . please . . ." Windsong rasped weakly, holding up a hand as she felt her vocal cords go numb along with the entire inside of her throat. The world swayed and weakness bled through her body.

"It's not up to me," the Demon said with a shrug. "What Ruth wants, Ruth gets. But trust me, my way of going about it is very much the better way."

She shot Windsong again, this time hitting her in a less vital area. The first drug was a paralytic, the second a sedative. Windsong collapsed onto the ground, unable to do anything to protect herself or escape.

The Demon popped out the second earplug and rolled her eyes at the Vampires, who were just breaking free of the Siren's spell.

"What a bunch of idiots," she said.

But it was the other Vampires, the ones who were coming toward them, threading through the trees to look down on the unconscious Mistral, who had been the real danger.

Yes. Her way was very much the safer way.

Adam had tracked more than his share of Demons over the years, but he had always had that little sense inside him to help him pinpoint their location. The absence of Ruth's presence on his internal grid made him just about useless when it came to hunting her. Or so he felt as he watched the Vampire track her from the caverns beneath the surface. Jasmine's senses and skills as a huntress were utterly remarkable to him. Mind Demons were difficult to track, what with their ability to teleport with a thought from one spot to the next, but if one knew what to look for, it was not impossible. Jasmine impressed him as she quickly traced the Demon's movements.

He had to confess to himself that watching her hunt was an incredible turn-on. His ineffectiveness left him with nothing to do but to watch her. Study her. Familiarize himself with every beautiful line of her features, the graceful length of her neck, and the curving arch of her back on into her rear end as she crouched down to study the signs she found and formulate her next plan of action.

"Must you stare at me so?" she asked with a put-upon sigh after a few hours of this.

Adam only smiled, unable to feel apologetic for being caught in the act. Too large a part of him wanted her to know he found her captivating.

"Cease being so fascinating and I will cease to stare," he offered.

Jasmine couldn't help smiling at that, looking up

at him from her position close to the ground. He was standing there with his powerful legs braced hard apart and his thick arms folded across his chest. He looked as though he were the master of his universe, in spite of the fact that he had currently lost his definition within it. She found that to be impressive and intriguing. He could have floundered around, waiting for others to help him define himself.

But not Adam. Somewhere along the way he had come to grips with the fact that his world had changed, that he needed to face facts and adapt or find himself hopelessly lost. Perhaps it was the act of the hunt that had helped it happen. He was in his element, the process familiar to him. He was hardly as useless as he thought he was, his well-trained senses and his experience lending significant guidance. But he was used to taking the lead in these things, used to being the solitary hunter. He wasn't used to following someone with better skills.

For the moment anyway. Had it been any other Demon they were hunting, Jasmine was certain Adam would have left her in the dust, but Jasmine had hunted Ruth before—knew what to look for, what she smelled like and what her tricks were. She supposed she could have enlightened him, taught him.

However, she was having far too much fun being ahead of him and leaving him with a great deal of time to simply watch her. There was something to be said for his regard. It was as if his eyes conveyed a physical touch. She felt them on her, felt exactly where they touched her at any given moment. She gave in to the temptation to bask in it. Unfortunately it was proving a huge distraction. A certain amount of heat came with his gaze, creating a steady sort of sizzle under her skin. It made her crave the time to do other things besides hunt the target she was seeking.

It was too much of a distraction. It had to stop.

Maybe.

"I have little else to do," he said absently, continuing to contemplate the curve of her ass rather shamelessly. "And I have had worse pastimes."

Jasmine stood up, smoothing her hands down her thighs and moving with a slow and sensual turn. She couldn't help the urge she had to tempt him, always tempt him, step after step—always one inch farther than before. She knew she was inviting trouble, that it was a bad idea all around considering her own unexpected reactions to him thus far, but still she couldn't seem to help herself.

He smiled, his knowing look telling her he was very aware of the purposeful way she toyed with him, and that he knew she did so in spite of her better judgment. He moved a little closer to her, close enough to touch, and even though he didn't reach out for her, it was as though he was doing so with every fiber of his being.

"I have felt attractions in my lifetime. I have been besotted with a girl when I was younger. I remember that. How she fascinated me and everything about her seemed so flawless. But all of that pales compared to what I feel when I am looking at you, little Vamp. And I cannot for my life figure out why that is."

"Perhaps it is just forbidden fruit?" she offered, brushing back her hair just so she could watch the way his eyes clung to the action, to the shift of the strands, to the way they resettled against her neck. She felt her heart fretting in her chest, the muscle wanting to beat despite its long-silent state. Beats and breath, so far he had inspired both. How was it he had the power to raise her dormant systems to life?

"Aye," he said. "It is very possible. But only this particular fruit, I assure you. Only you, little Vamp."

"Well, you have good taste, I'll give you that," she said with a smirk.

That made him laugh, a low rich sound, short-lived and yet beautifully male. It made her want to touch him so badly that she did. She was, after all, a sensualist. It was in the very core of her breed. It was how they tried to feel. So she reached out and drew a shaping hand over the powerful bulk of his shoulder and down the sinewy strength of his arm. An electric sensation jolted down the center of her body as she was forced to remember how he had felt above her, his strength and weight pressing into her, his heat penetrating her skin.

"Earlier, when I said you disappointed me . . ." she said softly, barely above a whisper, as if in confession, "I didn't mind the liberties you took with me. I only minded that you never followed up. I realize now that wasn't your fault."

"I could not have followed up in any event, Jasmine," he said. "The world being what it was at the time. Although I . . . I do not believe I would have been able to hold myself back. It would have taken others to do so." He spared a glance up toward the sky, then looked directly into her eyes. "At the time it was Beltane. Now it is Samhain. Perhaps I am victim to both powerful moons. Perhaps I am throwing away my normal care because I am so disembodied from my former life. But I much prefer to think it has something to do with the fact that you are the most bewitching creature ever to walk the earth." He took a breath, slowly, in through his nose, his eyes closing in obvious pleasure. "And you smell . . ."

She did the same, her eyes drifting half closed as she took in the smell of him. It was such a primal scent, so male and dynamic. She found him to be by far the most tempting pleasure she had ever come across.

"You are quite enough to tempt me outside my species," she admitted to him on a breathy voice. "I think, for the first time, I can appreciate the over-whelming attraction that Damien must feel for—"

She broke off, the words she was saying ringing sharp and yet discordant in her brain. She backed up a step, shaking her head. No. She would be damned if she would fall into the snare that currently held Damien in its grasp. To be so distracted that she would be willing to throw away everything that made sense?

No, she didn't want that.

She turned away and shook off his stunning physical spell as best she could, trying to refocus on her hunt. She had a job to do. A responsibility to thousands of people, if not the entire world, when she thought on it. Ruth was a curse on every living thing, and she must be stopped. Jasmine couldn't let anything get in the way of that. Too many of them had let their own personal distractions get in the way of destroying the Demon.

Adam sensed her withdrawal and knew it ought to feel like a slap in the face. One minute she was there, the next she was gone. But she wasn't truly gone. Not ever gone, he realized slowly as he continued to feel her presence against his skin as surely as if she were leaning against him. He felt as though threads of energy were somehow strung between them, and with every passing moment they grew stronger. Instinct told him that touching her would make it happen all the more quickly. He didn't understand how or why he knew these things. It wasn't logical at all, it wasn't some kind of learned information. It was purely intuition.

He reached for her hair, but his fingertips barely grazed her before she was leaping away into the air, moving to chase down her next lead.

Ah yes. The Demon. The traitor.

Jasmine had been regaling him with tales of Ruth's history. How nearly every major player in the Nightwalker world had gone up against her. Some had achieved victory, but it had proved fleeting and temporary as she escaped final judgment and came back stronger and more tainted every time. As Adam hurried after the Vampire, he knew that he would not let Ruth escape. He would sacrifice his life first. Especially since it was clear she was gunning for his brother's family. Adam could not allow that. It was his job, his life, to see no Demon harmed a human or Nightwalker. Catching Ruth was perhaps what he was most destined to do.

"Oh, how very lovely she is," Ruth remarked as her Vampire minions laid their Mistral captive out on one of Ruth's workbenches. "I had not expected her to be even prettier in person. They say Mistrals are as mousy in looks as they are beautiful in voice. Clearly that is not the case in this instance."

"No, mistress," agreed the petite black-and-gray-haired Demon who had followed the Vampires into the room. "She is heavily sedated," she said apologetically. "I thought it the best way to bring her to you

unharmed and"—she cast a look at the Vampires—
"unbled. I wished her to be in as pristine condition for
your needs as possible."

"You are so thoughtful," Ruth praised her. "Would
you like to see the spell I am working on, as a reward
for bringing me its most crucial component?"

"Very much so."

Ruth impatiently shooed away the Vampires who
were sniffing at the unconscious Mistral.

"Go, go! You'll have your fun later," Ruth assured
them. "Come closer, dear. You see?" She drew close
her papers, artfully interpreted pages of the hiero-
glyph spell of earlier. "It's very close to a spell I
used just a few years ago." Ruth paused for a private
chuckle with herself. "Idiots. They still have not realized they have been cursed. But *this* spell, unlike that
one, can never be reversed. Even if they kill me, it will
work its way through once the components have been
meshed and the phrases spoken."

"What will it do?" the Demon asked curiously.

"The other spell was a barrenness spell. But that
would not work here because the Queen of Demons
is already quite barren. This precious bit of work will
be much louder. More active. With this spell she will
simply go mad. No medic, not even Gideon, will be
able to cure her. And because of its nature, they will
quickly come to understand who is behind it. They
will know it was me. That is why it is important that
the spell be irreversible even should I die. Just in case
they hunt me successfully, I want to reach out beyond
my grave and make them suffer."

"It is quite a clever vengeance."

"It is a brilliant vengeance!" Ruth corrected her.
"Now tell me, how goes the hunt for Corrine?"

"I do not know. Shall I find out for you?"

"If you can. But this takes precedence," Ruth said, indicating her preparations for her spell. "When will the sedative wear off?"

"You have several hours."

"Oh." She looked disappointed. "No matter. It gives me time to double-check all my preparations."

"I will leave you to it," the Demon said with a respectful inclination of her head. "I will seek news of Corrine. If the hunt is not proceeding to my satisfaction, I will see to it for you."

"No doubt." Ruth smiled at her. "You have proved to be an eager and loyal pupil. I am so glad you joined us."

"There is no place I would rather be," the Demon assured her softly.

Then she made another bow and excused herself from Ruth's presence.

Damien bent over the back of the couch and pressed a soft kiss against his wife's temple. She leaned into the touch of affection, a smile warming her features.

"Where are the children?" Syreena asked.

"Playing in the garden. Annalise is watching them," he said. Siena, Syreena's sister, had come to visit, bringing the Demon children Seth and Leah with her. With all that Leah had been through that evening, Siena had thought that a change of scene was called for. That perhaps putting some distance between Leah and the ailing Isabella would benefit them both.

"I don't believe Seth has ever been here before," Syreena noted. "He's such a handsome little boy. Those curls of his are too adorable. His parents treasure him a great deal. He is a very lucky boy."

"Because he is a child of prophecy?"

She scoffed at that. "As someone who was raised with great expectations, I can assure you that is the least special thing he will have in his life. He will no doubt spend a great deal of time wishing he was 'normal.' But he has close and extended family that will love and protect him at every turn, so I have faith it will not be too terrible a burden for him, unlike the way it was for me. I meant only that he was lucky to have his family. I barely knew mine. Siena and I have only grown close over these past two decades. I imagine sometimes how much better my life might have been if only we had been allowed to be sisters together while growing up."

"Everything happens in its own way at its own time for a reason. Imagine if that were true, that one simple change in the fabric of history. You would have been a very different Syreena and would have acted in very different ways. Perhaps you would not have shown restraint and would have killed me the first time you laid eyes on me as I entered your vulnerable sister's sickroom. Then I would be dead, and you would be ever so lonely without me."

He smiled and kissed her on the corner of her mouth as she gently scoffed at him.

"You think so much of yourself," she teased him. "I could very easily walk this world without the great Prince of Vampires."

"Liar," he said knowingly. "You would be lost without me just as I would be lost without you."

Her charcoal eyes with their multicolored flecks lifted to meet his. She saw the truth in irises of deep midnight blue. But she did not need to see it to know it. She knew they were meant for one another. They could never part ways. Bond or no Bond, they were connected deeply beyond words, ceremonies, and the blood they had shared. Sometimes still shared, she thought with a sly smile.

"Ah, there it is." Damien took a deep breath, smelling of his wife slowly and sensuously. "I knew it was coming, but it is thoughts like those that make it clear you will be in heat any day now."

"I suspect I am always in heat as far as you are concerned," she said. "Perhaps I should have a snack prepared for the children." She stood up and moved away, very obviously putting distance and furniture between them. Damien narrowed his eyes on her and followed her quickly.

"You are many things, my love," he said as he caught her arm and turned her toward him, "but an artful topic changer is not one of them. You are horribly obvious. And it is the third time you have done so when I have mentioned your breeding cycle. What is wrong?"

"Nothing is wrong," she said with a shrug and eyes that hunted for stray bits of lint on his shoulders.

He caught her chin in his hand and made her lift her gaze to his.

She sighed in resignation.

"I've grown tired of this breeding carousel. My heat comes and I become a desperate little fiend demanding sex and frantically fretting over my fertility. I want a child so badly . . ."

"As do I," he said.

"Do you?" she asked. "I can't help wondering if I haven't just been dragging you into this maelstrom of mine and that you put up with it only because you wish to see me happy."

"Syreena," he said sternly, "one does not become Prince of the Vampires because he is easily swept away by the desires of others."

"This is different," she said with a small stamp of her foot. "Our connection makes it different."

"True. And yes, you do become a tad desperate during your cycle." At her stern look he edited himself. "Very well, quite desperate. But it all levels out afterward, leading me to believe that drive and desperation are probably a part of your breeding cycle and the hormones you are being subjected to at the time."

"Then why doesn't my sister behave likewise?" she wanted to know.

"Your sister is not you. And as you mentioned earlier, you are not like any other Lycanthrope. You are very much apart from others. Perhaps your dual animal aspects magnify your heat by two."

Syreena thought about it and gave a reluctant nod. "Perhaps."

"Damien."

Damien turned sharply at the intrusive address. His Vampires knew better than to intrude on his private time with his mate, but this was no Vampire.

Suddenly he could sense her, feel the wrongness of her. He thrust his wife protectively behind himself and hissed at the female. He mentally shouted for his guards, wondering how they had ever let such a creature get so close to him.

"Be at ease, I mean you no harm."

He did not believe her. She was a stranger and she reeked of foul magic, the stench of it emanating off her like a twisted perfume. She was a Demon, he realized, when he saw her with his infrared vision and deduced she was several degrees cooler than a human or Lycanthrope. The black-and-gray swirl of her hair was caught in a loose braid that snaked over her shoulder. A white scarf hung around her neck and shoulders, but the rest of her was clothed in sweeps of black fabric.

"You will forgive me if I do not take your word for it," he said as Vampires began to move swiftly into the room.

"I will be gone before any of you can touch me," she promised him softly. "Force me to leave, and I cannot give you the help you and all the Nightwalkers need."

"Wait." Syreena touched her husband on his biceps, moving to his side in a way that made him bristle. He did not like her being in the line of sight of this unknown threat. "Who are you?" she asked the delicate-looking Demon.

The Demon looked at them with the strangest eyes, the indiscernible color seeming to constantly shift across the grayscale spectrum.

"That is not important. I am not what matters. What matters is what I have done." And in an instant she was gone, disappearing in a strange pixilation of black, gray, and white, just out of the reach of a suddenly grasping guard. "I will not say this again," she said, suddenly behind them and forcing them into an about-face. "Waste your time on me and Ruth will slip free, gaining power you cannot imagine. This could be your last opportunity to stop her. Your last chance to live safe and happy." The female Demon fixed her gaze on Syreena. "Ignore me, chase me away, and you and your Prince will know nothing but sadness in the future."

"Speak, Demon. Quickly," Syreena encouraged. "My husband is impatient to have your head for daring to come so close to his loved ones with nothing but danger dripping off your tongue."

"Tonight I have kidnapped Windsong, the Mistral Siren, and delivered her to Ruth. She is safe and alive at present, but this will not last for long. You must find her and rescue her before Ruth can carry out her spell against the Demon King's mate. The spell requires the death of the Siren, and once cast, it will be unbreakable, even if the caster dies. Kestra will suffer and so will Noah. The Demons will lose their leader. The Nightwalkers will begin to lose the war against necromancers and the Vampire rogues. Your peace will dissolve. Your lives will unravel like a poorly crafted tapestry.

"The child of Time has saved you all from one fateful time line by sparing the lives of her parents, but by doing so she opened up an equally traumatic one. But this can be avoided if you save Windsong's life and defeat Ruth once and for all."

"If you knew taking Windsong to Ruth was going to lead to such terrible things, why did you do it?" Syreena demanded. She owed her very existence to Windsong. This news touched her close to home on so many levels. Yet instinct told her to listen carefully to this girl. This creature, spoiled with black arts as she might be, held crucial truths to Syreena's future. She could sense it.

"It is a trap. One of Ruth's tricks," Damien said dismissively when he heard the bent of his wife's thoughts.

"I captured her safely," the Demon injected, "because otherwise she would have been taken by a nest of powerful Vampires. In their victory they would have feasted on the blood of the most powerful Mistral alive today. That would have given them unspeakable power." She shook her head, seeming to be momentarily speechless. But after that moment passed, she continued. "By capturing her and tainting her blood with paralytics and sedatives, I managed to put them off their feast. Again, this will not last long. No doubt Ruth will let them at her as soon as Windsong regains consciousness and the drugs have left her system . . . provided it doesn't interfere with her spell. I cannot say. This I cannot see. I have already altered one thing, so what once was written has already been changed."

"Time," Syreena breathed. "She's come to change history as she knows it to be. You're from the future."

"One future. One possibility. One that still exists, I believe. If it didn't, then I would cease to exist."

"You are a Demon of Time?" Damien asked.

"No. I am . . . something else. And I cannot say more than that. All you need to know is that I have infiltrated Ruth's nest of rebel Nightwalkers. I have used magic, soiling myself as they are soiled in order to gain their trust. Just so I could be here for this moment. So I could protect Windsong for just a few hours. So I could come to you."

"And why should we believe any of this?" Damien wanted to know.

The Demon cocked a brow and inclined her head.

"In an act of vengeance, two years ago, Ruth cast a spell on Syreena so she could never conceive. That spell can only be broken with the death of the caster. You will never have a child so long as Ruth draws breath. Believe me or not, do as you will. But are you willing to take that chance?" The Demon turned up one side of her mouth in a smile that was not really a smile. "Also, your companion Jasmine and her would-be mate are about to stumble into Ruth's nest, not realizing that she has fortified her ranks with rogue Vampires and rebel Nightwalkers. Demons. Lycanthropes. Even Mistrals. Those who have been lured by Ruth's promises of power through black magic. She spins a very convincing argument, makes for a compelling leader when she wishes to. With a little more time, she will not be just a nuisance. She will foment civil war in your ranks. It will be the beginning of the end of peaceable life as you know it."

Damien scoffed. "Jasmine will never have a mate."

"You are correct. Because he will die when they fall upon this nest. And she will never be the same, I promise you. Think you she was melancholy before? Just try to keep her aboveground once he is lost." Again she gave them that smile. "These might just be words to you. But are you willing to take such a chance?"

And with that offering, the strange Demon female disappeared in a pixilated rush of grays and blacks.

Chapter 9

Adam followed Jasmine through the air as mist, sensing, as she no doubt did, that they were on the last leg of their hunt. They were very close to their quarry now.

And yet his mind was distracted from the imminent battle. All he could focus on, time and again, was the beautiful curve of a feminine cheek, the seductive length of denim-clad legs, and the way the wind whipped and twisted through her hair. He had come to know many things about her in just a few short hours, and somehow the new knowledge made his attraction to her all the more powerful. She was stubborn and dogged, beyond determined to see this Ruth come to an end. He was still fuzzy about whether it was personal or due to a deep-seated sense of right and wrong. She claimed it was because Ruth had detained her once, but he knew it had to be more than that. No one hunted with such passion because of what amounted to an inconvenience. And she was head of this Nightwalker law enforcement group. That didn't sound like something one did just for amusement.

He could believe it was to satisfy her bloodthirsty nature. It was very obvious she had one. But there were any number of violent pastimes out there for a Vampire. She could just as easily have turned rogue to get her kicks. Yet she had not. She had come down on the right side of the law. A lawfulness that, to be honest, surprised him when he saw it in a Vampire.

He had to remind himself that Vampires had changed and, clearly, grown in maturity and responsibility. Most of them, anyway. She was a strong example of the way Damien now led his people. It was impressive, to say the least.

Titillating.

Especially to one such as he, who lived and breathed the law. Strange as it was to entertain the idea, she was . . . very much like him. Close friend to a monarch. A powerful hunter. Employed to rein in those who needed reining in.

And all of this served to make their attraction toward one another all that much more powerful.

Damn it, he's staring at my ass again. I can just feel it . . .

Adam drew up short as her voice lilted through his brain. Startled, he dropped to the closest surface he could find and snapped into solid form.

Oh brother. Now what?

There it was again. Quite clear, quite obviously Jasmine's thoughts as she dropped down onto the stony outcropping where he had landed.

"Now what?" she demanded. "You know, Ruth isn't going to sit around and wait for us to catch her. She's very smart. She is very likely hauling up stakes as we speak and moving on. She's going to assume we are hunting her!"

"Yes, about that," he said a little numbly as he stared directly into her eyes. "It occurs to me we might be racing headlong into some manner of ambush."

Well, shit. If you want to be all logical about it . . .

"Perhaps. But I think she'll be too busy packing up her shit and running away," Jasmine said aloud.

Adam stared at her, slightly gape-mouthed. He had no doubt in his mind that somehow, for some inexplicable reason, he was hearing the gorgeous Vampire's thoughts. But that knowledge didn't startle him half so much as the understanding that she was actually being very honest with him whenever she answered him. She was, quite literally, speaking her mind.

"Are you as attracted to me as I am to you?" he blurted out before he could second-guess himself. Before he lost his nerve.

To say the question surprised her was understating things just a tad.

What in the hell is this all about? Talk about coming out of left field! But then after her surprise wore off, she leaned back ever so slightly, letting her eyes drift over him from head to toe.

"Wait. Before you say or . . . or *think* anything," Adam said with haste as his heart beat rapidly in his chest and chills of conscience walked his spine. "I think you ought to know that I am quite certain I can read your mind."

"As if!" She laughed so hard she snorted a little bit. Adam was shocked to realize he thought it was terribly cute. "And I am *not* cute. Look at me! Seriously, what do you see in this whole package that comes off cute?" She flung an indicative hand down the length of her body and its provocatively tight clothing. "You aren't a telepath," she went on to say. "You're just a

Water Demon. And even if you were a telepath, I am probably the second most powerful telepath on the planet. My defenses are quite significant . . ."

"Except when Ruth went ripping through your mind to gather information. You may as well have been a child, the way she pushed through you and mined you for information that proved harmful to the rest of the Nightwalkers."

It was, nearly word for word, the guilty thought that raced through Jasmine's brain right after her boast to him. He wasn't saying it to rub salt in her wounds, but to prove a point.

"Oh my God, you're reading my mind!" Jasmine looked at him in horror and shock. "How is that possible? You have to stop! I demand that you stop!"

"I do not know how. As you said, I am not a telepath."

"But then . . . how? What the hell . . . ?"

Adam reached out to take firm hold of her arm, stopping her suddenly agitated body movements. The outcropping wasn't big enough for her to pace across, and he didn't want her falling off and flying away.

"Be easy," he said as gently as he knew how. "First I would like to say that you are being somewhat unfair to yourself, as far as that encounter with Ruth is concerned."

"What do you know about it?" she demanded irritably. "You were four hundred years away."

"This is true," he agreed with a nod of his dark head. "However, even in my short time in your era, it has been made clear to me that this Ruth is a formidable opponent. A Mind Demon without equal. You cannot expect yourself to be more powerful than all things. It would be an unreasonable expectation."

She frowned, her eyes dropping down.

People died because I was so weak.

"People died because I was weak," she said.

Adam's lips lifted at the corners. Had he ever thought her to be duplicitous? Oh, he had no doubt that she was capable of it if her motivations were strong enough, but it would seem, at the moment, she did not see any reason to be so with him. It pleased him, giving him a sudden sense of intimacy with her. Again. It was so peculiar how that feeling crept up over him, seemingly out of nowhere, and so very strongly when it did.

"People died because someone wanted them dead. She would have gotten her information one way or another, Jasmine. You cannot fault yourself for Ruth's sadistic motivations."

"Says who?" she demanded petulantly. "I want to blame myself. I want to remind myself to do better. To get stronger. To never allow her to use me in such a way again."

"I can appreciate that," he told her. "But have a care. It is one thing to motivate yourself in such ways, and another to blind yourself with them." He reached to touch two fingers to the bottom of her chin, lifting her gaze to his. He opened his mouth to speak, but the words came to a screaming halt in his brain. She blinked questioningly at him, with eyes as green as jade.

As green as his own.

The truth struck him down like a thundering avalanche, overwhelming him, freezing him in place and leaving him breathless. He felt caught up and compressed from all sides, as though he were asphyxiating from the weight of it all.

Sweet Destiny, the Imprinting, he thought loud and clear.

And she heard it. Perhaps because she was a Vampire and a telepath, but more probably because they were deep in the stages of an Imprinting, and Imprinted mates formed a private telepathic pathway between them. They took up residence in each other's minds. All of their thoughts were constantly known to one another. The way it had been explained to him was that there was no real way to shut them out.

"As if!" she blurted out, her eyes wide with abrupt panic. "Vampires do not Imprint, and even if we could, I most certainly would not choose to Imprint with *you*! You are a dated, obstinate, Cro-Magnon, chest-thumping Alpha idiot and nothing about that appeals to me!"

For the most part, she thought. *Well, perhaps a little.*

Then her bright jade eyes widened as she recalled he could read her thoughts.

"Bloody freaking hell!"

Adam's only further argument was to cup his hands in the air, right in front of her face, and shift them into water. It swirled into a dark oval pool and then he forced it to become completely still, darkening the rear of it until the surface became a perfectly reflective surface. He showed her her own face, showed her the stunning new green of her eyes.

"No way," she uttered as she stared at herself. "No way am I going to let this happen. I am a Vampire! A *Vampire*!"

"So you keep saying," he said quietly. "And this evening I woke up at war with you. But that has changed. Everything has changed."

"You mean to tell me you are all right with this?" she asked incredulously. "You're going to sit there and tell me you wish to have a *Vampire* for your mate?"

"Jasmine . . ." He sighed and took a moment to rub at the painful ache knotting between his brows. "What I want is to be home, on the lands of my family, in the practice fields beneath my family standard with my mother harassing me to do this or that to keep me civil and respectable, instead of lost in this confusion of hunting and battle and one dire situation after another. I want to know the most stressful choice my brother needs to make is whether to chase after a Vampire for bounty or wrestle around with me in the practice ring. This is what I want. Or rather, 'tis what I wanted. What I thought I wanted.

"But I have learned in my lifetime that what we think we want and what is best for us may well be two separate things. I have also been raised to believe there is one absolute in the Demon world. One thing that cannot be questioned, cannot be changed, and cannot be fought. There have been those far better than you and I who tried to fight the inevitability of the Imprinting, and they were no more successful than either of us will be if we do the same."

"Horseshit!" she ejected hotly. "None of them were Vampires. The Imprinting is all about love and passion and emotion, all of which you yourself have been quick to point out I am not capable of! Certainly not on the grand scale of your mushy, lovesick, *disgusting* Imprinting!"

Jasmine leapt away from him, turning and pushing off the outcropping, leaping into the whipping breezes.

In a wild act of instinct, Adam leapt right after her. He launched himself onto her back, circling her neck and waist with his massive arms, feeling the jolt of gravity as they began to fall toward earth. She was unable to adjust her flight to his weight because she was too busy indulging in her fury to compensate. She struggled against him, her strength quite remarkable.

But only moments before he was going to morph them both into mist, she reacted with an unexplainable instinct, her fangs stretching free and long just as she grabbed his wrist and sank her teeth into his forearm.

Adam roared in pain, reaching to grab her by her hair and thinking he was going to rip her free of him.

But then time drew long, ticking into slower and slower instants as their bodies fell toward the ground at breakneck speed. His fingers were full of her hair, but all desire to detach himself from her was gone by the time his fingertips touched her scalp. Just as her desire to flay his flesh apart with the savage rip of her teeth vanished the instant his blood washed over her tongue. Their joined minds locked as if in mutual seizure as she tasted what she could only describe as ambrosia, the food of the gods . . . the most divine of forbidden fruits making good on its promise.

His blood, the essence of all that was Adam and all that was Adam's power, slid to the back of her throat and she couldn't even pretend to resist the urge to swallow. She groaned as the first mouthful burst down her throat as though she had swallowed fire, the overwhelming, sensuous burn rushing down the center of her body from throat to chest to belly and then onward into the lee of her hips and reproductive organs, burning a hot, wet path, it seemed, right back out of her body.

Water is my element. All that is liquid is mine to manipulate and harmonize with. Shall I tell you where you are wet, little Vamp?

Jasmine gasped for breath, removing her teeth from his flesh just before he was able to come to his senses enough to turn them into water, barely a second before they hit the ground. They dashed against the hard, cold earth, physics demanding their fluid forms spread far and fast over its surface.

But Adam defied those physics, instead rolling around with her and resolidifying their bodies once the initial danger of impact was past, sending them tumbling across the ground in a tangle of arms and legs. The Demon lay beneath the weight of the Vampire, both of them panting hard for breath. His blood was on her lips and he watched as a sensuous tongue came out to slowly bathe it away, felt his mind blossoming with pleasure as it exploded inside her senses. Her eyes rolled closed, her hands gripping his chest and shoulder where they lay. Her forehead dropped against him as if she didn't have the strength to hold up her own head. And he realized it was because she was too weak with bliss.

Then the next moment her head snapped up, her eyes popping open like suddenly released window shades. *Have her lashes always been so thick and so black?* he found himself wondering. Was it his imagination, or was she growing more beautiful every time he laid eyes on her? The brown of her eyes had been so sultry and decadent, but now the green she had acquired seemed bottomless and seductively mysterious. And there was something satisfying, soul-deep satisfying, about seeing a part of himself in her.

She took a breath, lowered her head, and was suddenly gazing at him through her upper lashes like a prowling jaguar eyeing its prey.

"More," she said in a voice that was far more growl than it was anything else.

He did not even pretend to mistake her meaning, nor did he pretend he didn't want it just as badly as she did. He reached for the collar of his new shirt, yanking it away from his skin in a tear of popping fabric and buttons. There was no preamble as she opened her mouth and attacked his throat in a quick in-and-out puncture of her wicked sharp fangs. Then before his blood could so much as bead in the open wounds, she had sealed her lips over the damage she had done.

Jasmine began to drink.

By the third sucking draw of her lips and tongue against his neck, Adam was as hard as pristine diamonds. It was as much because he was experiencing her compounding pleasure with her every swallow as it was the way she was writhing against him with such incredibly wicked sensuousness and need. That devious little body of hers could have raised a dead man's interest. And Adam was far from dead.

He had one hand gripping her hair so tightly it should have squeaked. The other had fallen to her hip, or rather the rise of her backside on the right side, and was mindlessly guiding the tease of her body more tightly and accurately against himself. It was utter torture, and absolute perfection. He could not possibly have wanted more. They did not need to be sexually joined just then because one of them had already penetrated the other. Now it was all about sensation and elation and the miraculous feel of things building stronger and stronger with every second that passed. She was moaning against him, her left hand rushing relentlessly up over her body and gripping at her breast through her shirt. Then she was pulling the fabric away from her skin, trying to free herself, trying to expose herself for her needs and pleasure.

Adam reached quickly up under the hem of her shirt and grabbed hold of the lace lying close to her skin. It took only a twist of his large hand to snap the thing free of her body, allowing him to discard the lace and boning. Quickly after, her breast was filling his hand, the soft heat of it divine and pleasurable. His fingertip found that metal ring she had lanced through the tip of her nipple and he toyed with it relentlessly, feeling her get as rigid and hard as he was.

Orgasm raced through her blood because of his, the power of it extraordinary, skipping from her and into him. Their bodies seized with awesome pleasure, liquid release throbbing from both of them. Adam felt light-headed as he fed her body in all ways at once, taking satisfaction in the idea that it went way beyond the sexual. The second thrust of her fangs into him was unexpected and ought to have been painful after he had been so wrung out. It was anything but. If anything, it kicked him back up into the wave of ecstasy she had swept him away with. They were both gasping for breath and groaning repetitively with pleasures no one else in the world could ever comprehend or perhaps even experience.

How sad for them, he thought as her mouth fell away from his skin at last. Adam recalled that a Vampire always bit twice. The first time to open a wound, the second time to inject the host with clotting factors and antibodies intended to close the wound and facilitate healing. But his technical understanding of it had never given him any idea what the experience would feel like. That there would be such bliss. Such overwhelming bliss.

"Because it is not supposed to feel like that," she told him on a soft, sleepy murmur near his ear. "I don't think any Vampire has ever felt like that during a . . . a . . ."

"Feed," he supplied for her.

"I cannot even call it that," she whispered fiercely against the rim of his ear, her hands gripping him with that impressive Vampire strength. "I cannot ever call it that. That was so far from being something so basic and rudimentary as a feed. Adam . . . Adam, it was amazing," she breathed. She lifted her head and looked down on him with starry jade eyes. "My God, is this what Damien feels when he loves his little Lycanthrope?" she wondered. "Well, then no wonder . . . no wonder . . ."

She sighed and rested her cheek on his chest, her ear against his heart even though her Vampire senses could easily make out the wild beat of his pulse. It was what she always supposed being stoned would feel like. It was the most amazing high anyone could imagine. Was this the way it felt for any Vampire taking any other Nightwalker's blood? If so, then she could see why some would be compelled to go rogue and want to feed on a plethora of Nightwalkers, if only to see what each tasted like . . . to see what it felt like.

But she was not so naïve as to believe that. She knew this experience was wholly different. This was special beyond even the Imprinting. Had she been afraid of this? Had she been resisting it?

"Yes, little Vamp. And you might again once you come down from your euphoria."

"Perhaps," she agreed with a nod. "Perhaps not. I am not as foolish as you think I am. Nor as stubborn."

He made a rude noise.

"Very well," she conceded good-naturedly, a smile spreading over her lips. "I am quite stubborn. But I am not an idiot." She lifted her head and moved to look down into his eyes, her hands brushing up over his face. "Do you think I like being so cold and so emotionally bland? Can you imagine what life begins to look like when year after year there is nothing to interest you? Nothing to stimulate you?" She touched a finger to his lips, tracing their generous shape. "All I can feel is physical pleasures . . . pleasures of the senses . . . and perhaps intellectual challenges. But my heart is cold. There is no true light for me. No *joie de vivre.*

"But this," she breathed as she touched her mouth to his in a ghost of a kiss, "this is life at its fullest. This is intense flavor and full-blown sensuality and . . . oh my God . . ." She gave a little groan before she caught his mouth in a deep kiss. Adam let her design the thing, let her set the pace and intensity. He understood that this was the first kiss she had initiated in decades. Perhaps even the better part of a century.

More than that. I will kiss Damien with warmth and affection, but no one else. I have not kissed with passion . . . until I kissed you.

That satisfies me greatly, he thought back to her.

She broke from his mouth to laugh.

"You see? You are such a Neanderthal."

"What I am is hungry. For you." He sank a big hand into her hair and pulled her down to his mouth. This time he was in complete command of the kiss, heat exploding like a bomb between them, the impact sweet and painful and so very full of fire. He reveled in the taste of her on his tongue as he played with hers. He kissed her until she was moaning in a sweet chain of sounds that, admittedly, revitalized his ego. Because even though he had been just as unsure about this thing between them as she was, her rejection had still hurt. Somewhere in his spirit he bore the bruise. But he knew she was equally wounded. She had hurt herself when she hurt him.

But all it had taken was a taste of blood to chase all opposition away. That exchange had done in an instant what might have taken days and a volatile Samhain moon to convince them of otherwise.

"Mmm . . . no. No!" She pulled back from him. "Bitch to hunt. Must hunt the bitch." She tried to sit up, but he only followed her, making sure she understood he was diametrically opposed to that course of action. For the immediate future, anyway. He did this by grabbing hold of her shoulders and dragging her back up against his mouth.

"The bitch has waited this long. Surely a little while longer will not make such a dramatic difference."

Jasmine sighed, a long, sweet sound, her entire body melting back against him as her arms wrapped around his neck. She succumbed to the workings of his mouth, telling herself she would only do so for a moment or two.

* * *

"There she is," Corrine whispered softly to the Demon by her side. She touched a hand of comfort to his shoulder, the action triggering him to breathe.

The redheaded Druid and the tawny-haired Demon named Aaron looked through the nursery glass at the squalling half-Asian, half-Hispanic infant, her tuft of black hair standing all askew in reflection of her obvious outrage at the world.

"Poor thing," Corrine said with empathy. "Such a hard start in life."

"This is such a difficult concept for me," Aaron confessed as he looked at the helpless human creature. "We take such care and thought before producing children in the Demon world. They are so precious to us, our offspring. It hurts and angers me to think a mother would poison herself with drugs while carrying a babe, knowing full well how that babe will suffer once born."

"Unfortunately drugs remove all manner of logic. With this particular drug, some of the mothers don't even realize they are pregnant for most of their term . . . or they simply don't care."

"And so she cries. My future mate. A female you say will be a powerful Druid one day if she survives this withdrawal. And I will see that she does."

Aaron moved to find entrance into the nursery, but Corrine held him back by his arm.

"You can't touch her, Aaron. Even as young as she is, you will very likely trigger those changes that will make her Druid, causing her to become dependent on you for the rest of her life."

"So? Is that not how it should be?"

"Perhaps. Or perhaps she should be allowed to

form a life as an individual first, before she feels the urge to become part of a pair."

Corrine could tell by the darkness flooding his handsome visage that Aaron didn't like the idea at all.

"Look what leaving her in the care of humans has done for her so far," he said bitterly. "And you cannot dangle her in front of me like bait, she who will be my salvation, and then force me to leave her unprotected amongst—" He came short of calling humans "savages," but the unspoken word hung in the air. "I am sorry," Aaron said quickly. "I know you are human."

"No offense is taken, Aaron. Your arguments are strong, unfortunately. We are very thoughtless and sometimes cruel with our own. And I don't suggest you leave her here abandoned and unprotected as she is."

Through the glass a plume of dark smoke suddenly appeared, the suddenness of it and the no doubt painful change in air pressure setting every single infant in the room to screaming. Kane reached out to touch the child in question, and before anyone could see him, he disappeared with her.

"There," she soothed the Demon beside her, who was itching to protect the girl child. "Kane is taking her somewhere safe where she will be raised by Demon parents in the Demon world until such time as you feel it is wise to introduce yourself to her. Perhaps in about twenty years or so."

"That is not long at all," Aaron said with a sigh of marked relief.

That made Corrine chuckle. Humans and Demons saw the passing of time so differently.

The lights in the hospital had been flickering angrily ever since their arrival, and were now fluctuating so wildly it looked as though they would lose power at any moment.

"Come on. Let's go," Corrine encouraged him. "Between your influence on the technology around us and the fact that a baby is now missing from the nursery, we had best leave."

"Of course."

Aaron reached out to take Corrine's hand, and in a burst of dust they disappeared from the hospital corridor.

Sometime later Aaron left Corrine in downtown Tokyo, where her husband had promised to take her out for a genuine Japanese dinner. Aaron the Earth Demon had agreed with her decision to keep the baby girl's foster family a mystery for now so he would not be tempted to interfere with her upbringing. But Corrine had a feeling he would be on her doorstep soon, fussing at her for the information. It really wouldn't matter too much. The foster parents she had chosen were powerful and strong-willed, and Aaron would have his hands full trying to get past them before they felt the time was appropriate for her to meet her would-be mate.

She felt compassion for Aaron. He had come to Corrine as Noah's new laws demanded of him, to have the Matchmaker seek his mate. Corrine had been learning the hard way that she would not always be successful in her search for specific Druids, however. Perhaps the Druid mate for the Demon in question had died or perhaps the mate had not been born yet. And then there were a number of other things that could go wrong or throw up an obstacle in the seeking process. Often it was the mental complexity of the Demon in question, the Demon's subconscious working against itself. And more recently she had realized that perhaps that Demon was not meant to find a Druid mate. Perhaps that Demon's soul mate was another type of Nightwalker breed completely. She did not have the power to find those mates. At least she didn't have that power yet. She was stretching herself, trying to see if she could do it . . . if she could figure out the path to that kind of ability. If she could find that power within herself, then she would be a true Matchmaker, with no obstacles in her way and no limitations to the mates she could find.

How beautiful that would be.

And that was why, after dinner, she was going to visit the Queen, Kestra. Kestra had a remarkable power that allowed her not only to map out the current abilities of a Nightwalker, but also to see that person's future abilities, and perhaps even guide them toward new powers. The one constant in the Demon and Druid races, as Corrine understood it, was that they never stopped growing in power and ability. Even Gideon, the Ancient, who was over a thousand years old, had learned the way to a new ability. And this was thanks to Kestra. Oh, he would have likely found the way on his own over many, many years of testing and practicing, but Kestra had dramatically cut down that learning curve.

Corrine was excited and nervous at the same time. What if Kestra saw nothing in her abilities that could lead her where she wanted to go? How could she truly call herself a Matchmaker if she could only make Demon/Druid matches? And if she could go beyond Demon and Druid, did that mean other Nightwalkers would come to her door seeking for a mate?

"Oh my God. It'll be a full-time job."

And protecting her had already become Kane's full-time job, it seemed. All of her consultations were now conducted with Kane right outside the door, making sure everyone inside was behaving themselves. If she cried out for him, he was always a quick teleport away. Ever since the fiasco with Noah losing control in his mad efforts to obtain Kestra, Kane refused to take any chances with her safety. Perhaps he wasn't as old and as strong as some of the Demons that came to her, and perhaps he might not win against them in a head-to-head, but he was damn well going to give it his all.

And she loved him for that. For that and a thousand other reasons. She had worried early on, a bit secretly, that they might grow a little bit bored of each other as time went on. That it would be exhausting being in each other's brains all of the time. Instead the very opposite had proved true. There wasn't all that wasted time wandering around wishing for this and that from her man. The minute something occurred to her, he heard it and responded. And vice versa. It had to be the most unselfish, reciprocal, and generous relationship she'd ever known.

And now here she was, in the middle of the overwhelming city of Tokyo, where she didn't know a single word of Japanese and kind of stood out like a sore thumb with her wild curls of red hair and her obvious touristy behavior. And this just because she'd had the passing thought earlier that she would love to eat and shop in Tokyo one day. Kane had suggested there was no time like the present, since they were so close.

So here she was, gazing into outrageous storefront windows, some with live moving people in them, showing off fashions and jewels. Corrine stared and watched and didn't care if she was playing the American tourist.

"Oh, excuse me," someone said after bumping into her.

Corrine instantly picked up on the sound of English, after spending nearly thirty minutes immersed in the Japanese chatter of people on their cell phones or having conversations she didn't have a hope of understanding. Kane would be there soon enough, but for the moment it was a relief to make a familiar connection.

"You speak English?" she asked the athletic-looking brunette. She was fair-skinned and willowy, her hair cut at short angles, shaping the dramatic bone structure of her beautiful face.

"Yes," she said with a smile. "First time in Tokyo?" she asked.

"Yes. I'm getting better at traveling, but it still amazes me what a culture shock some places can be. But not in a bad way. Look at all of this! There's so much light."

"I know." The brunette didn't seem as impressed. Clearly she was well traveled and very familiar with her surroundings.

"Well, I'm sorry. I didn't mean to hold you up," Corrine said apologetically.

"Not at all. I'm the one who almost plowed you down." She stepped closer, smiling with a strange sort of discomfort. It was the first indication Corrine had that she wasn't being entirely genuine. "I have a few moments," she said. "Can I help you do a little shopping or something? I love to shop."

"Well, actually I'm waiting for my husband," Corrine said, her feeling of unease growing. She couldn't figure out why she was uneasy, but she was learning more and more to go with her instincts.

"It will only be a few minutes. We can go in this store right here," the brunette said softly.

And just like that, the pitch in her voice seemed to change. She met Corrine's eyes directly, their bottomless brown suddenly compelling. Corrine felt drawn in and she wondered, with a mental laugh, why she had been so uptight about the generosity of a stranger. She really was so pretty and so sweet. Truly harmless.

"Come with me, Corrine," the woman said in dulcet tones that seemed to defy the noise and hustle going on all around them. All those distractions faded away as Corrine connected to this stranger in such a soulful way.

"What's your name?" Corrine asked with a genuine hunger to know. She suddenly wanted to know everything about her.

"Sana," she replied. "How pretty you are, Corrine," Sana said, reaching to stroke a graceful pair of fingertips down the side of the redhead's cheek. "You want to come with me right now, don't you?"

"Oh yes," Corrine agreed.

No!

In her head, the shout of the voice she knew as well as her own was cold and sharp, shocking like icy water dashed across her senses. Corrine stepped back suddenly, surprised to see how close she had gotten to Sana. They were practically embracing.

No, sweetheart! Look away from her eyes and do not meet them again, Kane instructed her sharply. *She is a Vampire and is trying to mesmerize you with her mind. And no doubt she is realizing this instant that you are breaking free of her spell. You need to get away from her!*

Corrine felt her heart jolt into overdrive as an aggressive change washed down Sana's body. Corrine looked away from her and desperately sought some kind of safety. But what safety could there possibly be for a defenseless Druid facing off against a powerful Vampire? And Corrine was no idiot. She knew there was only one reason a Vampire would want to lure her away.

The only thing she had going for her was the fact that they were in a crowd of humans. As a rule Vampires didn't do things that might expose their true nature to the human public.

But rogue Vampires didn't really much care about Vampire rules and regulations, and she was willing to bet this one could give a merry shit whether attacking her in public drew some attention.

"Touch me, and the Demon King and all his brethren will hunt you into the ground. You, Sana. Personally. My husband will see to that," Corrine promised in a low hiss of threat.

The Vampire smiled. She clearly didn't seem to care about the prospect of being the target of all Demons everywhere.

"I'm going to devour you," she said in a low sort of growl.

Then she reached out and grabbed Corrine by the collar of her shirt, jerking her up close against her body. Sana opened her mouth, flexing a wicked-looking set of fangs.

Then she jerked sharply, her body turning a little oddly.

Suddenly she seemed to dissolve away right before Corrine's shocked eyes. And as the Vampire disappeared, a second woman appeared, little dots of black-and-white at first, like a low-resolution photograph viewed too close. Slowly her image focused into the picture of a small woman with exotic features, eyes of indeterminate color, and long, black and gray hair.

The Vampire was nowhere to be seen.

"There's a pack more of them right around the corner. They'll be on us in a second. Come with me!"

I don't know who this is! I can't even tell what she is! I am coming, Corrine. I'm almost there!

She could feel his imminent arrival. She knew he was close and rushing to get to her.

"What . . . ?"

"Ah hell, Corrine, why do you always have to over-think things?" the young woman said with exasperation. Then she grabbed Corrine by the wrist. The sensation that came over Corrine was like turning into champagne, little bits of herself fizzing and bubbling away. Before she faded completely, she saw a cadre of Vampires rushing at her from all directions. But their grasping hands went right through her and the mysterious woman. Then she was gone in a swirl of white and black. When her body rushed back together, she found herself on another street in Tokyo, this one perhaps only blocks away from her previous location. She was struck by a wave of incredible nausea.

"That will pass," the dark-haired girl said with scant compassion. But to be fair, she was distracted by checking their surroundings for any further threat. "Kane is almost here. Instants away. He will be happy to know that this time he wasn't too late." Her strangely shaded eyes fixed on Corrine's for a moment. "This probably won't make sense to you for a long time. If ever. Just know that you have avoided danger. You are safe. That's all that matters."

Then a huge shift in air pressure heralded the

thunderous appearance of Corrine's mate, the black cloud of sulfuric smoke accompanying him out of control as it tended to be when he was upset or emotionally stressed. His skills as a Mind Demon altered the perceptions of all the humans nearby, so that they saw none of it for what it was. And by the time the smoke cleared and his arms wrapped around her, the mysterious dark-haired girl was gone.

"Okay, what the hell was that?" Corrine demanded as her husband swept her up tight to his body and prepared to teleport them far away and to better-assured safety.

"A hell of a guardian angel," Kane said, and he breathed a sigh of relief into her beautiful riot of red hair.

Now that he had hold of her, nothing could hurt her.

He teleported them away.

The young female Demon reappeared on the Tokyo street in the midst of four angry Vampires that had been cheated out of a powerful meal. Sure, they had been instructed to keep Corrine alive, but that didn't mean they couldn't feast on her quite a bit in the process.

They had seen her. Recognized her. And she couldn't take the chance that they would report back about her actions. That would ruin everything. So she whipped out the dart gun she had used earlier and shot the loaded dart into the left eye of the first Vamp, sending him down into a screaming fit of pain. The second grabbed her by her hair, forcing her to turn hard around and head-butt her right at the zygomatic arch. The maneuver cut open a gash in her face, but it also sent shards of bone shooting into the Vampire's frontal brain, dropping her like dead weight.

She pulled a modified ice pick from her belt as she whirled to stuff it and her fist as far as she could through the soft throat of the third Vamp, severing the brain at its stem.

By the time she jerked her hand and weapon back, the fourth Vampire had come to the conclusion that he wanted no part of someone who could take out three of his brethren in under sixty seconds.

He began to run.

She sighed.

She really did hate to run.

Jasmine moaned with the incredible pleasure racing through her veins, like the pulse she normally didn't have. But something about this Demon brought every last part of her to life, from breath to heartbeat to stunning multidimensional emotions. More than anything, he brought pleasure. The stroke of his hands as they mapped her body completely from head to toe was unparalleled. He made her want to crawl out of her clothes, to strip down to utter nakedness and just rub her bare skin all over his. The craving was as dizzying as it was overwhelming.

"No," she cried a bit painfully, the word a cross between a moan and a whine. "Demon bitch. I have to go get her. I cannot . . ."

Fail.

Jasmine felt the bitter taste of the word in her mind and it was a powerful countercoup to the incredible pleasure he was making her feel. It was, perhaps, the only thing strong enough to entice her away from all the promises his touch and closeness and extraordinarily sexy body were tempting her with. Oh, how she wanted all of those things he was trying to give her. She was not afraid to admit that she had wanted them for quite some time.

But she wanted them free of this albatross swinging from her neck. She had to find her white whale and destroy it before it had the chance to hurt anyone else. She couldn't be at peace, couldn't relax and enjoy this new state of being, until she had extracted this poison from her life. From everyone's life.

Adam felt what she felt the very instant it fell over her. He felt the passion of her hatred for Ruth, and for the first time Ruth became more than just an average quarry to him. He felt Jasmine's pain and frustration. He recalled her most significant battle with Ruth as if he had been there himself the day Jasmine, Damien, and Syreena had stumbled upon the traitor Demon and her avaricious Vampire mate in the woods and almost lost their lives to her cunning ability to fight and spellcast. Because of Jasmine's experience, he was finally able to appreciate the enemy he was hunting. For the first time he was forced to question the wisdom of taking her on alone.

"Jasmine," he said, his voice rough with the physical need for her that still flooded him. "We will get your Demon. But perhaps we should reconsider facing her alone."

And just like that, she turned cold in his arms. She pushed him away, stumbling to her feet as she jerked her clothing back into place and tried to run her hands through her tousled hair, as if smoothing the look of it would make everything they had shared disappear.

"Horseshit," she sputtered. "Are you turning soft on me now, Enforcer?"

"Far from soft," he reminded her wryly as he drew himself to his feet and his full height. His body was heavily and quite obviously aroused. He adjusted himself a little bit, drawing her attention to the fact against her immediate will.

God, I have got to get me some of that, she thought fiercely.

It made Adam smile to hear it. Regardless of what she wanted or felt about anything else, she wholly admitted to herself that she craved him. As angry as she might be at him in the moment, she had to acknowledge that their attraction was not going to simply stop because she willed it to be so. She wasn't going to be able to brush him away like a few tangles in her hair.

"Fine! All right! I am hot for your body and all of that," she blurted out with exasperation. "That doesn't mean I'm not going to be all kinds of pissed off if you back out of this on me! I'm not stupid and I'm not so arrogant as to think I could take her on by myself," she said hotly. "I need you. The Enforcer. This is what you do! You snap Demons back in line. And if they won't get back in line, you do what needs to be done. I need that, Adam. I need you to come with me and do *what needs to be done*! That last fight she had Nico on her side and yes, it made her unbelievably strong, but you killed him. He's dead now! She's all alone, except for the odd minion or two. We have to strike now before she can recoup, before she can start to recruit new blood, take a new mate or even start Summoning more Demons to use against us."

"Black magic," he spat, the taste of it on his tongue as vile as the notion of it. It was the ultimate perversion. A Demon Summoning Demons. "It must be stopped," he agreed. "I am only suggesting that the best way to do this is with a strength of numbers."

"If we go back now for help, she will disappear again as she always does. This time there will be no trail. She will have time to do whatever it is she does to make certain of it. Adam, you have to believe me," she said, stepping forward and reaching for his hand. She grasped his palm and fingers, squeezing with her wonderful strength of breed and the passion of her feelings. True, deep feelings. Feelings that had been inside her long before he had come along. "I am not as reckless as others may think I am. I am not doing this in the heat of the moment. I am doing this with the conviction of my beliefs. If I am wrong, if I die, then so be it. It will be worth it if I can hurt her enough to make a difference. To cut her legs out from under her so she can never get her footing again. I'll die dragging her down with me the whole way. I know you believe in destiny. So feel me, feel my soul when I swear to you that this . . . this is *my* special destiny. I was put on this earth, here and now, in this place and time, to destroy the Demon Ruth. Help me. Please help me to do that."

The passion of her emotion moved him. He could feel it as it stung across her eyes and sinuses. She turned away a little, as if to hide her weakness, but she recalled how useless that was when he was so clearly entrenched in her thoughts and emotions. In fact, she wanted him to know just how genuine all of this was for her, so she embraced it. She let the tears fill her eyes.

"A cavern full of innocent Nightwalkers died because

of the way she used me to get to them. My fault or her fault, wherever the blame lies, she has to answer for it. She has to answer for all of her crimes."

"And so she will," Adam said with a firm nod of assurance. He drew their joined hands up to his lips and pressed a kiss against her fingers. "You and I together. There is great power in this thing between us. It goes beyond shared thoughts and this magnificent lust. Together we will be a force to reckon with. I feel it in my soul. And we will start with your Demon bitch, eh?"

"You got that right!" she declared, letting out a whoop of joy. She leapt for the sky, flying fierce and free into the night.

Dawn was only a short time away. They were running out of time. Adam could tolerate a portion of daytime hours, but his Vampire mate could not. The sun would roast her like a chicken on a spit, slowly and painfully cooking her from the skin inward.

The thought propelled him off the ground and after her. He followed with as much haste as he could muster in spite of his limitations. He skipped after her, following cloud after cloud, jumping them like a frog jumps lily pads in a pond. Now that he had resolved himself to doing this thing once and for all, he felt almost euphoric. It took him several minutes to realize that euphoria was not entirely his own. It would take some time, this getting used to the presence of another in his mind and emotions. He had his own individual thoughts as he always had, but now her thoughts were inside him and also this strange sort of blending of the two that was growing stronger with every passing second. The Imprinting, he recognized, had already been occurring in earnest, but since she had taken his blood it had taken on a whole new and powerful dimension.

It was almost astounding to him, the idea that he had let a Vampire drink from him. Considering the world he had been living in when he had woken that evening . . .

No one can accuse me of inflexibility ever again, he thought with amusement.

I agree. When I think of the look on Damien's face . . .

It should have been strange how easily they fell into communicating with one another through this powerful mental passageway, but it was as natural as breathing. Perhaps that was what made her fall silent, or perhaps it was her thoughts about Damien and all the baggage she had accumulated with him and his relationship with Syreena. Adam could see it all so clearly as it churned through her mind.

You were jealous of her, he noted carefully. He had long since realized she didn't particularly care to be called out on her flaws. She much preferred to admit them in her own way and in her own time.

But to his surprise, she didn't become angry and she didn't shut him down immediately.

I think I was more afraid she would become so important to Damien that my relationship with him would fall completely by the wayside. And while there have been changes and I spend less one-on-one time with Damien, I have to admit he juggles us well. We are both important to him and he wishes to please us both, to keep us both happy.

Still, you are verbally abusive to the woman he loves, Adam noted.

Not as much as before, she tried to excuse herself. *Time has begun to mellow me toward her.*

Adam laughed. *I wonder if she would agree with that assessment.*

He felt the sheepishness that skimmed her thoughts. He realized then how much he had underestimated her. He comprehended how little he truly knew about her depths, her passions, and her flaws. But this connection between them was closing the gap rapidly, filling his mind with her in extraordinarily full dimensions. And with each dimension she seemed to grow more beautiful. The wind whipping through her hair, twisting it to and fro, made her look like a storming goddess, a powerful woman in charge of all the elements around her. In a way it was an amusing comparison since he was the only one in control of any elements. Yet cold hard facts had no place in his vision of her, although he had never seen her more clearly. Had never seen anyone so clearly.

"Easy there, Romeo. Don't get carried away on a wave of romantic drivel," she shouted to him.

That made him laugh. Perhaps he was romanticizing to some degree. It seemed he couldn't help himself. Normally he was a creature who worked in logic and stone-cold truths, who clearly saw the line of the law and would not allow himself to see shades of gray. The fact that he had stars in his eyes as he looked at her could be construed as very amusing. His brother would never let him live it down.

At least, the Jacob he knew would have had fun with it. But now his brother was a stranger to him. And he had yet another brother whom he had not even met. His life was in a state of turmoil . . . so how was it that he felt so calm and so incredibly centered?

Jasmine felt herself smiling as his thoughts ran almost musically through her head. As a telepath she

was very comfortable walking through the thoughts of
others, but her ability forced her to do the seeking. This
connection with Adam was proving to be like a light
that was left on all the time. It was a wonder Imprinted
mates didn't burn out after a while, what with trying to
manage and catalogue the thoughts of two beings at
once. But as Adam had noted, there was nothing in-
nately stressful about what they were experiencing. It
was just unusual. Alien. Yet quickly growing familiar.

She ought to have been more upset about this
whole thing, his invasion of her space and mind, the
severe alteration of her body and her soul.

She was not. She could not make herself be. Because it felt too much like coming to completion, becoming suddenly whole. Had someone asked her
yesterday if her life was complete, she would have absently said yes, disregarding all the empty places she
had covered up these past four hundred years, and
others that had existed even before she had ever encountered Adam. But for the first time . . .

For the first time.

For the first time her body was singing and her soul
was in chorus with it. The mixture of their thoughts
in her mind and the blood she had taken from him
swirled into the choir of it.

Good God, she was on the verge of skipping through
a field of daisies in a gauzy white dress with freaking
flowers in her hair.

She laughed with him at the imagery. He didn't
understand the reference completely, but he could
appreciate the absurdity of it nonetheless.

They both stopped laughing at the same moment, as
if it had been planned, when each felt the overwhelming sense of wrongness that echoed in Adam's blood.

All of the Enforcer instincts that had been muted for some reason until that moment came screaming to life. Suddenly every cell in his body went off as though each was an individually screaming klaxon. The Water Demon shot to the ground as quickly as he could, his form shifting from mist to flesh like the whipping back of a curtain to reveal a magic trick. There was, however, no grace to it and no showmanship intended. He was driven down to a single knee as he tried to brace himself against something that was happening from the inside out.

And because it was stripping through him, it was stripping through her. Though certainly not as powerfully. Her advantage was her extensive familiarity with her enemy.

She quickly stood before him, taking his face in her hands and leaning his forehead against her solar plexus. She comforted him by running her hands through his hair and gave him a moment to compose himself.

"She's very close. Within a mile," she told him. "What you are feeling is no doubt the effects of some kind of spell intended to put off the Enforcer, using his own power against him. It was perhaps meant for Jacob, in case he came hunting her."

"No doubt the components of it are attached to those things within us that make me and Jacob brothers as well as Enforcers," he said tightly. "I fought many a necromancer in my time. I am familiar with their tricks. Although I confess, this is something altogether different. A Demon casting spells. It is as unnatural as one can possibly conceive of."

"Yes. Very much so. As unnatural as Vampires killing in a feed or . . ."

"Drinking the blood of Nightwalkers," he finished for her when she trailed off. "But one taboo broken has led to nothing but pain and misery, while the other," he said, looking up into her eyes, "has led to us. There is no such thing as good magic. And all I see in this connection with you is goodness."

"I look forward to introducing you to Valera," Jasmine said with lips turned up in amusement. "She is a natural-born Witch staying in the Vampire court at the moment with her Shadowdweller mate, Sagan. She is living proof that a human with magical inclinations can use magic in a good way. Holistic magics. Defensive magics. Well-intentioned magics. We have begun to call it white magic or sometimes clean magic. It is quite something to see."

Adam sighed deeply, resting his head against her again for just a moment. Talking to her was easing the pain inside him, helping him get a handle on it, helping him to compartmentalize what was necessary to finish his hunt and what was not.

The world has changed so much, he thought wearily.

"Don't let it overwhelm you now. You've barely scratched the surface of the changes you will see, and you cannot let despair take you over. And for every bad taste, I promise you there is an equally good one waiting for the curious touch of your tongue."

Jasmine felt the mischievous quirk of the smile that touched his lips.

Her soothing hand in his hair quickly wrapped around a few locks and gave a hard tug.

"Ah! Vicious woman," he cried, grabbing hold of her wrist as he surged up to his full height. "Give me some time to learn to censor my thoughts better before you start to punish me for them! I am unused to every stray idea being monitored. It takes a large measure of control to filter what goes through my mind from coming past my lips."

"Oh, as a lifetime telepath, I am very aware of this," she assured him. "I did not punish you for the thought, merely for having it in a situation where I could do nothing to take you up on it. I rather hate being put in the position of having to be responsible."

"That is a merry lie," he accused her. "Everything you do reeks of responsibility."

She visibly winced.

"Ouch. You really know how to hurt a girl."

"Confess," he urged her. "I know you must see it as clearly as I do. You are the right hand of a powerful monarch. You are in charge of a multitude of subordinates who are not always used to being subordinate to others, never mind a Nightwalker of a different breed, and you dance attendance on the leaders of other nations. You might wish others to see you as being a long-legged sack of trouble, but I think you are failing miserably."

"Mmm, well . . ." She tilted her head back so she could look up into his eyes, their stunning green so incredibly pretty in the face of someone so incredibly male. "I bet no one else would ever dare say that to my face. That has to count for something. And the only reason you are getting away with it is because . . . I'm in a mellow mood."

"Admit it, you rather like me," he needled her, cupping her jaw and tilting her face to his dropping lips.

"You're not bad, as far as obnoxious, arrogant asses go," she relented with a smirk.

"Bah!" He pushed her face aside, not bothering to

hide the irrepressible grin she inspired. "Let us get this over with."

"Acting with haste as usual, Jasmine?"

Jasmine tilted her head to look at the Vampire intruding on her private exchange with Adam. She had sensed Damien's approach somewhere in the back of her mind, but had been more focused on Adam and his needs of the moment. She was not foolish enough to disregard Damien's value in the encounter to come. She wanted a successful vengeance, not a private one. That was why she had been so eager to have Adam by her side. However, Damien was a much cooler head and knew the enemy far better than Adam did. She had played on Adam's arrogance and confidence a little in order to recruit him to her way of thinking.

A trick I will not fall for twice, he thought admonishingly to her.

The grin she flashed at him was as unrepentant as the one she gave to Damien.

"That implies I had not put a great deal of thought into my actions. I assure you, Damien, I have done little else." She raised a brow when she saw Syreena at Damien's side as well as Valera the Witch and Sagan the former Shadowdweller penance priest. Sagan had given up his calling as one of the most powerful warrior priests to stand protectively at his mate's side. He was a fighter of incomparable skill, and at present armed with the notoriously vicious *khukuri* blade he wielded so proficiently.

"This is not a wise battle for a Shadowdweller," Jasmine noted. "The light that emanates from Ruth's magic will burn you to a crisp."

"I have a protective spell for that," Valera countered proudly, her hand drifting to rest on Sagan's powerful forearm. "It covers him in shadow, a personal bubble of darkness. Don't worry about us, Jasmine. It's Ruth you need to worry about. She's going to sense us here soon and we'll lose all advantage, if we haven't already. The spell affecting him"—she nodded to Adam—"probably has an alarm tethered to it."

Valera stepped up to Adam and reached out a hand to touch him. To her surprise, Jasmine suddenly hissed at her and body-blocked her. The women looked at each other, and it was hard to tell who was more surprised.

"I was only going to ease the pain he's feeling," Valera reassured the possessive Vampire.

"So it is true," Damien noted with a grave measure of surprise as he stared at Jasmine and Adam. "He is your mate."

Damien sounded as flabbergasted as Jasmine was feeling.

"Some joke, right?" she remarked in return. "But not what's important at present," she brushed on. Neither was her curiosity over how he'd come to be there. No doubt he had intercepted their trail at some point, and Damien's familiarity with her scent had allowed him to track her twice as fast as she had been tracking Ruth.

"Dawn comes. The fighting force will be devastated by its arrival," Adam noted. "Is an hour enough to do this thing?"

"We will make it enough," Sagan said grimly. "Damien says this is our last chance to bring her to heel. Let us go."

It was true. It was time. All the other hashing of questions and details could wait until it was over.

Chapter 10

Windsong had slowly been coming conscious over the last half hour. Conscious, aware, and yet unable to move because she was tightly trussed to a hard, flat surface. A table about three feet up from the floor. When she looked to the left she could see a bed with a Vampire in it.

A dead Vampire.

She could tell he was dead because death held him in the shocked, gripping position he had no doubt died in, and she knew he was a Vampire because that position included a gape-jawed extension of his fangs. It was hard to tell if the smell of him was decomposition or the same malodorous stuff that sloughed off the other occupant in the room.

Ruth.

Infamous Ruth. Evil-to-the-core Ruth. And now Windsong was her prisoner, for whatever reason. Windsong had realized she had the dubious luck of being held captive by a gloater and a sadist. Whatever Ruth's motives, Windsong had no doubt she would reveal them soon enough.

"How good to see you awake," Ruth greeted her as she worked busily at a mortar and pestle. "Do not bother trying to speak. You are gagged for the time being. But do not fret. We will want your voice soon enough." Then she shouted toward her workroom door. "Girl! Get in here!" To herself she muttered, "What is her name? I can never seem to remember it."

The door opened and in walked the girl who had tranquilized Windsong.

"Yes?" She bowed her head respectfully as she shut the door.

"Help me with these last components," Ruth ordered her. "Grind them together."

"Of course." The girl hid behind the loosened fall of her hair. She looked as though she'd been in a fight and had hastily put herself back together. She had a wicked-looking cut down her face from the corner of one of those disturbing eyes of hers. She moved to the table, taking over the mortar and pestle for her mistress, but sparing a glance at the tied-down Mistral. "I'm sorry we couldn't get the Druid for you," she said carefully.

"You were ambushed by a pack of Demons," Ruth said dismissively. "What were you going to do? You were fortunate to make it out alive. The others did not."

"I suppose."

Windsong was astounded. In spite of not having telepathy or any great special senses, Mistrals could sense quite easily when someone was lying to them. Windsong's senses told her that this girl was telling a massive lie to her mistress.

Strange. Ruth was a Mind Demon. Couldn't she read her subordinate's thoughts and discover the same thing? And surely the Demon girl knew a Mistral would catch her lying, so why bring up the topic at all in front of her? Windsong sensed it was not a detail she should dismiss, but neither should she think any more about it. Ruth most certainly could read *her* mind at whim while her voice was out of commission.

Luckily, Ruth was distracted by the obviously huge project she was embroiled in.

A spell, Windsong realized.

"Almost complete. The last and most powerful component comes during the casting," Ruth said, pausing to look at Windsong and smile. "The death screams of a powerful Mistral. The older and more powerful the Mistral, the more powerful the spell. So you can see why I needed you. Nothing but the best for Noah's Queen."

"What does this spell do again, exactly?" the assistant asked.

"It is simple," Ruth said impatiently, clearly having explained it before. "It will carry her screams to the center of Kestra's mind. Softly at first. But then the sound will grow until it is loud and incessant. Kestra will go quite insane from it. I imagine she will break at some point and take her own life. Noah will follow quickly after, if he does not also go mad, since their precious little Imprinting makes them share thoughts."

Ruth was so delighted by the idea she danced a little bit on the tips of her toes. Her airy dress floated around her as she moved, looking something like a demented ballerina. But she quickly recovered her decorum, running her hands back over her smooth blond hair and smiling like the cat that had swallowed the canary.

"Vengeance is so beautiful. Is it not, dearest? And

once this is done, I can fully focus on your resurrection. Even now our children are researching the Egyptian—"

She broke off awkwardly, her head jerking and tilting as if someone had smacked her in the back of her head.

"No! Damn you, not now!" Ruth growled out a curse angrily, picked something up and threw it against a wall, the clay container shattering into dust from the power of her anger and strength. She stormed over to a table and began searching frantically for something; then with a shout of triumph she found it, thrusting the bejeweled dagger into the air. "Ha! Very well then, come if you must. I will make you choke on the very dagger you used to kill my mate. You!" She turned to her assistant. "What is your name? Damn it. I have no time for such trivialities! You come with me."

The female with the black and gray hair laid down her pestle and closed her eyes a fraction of a moment, taking a breath as her hands curled into fists.

"Yes, Ruth. I very much wish to be by your side in this battle."

And that, Windsong could see, was the complete truth.

Ruth appeared in the thick of the woods with a tide of Vampires and Demons at her back. It was a small contingent, but in it was packed a great deal of power. More than enough, she thought, to overwhelm the Enforcer.

He was there, leaning back against a tree, sword in hand, the tip of which he was tapping against the heel of his shoe. He looked bored, impatient, as if he had been waiting a long time for her to get there.

"Waiting for me, Enforcer?" she asked him archly.

"All of my life," he said, straightening from the tree to make her a flourishing bow. "Many have told me you are the consummate enemy. That I would die, should I be foolish enough to take you on by myself."

"Mmm, and yet here you are. Did you not believe them?"

"If I did not believe them, I would not have come."

"So you have a death wish," she observed.

He laughed at that. At her. It made her prickle from head to toe with fury.

"Your logic is flawed, you traitorous bitch. Your assumption is that I am foolish. Foolish enough to come alone."

Jasmine stepped out from behind the tree.

"But you are not foolish," she observed with a *tsk*.

"Not at all," he agreed.

Ruth felt a flash of irritation at herself. She had not taken the precaution of scanning for other minds. She did so then and felt only Adam's strong thoughts. But it was like hearing an echo. She heard them twice over. It was an effect she was used to when she confronted Imprinted couples. But this was a Demon and a Vampire. A Vampire whose thoughts she had once mined quite easily. But Jasmine had grown quite a bit stronger since their last encounter. She could barely make out her presence. The Enforcer was schooling his thoughts very well. Impressively well. But that was a skill even his brother had shown. It seemed to be something innate in their hunting strength.

"So how do you find the future, Enforcer?" she baited him, knowing it would be a point of disturbance for him. No one could leap through centuries and adapt perfectly in a matter of hours.

"I find it very much the same. Demons in need of hunting and clearly in need of punishment."

"I dare you!" She laughed. "You are a fool after all!"

"Does your dead Vampire mate think so, too?" he asked.

Ruth's temper exploded, as did she. She leapt with her bare hands reaching for him, crooked into claws. She sent mental commands to her fighters, and they, too, moved forward. But in her rage and in her vain need for personal vengeance, she directed them toward the Vampire, keeping the Enforcer for herself. She couldn't care less about Jasmine, even though she did owe her a little payback as well. That could come later. Right now she wanted this archaic Enforcer. She knew he was a duck out of water, for all his bravado. He had never fought a full-strength Elder Mind Demon before. She and Lucas had not yet been fledged back then, and they had been the first of their kind. Elder Mind Demons, male or female, had not existed during his time, much less Elder Mind Demon necromancers.

She began to cast as she closed the distance between them.

Jasmine felt a beautiful sort of power come over her as she watched Ruth lose control of her temper and leap for her mate. She had shared with him that the traitoress's madness was her one true weakness. Ruth did not like to lose, but personal loss was an even sorer point for her. And her mad rages kept her from thinking clearly. Weakened her. Adam had played Ruth like a cheap instrument, his powerful calm and awesome mental self-control an impressive side of him Jasmine had not yet had the opportunity to see. All of her dealings with him had been so volatile, so influenced by the uncontrollable urges the Imprinting impressed upon him.

But now he was as placid as a pool. Even Ruth's attempts to toy with his insecurities about his future had failed. He had compartmentalized that far away from himself. And he had used thoughts of Jasmine to do it.

So long as I have you, my mate, I have found my place.

Jasmine moved away from Adam, leaping into the sky and forcing her enemy to follow. She felt so empowered by Adam's calm in the center of her mind and deep within her soul. It should have been disconcerting for her, but again it played like the most perfect music. She began to appreciate why the Imprinted couples she had become acquainted with were so very strong.

She landed a little distance away, ready to do some damage.

She faced a foursome, two Vampires and two Demons. One Demon was of the Wind, the other of the Earth. Easy enough to determine because each had shifted into his respective element in order to follow her, not realizing that was part of her strategy. They had given away crucial information about their abilities without even realizing it. It was an old trick she'd used often whenever she'd been forced into a head-to-head during the Vampire/Demon wars.

"Suckers," she said, smirking before launching her attack.

Adam didn't blink when Ruth lunged for him; he didn't so much as twitch when his own dagger appeared in her hand the second before she made contact with him.

As he brought up his sword to bring her wild stab at his heart to a metal-clashing halt, it was almost absently and automatically done. He had been told she'd been one of the finest Demon warriors at one time, trained by Elijah himself. He gave that history the respect it was due, the attention it was due, but there was a part of his brain calculating the four-to-one odds Jasmine was facing and not liking them very much at all. But he reminded himself he had to have faith that he wasn't the only significant warrior on the field. A distraction, however small it might be, would be just what Ruth needed to earn an advantage.

So with his full attention on the Demon traitor, he grabbed the dagger by its tail, forcing the blade upward and rotating it against the fixed point in Ruth's wrist. She had to either let go or her wrist would snap. Let go she did, and with a practiced move, the weighted hilt jumped into his palm and he stabbed it hard and true into the juncture of her neck and shoulder.

But instead of sinking into her flesh, the metal was deflected off her skin just as it would have had she worn the heavy metal armor breastplates of his time. And it was deflected even though the maneuver he had made was designed to get through the weak spots of such armor.

"Did you really think it was going to be that easy?" she hissed in his face.

Then she clapped her hands together, speaking a Word. The thunderous force of it sent him exploding backward, slamming him into the tree behind him. The impact knocked all the breath out of him, sent pain bursting through his entire body. But when he dropped down, he landed hard on his feet, shook the pain off, and glared at his adversary.

"I would have wept if it were," he told her, forcing the words to come steadily despite the good bruising his lungs had just taken. It was worth it. The steel of his voice and the way he shook off her attack seemed to give her an instant's pause. But he wouldn't give her that instant. It was time she would use to think, to center herself, to let logic come in where anger might be instead. "Your lover was enough of a disappoint-ment for one night."

Ruth screamed at him. Rage at its purest.

She tried to funnel that rage into her next feat of magic, flinging a torrential spell at him, only to real-ize he was no longer there. Adam deconstructed him-self into mist, rolling low past her feet and coming up behind her. He ringed an arm around her neck, the powerful muscles yanking her back off her feet and into his body. He did not have mercy because she was a woman. He had never had a problem discarding the polite gentleman in himself when in battle. There was a time for everything, and politeness had little place in battle of any kind, whether with male or female ad-versaries. After spending time in his mate's memories of this creature, he could think of no one less deserv-ing of niceties.

"Evil. Through and through," he ground out in her ear as he cut off her oxygen and her voice. "Worthy of nothing but destruction. And yet, it is too slight a punishment for the likes of you."

But before he could jerk his arm aside and break her neck, she suddenly wasn't there.

Impressive, he thought as he quickly turned around.

She could keep her cool enough to teleport even when unable to breathe. Most would simply panic.

She was notorious for teleporting behind her victim and backstabbing them. Too notorious. It was the first thing he had been warned about. So as Ruth materialized behind him, she found herself face-to-face with Adam. She spoke a brief spell and a cloud of black arrowed into her hand, resolving itself into a double-pointed weapon, foot-long spearing tips sprouting out of a center handle. The handle, made of some kind of wood, protected the wielder from the shafts of iron.

Iron. The one element of the earth that could hurt or kill a Demon.

She wasted no time before trying to imbed the vicious metal in his flesh. Not expecting to fight a Demon wielding what amounted to poison for both of them, Adam stumbled back.

"The time of the law-abiding, simpering, weak Demon is over," Ruth hissed at him as she thrust again with impressive strength, forcing him to swing his sword up to block her, and locking them together too close for his liking. He countered with his dagger, and again it deflected off her as though she were completely wrapped in protective armor.

Sweet Destiny, how was he going to get to the bitch if he couldn't make a killing blow?

He was going to have to resort to hand-to-hand. But she could teleport away so easily. It was like fighting an opponent covered in animal fat. As soon as he got a grip on her, she'd slip away.

Adam realized the truth of the matter.

There was no way he could kill her on his own.

Luckily, he wasn't on his own.

Adam went to disarm her of her latest weapon, wanting to take it out of play, even though it was very likely she could just conjure another. However, magic took energy and power to perform. He had no doubt that she was very powerful and had a great store of energy, but she couldn't keep up her tricks forever. She would eventually wear down. He made the unexpected move of grabbing the thing by one of its necks with the haft of his dagger and his bare hand, ignoring the vicious burn in his palm as he came into contact with the poisonous metal. He yanked at the thing with all his significant strength, while at the same time flipping his sword so the blade faced her gripping hand. He sent the honed edge toward her hand, hoping her fingers weren't as protected as her body seemed to be, loving the idea of removing a few of her digits.

Unfortunately, the moment the idea entered his mind; she was able to anticipate him. She let go, teleporting again, allowing him to throw away the iron weapon but giving him no satisfaction or opportunity to wound her.

He stepped around again, watching his back. He glanced upward when a black raven squalled in the trees, flapping its large wings. And just like that Ruth reappeared. With her very next breath she cast again, throwing her hands forward.

She wasn't taking any chances by getting too close to him anymore, acknowledging that he was the stronger Demon and perhaps even a cleverer fighter than she was when it came to hand-to-hand and close-in fighting.

As she threw her hands forward, a collection of iron nails appeared in motion, as if they had been shot out of a cannon toward him. He barely had enough time to alter form, shifting to water and falling to the ground in a rushing puddle.

As he reformed into flesh on his knees he felt fire and agony in his arm and upper chest. He'd been hit by a couple of those projectiles, and though the iron itself now lay harmlessly on the ground, the wounds the nails had caused burned with the shavings of metal left behind.

There was nothing he could do about that. And nothing he could do about the free-flowing blood that began to saturate his shirt.

"Damn," he said, giving the torn fabric a little tug. "I rather liked this thing." He looked at Ruth and gave her a smile that had no humor in it. "Send more iron," he beckoned her. "Prove to me how truly corrupted you are. It only makes me want to put you down all the harder. And I will find the way, I promise you."

"Find your way around this, Water Demon."

This time she conjured fire, as though she were Noah himself, a great ball of it forming between her hands before she threw it at him with all the strength of the magic in her body.

The ball exploded against the tree behind where Adam had been. As he reformed a few feet away, he laughed at her.

"Please," he taunted her. "I grew up with the Demon King as a playmate, and he wielded Fire a thousand times better than that. You are going to have to do much better."

"Very well then, I will!"

She began to speak a spell. And as she did, the black raven speared down out of the tree and tackled the blond Demon to the ground as it changed on the fly into the massive physical form of the Vampire Prince.

* * *

Jasmine smiled as she faced off against her enemies.

"Looks like we're having Vampire for dinner," one of the Vamps remarked blithely.

Jasmine snorted out a laugh.

"I'm going to string your fangs on a chain and wear them for jewelry," she promised him.

"We're not afraid of you," another said.

"You should be," she countered before leaping toward them.

She crashed into the first one so hard that the sound of their skeletons smacking together echoed into the woods. She sent him sprawling into the bracken, the leaves alleviating friction in such a way that he slid a good distance before stopping. Dazed, he shook his head, trying to resuscitate his brainpan.

Meanwhile, Jasmine turned to face her three remaining adversaries, smiling at them through the blood dripping down her face from the gash in her forehead. Then she held up her hand, showing them something long and white, covered with blood.

The Vampire on the ground began to scream as Jasmine proudly displayed his fang to the others.

"Next?" she invited.

The remaining Vampire suddenly didn't look too sure of himself. The Demons, however, were not as intimidated. After all, they had no fangs to lose. Plus, they had magic on their side. They considered that a great advantage. To prove it, they began to cast. The ground beneath Jasmine's feet turned to quicksand. But she was faster and she levitated several inches above the affected area. Jasmine didn't take any time to be astounded by the sight of other Vampires and Demons working magic in service to Ruth. Frankly, when it came to that demented Demon, nothing surprised her any longer. But she did recognize that had it truly been only herself and Adam confronting this small but powerful army, there was little chance they would have come out the victors.

However . . .

While her enemies were focused on her, a creature blending perfectly with the shadows behind them grabbed one by the scruff of the neck, leaving the throat open to the quick, deadly slash of a *khukuri* blade. One Demon crumpled to the ground before the second even had time to register the Shadowdweller's presence.

Sagan's attack was enough to startle the Demon necromancer, throwing off his focus and concentration, destroying his spell. He was too young and too unskilled in his new craft to recover immediately. It opened his mind and nerves to the scream of the falcon that swooped in from above him. That scream had the power to strike fear in the hearts of those who heard it. By the time the falcon landed in the running form of Damien's wife and Jasmine's frequent adversary in life, Jasmine had taken advantage of the opening Syreena had created for her and leapt on the Demon's shoulders, using the powerful strength of her legs around his neck to snap it in two. Perhaps even three, given the violence she used to wrench it around nearly 180 degrees.

Jasmine landed on her feet and found herself facing Syreena. She met the Lycanthrope's charcoal and wild-colored streaked eyes. She smoothed back her hair with one hand and shrugged her opposite shoulder.

"Thanks," she said.

She didn't have time to appreciate the expression of surprise Syreena gave her. Although in the back of her mind she acknowledged exactly why Syreena would find even the smallest of common courtesies from her surprising. She had probably never given her one before. Certainly not with any sincerity.

Perhaps that had been wrong of her.

Perhaps not.

Jasmine didn't have time for much in the way of soul-searching. When she had taken flight early on, she had separated the forces Ruth had sent against her. Now the rest of them had caught up to her, Syreena, and the remaining enemy Vampire, who had slunk aside and tried to move away unnoticed. Somewhere in the shadows was Sagan. He would not move forward until needed.

Jasmine didn't care what Valera said about magic users being redeemable, about addictions and withdrawal and all of that touchy-feely nonsense. The equation was simple for her. If they threatened her life, she would respond in kind. They had made a free choice to immerse themselves in this wickedness long before it had tainted them with addiction. As far as Jasmine was concerned, that act of free will made them fully responsible and fully deserving of the death she would deliver.

She turned to face the newcomers, Syreena stepping up to her side.

"I'll take the two on the left, you take the two on the right?"

"Yeah, right." Jasmine laughed. "Give me a sec and I'll be able to help you with your two."

Together the women launched themselves forward.

Ruth mentally and magically regrouped.

She had been blindsided by Damien's sudden appearance and attack. But she had been a warrior serving under the Demon Elijah for over two centuries, battling her way through Vampires and Lycanthropes when the Demons had warred with each in turn. She had learned to shake things off quickly. She teleported out of Damien's reach, out of all their reach, and took a breath to scan the scope of the battlefield in front of her. It was clear Adam had not come alone. He and Jasmine had somehow snuck others in under her guard. How? Had she not scanned mentally for others? She was the most powerful Mind Demon alive. No one could shield their thoughts from her. Yet now Jasmine had somehow managed to do so, and these others as well? Damien she could understand. He was an ancient Vampire, his mental powers certainly above all others. But his Lycanthrope trollop? She was as weak as they came. Her only claim to power was her ability to shift into two forms. Ruth had once kidnapped her and tortured her with ridiculous ease, and she would have killed her, too, had Damien not interfered. However, that, too, had played in her favor. Damien's rescuing Syreena had set off a chain of events allowing Ruth to find Nicodemous and an alliance that had doubled her power.

If only she had had time to resurrect him!

Just the same, she had confidence that she was powerful enough to take on an entire army of Vampires and Demons. There was nothing any of them had that she had not seen before and had not learned how to defeat.

It was time to stop toying with them and get to the serious business of eradicating the pests once and for all.

The locking spell . . .

Ruth was a master of thoughts and the Mind. Enough to recognize when a thought was not her own. Most female Mind Demons were only empaths, unable to read the thoughts of others, but she had grown beyond that limitation and, she believed, in the short time since then had learned how to surpass even her male counterparts who were proficient telepaths.

The thought felt strange, but she had been inside the mind before. Enough to recognize it. She glanced to the right and saw her latest protégée, the black-and-gray-haired girl whose name she could never remember. She met her eyes and spoke the thought again in her mind.

The locking spell.

So simple. So perfect! However, it took some time to lay the groundwork for the spell, and she was in the thick of battle.

Begin the spell. I will take over once you near completion.

The girl nodded assent and began to cast, blue light swirling from her hands, wrapping around her, spreading over the ground in a small circle until she was completely enveloped in a cylinder of blue electricity.

Ruth focused on her enemies with more aggressive spells. Quicker spells. The power snapped out of her like lightning, feeding her even as it drained her. Savage bolts leapt from Ruth's hands, striking the

Vampire Prince and the Enforcer. There was nothing either of them could do to escape the attack. It would ravage the Enforcer no matter what form he shifted into; and no matter how strong and ancient he was, no matter what animal he was now able to shift into thanks to feeding off his Lycanthrope bride, the Vampire would be equally unable to avoid her attack.

Both men were struck, flung back like a couple of boneless dolls being tossed from the jaws of a playful dog. Then the maw of that dog caught them up again, power compressing them with an unbearable strength. A strength they could not escape. Had she been fresh into the spell, she would not have needed the locking spell. She would simply crush them until they popped like overcooked peas under a treading foot.

But she was tiring, and the spell took a great deal of raw personal power. Power she had initially wasted while Adam toyed with her. She realized now that had been his plan all along. To trick her into tiring herself out by dangling himself before her like bait while the Prince held himself in reserve.

Tricky, tricky. She might almost be impressed, if not for the fact that she knew she was about to strike them a lethal blow.

She had to disengage when she felt the locking spell had reached critical mass. She reached to take the spell over, creating the receptacle. She shaped a crystal ball into her hands, the clear glass of it the purest thing anyone would ever see. She magically lowered it to the ground and opened it up. Light from it sparkled in an upward cone, and she carefully moved away from it.

Now the trap was ready.

She teleported away, appearing at Adam's back.

The Water Demon was on his knees, gasping for breath as he tried to recover from her previous attack. She leaned forward and whispered.

"You are going to wish you'd never met the future," she promised him.

And with a lightning-quick movement she hurled an explosive force against him, sending him flying toward the cone of light. He was headed into it, nothing to stop him.

Yet suddenly he sprang to a stop, as if an invisible safety net had caught his big body. When he touched the net it sparkled into existence, blue light etching the shape of it, sending him rolling safely to the ground.

Infuriated and shocked, Ruth twisted to and fro, searching for the necromancer who had turned against her, the necromancer who dared to cast magic counter to her own.

She saw her then, a curvy little redhead kneeling behind a tree, her hand extended toward Adam, her fingers curling to withdraw the energy so it wouldn't be wasted once she was certain Adam was safe. Then the woman looked Ruth dead in her eyes, and Ruth could see the fear inside her. She was strong, Ruth sensed. A natural-born Witch. A being who, unlike Ruth, had to speak spells aloud or in her head, could call magic from herself and from all around herself as naturally as she could draw breath. She had been born to make magic.

Yet Ruth saw into her mind and saw she was afraid of her own gifts. She saw the woman was limited by her fears and limited by her conscience. She would only use defensive magics. She would only use magic to protect herself and others.

Ruth laughed at her.

"You idiot! You think what you do is good magic? Clean magic? It is the same as mine. You are as deep into it as I am, and going deeper with every spell!"

"You're wrong," the redhead said, her lip moving nervously between her teeth. She glanced around, looking for someone. Someone who could comfort or support her. But there was no one.

She would be so easy to destroy. Ruth could easily jump into her mind and twist that fear into something the little Witch would never be able to escape.

The portal . . .

Again, a thought not her own, but a gentle reminder that the locking spell was drawing on her energy every moment the portal stayed open. It drew her attention away from Valera and brought her back to Damien and Adam, whom she deemed the bigger threats. She had to get rid of them, just in case her companions were not able to manage Jasmine and Syreena. She was strong, and her protégé was proving to be a huge asset, but they would not have much success if they were so thoroughly outnumbered. And who was to say what other Demons or Nightwalkers were waiting in the wings? Ruth couldn't take any more chances. It was unwise to do head-to-head battle with these brethren. She had always understood that. It would benefit her far more to escape for the moment and get back to her workroom, where the key component of her most powerfully destructive spell ever lay trussed to her workbench.

She would have far more victory over the Demons by destroying Kestra and Noah than she ever would fighting them like this. So Ruth cast a snare, snatching Damien up into it, pausing only a moment to enjoy the fruitlessness of his struggles against the power that held him. There were no hands to hit, arms to break—no weaknesses to exploit so he could free himself. All his ancient power was for naught as she pushed him toward the portal.

That was when a vine burst out of the ground and lashed itself around her calf. The living thing, made strong by magic, yanked at Ruth, pulling her off her feet and slamming her hard to the ground. Once her concentration was broken, Damien was freed. He hit the ground hard, rolling and attempting to get to his feet, but she had abused him greatly and there was no quick recovery from that. She took satisfaction in his pain even as she threw her attention back to the little Witch cowering behind the tree.

"This?" Ruth laughed with contempt. "I am the master of this spell!"

Jasmine and Syreena each recovered from her final opponent simultaneously, throwing back their heads and their hair to take stock of what was happening around them. Their eyes met and each woman had a heartbeat of time to appreciate the deadly skills of the other. Syreena's ability to shift form on the fly had always been her greatest strength, and she had also spent her entire lifetime training in the fighting techniques of the Monks of the Pride. Ancient and powerful, she had been blessed with their knowledge and had always been their best student. And even though she had outgrown that part of her life long ago, the skills would always be at her fingertips whenever she needed them.

Jasmine acknowledged Syreena's strength for the first time. She appreciated it for what it was. Suddenly she felt like she was seeing a completely different

Syreena than the one she had known for the past two years. She didn't fully understand why, in this moment of all moments, it was happening. They had fought together before. Jasmine had seen her move and fight and draw on the most incredible ingenuity.

She had simply never felt true appreciation for it before.

There was no time to dwell on it at present either. Simultaneously the two women recalled the Vampire who had been sitting by the wayside, watching to see how the battle turned. He and the Vampire Jasmine had originally attacked were the only ones not dead. There was no sense in leaving them at their backs, a potential threat that could attack later while they were fighting Ruth. Though both women were itching to get a piece of that deceptive traitor, each for her own reasons of vengeance, they had to finish their part of the battle first.

They couldn't see either Vampire, though.

But suddenly the shadows resolved into the shape of a man. Sagan and his bloodied *khurkhuri* blade stood strong in the nearly full moonlight. He tossed something in Jasmine's direction, and her preternatural instincts and reflexes allowed her to snatch it out of the air.

She opened her palm to see the long white match to the fang she had in her pocket.

"I thought maybe a nice pair of earrings," Sagan offered.

Jasmine laughed.

"Perfect. Did you get both Vampires?"

He nodded. A simple gesture, but one that spoke of the fabulous strength and skill of a Shadowdweller penance priest. He might have resigned from his position, but he could never resign from his skills.

Then suddenly, he gave a jerk, as if someone had stabbed him through the head. The expression that moved across his face was a combination of fear and fury the likes of which Jasmine had never seen before.

"Valera needs me. The battle does not go well."

He took off at a run, leaping through the forest, dodging trees and low scrub that seemed placed in his way just to slow him down. Nothing could keep him from the side of his mate when she needed him. Nothing but . . .

Light.

Sagan jolted to a stop, dodging behind a tree to protect himself from the blue light bursting in all directions on the battlefield. Even so, he was scorched all over his exposed skin. Somehow, Valera's protective spell had worn off. Probably because of her broken concentration. Now, as long as light stood between him and Valera, there was nothing he could do to help her. And in his mind he felt her desperation and insecurity. She had come to this battle knowing she had never hurt or killed anything in her life, that it was because the core of her soul was so opposed to the idea of harming another that she was able to break free of her black magic addiction in the first place. Without that powerful core belief, she wouldn't be who she was.

And yet she had insisted on coming. She had known that the best way to gain advantage in a battle of magic was to use magic in return. She knew she could help protect the others. She had developed an affection for Damien and Syreena during her time in their court.

Indeed, she felt strongly for all the Nightwalkers she had met. She couldn't find it in herself to sit idly by while they fought their worst enemy and battled for their futures.

This was why he loved her.

This was why it was killing him that he couldn't get to her. He could fade into Shadowscape, the parallel dimension that the Shadowdwellers often traveled in. It was identical to this plane, except there were no people and there was no light. He could cross the field and come out of Fade right by her side.

But still the light would be there and she wasn't in a position to recast her protection spell on him. Now that Ruth had engaged her, Valera wouldn't have the focus to cast the spell. Sagan wondered what had happened. She was supposed to have kept low and quiet until she was needed most. How had she exposed herself?

Now as he watched her coming out of her crouch, his eyes burned as blue energy was expelled from her graceful fingers and she faced off against a necromancer who was ten times superior to her in skill and power.

"Well, she's going to get herself killed," Jasmine noted, making him realize Jasmine and Syreena had followed him and were now watching the same scene he was.

"I cannot protect her," he said with frustration. "You must help her."

"If you insist," Jasmine said, giving him a cheeky grin.

Ruth was dragged across the ground several feet by the fingers of animated vines before she teleported out of their grasp. She reappeared only a few yards in front of the upstart Witch who thought she could go head-to-head with her. However, before she dealt with her, she threw instructions at her protégée.

"Get one of them in the lock," she commanded. "I do not care which! Whichever you think you can manage."

"Oh, I think I can manage one," the black-and-gray-haired girl said.

Ruth smiled and turned to face the Witch, letting magical blue power pulse from her hands like someone firing a warning shot. The energy burst above Valera's head, the sound and force of it making her flinch hard.

"Oops. I missed." Ruth tsked. "I promise, it will not happen again. You might consider giving in to that wild urge to run that is going through your mind right now."

"Or she can stay and watch me kick your ass."

Jasmine grabbed Ruth by her hair with both hands and yanked her back off her feet.

"Concentrate now, bitch," Jasmine spat as she dragged Ruth over the bracken by her hair. Jasmine heard Syreena whoop out a cheer. Of course, the Lycanthrope had cause to cheer this tactic. Ruth had once ripped out half of Syreena's hair, and left her maimed because of it. Lycanthrope hair being what it was, alive with nerves and blood supply, it had been a devastating blow.

So Jasmine took pleasure dragging Ruth to heel. Whether she liked Syreena or not, no one deserved to suffer like that. Just as those innocent people in the hidden Nightwalker library had not deserved to die simply because Ruth had wanted to pillage it for spell books.

Jasmine built up momentum, swinging Ruth over

the ground by her hair and slamming her into a tree. She didn't want the Mind Demon to adapt and recoup, to gather her thoughts and teleport out of her hands. So she beat her against the tree like a dirty rug that needed cleaning. She was about to swing her into it a third time when suddenly a black-and-gray-haired Demon girl appeared at her side, having stepped up so quietly Jasmine didn't notice her until she was practically on top of her.

She could smell the vile magic on her, pegged her instantly for an enemy, and coiled to protect herself or attack as necessary.

"The portal," the girl said quietly. "Throw her into it. Quickly, before she recovers."

She pointed to the conical display of light coming from a crystal ball sitting in among the brown leaves waiting for winter to hurry their decay. Jasmine hesitated, not trusting the girl.

Do it.

Adam's voice in her head rang sweet and clear, sharing a confidence and strength she found to be beautiful and empowering in that moment. Hesitation disappeared and she lurched toward the cone of light, dragging her captive roughly behind her. She only needed to take a few steps to build up enough momentum.

She flung Ruth into the light like a shot-putter, hauling her off the ground and into the air by her grip on the bitch's hair. The traitor Demon flew into the light screaming with fury, trying to come up with threats and curses but too overwhelmed by the understanding that everything she was, everything she had striven for, was about to come to an end.

She hit the light and magic burst up around her,

magic powered by her very own energy and strength, and it welcomed its creator with powerful, grasping arms. Ruth was swallowed up in a rush of blue energy, then, her screams still audible, was dragged violently down into the crystal ball.

There was a final flash of electric blue light and then, suddenly, everything fell dark and silent. The only light remaining was the glow of the moon in the sky and the barely perceptible glow of the crystal ball sitting in the leaves.

Jasmine walked up to the ball and nudged it with her toe. The light within swirled for a moment, the smooth crystal inside gleaming and showing the face of a familiar blond Demon, her expression contorted into rage.

Impotent rage.

"Can she get out of there?" Jasmine queried.

"No. Not unless someone casts a very powerful counterspell to free her," the dark-haired Demon said. "The only person powerful enough to do so at the moment is now inside the lock. But you ought to destroy it. Crush it to dust. Then you will be assured no one can free her."

Jasmine picked up the ball, turned it in her hands a couple of times so she could catch glimpses of Ruth's infuriated face, and smiled.

"You know, I think I'll keep it. It'll look rather nice on my vanity," she said.

The Demon looked at her a long moment, her strange eyes shifting through grayscale as Jasmine watched.

Then she turned up her lips in a small but genuine smile. Somehow, Jasmine got the feeling that she didn't have much opportunity to smile. Impulsively, she went to search the stranger's thoughts, but found she was thoroughly blocked out. Was she a Mind Demon, then? If so, she had to be a very powerful one to resist a telepath of Jasmine's strength.

The rest of the fighters had slowly come toward the two of them, gathering around to look at the prison Ruth had made for herself. Then all attention turned to the Demon who reeked of magic and unclear motives.

She cleared her throat.

"About half a mile away you will find Ruth's lair. There are others there to be dealt with. In her workroom, though, you will find Windsong held prisoner. You should go quickly before the unsupervised Vampires there get it in their heads to feed from the most powerful Mistral of all time."

She then turned to Syreena, who was helping Damien keep his feet, letting the Vampire Prince lean his significant weight against her.

"In that workroom there is a charm kept inside a locked box. You will recognize it easily because the charm is wrapped up with your hair, Syreena. The hair that Ruth once ripped free of your head, she later used to keep you from getting pregnant. Since you do not plan to kill Ruth, you must burn the charm to ashes, and it will release the binding."

"Who are you?" Adam demanded, moving forward to get in her face. "Why should we trust anything about you when you stink of magic? You even helped Ruth cast that thing she was going to use to capture me and Damien!"

"But she did not capture you, did she? All I have done is help cast the trap that finally caught the Demon traitor Ruth. Think on that a moment."

She moved slightly, tipping her head back and

taking a deep breath. It was as if she were breathing in freedom.

"Ah . . . here it comes," she breathed.

She held out her hands and Jasmine could see the tips of her fingers fading away. For the first time, emotion broke through the girl's features. Tears filled her kaleidoscoping eyes.

"It means it's all changed," she breathed to Jasmine. "It means I did what I was supposed to do. I only pray this time things turn for the better." She looked at Jasmine with a momentary flash of worry. "It will be better now, won't it?"

The girl was fading quickly, but Jasmine felt her pain and thought she understood, at least in a small sense, what was happening.

"Yes," she assured her softly. "Trust us. We'll make it better for you."

The girl let out a stark sob of relief.

And then she was gone.

Chapter 11

"Who do you think she was?" Adam asked.

It was the question on everyone's mind as they sat in the main salon of Damien's citadel, an impromptu after-the-battle party. Apparently Valera was something of a cook, a skill that was rather wasted in a household of Vampires. She was tickled to have someone other than her mate to cook for. She served them dishes and cocktails, urging them to eat and replenish their strength.

Adam felt something brush against his legs as he stood in his usual stalwart manner. He looked down to see a fat cat winding around his ankles. *Since when do Vampires keep pets?* he wondered.

Since we decided to have the Witch as our guest, Jasmine provided for him. *She has three of them. And they communicate telepathically . . . when they feel like it.*

Truly? What exactly does a cat have to say?

Mostly, they like to explain how we are doing everything wrong, Jasmine thought with an internal chuckle.

"I think it is clear she was from the future," Damien said carefully.

"Do you think she was sent here by my . . . my niece? The same girl who brought me here? Can she send someone else through time without going, too?" Adam asked.

"Yes. That is how I obtained my bride." Noah spoke up from the doorway he had suddenly appeared in. He nodded his dark head to Damien, his gray and green eyes full of unspoken emotion. "Is it true? Is Ruth gone? For good?"

Jasmine reached for the ball that sat on the table in among the plates of food, looking very much like the perfect centerpiece. She hefted it for a moment, then tossed it to Noah. The Demon King caught the thing and turned it over in his hands slowly, watching as that hated face flashed briefly into view while Jasmine quickly recounted the story of Ruth's capture.

"Hmm. She looks pissed," he noted. Then he smiled. "Do we destroy the thing and her with it?"

"I was rather hoping to keep it as a souvenir," Jasmine said. "Or perhaps trophy is the better word."

Noah nodded and tossed it back to her.

"You captured her; it seems only right that you be her jailor."

Jasmine turned the ball around in her hand.

"That girl—whoever she was, she took small, precise steps, even went so far as to learn magic and poison herself with it, just so she could be there at that moment and influence events so this could happen."

"She came and warned us to back you up," Damien said.

"She also stepped in to rescue Corrine from attack," Noah injected. "Corrine described her guardian angel very clearly. Those shifting eyes . . . that black and gray hair."

"She was not like any Demon I've ever seen before," Jasmine said. "She had a strong mind, could resist telepathy . . ."

"She made a short teleport while rescuing Corrine, if you could call it a teleport. Corrine's description was quite . . . odd."

"If she came from far enough into the future, she could have been a new breed of Demon we don't yet know about," Syreena posited. "Or perhaps she was mutated somehow. Maybe by an Exchange?"

The room fell quiet and Adam, who had been distracted by the waves of his mate's hair and was presently toying with the fragrant curl of it, became aware of many eyes falling on him. He felt Jasmine stiffen under the attention, felt her bristle suddenly under the implied expectation in the thoughts of those around her.

Hush, little Vamp, he soothed her softly. *The only expectations that concern you are those of your Imprinted mate. And if you noticed, I have not made any demands of you.*

And why is that? she wanted to know, turning to look up into his eyes and dismissing the rest of the room. *You are pushy and possessive. Why would you not demand the Exchange of me? You would have me all to yourself then. I couldn't back off or walk away. We would be joined forever.*

Jasmine, have you not been paying attention? We are Imprinted. We already are joined forever. Nothing else we do can ever change that. Death is the only thing that can break this connection.

"But I'm a Vampire," she said softly, moving close enough to let their bodies touch. "What makes you so certain it will be the same for me as it is for a Demon?"

"Look at how you lean into me. How you touch me. Even when your mind runs with doubts and little resistances, you are still here. Still connected to me. Vampire or Demon, it does not matter, Jasmine. You are mine and I am yours. And nothing from the past or the future can ever erase that."

Jasmine broke away from him, stepped back, unable to help the urge to defy the connection, even as the greater part of her was delighting in the understanding that he was hers, that he had added more feeling and color to her life in a single day than she had known for centuries.

"Excuse me," she said brokenly as she stumbled away from the gathering, the crystal ball still in her hands.

Adam found her in her rooms only minutes later, and stood as unobtrusively as an Imprinted mate possibly could in her doorway as she leaned against her vanity, spinning the crystal ball like a top on its surface, over and over again.

"I'm going to make her so violently ill that she pukes up all over herself," Jasmine said with a bit of a pout to her soft lips.

"I wonder if she even feels the movement of her prison," he said.

"Don't spoil it for me," she insisted, giving the ball another spin. "Later, I plan to boil it in water. How about it, Ruth? Up for a long overdue disinfection?" Jasmine smiled a little at the idea. "I wish I could put it in an autoclave. Now, that would sterilize the bitch. Maybe see how it feels to have someone sterilize *you* for a change?" she shouted at the ball.

"I think Syreena will find it cathartic enough to burn the talisman."

"Well, maybe I don't. Maybe I think Ruth got off too easy."

"Perhaps. But what purpose will it serve to torment her now?"

"You mean besides making me happy?"

"Will it? Make you happy?"

She shrugged. "Maybe. Or maybe it will just satisfy me a little. Something." She sighed and finally looked up at him. "Everything is changed. All in a single day. I've caught my white whale. I'm permanently glued to you. Now Damien and Syreena are going to start making babies." She sighed. "It's all different and I feel out of place."

Adam laughed at that, shaking his big shaggy head, his fair green eyes alight with merriment. "I think I can safely say I know how you are feeling. Though I do not know what a white whale has to do with this, I can definitely empathize with your feelings of displacement."

Jasmine had to grin.

"I suppose everything is relative, is it not? There is no one here who has a better claim to feeling displaced than you do." She lifted her eyes, the malachite color of them unbelievably beautiful, so indicative of how enmeshed they were on a spiritual and physical level. Then her eyes suddenly widened and he felt the thought that streaked through her mind long before it ever reached her lips.

"I cannot answer that question," he said hastily. "But as I understand it, there has been one other unusual Imprinting that crossed unexpected breeds. When Demon and Druid mate, the Druid becomes physically dependent on the Demon mate, but when Demon and Demon Imprint, that is not the case. Tell me, what of Elijah and the Lycanthrope Queen? Is she symbiotically dependent on him? If Elijah is killed, will she die of energy starvation?"

"I don't know. I don't think they even know. But I think they both realize that neither of them would survive for very long without the other. And yet . . . I survived four centuries without you . . . even after you had already touched me."

"And you suffered for it the entire time," he said gravely. "You said so yourself. Not from lack of energy, but because I woke something inside you and did not fulfill the promise of it. Not until today."

"Today. And today is over. The sun is climbing outside of the citadel. I can feel it. Sleep pulls at me." She tilted her head. "You pull at me. In ways I'm afraid to be pulled. Your blood has been moving through my body like . . . like . . ." She didn't want to say "poison." She wouldn't insult him like that.

"Like laudanum," he supplied for her.

"But nothing so harsh or so dulling. Nothing so false. Instead it's awakening everything. Things I didn't realize were asleep inside me. I feel . . . stronger. That battle went far more easily for me than it should have. I am old and I am strong, never doubt that, but I had advantages I never had before. I could sense things. Anticipate things. I think . . . I think you gave me what it is inside you that makes you such a fine hunter. Makes you Enforcer."

"That has less to do with my blood, I think, and more to do with the way our minds are connected. I could feel your every moment, and instinct joined my thoughts to yours, urged you to act and react. Just as I felt the same from you." He moved into the room, coming up to her side and brushing gentle fingertips over the curve of her shoulder. Then he reached to touch the gash in her forehead that was already knitting and healing. "I am notorious for cracking my head into my enemy's to throw off his senses."

She laughed softly at that. She touched the spot as well, their fingers meshing gently. "I wondered where that came from. And to be honest, defanging a Vampire is akin to kicking a guy in the balls. Guys don't kick other guys in the balls and Vamps don't defang other Vamps."

"Ah well . . . perhaps that was a holdover from *my* Vampire fighting instincts."

"Famous for defanging Vampires, were you?"

"Actually, Jacob was the best at it. I will never admit it to him, but I honed the technique watching him."

"Jacob? Really?" She looked utterly stunned. "Mr. Do Good?"

"Well, you were asleep for the meat of the war, so you did not know his reputation as a Vampire hunter."

Adam raised a brow. "My brother is a man who does much good?"

"He's a stickler for the law. For peace. For doing the right thing at all costs. It's a wonder he ever crossed the line and took Bella to mate. They were the first, you know. They were everything the rules said shouldn't happen. But he did it. This Imprinting thing . . . it changes people, I guess."

Adam could feel her following thought. She didn't want to be changed so much and enmeshed so much in someone else that she lost herself. The way she felt Damien had done with Syreena.

"But now that I look at it," she said quietly, "the essence of who he is hasn't changed. He is still the strong, implacable ruler I have always known. And yet . . . he's also more. There's more depth to him. More contentment. More . . . color."

"Do you not want color?" he asked her, his thumb turning to drift against her cheek. Her skin was so smooth and his calluses so rough in contrast. He had a swordsman's hands and she had the skin of a lady.

"You know I do," she said.

Jasmine finally turned toward him, opening her body to his, opening herself to him in general. Not that she had much control over that. The pull of him was incredible. Her upper jaw actually ached with the craving to sink her teeth back into him. She wanted to taste that magnificent flavor again, to feel that extraordinary pleasure.

Her entire body went hot with the thought of his blood on her tongue.

"I will be happy to accommodate your cravings, little Vamp," he said breathlessly as her thoughts and feelings swirled inside his brain. "But I was hoping we might discover more traditional pleasures." Adam slid his fingers around the side of her neck, his thumb tipping her chin up so she was looking into his eyes. He paused a moment so he could casually trace his eyes over the beautiful curves and sweeps of her face, acknowledging just how quickly it had become familiar to him, essential to him. He watched how her lips curved in and out of a series of little smiles as she let him take his time studying her. "I like that," he told her softly, his breath brushing the crest of her forehead a moment before he brushed a gentle kiss to it.

"The way I smile?" she queried.

"The way you smile because you know just how

beautiful you are. You take pleasure in your power over my needs and senses. No doubt you are quite the accomplished flirt, enjoying the way you play men."

She made a noise. "Humans were too easy. I never even had to use my Vampire power to coax and capture their minds. Well, almost never. There were, I admit, one or two with surprising strength and clarity of mind. It was those who truly engaged me. I would never lower myself, of course."

"Of course," he agreed seriously, although humor still flooded his mind.

"However, the game was entertaining. Their minds were surprisingly complex. For humans. Of course, they were still men and, in the end, it would all dissolve into their demands for the sexual. Demands I would never give in to."

"And what of my demands, little Vamp?" Adam pushed back her hair near her neck on the right side and leaned in briefly to draw his lips and the warmth of his breath up along the length of it, from the crest of her shoulder to the point just below her ear. "What do you feel when I request things of you that you are not used to giving?"

Jasmine shivered, her hands coming out to grip at his clothing. The silk of his shirt made a crisp, crackling sound and she opened her eyes, recalling he had been injured and had bled heavily into the fabric. Even now there were wet edges around the hole the nail had struck through. Wounds of iron did not knit and heal well on a Demon without outside assistance. Objects of iron tended to rust, flaking off into the wound, where it continually poisoned and burned the Demon.

"You need a medic," she noted.

"You need to face my question, Jasmine. You need

to realize your thoughts skip away and you try to fly off whenever you feel the slightest bit uncomfortable with intimacy of any kind. But you do not have any escapes available to you any longer. I am in your mind, sweet Jasmine. My blood is in your body. I do not wish for you to feel trapped by this knowledge. I want you to embrace it. To luxuriate in it, like a creature that craves seductive pleasures ought to embrace it."

"But it comes with so much . . . baggage." She made a frustrated noise even as she tilted her head and allowed him to travel the length of her neck in the opposite direction. The neck of a Vampire was a major erogenous zone. Clearly he had figured this out. Was it previous knowledge that allowed him to exploit her weakness, or was it the unprotected access he had into her brain?

"No." He made a hard sound with his tongue and grasped hold of her chin, forcing her to meet his gaze. "This is not like the mental rape Ruth put you through, and I will not have you equate the two. This is something with pure intentions, open emotions, and a reciprocation that will never cause harm to either of us."

"How can you say that? You will forever be a weakness to me now. I will always be distracted by you in a fight—"

"And you will always be fortified by me in that same fight. You will worry about me, and I will worry about you, but that will trigger each of us to lend the other our best strengths and skills. Just as we did today. I was wrong when I assumed Jacob was weakened by his mate. When I thought he had failed his duty when it came to Ruth. She was an extraordinary enemy. Look how many of us it took to capture her at last." He reached out and pushed at the ball.

Jasmine stopped it just before it dropped off the edge of the vanity.

"I did not feel weakened by you today," Adam said softly to her. "I realized today that you multiplied all' my strengths. I could feel it like a fire in my soul. The only thing that burns more fiercely is the way I burn with need for you."

He could be gentle with her, understanding and thoughtful, pussyfooting around her insecurities until the cows came home, but his nature and hers called for a more direct approach. Adam placed a hand on her back and jerked her up against himself. It was instantly like connecting two strong magnets. The sound that escaped him was low and primal, coming from a place in himself he was only familiar with during the height of battle. But here it was, jumping between them, raw and fierce. And Jasmine echoed the sound, the ferocity of need it implied just as strong on her part as it was on his. Her hand curled into a fist, and it hit against his shoulder without real physical strength, but full of emotional protest. She hated that she couldn't control this thing inside her, that she was as weak to it as he was, as so many men in the past had been weak to her manipulations of their needs.

"Look for the strength in it," he said roughly to her. "See the strength in it."

He moved his mouth against hers, inhaling the breath she suddenly exhaled, taking immeasurable satisfaction that he had provoked her into breathing. He tightened his hold on her when he felt her bristle against his thoughts. She was the one who was supposed to be taking satisfaction in the things she provoked in others, not the other way around!

"Then do what you do best," he taunted her. "Make me weak to you. Show me your power."

It took a minute, but the rigidity of her body slowly eased, a softened curve in her spine causing her gorgeous body to cling to his in ways he hadn't thought possible. He knew then that he was going to suffer beautifully for the challenge he had thrown at her feet.

Jasmine tipped her head back, letting her hair slide down behind her shoulders, falling over the wrist and forearm that had caught her, letting the soft, smooth weight of it tickle the skin and hair on his arm. She exhaled that breath that so pleased him across the side of his face and beneath his hair, the sound of the most delicate pleasure teasing at his ear.

The motions were so simple and yet so complex all at once. It was pure artistry, perhaps because he felt it was less about challenging him and more about giving him pleasure as the impulses skipped through her thoughts. She might want to fool herself into thinking it was a battle of wits and will, but he knew it went much deeper than that.

She wanted this as much as he did. She had since the moment she had tasted his blood—since the moment she had met him, if she were clear and honest with herself. She had wanted to feel his embrace for four centuries, had felt its absence like she had never felt anything else. Jasmine had become an expert at repressing the need, at dismissing it from her daily world, drenching herself in the bitterness left behind and taking it out on every less-than-adequate male to cross her path since then.

But there was no longer any need for any of that.

Finally he was there and she was able to rewrite all that she had become. But Jasmine worried that it had been too long, too many years and too much pain and deprivation ever to make her right again. She feared she wouldn't have it in her to be worthy of this connection fate had dropped onto them.

In spite of all those doubts and fears, Jasmine let her hands move slowly up the massive strength of his arms, traveling onto his shoulders where they continued to his neck. Her fingers moved past his collar until the tips were toying with the prominent pulse in his throat. Touching that vital spot was like having someone lick her across her clit. It was stimulating beyond all reason, made her suddenly wet with craving and desire. There was no feeling like it in the world, and she had never experienced it before.

She couldn't resist pushing herself up onto her toes and touching her mouth to his pulse, her tongue coming out to lick flatly along its length. She could smell the heat of life and arousal on him all at once and it was a potent combination, the perfect Vampire aphrodisiac. She was a little dizzy with it, so she moved away briefly to bite his ear with the tips of her front teeth.

Her mouth ached where her fangs had made a demanding appearance. They knew what they wanted, whether she was sure or not. Instinct and need pressed onto her, making her hungry on physical and spiritual levels. Levels she had never experienced before. There was such depth to it, such stunning dimension.

But before she could move back to his throat, he brought his hand up to her mouth, covering it and pulling back so he could meet her eyes. The jade color had gone smoky with appetite, and he had never seen anything so erotic and compelling in his life. If he had not already been hard from the mere closeness of her body, he most certainly would have become so just looking into her eyes.

"You can feed all you like—after you feed me."

With that he grabbed the bottom of her shirt and in a single sweep of motion stripped it up over her head. He let it fall carelessly to the floor, his eyes and attention better spent staring at the alabaster beauty of her shoulders, breasts, and midriff. She was like a statue come to life, only not so cold and far more essential. He encompassed her back in both of his hands, the masterful grip on her making him realize that she was actually quite small. Her vibrancy and cocky strength made her seem so much bigger than she was in actuality.

Adam was not intimidated by the realization. He knew there was nothing delicate or fragile about her, and if he entertained the thought for even a second she'd probably take great pleasure in painfully proving to him otherwise.

He was not in the mood for her enmity. He'd had more than enough. Now he was ready for the purity of her passion. An undaunted passion.

"Sweet Destiny, you are the most beautiful thing I have ever beheld," he breathed over her mouth as he pulled her lips to within an inch of his own. "Then I look again and you have grown even more beautiful. Then again, and you stun me, flood me with urges and craving I cannot control. No matter how I tried, no matter what I wanted my mind to do, it has had its own will where you are concerned, until I no longer know myself. And yes, it does frighten me, too," he admitted to her. "Or it did. How easy it is for me to give in when it means I will have my mouth all over your skin."

Jasmine felt her entire body go liquid with need as his words sank into her brain, and deeper still into her soul. He was right. What did it matter anymore? All the struggling and the resistance. Why bother when giving in meant such sublime pleasure awaited her?

Her lips parted just as he pulled her up to his mouth, kissing her more deeply than he ever had before. She realized then how much she had missed the complex pleasure of a kiss. But no others had satisfied her like this. They had only frustrated her to a point of fury, compelling her to edit them out of her life completely because they failed to live up to what they should be.

This was what they should be.

Hot and wet and sensual to the point that her thoughts completely hazed over and thinking became utterly impossible. There was no part of her body left untouched by his kiss as it shifted from wild to sensual to dynamic by turns.

Before she realized it, she was unbuttoning her jeans and pushing them down her legs, kicking them away so she could touch her skin to his. But he was still dressed, so she immediately began to work on his clothes. She encountered his own impatient hands as he helped her in her task, but she was far more familiar with the way his clothes worked than he was, and he lost patience. He turned to water, splashing into her body and face, running down through the length of her hair, the temperature of him just as warm as his body was.

Jasmine barely realized his empty clothes hung from her hands as she felt liquid eddy and cling to every inch of her body. She felt him moving up the insides of her thighs, her body trembling as the water wetness of him combined with the wet need her body had expelled in response to his kisses. The sensation was the same as if a soft mouth and tongue were swirling their way across her flesh, teasing at her clit even as the rest of her was being stroked until every nerve of her body was stimulated at once.

Unable to bear her weight, her legs folded and she found herself on her knees with Adam continually moving over her skin and hair. He slid through her hair from roots to tips, then rained off the ends and onto the small of her back, dripping down onto her backside and slicking his way through every crevice he could find before shifting over her to do it all over again.

Jasmine had only tasted a few instants of this four hundred years ago, but even then she had never comprehended just how overwhelmingly erotic and pleasurable such a thing could be. She found herself on the verge of an orgasm she could barely grasp. She felt him inside her body, felt him flowing into her in a liquid penetration that was deceptively simple, yet nothing of the kind.

Adam drew back and solidified into the burning flesh of a man, his senses inundated with everything he had discovered about her, and his hard shaft buried deep inside her. The alteration from water to flesh was simple and shocking all at once. Adam's hands were pulling her up onto his braced thighs, seating her astride him and pushing his erection much deeper inside her.

Jasmine gasped in a hard breath, gripping his shoulders with all of her strength, unintentionally pulling at the wound he had suffered and making it bleed afresh. But for the first time in her life, Jasmine had found a call far more compelling than the scent of fresh blood. Even more compelling than the scent of the blood of her mate.

When? Oh, when had she last felt so much pleasure from the physical connection of her body to that of another? Never. Oh, never. She admitted it wildly and freely to herself. She had just come home. She had found the place she had always been searching for. This, she realized, was the place she would always be able to stay. This would keep her aboveground. This would make the world a gorgeous, irresistible pleasure every single day of her life to come.

Jasmine came hard and with incomparable ecstasy.

Adam felt the bliss in her thoughts, and it overwhelmed him even as he was feeling his own wild sense of having come home at last. He felt the orgasm hit him like a ton of bricks and he wanted nothing more than to fling himself into it, to let them both indulge in their realization that they had quite simply been made for each other. As though they had been whole at one point, split apart, and were now reunited at last. It brought tears to his eyes. Partly because he knew how important this sense of coming home was going to be to him in the future as he learned how to adapt to the new world he found himself in. This, he knew, would be what kept him sane, would keep homesickness at bay, would make his losses feel less and his fortunes seem so much more.

"Sweet Destiny. Sweet, sweet fortune. Can a man find love in only a day?" he asked her even as she threw back her head and shouted out to the ceiling. He saw tears leaking from the corners of her eyes, and it made him happy he had held himself back. He wanted to give her that pleasure again. And again.

The locked tension in her body suddenly released and she relaxed in his hold, her torso a liquidy ooze of flesh against his own. She gasped for breath she didn't need, her hands alternately gripping at the muscles of his arms, then relaxing.

"Is it love or just this crazy genetic predisposition?" she asked softly. He had not realized she had even heard his uncontrolled utterance. He was also surprised she was being so calm about it. The idea of love must be everything she feared the most.

"I don't fear it," she corrected him. "I fear being disappointed by it."

She lifted her head and met his eyes, understanding that the deep green she saw was a reflection of her own now, in more ways than she could possibly think of in that moment.

"I am not afraid," he heard himself say, even as he surprised himself by saying it. "No, it is true. The Imprinting was such a distant dream for me. So distant I just assumed it would never happen. But the moment I understood it had happened, whether to a Vampire or a speck of dust, I understood it was destined. It was meant for me and it would be right for me."

"I like that, I'm no better than a speck of dust." She sniffed at the idea, but he knew she was playing.

"Perhaps you ought to prove to me otherwise, eh?" Adam lurched forward, throwing them both on the floor, her back hitting a tapestry rug and her body swallowed up under his.

"Perhaps I should," she agreed. Then using the strength of her entire body she pushed him over, reversing their positions on the rug. She sat up over him, a proud and fantastic woman, more than he would ever have asked for, more than he would ever have expected. "Aye, you should remember I am better than a Demon like you deserves," she taunted him.

"Keep teasing, little Vamp. I am your only source for dinner tonight. Methinks I will not feed you."

"No?" She moved in a wicked undulation of her body, riding tightly over him, sending chills of delight all over his body. "But you have such mighty appetites of your own. Why not feed together?"

He groaned, reaching to grip her by her long, sleek thighs.

"I might be so convinced," he confessed on a rough exhalation.

Jasmine smiled.

He should have known just by the smug turn of her lips that she was up to something.

She rose off his body, letting him slip free of her warmth and wetness, making him utter a clear sound of protest, his hands trying to grasp for her before she could escape him further.

But she wasn't going far. That reflexive breath of hers skimmed his belly as she resituated herself, bringing her mouth to the level of his waist, her tongue darting out immediately to lick the length of him from tip to base and then ever more slowly back again. Adam's hands fumbled blindly into her hair as his eyes rolled closed with pleasure. She dipped her head and took him into her mouth, a strong seal immediately following as she sucked him hard against her palate again and again. Then she eased up a little, her saliva wetting him as her tongue danced over him in teasing sweeps of pleasure.

Adam had never felt anything like it. He was so

hard and heavy, growing more so by the second . . . or so it felt. The urge to come flooded over him as sharply as it had when he'd been inside her. His hands fisted sharply in her hair and he ejected a harsh sound of need.

I need you!

And I need you, she countered.

And that was the moment he felt her fangs skipping along his length.

She bit down hard.

Under any other circumstances, Adam imagined his first instinct would have been to backhand her across the room and then curl up into a wounded little ball of damaged manhood.

But this was not other circumstances.

This was his Imprinted mate, and her bite had proved to be the closest thing to nirvana he would ever know. He exploded into her mouth, a mixture of blood and all his most primal essences. He came in a way that went beyond the physical, the orgasm clawing up out of his every blood vessel and every nerve all at once. She drank from him as though she had been denied food all of her life and was finally given the chance to suckle. He felt the pleasure flooding through her mind, felt how it numbed her and invigorated her all at the same time.

Then he felt her reach her threshold of pleasure and of physical satiation. He braced for the second bite, but was still unprepared for it. He felt the coagulants and antibodies burning through him, but it was like a whole new act of bliss instead of something practical and helpful. Adam fell flat on his back, his hands leaving her hair and driving through his own. He had to close his eyes because whenever he looked up, the etched stone ceiling and the Moorish arches in her room began to spin around him, making him feel incredibly dizzy and unanchored from his world.

Her tongue brushed over him and he felt the skin on his body flinch. It was all too much. More than any one creature could possibly withstand. The impression must have flitted through Jasmine's mind, because she immediately backed away from him. She climbed up the length of his body and dropped down heavily over him. She began to chuckle in soft outbursts of humor, rolling a bit to and fro, like a woman deep into the high of her life.

"You know what I like best about all of this?" she asked him.

"Hmm?" he grunted.

"We are never going to have just boring old sex. Neither of us has it in us to be drab and conventional."

"I should hope not," he agreed.

"So . . . I guess that is kind of cool. I wouldn't mind that too much."

Adam laughed. "Well, I am comforted."

"I am trying to say I accept this Imprinting of yours," she pointed out.

"I realize that," he said. He didn't bother pointing out to her she really didn't have any choice in the matter. They'd already been over all of that. They were both very aware of it. This was Jasmine's way of taking control of something she simply couldn't control. "I am glad. I have decided I really rather like you, Jasmine."

"You said you were in love," she pointed out. "And in less than a day." He opened an eye to see how smug she looked, because she certainly sounded it. She was obviously very pleased with herself.

"That I did. I have to admit, I find your irascible nature, your quills, and your tendency to want to torture those around you to be rather charming."

Jasmine laughed at him. "True. I am all those things," she said, sounding very proud of herself for it.

"But you are also more sensitive than you care to admit to others, capable of craving beauty in all the things around you, and loyal to those who have been blessed to earn your loyalty. You are firmly for the moral right, although your methods might skirt the appropriate." He reached out to push the edge of her hair back. "You are lovely, evocative, and I have never met your match. Tell me what in all of that I could resist loving?"

Jasmine suddenly sat up and moved away, snagging her robe from the hook near her vanity and cocooning herself within the plush fabric, tying the belt extraordinarily tight.

By the time Adam gained his feet she was spinning the crystal ball again, occasionally breaking from her study of it to glance up into the mirror above the table. He felt her insecurity, her fear, and the racing of her thoughts.

Adam came up beside her, reached out to cup the side of her face in his big hand. Despite her resistance, he made her look at him.

"I will not hide or lie. I do not wish to," he said softly to her. "There can be nothing but truth between us, even when we wish to lie to ourselves."

Her breath caught.

"I don't love you," she burst out, the statement a bit more painful than he had anticipated it would be.

"Love will come when you are ready to let it come, Jasmine."

But I know it is already here.

"Stop it! I do not love you!" She picked up the ball with one hand and threw it into him as hard as she could. He caught it against his sternum with a grunt of pain. She used the action to push past him, to leap right through the blackened glass and out the window.

"Jasmine!"

He bellowed her name, racing after her, diving after her even before he heard her scream.

Sunlight.

Everywhere, all at once. Desperation and emotional pain had overwhelmed her instincts, making her forget that the sun was high in the sky. There wasn't a cloud in sight, but they came as he plummeted after her, falling at breakneck speed down the massive height of the citadel walls. The clouds came with more speed than he had ever managed before, but not fast enough to keep her skin and hair from bursting into flames. He reached out with both hands, knowing he couldn't grab her, but willing himself to do something. Anything.

And then suddenly he felt a source of water appearing before him. Jasmine, yet more than Jasmine. The fire along her body doused itself as her skin turned liquid, flinging droplets back at him.

They hit the ground, Jasmine first, in a violent splash of water, and Adam second as the same. But Adam knew how to draw himself back into a cohesive shape and Jasmine did not, so he had to gather up all of the water molecules that she had become, and slowly, with his arms around her, he reformed her into what she should be.

Her hair was burned, her skin, too, but she was Jasmine again. Jasmine his mate. Jasmine the beautiful. Jasmine the Vampire.

Jasmine who could become Water.

The clouds sealed away the sun, rain falling to keep her cool and protected as he took her to the nearest entrance of the citadel and finally was able to close her behind a sheltering door. She was groaning in pain, too weak to hold herself upright, staggering as he tried to avoid touching her at first. But he gave up on that, turning to Water and wrapping himself around her in a cooling, protective sheath. He buoyed her, helped strengthen and guide her steps. He didn't want to change her form while she was so injured and damaged, not knowing what further harm it might do. When Demons were wounded, changing their molecular cohesion could cause a great deal of harm.

He found a bath nearby, herded her in, and, filling the tub, he lowered her into the water. The tub was wide and deep, allowing her the opportunity to float free of the hard, cold sides.

"I will heal," she croaked, her voice scorched by the flames that had been swallowed down her throat as she screamed.

"I know you will. I know it takes far more time than a pair of minutes in the sun to kill a Vampire. It is . . .

it is one of the best ways to torture a Vampire. Stake them out in the sun and let them immolate for hours."

"And you know the technique well," she rasped. "How can you love something you hated for so many years?" she wanted to know.

Adam realized it wasn't that she doubted his feelings. She wanted to know how he had managed to change himself in so short a time. She wanted to know if she was ever going to be able to change.

"To me it is not about Vampire or Demon. Not when it comes to you. It never was. I tried to hold you up to my ingrained hatred of your kind and failed time and time again. It was not the Vampire I was coming to love. It was Jasmine," he said softly to her, brushing his fingertips, turned into water, against her temple. "It was always Jasmine. And once I realized you could never fit my preconceived prejudices, those prejudices had to melt away. They were designed to fit all Vampires. All Vampires were this. All Vampires were that. But you were none of it, so I learned I could not continue to make such encompassing assumptions about your kind. It made me realize how hard I had been working for some time to hold on to those assumptions.

"So tell me, little Vamp, what are you trying so hard to hold on to that I am not fitting into properly?"

Jasmine turned her face away, let herself soak quietly in the water for a long minute. He felt thoughts ghosting wildly back and forth in her mind.

"Emotions have always disappointed me," she said at last, her voice already sounding smoother. She had lost her brows and eyelashes, and her hair was breaking off into the water. "For five hundred years I have longed to feel more than I do, but it never changed. No matter what I sought out, how I tried. So I gave up. I just . . . gave up. Then Damien told me he had found the answer. But how could he?" she demanded angrily. "I had already written it off. It was over. And I couldn't take the chance that he might be wrong. Clearly love was working for him, but what guarantees did I have it would work the same for me?

"You said I was jealous of Syreena? I wasn't," she said softly.

"You were jealous of Damien," Adam realized gently.

Jasmine burst into sobs, her hand trying to cover her face, but her face was too tender to touch. She was left raw and exposed in more ways than one. Adam climbed into the bath and surrounded her softly, combining with the water around her to tenderly wash up against her. But he left his shoulders, chest, and neck whole, giving her a point of strength to hold on to. He touched watery fingers to her face, absorbing every salty tear as quickly as it fell so it wouldn't have the opportunity to sting her.

"Jasmine," he whispered hushed into her ear. "I am not going to leave and I am not going to take my love, your love, and all those brilliant emotions you are finally feeling away from you. We are all here to stay. You need to give yourself permission to enjoy them. You have waited so long for them." He took a breath. "I know. I know I left you once. But had I known . . ."

"You still would have gone to save your brother," she said. "And neither you nor I will ever know how many lives you changed by doing so, Adam. Ruth is gone. Defeated at last. I think I am glad I suffered a drab life for a few centuries rather than consider the possibilities. Can you imagine what it would have been like, ten years from now, had Jacob died at Ruth's hands? Twenty years? Can you imagine the power Ruth would have gained with Nico still alive at her side? The people she would have hurt?

"I saw that girl's eyes, Adam," Jasmine said softly. "She was dead inside. She was . . . she looked like she had waited four hundred years just to feel that one moment of life the way it was meant to be felt."

She turned in his watery embrace to look up at him.

"I should take that lesson to my heart," she said. "The present is so precious. Not to be wasted. Oh my God, look what I almost did!" She lifted her scorched hand to his face, touching the roughness of a cheek in need of grooming. The detail, the dimension of it, the reality of it, made her chest expand with emotion.

"You never meant to hurt yourself," he said, covering her hand where it lay against him. "Only to run away."

"Never in my long lifetime have I lost track of the sun. How is that even possible?"

"Fear can blind us to a great many things. Just as prejudice can. I might well have killed you the moment we met. I would have destroyed my own heart without realizing it."

"It makes me wonder how many of us have done just that? All these years of various wars with each other. How many Nightwalkers have destroyed their own happiness in the name of something as foolish as wars, or boredom, or laws, or the dozens of other types of nonsense we have put in our way?"

"Ten? A hundred? Thousands? We can never know about the past. Only move on into the future."

"Yes," she breathed, pulling him to the reach of her mouth, "let's do that. Let's move on into the future, Adam."

Adam smiled, touched his lips gently to hers, and gave her a steady nod.

Epilogue

Windsong stood in the meadow, letting the wind blow over her body, through her hair and against her ears, the sound its own special sort of music. Harrier sat on a rock a short distance away, keeping an eye on her. He had barely let her out of his sight since Damien had returned her to *Brise Lumineuse*. Her kidnapping had wildly reinforced the village's fears about strangers and letting others come into their sphere. They foolishly thought that if they kept their heads down, all would be well.

But Windsong believed the Mistrals were only destroying themselves with their paranoia and fear. Their isolation kept them from socializing even with other Mistrals. Their birthrates were nearly at a standstill. Windsong couldn't even recall the last time a Mistral couple exchanged vows. Became a family.

Harrier leapt down off his rock and came over to her, the breeze ruffling his beautiful hair, making her understand how handsome he was and what a shame it would be if he never ventured forth and found himself a bride, never found himself someone to make equally beautiful babies with. And that wasn't even taking into consideration the extraordinary gift of his voice. The world would suffer a tremendous loss if that gift were never passed to later generations.

But like her, she knew, Harrier believed the insular Mistrals were headed for eradication in the future. At least, that was how he had felt before her capture. She wondered if fear had been revived inside him. If his view had changed.

"Harri, we are the oldest of our kind. We are responsible for the future of our people. You know that, right?"

"I have always known that," he agreed, sitting beside her and circling an arm around her shoulders. "I have also always known you see the future more clearly than anyone else I know. I believe . . . part of me believes you let yourself be captured, Windsong, in order to bring certain things to pass. I find it hard to believe you did not have vision of that encounter."

"Not entirely," she hedged. "Nothing is ever that clear for me. But I have seen many other things. I see other ways in which my interference is needed." She smiled softly at him. "My personal happiness . . . there will be some years to pass before we reach that point. But you and some others, Lyric and her little friend Thrush—you will never find your futures if you all continue to hide from the world. None of us will."

"The villagers will not believe that. They are set in their ways. They are afraid."

Windsong met his eyes firmly.

"Then I must find a way to break their fear."

Harrier nodded.

"If anyone can, it will be you, love."

* * *

Jacob was wandering the caverns a short distance away from where Bella lay resting and recovering. Only she wasn't quite all his Bella yet. She was conscious, and she was improving every day, but it was as though she had suffered a traumatic brain injury. Her speech was slow and difficult, her thoughts were disjointed. She had horrible nightmares caused by the infusion of raw evil and tainted magical power she had taken into herself. The mental telepathic connection they had created together when they had Imprinted was silent.

Gideon said she would heal in time, and that all would return to normal one day. She would sleep in peace, she would scold him in his head, the unity and harmony that flowed between them would slowly come back to them. She just needed to heal. Heal in a way that Gideon's impressive medical skills and powers of the Body simply could not accomplish.

"The Mind and the human brain are very complex," Legna had said when he had tried turning to her for help as well. "I can work with her to help bring her along, but this trauma will only heal itself in its own time. It will not adhere to our impatient schedules, it will not bend to our desperate wishes to see her back to normal. It has its own methods, and often those are the best methods. If we rushed her back, it could cause more harm than good. Isabella is the most complex and most powerful Druid of her time. Her power knows no equal and, so far, knows no real boundaries. Everything she experiences seems to make her grow in strength almost at an exponential rate. I can only believe that when she comes back from this trauma she will be herself and even more than she was before. Do not worry, Jacob. I feel very strongly she is on her way back to you."

Jacob felt it, too. Not at first. It had taken almost a week of watching her stammer and stutter her way through the simplest of sentences, having difficulty remembering who he was, who her daughter was, before he had finally seen the small glimmer of hope he had been looking for.

"D-did t-the g-girl co-ome tuh-tuh se-ee me?"

"Her name is Leah," Jacob reminded her gently for what had to be the twentieth time that evening. "And yes, she came to see you. But you were sleeping. She is off playing with the Lycanthrope children. Do you want me to bring her to you?"

"N-no. L-let her ha-have fun."

Jacob nodded, sitting beside her in bed with a hair-brush in hand.

"Let me brush some of the tangles out of your hair," he said quietly.

"O-okay." She leaned forward, her body jerking as she tried to correct her balance and control her move-ments. Then she rested her cheek on his shoulder and he sensed she closed her eyes. He brushed her hair in silence, needing a few moments of quiet, a few mo-ments in which she wasn't struggling for everything she did.

"A-Asher," she said softly.

It was peculiar to hear his father's name on her lips. He hadn't even realized she knew his parents' names. He leaned back and tipped her chin so he could see in her eyes.

"What was that, little flower?" he asked her.

"A-Asher. F-for t-the b-boy." She closed her eyes and

shook her head a little, clearly forcing herself to get it right. "The ba-baby. O-our son."

And there she was. Bella. His Bella. In her eyes and in that stubborn moment of fighting her way through, he saw his wife, her spirit, for the first time in days. Tears had come quickly, and he had been forced to work hard to keep control of them. He wouldn't let her see his fear, even when the reaction was relief from that fear.

"It is a good name. A strong name," he said.

She nodded. A smooth, decisive nod.

And so they had named their son.

Now, in the solitude of the cavern, with nothing but etched walls surrounding him, he let himself exhale a shaky breath, let himself lean against one of those walls for support.

"Jake."

Jake. He hadn't let anyone in four hundred years call him that. Honestly, Adam had been the only one he'd ever let call him Jake. It had been special. Personal. A connection that had signified Adam was the elder brother and Jacob the younger. Adam was the protector and mentor, and Jacob the one he sheltered and cared for.

He had not had the benefit and comfort of those things since the day Adam had died.

Disappeared.

Been taken away.

"Adam." Jacob opened his eyes and turned his head to look at his brother. It was like a vision. Or perhaps a hallucination. The Adam he knew was all there, big and powerful and taking up so much space in the closed-in caverns with just the energy of his presence. Only he had been tucked into modern clothing, his hair had been shaped closer to his head and trimmed short against his collar. He was incredibly kempt. It made Jacob chuckle.

"My metrosexual brother. I would never have imagined it."

Adam raised a brow. "I hope that was not an insult. You are older than me and no doubt more skilled, but I have no doubt I can hold my own against you. I will not tolerate you disrespecting me."

Jacob had to smile. "It is true. I am actually the elder brother now." The thought amused him. But not for long. "I would rather not be," he said gravely. "I—" He stopped. He wasn't going to spend time or energy wishing for things that simply could not be. "I feel I have to apologize. First for my daughter and what she did to you. It was selfish and very unfair to you."

"And yet," Adam said, "she saved countless lives. Protected a number of innocents, including Noah and his Queen. If I had not been here, I could not have played a crucial part in Ruth's capture. And your daughter brought me to this time, this perfect time, where I could claim a Vampire as my Imprinted mate."

"A Vampire . . ." Jacob gaped at him. "A *Vampire?*"

"Jasmine and I are Imprinted. Something that never would have been accepted—"

"Jasmine!" Jacob blurted out incredulously, cutting his brother off. "*Jasmine?*"

Adam cocked his head and narrowed his eyes on his sibling.

"Is something wrong with Jasmine?" he asked coldly.

"I . . . uh . . . no," Jacob said wisely. "I like Jasmine a great deal. She is a strong fighter and is doggedly loyal to Damien. She has made a fine commander of the Nightwalker Sensor Network. She . . ." He looked at his brother, his brows lifting in a bit of surprise. "She is rather a great deal like you in those aspects."

"I think I will take that as a compliment," Adam said with a smug little smile.

"Enjoy it. I doubt you will have many more from me," Jacob shot at him.

And just like that, four centuries melted away from Jacob. It was as though they were standing around the practice ring again, trading barbs and boasts. As if no time at all had passed.

Adam smiled and sighed, glancing at his brother through lowered lashes. "Was it very hard on you? Like you said? Whether I meant to leave the job to you or not . . . it became yours. And I know very well the weight of that mantle. How heavy it can be. But to inherit it in such a way, and when you never aspired to it . . . I can only imagine how hard it must have been for you."

Jacob drew a breath and let it out slowly as he looked into those light green eyes he remembered as sure as he knew his name.

"I was alone, Adam. Very alone. The worst of it was not so much being compelled to become Enforcer; it was becoming Enforcer without benefit of your guidance. I missed my brother. I could not figure out what had happened to you. I searched for answers, but there were none to be had." Jacob shrugged. "None of that matters now. I have my answers and I have my brother. I was wrong to lash out at you. I was wrong to feel anything but grateful that you are here."

Jacob reached for Adam's hand. His brother caught hold of it and pulled him close. Adam embraced Jacob with love and strength, with affection he probably wouldn't have shown him four centuries ago. But this past week with Jasmine had taught him a great deal about exposing his emotions and acknowledging them quickly, because there was no telling if he would have the opportunity to do so ever again.

"Come," Jacob said with the first real sense of rightness he had felt in days, "there's someone I want you to meet."

Jacob brushed off Adam's curious expression long enough to take him back to Bella's room. Adam saw his brother's wife, conscious and seemingly alert. A beautiful woman with a cape of red curly hair was sitting on the bed by her side. She and the man standing beside her looked up at him in unison when he entered.

He was a dead ringer for Jacob. A little stockier, perhaps . . . but there was no mistaking the blood that ran through his veins.

"Adam," Jacob said, "I want you to meet your brother, Kane."

If you loved *Adam*, please turn over
for a sneak preview of *Jacob* . . .

JACOB

How ridiculously simple it would be to cause them harm. From far above, he watched with unwavering dark eyes as they walked down the shadowy street. The human male was so absorbed in his flirtation with his female, he would have no chance of protecting her from harm should they be surprised by a threat. What if he were to drop onto them from his current height?

Although in that instance, "surprised" wouldn't be an adequate descriptive. The debate of defense would be futile as well. A human versus one of his ilk?

Jacob the Enforcer exhaled a sardonic laugh.

The redheaded woman had chosen poorly, in his opinion. No respectable male would have encouraged his partner to venture out on such a forbidding night. Mystical portents aside, the street they walked was notoriously disreputable. Menacing shadows shifted with threats unknown to simple human senses as clouds skimmed over the fickle light of the moon.

The couple walked beneath him, oblivious to his camouflaged presence.

Not to mention the coming of the other.

Jacob cocked his head, taking careful note of the other's distant movements. Though the man-made features of a glass-and-concrete city numbed the Enforcer's favored senses, he could still follow the comer's progress easily. The younger, less experienced Demon was being careless, his focus riveted to his objective.

The human female.

Jacob recognized the younger Demon's hunger, feeling it as it eddied into him, oppressive and pungent with the musk of unrestrained lust. The young Demon, Kane by common name, was stepping in and out of solid existence as he progressed toward the redhead. Kane's fixation was making him uncharacteristically single-minded. He had no idea that the Enforcer had pursued him, that he was now lying in resolute wait for him.

Kane abruptly appeared on the pavement below in a burst of roiling smoke and the distinctive odor of sulfur. He was several yards behind the unknowing couple, his teleportation going completely unnoticed despite its display.

Jacob waited, the tension stretching his nerves taut. Although it pressed on him to interfere, it was his duty to let the other Demon commit to his course. Only then would he have justification for bringing the laws of their people down on him. All the while, he prayed to Destiny that Kane would regain control and walk away.

As Jacob gave the other Demon his chance to change his mind, he sat as still as a stone, watching Kane step into the recently trod path of the couple. When he passed beneath the Enforcer's unseen perch up on the light pole to gain on his prey, Jacob launched upward into the air in a light, airy leap from one lamppost to the next several yards down the sidewalk. There was no sound as his feet touched the cool metal, no rustle of the clothing he wore as he crouched down once more in perfect balance. The only telltale sign of his presence was the sudden flickering twitch of the light. It only took him a moment to compensate, making the others below him perceive all as normal, though in actuality the light continued to flash with increasing spasms of protest.

He kept his thoughts hidden behind this projected camouflage as well. He knew that even in the grip of these basest of instincts, Kane would sense him if he did not. And yet, a whisper in the back of his mind was begging the Enforcer within him to just once, only this once, make an error. *One small error,* it murmured, *and Kane, who is so dear to you, will sense your presence and your thoughts. Let him have the chance that you have denied so many others.*

No one would ever know what Jacob sacrificed to deny that insidious whispering. Regardless of the voice's entreaty, he could not forswear his duty.

So instead, he watched as Kane sent out his summons to the vulnerable couple. Abruptly, the male human turned and walked away from the female, abandoning her without reason or the awareness that he was doing so. The redhead turned completely around, facing the approaching Demon. She was quite beautiful, Jacob noted as she faced the lamplight, with a lush, long body and auburn curls hanging in lengthy coils down her back. It was clear why she had attracted Kane. It wasn't the Enforcer in Jacob that allowed a small, quirking smile to play at the corner of his otherwise grim lips.

Kane sauntered up to her, completely confident of

his power over her, and reached to touch her face. Jacob could see the thrall in her eyes, the manipulation of her mind making her soft and pliant, making her turn her cheek into his affectionate caress.

The affection was a lie. What would start with this gentility could not possibly end with it. It was the nature of the creatures that they were, and it was inevitable. This was why he could never have allowed Kane any more warning than he had already given hundreds . . . no . . . thousands of times before this.

Jacob had seen enough.

He leapt lightly into the air, his long body tumbling gracefully in a backflip until he came full around and landed soundlessly behind the redheaded woman. He discarded his camouflage so abruptly that Kane sucked in a loud, startled breath. He froze when he saw Jacob, and the Elder was easily aware of what the young Demon's thoughts must be.

The Enforcer had come to punish him.

It was enough to make Kane swallow visibly in apprehension. His hand jerked away from the redhead's cheek as if she'd burned him, and his concentration broke from her. She blinked, suddenly becoming aware that she was sandwiched between two strange men and had no idea how she had gotten there.

"Take hold of her mind, Kane. Do not make this worse by frightening her."

Kane obeyed instantaneously and the lovely woman relaxed, smiling softly as if she were in the easy company of old friends, now completely at peace.

"Jacob, what brings you out on a night like this?"

Jacob wasn't deterred by Kane's casual quip or his attempt at saving face through levity. The Enforcer already knew the other male was not wicked at heart.

Kane was still relatively untrained and, considering the conditions of the night, it was easy for him to be led astray by his own baser nature.

That did not change the stark facts of the moment. Kane had literally been caught with his hand in the cookie jar. His knee-jerk reaction, understandably, was to bargain his way out of the punishment he knew was impending. He would start with humor and continue on to every other tool in his arsenal.

"You know why I am here," the Enforcer said, nipping those tools right in the bud with a chill, disciplined tone that warned Kane not to test his mettle.

"So maybe I do," Kane relented, his dark blue eyes lowering as he shoved his hands deep into his pockets. "I wasn't going to do anything. I was just . . . restless."

"I see. So you thought to seduce this woman to appease your restlessness?" Jacob asked bluntly as he folded his arms across his chest. His entire manner radiated the image of a parent scolding a wayward child. It could be an amusing thought, considering Kane was just about to enter his second century of life, but the matter was too serious by far.

"I wasn't going to hurt her," Kane protested.

Jacob realized that Kane actually thought that was true. "No?" he countered. "Just what were you going to do? Ask politely if you could visit the savageness of your present nature on her? How does one word that, exactly?"

Kane fell stubbornly silent. He knew that the Enforcer had read his intentions from the moment he'd decided to stalk prey. Arguments and denials would just worsen the situation. Besides, the incriminating evidence of his transgression was standing between them.

For a brief, passionate moment, Kane's thoughts filled with vivid mental imaginings of what could have been more incriminating. He suppressed a shudder of sinful response, his eyes falling covetously on the woman standing so beautifully serene before him. Had Jacob been even slightly off his irritatingly perfect game and come into the picture a half hour later . . .

"Kane, this is a difficult time for our people. You are as susceptible to these base cravings as any other Demon," the Enforcer said with implacable resolve. It was as though Jacob were the one who could read Kane's mind, rather than the other way around. "Still, you are a mere two years from becoming adult. I cannot believe you have me chasing you down like a green fledgling. Think of what I could be accomplishing if I were not standing here saving you from yourself."

Kane's rugged features flushed red with the shame Jacob intentionally laid at his feet. It relieved the Enforcer to see the reaction. It told him that Kane's conscience was once again functioning, his usually smart sense of morality closer to restoration.

"I'm sorry, Jacob, I really am," he said at last, this time with sincerity rather than as another ploy to try to disarm the Enforcer. Jacob could tell he was sincere because he finally stopped staring at the redhead as if she were due to be served to him on the proverbial silver platter.

As the Enforcer's dynamic presence stabilized his principles, Kane was realizing that he'd placed Jacob in an untenable position, perhaps in a way that might forever mar their relationship. Kane's throat closed with the sharp sense of remorse that knifed through him.

It was as overpowering as the dread that was welling up within him. He'd betrayed the sanctity of their laws,

and there was punishment for that—a punishment
that made an entire species catch their breath and
back away whenever the Enforcer entered the vicinity.
Kane could suddenly feel the weight of Jacob's position, and it sharpened his regret to a point of pain in
his chest.

"You will send this woman home safely by reuniting
her with her escort and making sure she remembers
nothing of your misbehavior," Jacob instructed softly
as he watched the tumult of emotion that swam across
Kane's face. "Then you will go home. Your punishment will come later."

"But I didn't do anything," Kane protested, a swift
rise of inescapable fear fueling the objection.

"You would have, Kane. Do not make this worse by
lying to yourself about that. You will only convince
yourself that I am the villain others like to make me
out to be. That will only cause us both pain."

Kane realized that truth with another upsurge of
guilt. Sighing resolutely, he closed his eyes and con-
centrated for all of a second. Moments later, the redhead's escort loped back across the street with a smile
and a call to her.

"Hey! Where'd ya go? I turned the corner and suddenly you weren't there!"

"I'm sorry. I was distracted by something and
didn't realize you'd gone, Charlie."

Charlie linked his arm with his date's and, completely oblivious to the two Demons barely a breath
away, drew her off.

"Good," Jacob commended Kane. It was simple
and to the point. The younger Demon was becoming quite efficient as he matured.

Kane sighed, sounding gravely bereft.

"She's so beautiful. Did you see that smile? All I could think about was how much I wanted her to smile when . . ." Kane flushed as he looked at the Enforcer. Jacob was well aware that her smile hadn't been his only motivation. "I never thought this would happen to me, Jacob. You have to believe that."

"I do." Jacob hesitated for a moment, for the first time making it obvious to Kane that this had been a terrible struggle for him, no matter how well he projected otherwise. "Do not worry, Kane. I know who you really are. I know that this curse is hard for us to fight. Now," he said, his tone back to business, "please return home. You will find Abram there awaiting you."

This time, Kane brushed away the welling trepidation within himself. He did this for Jacob's sake, knowing how deeply this cut the Elder Demon, even though his thoughts were too carefully guarded for Kane to read. "You do your duty as you would with anyone. I understand that, Jacob."

Kane then gave the Enforcer a short nod of kinship. After glancing around to make sure they were unobserved, he exploded into a burst of sulfur and smoke as he teleported away.

Jacob stood for long moments on the sidewalk, his senses attentive until he was confident Kane was truly returning home. It wasn't unprecedented for a Demon to try running away and hiding for fear of impending punishment. Nevertheless, Kane was on the proper path, in more ways than one, once again.

Jacob turned and glanced up the street in the direction the human couple had taken. It never ceased to amaze him how lacking in instincts humans were. For all their civilization and technological advances, they had truly lost something valuable in trading away their animalist intuitions. That woman would be forever ignorant of how close she had come to danger. Meeting a wayward Demon in the shadow of a cursed moon was something no mortal wanted to be a part of.

Jacob released himself from the hold of gravity and rose into the air, barely causing a displacing breeze as he did so. His long, athletic body cut through the night like a beautifully honed blade. He soared past high-rises, some of the lights in the nearest occupied windows flickering in complaint at his passing. He burst up into the clear night sky.

Here, Jacob hesitated. He paused to study the bright, waxing moon with a frown he could not suppress. This was the way it was the weeks before and after the full moon of Beltane in spring and Samhain in autumn. These holidays were held Hallowed by Demons, but at the same time, they were the center of their curse. Restlessness among his people would only grow worse this coming week; peaking at the fullest moon. There would be more straying in the fledgling and adult generations. Even Elders would find their control sorely tempted.

Jacob had been chosen as Enforcer for a reason. His was a control beyond measure. Even the Demon monarch was considered more susceptible to this madness than he, and that was saying a lot considering that in all his four hundred years as Enforcer, Jacob had never been called to pull Noah, the Demon King, into check.

Jacob was grateful for that. Noah's powers were not something he would relish going up against. Their King hadn't earned his position by mere bloodlines like those in human histories did. Noah had earned his place based solely on his leadership and superiority of power.

As Jacob flew onward, his thoughts turned philosophical. Was it harder to be Enforcer or to be the King who must choose the Enforcer, as Noah had chosen Jacob? When making the choice, Noah would have been forced to acknowledge that there was an equal chance that he might one day find himself face-to-face with the Enforcer.

It was a brave leader who could still make the best choice knowing that one day he might live to regret it.

Do you love fiction with a supernatural twist?

Want the chance to hear news about your favourite authors (and the chance to win free books)?

Keri Arthur
S. G. Browne
P.C. Cast
Christine Feehan
Jacquelyn Frank
Larissa Ione
Sherrilyn Kenyon
Jackie Kessler
Jayne Ann Krentz and Jayne Castle
Martin Millar
Kat Richardson
J.R. Ward
David Wellington

Then visit the Piatkus website and blog
www.piatkus.co.uk | www.piatkusbooks.net

And follow us on Facebook and Twitter
www.facebook.com/piatkusfiction | www.twitter.com/piatkusbooks

piatkus